Initiation Into Ecstasy

"Sweet Mary, but I love you, Lea," Roger said as he came into the bed beside her and enveloped her in his arms.

"I will do my best to please you."

She pressed against him, warm and trusting.

"Would you have the candles doused or left lit?"

" 'Tis up to you," she murmured against the hard flesh of his shoulder.

"I would see you," he answered. "Aye, I would see your face."

He explored her with his mouth—her lips, ear lobes, neck and shoulders, while with his hands he stroked the silky softness of her body.

"Do not draw away now," he whispered hoarsely. And she obeyed, clutching his waist half in fear and half in hunger of what was about to happen. . . .

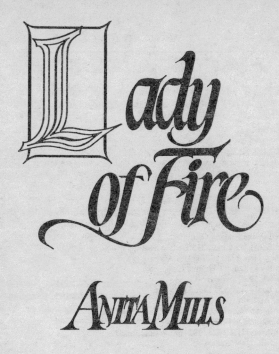

Lady of Fire

Anita Mills

AN ONYX BOOK

ONYX
Published by the Penguin Group
Penguin Books USA Inc., 375 Hudson Street,
New York, New York 10014, U.S.A.
Penguin Books Ltd, 27 Wrights Lane,
London W8 5TZ, England
Penguin Books Australia Ltd, Ringwood,
Victoria, Australia
Penguin Books Canada Ltd, 10 Alcorn Ave., Suite 300,
Toronto, Canada M4V 3B2
Penguin Books (N.Z.) Ltd, 182–190 Wairau Road,
Auckland 10, New Zealand

Penguin Books Ltd, Registered Offices:
Harmondsworth, Middlesex, England

Published by Onyx, an imprint of New American Library,
a division of Penguin Books USA Inc.

First Printing, August, 1987
12   11   10   9   8   7   6   5

 REGISTERED TRADEMARK—MARCA REGISTRADA

Printed in the United States of America

PUBLISHER'S NOTE
This is a work of fiction. Names, characters, places, and incidents either are the
product of the author's imagination or are used fictitiously, and any resemblance to
actual persons, living or dead, events, or locales is entirely coincidental.

BOOKS ARE AVAILABLE AT QUANTITY DISCOUNTS WHEN USED TO PROMOTE PRODUCTS OR SERVICES.
FOR INFORMATION PLEASE WRITE TO PREMIUM MARKETING DIVISION. PENGUIN BOOKS USA INC..
375 HUDSON STREET, NEW YORK, NEW YORK 10014.

This book is dedicated to my family, without whose support its inception and creation would not have been possible: to my husband, Larry, for his encouraging me to write it and his determination to see it through to the end; to my daughter, Tracy, for listening to my moans and groans when I couldn't come up with just the right word or phrase; to my son, Corey, for not complaining about skipped or late meals; and to my sister, Deborah, for having the patience to read and critique my every word. My heartfelt thanks to each—I could not have done it otherwise.

May, 1085

1

An expectant air hung over the small high-walled garden set within the lower bailey at Nantes. Herleva, nurse to Count Gilbert's three daughters, fought a losing battle to keep her young charges busy, while the sounds and smells of festival preparations competed for their attention. Somewhere in the town below the castle, carpenters hammered on stands and hung gaily dyed bunting, while cooks tended pits and spits of roasting meat and bakers kept ovens going day and night baking enough bread and pastries for noble and peasant alike. From time to time, the clatter of newly arriving lords and their retinues carried upward from narrow cobblestone streets. Most would seek lodging within the town, but a few of the more distinguished of the nobility would enjoy Gilbert's own hospitality.

Herleva watched as the eldest girl, twelve-year-old Eleanor, struggled reluctantly with her needlework. The girl held up the altar cloth she had been working, surveyed it with disgust, and slowly began to pick out the stitches she had just completed. No, the girl would never be noted for her skill with the needle—or for any other housewifely accomplishments. Well, it would be a rare lord that would care, anyway, because the girl was already much remarked for her beauty. Unlike others her age, Eleanor of Nantes lacked that awkwardness so often associated with the approach of womanhood. With long dark hair that hung in a thick curtain to her tiny waist, clear fair skin blushed with health, and a pair of fine brown eyes fringed with thick black lashes, she presented as pretty a sight as flesh and blood could make. At twelve, she was small

7

and delicately made, but her young breasts already outlined the smooth samite of her silver-threaded purple gown. It was rumored that Count Gilbert intended to negotiate for her marriage soon, and the servants of Nantes hoped that their Demoiselle would go somewhere where she would be more valued.

A mild oath escaped the girl's lips as she threw her work down in frustration. Abruptly she stood up and began to pace impatiently back and forth along the narrow flagstone walk.

"Demoiselle!" Herleva's voice rose in reproof.

"I don't care," Eleanor muttered mutinously. "It is easy to chide when you sew a fine hand. Mine is naught but a batch of knots that I should be ashamed to offer for Christ's altar." She kicked the crumpled cloth with a dainty leather-clad toe.

"Child, would you have it said that I taught you nothing?" Herleva asked quietly.

"Nay, but I cannot be what you would have me." The girl looked longingly at the high rock wall that enclosed them. "I would rather be a peasant out there tasting, seeing, feeling the festival. Instead, I sit unraveling poor stitches—and so it goes on and on." She hugged her arms to her. "Why is it that none but Roger can understand?"

The old nurse sighed in sympathy. "You cannot follow Roger around much longer, Demoiselle. It will soon be time to prepare to be a lord's lady." She stooped to retrieve the discarded cloth. "Here—it cannot be so very bad. Let us work on it together." Closer inspection caused her to shake her head.

"See—even you who love me must own it hopeless."

"Let me see," piped ten-year-old Margaret, "though I know mine's better."

Herleva whisked the cloth behind her. "As for you, little Margaret, you need to know there's more to being a lady than stitching," she admonished the younger girl.

"At least *I* do not spend my time in the courtyard with a bastard stableboy," the child retorted. "Maman says ladies do not follow stableboys."

"He's not a stableboy! For shame, Maggie—he's your own brother."

"Half-brother," Margaret sniffed disdainfully, "and a bastard at that."

"Through no fault of his own," Eleanor defended.

"Roger's a bastard," seven-year-old Adelicia chimed in. "Everyone knows he's a bastard."

"See—even Lissy knows what he is. Maman says he is only fit to feed the horses."

"Maman is just jealous because she never had a son," Eleanor shot back.

"Mmmmmmmmm—I'll tell Maman," Adelicia threatened.

"You'll do no such thing," Herleva intervened, "unless you want to spend Festival in the nursery while the rest of us see the company. The duke himself comes to Nantes."

"The Old Conqueror?" Even Eleanor was diverted by the news. "I thought him on the French border. Will he bring England's crown to wear?"

"As to that, I cannot say. All I know is that I heard he comes to ask for the count's levy against King Philip."

"Well, he wastes his time," Eleanor pointed out with an insight beyond her years. "If he would have Nantes' levy, he'll have to demand it. My father is too careful of his own skin to fight another man's war. He'll claim he cannot fight because he is a vassal to both Duke William and King Philip."

"Nonetheless, he comes here—mayhap today or tomorrow."

But Eleanor's attention suddenly became intent on sounds coming from beyond the castle wall—sounds of a fight brewing in the field by the drainage pond. She could barely make out taunts of "Bastard! Bastard! Your mother's a Saxon whore!" Instinctively she gathered up her skirts and moved purposefully toward the gate.

"Demoiselle! Eleanor!" Herleva implored. "He can take care of himself!"

Eleanor broke into a run, passing sentries who hesi-

tated to lay a hand on the heiress. As she cleared the
gate, she could see a crowd gathered at the edge of the
foul-smelling ditch. It appeared that Roger was cornered at water's edge by a group of boys brandishing
swords. He was parrying off thrusts with a stout pole
held in front of his chest. She hurled herself headlong
into the startled group, panting for breath and pushing
her way to the forefront. That these boys were sons of
the greatest noble houses in Normandy, Maine, and
Brittany bothered her not at all—to her they were
nothing but a group of bullies intent on harming her
brother.

"Foul! Foul!" she cried. "Does it take all of you to
beat one boy? For shame! Where is your honor? Where
is your chivalry?"

Roger's chief tormentor, a tall black-haired boy,
growled back, "Hold her—she can watch me drown
the bastard."

The others were hesitant. By the richness of her
gown, it was evident she belonged to a great family.
She took advantage of this hesitation to rail against
them. "Fools! Dare you put a hand on Nantes? I shall
have you whipped if you do!"

"Lea, get out of here!" Roger called to her. " 'Tis
no place for a maid!"

"Nay, brother, I'd not see you harmed in an unfair
contest." Turning back to the group, she continued,
"Art cowards all! He can take any one of you—why
must it be all against one?"

"Nay, he cannot take Belesme," someone called
out.

"Then let Belesme fight him alone."

The black-haired boy sneered. "I'd not sully my
honor meeting the Saxon bastard."

"Fie! Shame! You call it honorable to fight eight or
ten to one? You are not fit to bear the sword you
hold!"

They were so intent on each other, girl and squires,
that they did not notice the approach of several riders.
It wasn't until the leader, a thick-set graying warrior,
rode straight into their midst and dismounted that he

got their attention. Expressions of shock, disbelief, and horror spread across the boys' faces. From behind Eleanor the old man called out, "What goes here?"

The crowd fell strangely silent and uncomfortable. Eleanor whirled to face the newcomer while the others looked at their feet. The old man's black eyes raked the group until they focused on her. "Well," he asked finally in a rough and raspy voice, "is there not a man among you save for the maid? She stands brave whilst you cower." In spite of the challenge, none dared to answer. "Well, Demoiselle, I leave it to you to answer—what goes here?"

"These . . . these squires thought to amuse themselves by harming my brother for no reason other than that he is bastard-born." She pointed accusingly at the tall boy identified as Belesme. "He threatened to drown him."

"Robert"—the old man scowled at the black-haired youth—"is this true?"

Robert's answer was evasive. "Sire, he would use the quintains with us and he has not even fostered. 'Tis plain he's baseborn and not fit to meet with us."

"And why should he not use the quintains?" Eleanor questioned hotly. "They are his—he set them up and this is his practice field." She faced the tall boy defiantly. "What right have you to come to Nantes and to taunt Nantes' son?"

"If he's so noble, why hasn't he fostered?" Belesme countered.

"Silence!" There was unmistakable authority in the old man's voice. "I would only know if the quarrel is over bastardy—is there any here who can say it isn't?" He motioned Roger forward and stared hard at him. "Well?"

It was obvious that Roger had no wish to be a talebearer, but Eleanor refused to allow his tormentors to go unpunished. "Sir . . . my lord," she cut back into the old man's attention, "they were all taunting him—calling him a bastard and calling Dame Glynis a Saxon whore. They fault him for that which he cannot help."

"I know much about bastardy, Demoiselle," was the terse reply. "Gilbert's by-blow, eh? You have not the look of him."

"I favor my mother, my lord." Roger met the black-eyed gaze squarely. "My mother is daughter to a Saxon thane and no baseborn whore."

The old man rubbed his chin thoughtfully. "A pity Gilbert's only son had to come from the wrong side of the blanket. I wonder . . ." He let his train of thought trail off unsaid. "Never fostered, eh?"

"My mother would not hear of it." Eleanor inserted herself back into the conversation. "She hates him."

"I can well believe that of Mary de Clare," he commented dryly. "How are you called, Demoiselle?"

"I am Eleanor, heiress of Nantes," she answered proudly, "and this is my brother, Roger, called FitzGilbert."

"I see. And how old are you, Roger?"

"He is nearly sixteen, my lord," Eleanor responded.

"Demoiselle, he does not appear addlepated," the old man told her. "Surely he can answer simple questions by himself."

Eleanor reddened and bit her lip to stifle a retort. Roger had to smile at her discomfiture as he answered for her this time, "Your pardon, my lord, but Lea is strong-minded and always ready to speak on my behalf whether I need the service or not."

"I see. Well, Roger FitzGilbert, you have not trained in any household, yet your sister says you can fight. Can you indeed acquit yourself with any skill in combat?"

"Aye, my lord, I can fight with a lance, ax, or sword," he answered simply.

Those around them laughed derisively. The one called Robert of Belesme snorted, "That marks him for a liar, Sire, for a broadsword is nigh as big as he is."

"I think we'll see, Robert." The old man glowered warningly. "If this fellow can account for himself against you, I'll foster him myself. When all's said, I think we bastards should stand together."

Roger was dumbfounded by this sudden change in

his fortune. When he could finally find his voice, he managed, "But . . . my lord, you do not know me— nor do I know you."

This brought another snort from Robert of Belesme. "The fool knows not Normandy and England, Sire."

A boy little older than Roger edged his horse forward from where he had been watching with the others who accompanied the old man. "Aye"—he leaned forward to address Roger—"FitzGilbert, you stand before your duke." His face broke into a friendly smile even as Roger's reddened, adding not unkindly, "My father will give you justice even though you recognized him not."

Both Roger and Eleanor sank to their knees beneath Duke William. The newcomer turned his attention to the kneeling Eleanor. "Art a fine champion for your brother, Demoiselle. I would that any of my sisters were half so spirited in my defense."

William gave the crowd one last withering look before raising them. With his own hand, he lifted Eleanor to her feet and studied her intently. Apparently he liked what he saw, as his face softened into a smile.

"Henry," he addressed the rider above them, "see the Lady Eleanor back inside whilst I deal with those who would taunt a bastard." His weather-roughened hand still enveloped hers in a firm grip. "Are you betrothed as yet, Demoiselle?"

Eleanor colored under his gaze. "Nay, my . . . Sire."

"Art a fierce little maid, Eleanor of Nantes, and worthy to be a warrior's bride. Mayhap I should speak to Gilbert about a suitable husband for you." He released her hand with a sigh. "I've five daughters of my own, and not one has your spirit. I pray you are allowed to keep it." Motioning her over to his son's horse, he bent and cupped his hand. "Up with you, child," he rasped as she hesitated before stepping into the palm. With a quick boost, he put her in front of the prince. Henry slid back on the saddle to make room for her slender body and slipped an arm easily about her waist to steady her.

"Sometimes my father finds particularly pleasant

tasks for me, Demoiselle," he murmured from behind her.

"Wait—what of my brother?"

Duke William answered her. "Your cousin Walter will lend his mail so that young FitzGilbert has his chance to meet Robert in a fair match. After that, I intend to birch Belesme myself."

Prince Henry twisted behind her to loose his sword. Raising it hilt-first, he proffered it to Roger. "Give a good account of yourself, FitzGilbert, and when you join my father's household, you shall ride in my train. Until then, I lend you Avenger. Use it well, boy, because you have a chance to do that which I have oft longed to try."

"But never dared," Belesme taunted.

The prince ignored the gibe. "Remember, FitzGilbert, you shall ride with me."

"Henry," the Conqueror warned his son, "I would have him learn warring rather than wenching."

The remark drew laughter from the rest of the boys. It was well known among them that the seventeen-year-old prince had an eye for beauty and a lusty appetite for the favors of some of the married ladies at his father's court. Henry laughed good-naturedly with them while tightening his arm around Eleanor. "Pay them no heed, Demoiselle, for today I am slave to you."

Roger frowned, his blue eyes narrowing at Henry's words. He moved protectively toward his half-sister, but stopped when he saw nothing but open friendliness and teasing in the prince's expression. Instead, Roger tweaked the toe of Eleanor's shoe for attention. "Lea, if I am to meet Belesme, I would wear your favor."

She flushed with pleasure at the request given as gravely as though they were knight and lady. Nodding, she removed the enamel brooch she wore pinned to her shoulder. Leaning as far as she dared while Henry held her waist, she tried to pin it in the rough wool of Roger's tunic. The task completed, she kissed him solemnly. "May my token bring you good fortune today, brother."

Prince Henry nudged his horse away. As they began the climb up the rocky road, Eleanor strained to watch as Walter de Clare began divesting himself of his mail and his gambeson.

"Do not fear for him, little one," the prince reassured her. "While I doubt very much that your brother can best Belesme—I doubt anyone can—you may be assured that my father will not let the boy come to harm."

It was then that the full import of the day's event came home to Eleanor and she fell silent. For Roger, gaining a place in William the Conqueror's household was a great honor. For Eleanor, it meant losing the person dearest to her heart. She tried hard to focus on the thought that it was at least an opportunity for him to make his way in a world that denied him an inheritance. Besides, had he been a legitimate son of a noble house, he would have fostered at seven or eight. At least she'd had him a lot longer than most sisters had their brothers with them.

"Why so silent, Demoiselle? You were full of words back there."

"I . . . I shall miss my brother," she managed.

"My sisters could scarce wait to see me gone," Henry told her conversationally, "and I thought much the same of them. My sister Adela has the temper of a viper."

Eleanor spoke before she thought. "It cannot be the same for you, Your Grace. Your father does not hate you for being a girl, and I am sure that your mother did not hate you either. My parents have never forgiven me for that which I cannot help. I suppose that is why Roger and I have always meant so much to each other—we are both despised for what we were born. Only he, Dame Glynis, and my old nurse care about me. And I love Roger above all things." Her shoulders began to shake slightly.

"Demoiselle, you weep too soon. Your brother will be back often enough to visit, I promise you." Henry's words only seemed to increase her anguish, causing him to try another subject. "Even if your lot is unhappy for the moment, little one, it will not be too long before you will be betrothed to a lord that loves you." He shifted his arm to cradle her against him. "Nay, sweet child, none could look upon you and not love you."

"You are kind," she sniffed, "for you do not know me. My lord will most probably beat me because I cannot sew and I have not the least ability in household accounts."

Her innocence brought forth a fierce desire to protect and comfort her. "Believe me," Henry told her, "when I say that such accomplishments are commendable but have little to do with a lord's love for his lady. A man can pay to have his sewing done, and he can get a steward and a seneschal to run his household. On the other hand, it is a rare marriage contract that yields a beautiful wife."

"Your Grace—"

"Demoiselle, you may call me Henry—come, I am not much older than your brother. Can we not be friends?"

She half-twisted her body to look at him. The friendliness in his face was unmistakable as she studied him. Unlike his father, he was not dark. His open countenance was framed with light brown hair cut straight across the forehead in Norman fashion, and his eyes, while brown, were not nearly so dark as the Old Conqueror's. But it was his easy smile and gentle manner that made her think that this surely must be the best of Normandy's sons.

"I am but seventeen and yet to be knighted," he continued. "While there is some small difference in our ages, I hope your brother and I may become friends. Perhaps we will both be able to visit you, and mayhap my father will order you to court when this quarrel with France is done."

She leaned her head back against his chest much as she would have done with Roger. As the prince's arm tightened protectively around her, she was suddenly

struck by the picture of impropriety they must present.
She tried to sit upright before any could see her, but
found herself held so tightly against him that she could
feel his heartbeat.

"Your Grace . . . Henry," she protested, " 'tis unseemly that you hold me thus—though the fault is
mine."

He relaxed his arm reluctantly. "Nay, Eleanor, the
fault is mine."

"The black-haired one—the one called Robert—I
didn't like him at all," she changed the subject to safer
ground. "Is he always like that?"

"Always. The young Count of Belesme is excessively proud, excessively cruel, excessively vain. No
one likes him and everyone is afraid of him. He's
Mabille's spawn."

"Mabille?"

"They say she's a witch." Henry crossed himself
with the hand that held the reins even as he added, "I
do not put much store in such tales, but she is said to
have poisoned Robert's father. There are other things
said of Robert and his mother that I dare not tell
you."

"What things?"

"I say too much. What I have heard is unfit for your
ears. Suffice it to say that my father is the only thing
Robert of Belesme fears. When he is gone, I fear the
Devil will be loosed."

"And you, my lord—are you afraid of him?"

He shrugged behind her. "I? I am not much the
soldier, Demoiselle. I fight if I must, but I'd rather
not. I have not the quarrelsome nature of Curthose
and Rufus. Besides, as the youngest son, I have little
enough to fight for." There was a faint trace of bitterness in his voice that faded as he added, "Alas, Demoiselle, we are arrived, and by the look of things, you
have been missed."

2

"Gilbert, I tell you I won't have it! William the Bastard can order your service, but he cannot order me in my household!" Lady Mary's voice was shrill and strident, carrying well beyond the confines of her solar.

"Mary . . ." Gilbert of Nantes' tone was placating.

"Mary nothing! The boy is naught but stable fodder, and the girl shames us with her boldness! I say they can both live on bread and ale dispensed in the kitchen during Festival. I will have neither at my table!"

"And I tell you that Normandy demands their presence—before I could whip the girl for her unseemly behavior, William's whelp warns me, 'I'd not mark her were I you, for my father would have her sup with us tonight as reward for her bravery.'" Gilbert nearly strangled at the recollection of Prince Henry's coolness toward him. "Whilst you and I consider her overbold, the duke considers her brave, so we must hold our tongues. She sups with Normandy himself, I tell you! Would you have him bring his mailed fist down on me because you hate your daughter?"

"'Tis you who curse her for not being a son!" Mary shouted back.

"Aye, but she may have some value to me yet, wife."

"Then let the little strumpet appear at supper and nowhere else—but I warn you, Gilbert, I'll not have your harlot's son in my hall."

"Nay, there's little enough harm in the boy, Mary, and 'twould seem he's caught William's eye. Walter tells me he means to take Roger into his service."

"The son of a Saxon whore?" Mary curled her lips in sarcastic disbelief.

"The grandson of a Saxon thane. He could be a credit to me yet."

"As much credit as the little strumpet, I'll warrant."

"Eleanor? Nay, whether you care to admit it, Mary mine, the girl's a beauty. I can aim high for a son-in-law, I tell you."

He could not have chosen his words with less care. Lady Mary was intensely jealous of the girl's looks and could not abide even the faintest praise of her beauty.

"Husband, are you daft? She'll naught but shame you! What worth is there in a maid so lost to propriety that she'd mix in a common brawl? Let her go to a nunnery and cast about for a husband for Margaret. Nay, I've changed my mind. You will tell Duke William she is ill."

Gilbert's patience was strained. "By all the saints, but you are a fool, Mary. 'Twas her boldness that lets me look high. Normandy notices her now and hints an interest in her marriage. And you, jealous fool, would hide my chance for gain. Sons of great houses ride in Normandy's train—sons who could make Eleanor a countess or more. I say dress the girl in finery, deck her in jewels, and see what comes of it."

"If you have her at our table, I'll not be there," Mary threatened.

Gilbert unclenched his fist and gave her the open palm of his hand across her cheek. She reeled from the blow, her expression one of shocked disbelief. Her hand went to her face as she screamed, "You hit me!"

"Aye, I did—and I'll do so again if you defy me. You listen to me, Mary mine! You've done naught but stand in my way since you came to me. You would have me disobey my liege lord to satisfy your meanness, wife. And what have I ever had of you?" His voice dropped to a menacing growl. "I'll tell you what—a lot of whimpering in your marriage bed and naught but three girls to show for thirteen years as a wife. You would taunt Glynis and make her life hell, but at least she knows how to make a son."

Mary's anger made her reckless. "Really, Gilbert?" she challenged. "And did she make one for you? I doubt it—I always have. Roger Bastard bears little likeness of you, my lord, yet you parade him around here like you are a randy rooster, flaunting him as a symbol of your manhood. Well, what of me? I've conceived three live and four stillborn girls, Gilbert, and if I've not borne a son, it's because you've not sown one." Her voice sank to a spiteful whisper. "Nay, husband, you do not have it in you to make a male child."

Gilbert reached out and grasped her chin painfully. "Have a care what you say to me, my lady, else I will put you aside. D'ye hear me, woman?" He released her and stepped back. "Now—Eleanor will sup with us and you will appear the proud parent. And if you beat the child and mark her, I'll mark you. As for Roger, you'll see him decently outfitted if you have to strip one of your fawning relatives to do it. I'll not send him to Normandy in rags. If you do not appear, you will be put out of my house."

He'd won his point. Mary stood before him with blanched face and enormous frightened eyes. Abruptly he turned on his heel and walked out, brushing past his eldest daughter on the winding stone stairs.

Eleanor had heard it all and, poised indecisively, tried to decide whether to go to her distraught mother or to follow her angry father. She finished climbing the few steps to Lady Mary's solar, where she found her beautiful mother still shaking, her hands held to her cheeks. Eleanor's first impulse was to reach out and comfort, but she drew back as Mary saw her. The hatred in her mother's eyes was unmistakable.

"There you are, you stupid girl! I hate you—get out of my sight!"

"Maman, please—"

"Get out! Whatever happens to me, you are to blame for it!"

His elation tempered by his aching limbs, Roger leaned forward on the bench while his mother tended

the ugly bruises on his arms and torso. It had been a
hard-fought contest between him and Belesme, one
that the bigger boy had eventually won, but he knew
he'd impressed those who'd watched with his own
skill. And when the Conqueror had called the halt,
he'd clasped Roger firmly by his sore shoulders and
told him he could join the Conqueror's train, a signal
honor even for the legitimate sons of great barons.
Robert of Belesme had thrown his sword down in
disgust at the news, but even he dared not defy Old
William.

"There," Glynis murmured as she rinsed the cloth
in the bowl of water, "you've nothing to stitch up at
least. Now"—she set aside the water and dropped to
the bench beside him—"tell me again how this came
about."

"There's naught to tell, Mother, that I have not
already said." He looked up into Glynis' blue eyes and
read the pride there and relented. "All right, 'tis as I
told you—I was practicing with the quintains where I'd
set them this morning. Anyway, several others stopped
to watch and then an older one, Robert of Belesme he
is called, came up and said I belonged in a stable—
that I was naught but a bastard, and a coward's bastard at that—and that they ought to throw me into the
drainage ditch for daring to try a noble's sport. I had
but the pole I was using for practice and he had a fine
sword. Anyway, he would have done it had not Lea
come running out to save me." He broke into a broad
smile at the memory and nodded. "Aye, I would that
you could have seen her, Mother. She marched right
through them and faced Belesme, calling him a coward and forbidding him to do it. When they would
hold her, she dared them to touch Nantes' daughter
and they did not. Anyway, we did not hear the riders
coming until this old man in mail rode up and demanded to know what was amiss. Lea would not let
me get in a word as she told him about it. You cannot
imagine our surprise to find that it was the Old Conqueror himself and he was most displeased to learn of
Belesme's part in the matter. He had Walter de Clare

give me his mail and his sword and told the young
count he'd make it a fair fight. Jesu, Mother"—Roger
winced in remembered pain—"But Belesme fought
as though possessed by the Devil—I think he would
have killed me had not Old William been there."

"But he did not, my son, and now you have your
chance."

"Aye. Had it not been for Lea, 'twould not have
happened." His face clouded at the thought of telling
Eleanor he was leaving. Her life at Nantes was little
better than his own, given Lady Mary's spitefulness.
"She will take the news ill, I think."

"She is but a child, Roger—she will recover from
the loss."

Somehow the thought was small comfort to him.
For some perverse reason, he did not want to think of
her not missing him—not that he wished her any pain—
quite the contrary, in fact. But they had endured so
much together that there was some special bond that
he was loath to break at all. No, aside from Glynis,
she was the most important person in the world to
him. He shook his head. "Nay, I will not recover from
the loss, Mother."

Glynis looked up sharply and frowned. "Mayhap 'tis
a good thing you go, Roger. You and Eleanor cannot
be together forever, you know. Soon she will be betrothed to a young lord and neither of you will have a
say in the matter. Nay, mayhap 'tis better to part now
and cry Godspeed to each other."

He thought of Lea with those great dark eyes and
that thick dark mane of hair and felt an overwhelming
protectiveness for her. No matter how they were separated, no matter how far apart they were, he knew he
would feel the same about her. Finally he nodded.
"Aye, mayhap you are right, but if I am ever in a
position to serve her, I will."

"Would it be easier if I told her?"

"Nay. Without doubt, Gilbert will have given her
the news even now. He is as swollen with conceit over
this as the cock on the wall." His voice betrayed his
disgust. "It isn't as though he ever thought to do more

than feed me and put a roof over mine head, Mother, but to hear him tell it, now that I am to join Duke William's train, my blood will tell. My blood will tell, Mama! Sweet Jesu, but who does he think he is? Can he not know how he is regarded? His cowardice is scoffed at from one end of Normandy to the other! Does he think I can be proud of that? My blood will tell, he says! Mother of God, but I want to hide the blood I have of him!"

"My son, there is no need for shame over Gilbert." Glynis leaned closer to put a comforting arm around Roger's shoulders. "Aye," she murmured at his questioning expression, "you are not Gilbert of Nantes' son."

He stared at her for several seconds until he comprehended the full import of her words. "Not his son!" he echoed blankly. "But how can that be? I have lived in his house since my birth—he has acknowledged me."

"Aye, but you are not his son," she repeated firmly. "When he brought me to Normandy, it pleased him to think he'd gotten a son, Roger. God forgive me, but it was the only chance you had, so I did not tell him otherwise."

"But you are his leman."

Glynis winced at the hated word. "I am his leman," she agreed, "but he was my second lover. Your father was a Norman and his keep is in England. I loved him once, believed in his lies, and went to him, but he betrayed me to Gilbert." Her mouth twisted and her voice turned bitter. "Aye, I was sold to Gilbert of Nantes even as I carried you in my belly, Roger."

"Sweet Mary! Mother, my father—*who* is my father?"

"Nay"—she shook her head—" 'twould serve no purpose in the telling. Let it be only said that you've naught to fear of cowardice in your blood. Your father, as young as he was, fought well against my people in the Wake's rebellion. Aye, and was rewarded with a Norman heiress."

"Then Lea is not my sister." The flat statement did not begin to reflect the sudden conflict of emotion he felt at the thought. For years it had comforted him to think of their shared kinship, but now . . . He dared not even think the impossible fleeting thought that came to mind.

"Roger, you will not tell her."

"Why?"

Glynis twisted and then smoothed the fabric across her lap. Raising her eyes to meet her son's squarely, she answered simply, "Think you I do not love her also? It is bad enough to have been her father's leman these many years, Roger, but to admit I lay with someone else also—can you not see, 'twould brand me the harlot in her eyes."

They were interrupted by the sounds of several men coming up the stairs to Gilbert's chamber. Glynis rose hastily and picked up the bowl of water. Roger shrugged his rough tunic over his head and pulled it down to cover his discolored rib cage. As Glynis finished tidying the clean-swept chamber, servants unknown to either of them rounded the last step and surveyed the room appraisingly. Apparently satisfied, one nodded to the others. "Aye, 'twill do—bring up his things." Turning to Glynis, he bowed slightly. "Art the Lady Mary?"

"Nay."

The man's gaze traveled over her with new interest, his eyes taking in the fineness of her clothing, his thoughts reaching the obvious conclusion. And even as his manner changed to her, she appeared to color slightly. Roger watched and wanted to wipe the knowing smile off the fellow's face. But at that moment he recognized the badge of Normandy on another servant's breast and he forced himself to hold his temper in check. His mother sensed his tension and sought to divert him. "You have much to do, my son, if you would be ready to leave with the duke. You'd best seek out Herleva and see if she can lengthen any of your tunics whilst there's still time."

Having unceremoniously taken over Gilbert's own chamber, Duke William soaked in his great oaken tub.

Glynis stood over him with a soapy rag, ready to assist in the ducal bath.

" 'Tis silly enough to think me incapable of washing myself," William grumbled, "but if you must do it, have a care for my eyes—they are not what they used to be, but I've still need of both of them."

Glynis' voice was soft and musical as she leaned to soap his battle-scarred back. "I've bathed many a man, Your Grace, and I've yet to blind any of them."

"You've a Saxon accent."

"Aye, I was brought over here during Hereward the Wake's rebellion—my father sided with the Wake. I long to go back, but there's naught of what I used to know still there."

Prince Henry rose for a closer look. "Can you be young FitzGilbert's mother?"

"Aye."

William looked up, his eyes squinting at her appraisingly. "Gilbert's leman, eh?"

"Aye."

"A pity he did not wed with you rather than Mary de Clare."

"I had nothing to bring him, Sire, and had I the choice, I should have refused." The musical quality left her voice and it became low and flat.

"Yet you bore him a fine son. Though outmatched by two stone and a full hand in height, your Roger fought well today. With training, he'll make a good knight."

"I should have thought he lost badly, Sire, for there's scarce an inch of his body unbruised."

William stood to be rinsed. "If that is so, he took a beating before we arrived. Once he had a sword and shield of his own, the boy gave nearly as many blows as he received. It pleases me to foster him."

"And grieves the little maid. She would not part with her brother, Papa." Henry would know more of Eleanor if he could prompt Glynis to tell them.

"Well"—she began rubbing William vigorously with a rough towel—"it is best for both of them that Roger leaves now. They have been overmuch together and

the time nears when she will be betrothed, anyway. As
it is, they protect each other too much for either to
grow strong."

"Is her lot that unhappy?" Henry pressed.

"She is not a son," Glynis answered simply.

"But she is truly beautiful. How could anyone not
love her?"

"Henry—" William's black eyes warned his son.
"You'll not play the rutting boar here. Good dame,
that's enough—old wounds heal slowly at my age."

Glynis would have clapped for William's man, but
he stayed her. "I would dress myself." She shrugged
slightly before sketching a hasty curtsy and departing.

"What did you think of her, Papa?"

"Gilbert's leman?"

"The Demoiselle."

"She is old and wise for her years. Were she fifteen
or sixteen, she would make a good wife—especially
since she brings Nantes with her when Gilbert dies."
William reached for his tunic and shrugged it over his
head, muffling his voice as he added, "I find her
enchanting."

"And you are fifty-eight with a houseful of heirs,"
Henry reminded him with alarm.

"I have no need of a wife," William agreed mildly
as his head emerged again. "I was thinking of Rufus.
Robert is wed—much good that does us, since he sits
with my enemies—but Rufus is not."

Henry fought the urge to vomit. The thought of
sweet Eleanor and the crude violent Rufus caused his
gorge to rise. Nay, Rufus had no use for a woman.
She'd have a better chance of winning his love if she
were a pretty blond boy.

"Your brother will have England, Henry. I cannot
stop Robert from claiming Normandy as his birthright,
but, by the saints, I can bestow England on the son
who stands by me. The little maid of Nantes could be
a good influence on him, Henry."

"Nay! You would not! You could not! Think—Rufus
would not know what to do with one such as she is.
Nay, he would not want her!"

The old duke wrapped his cross-garters over his chausses. "I am well aware of your brother's strange appetites. You need not remind me."

"Papa, there are other considerations besides Robert and Rufus." Henry's voice took on an intensity not often used with his father. "Robert gets Normandy, Rufus gets England, and I get nothing. The Demoiselle brings Gilbert and all he has—yea, even Nantes one day. She is everything a man could wish for—beautiful, intelligent, strong-willed, and loyal. Can she not come to me?"

"Henry, is this your heart or your loins speaking?"

"Both. I would be lying if I denied it."

William sighed as he regarded his youngest son. "A man in your position cannot afford to wed where he wishes. You must always weigh the politics of your decisions because I have no land to leave you. There's money enough to make you rich, but there's no land."

"She can bring me land. Surely Gilbert will dower her well—and then there is Nantes. She can bring me Nantes, Papa."

"She is but twelve years old. What if she does not live long enough to give you an heir? Her land will go to the next sister, not you. And have you considered that it will be two or three years before you can bed her?"

"And what of Rufus?" Henry argued back. "I doubt he would ever bed her—not even for England's sake. She is more like to die in his care than mine, I'll warrant."

William wavered. This boy was much he wished to be—intelligent and cunning, educated beyond his peers, even-tempered, and loyal. Oh, if he could only disinherit the feckless Robert and provide for Henry. Nay, the baronage would revolt against the very idea that the eldest son did not inherit. Then too there had been his promise to his beloved Mathilda—Robert had always been her favorite. As for Rufus, William could not deny him either. Harsh, crude, with a streak of cruelty, Rufus nonetheless always stood firm with his father, taking the field on William's behalf time and again, putting his very life on the line to keep William secure on England's throne. He could never deny Rufus. But Henry was right—Rufus would not want a queen.

Henry watched intently as his father thought. In the space of this brief conversation with William, little Eleanor of Nantes had become very important to him. He not only wanted her for her extraordinary beauty and her wealth—now she had become a symbol of his own worth to his father.

Finally William spoke slowly and reasonably. "There is much to what you say, my son, but I think Gilbert would prefer Rufus for his daughter because of the crown he will wear."

"I doubt he dares aim so high. I'll warrant he'd take any of us for a bridegroom."

"And what of the Demoiselle?"

Henry doubted that she cared much about marriage to anyone, but he had something to sweeten the bargain. Betrothed to him, she would come to court to be educated and there she could see her brother often enough. A smile spread across his face. "She'll be pleased enough."

"Let me approach Gilbert on the matter. Say nothing to the girl until it is agreed on with him."

"So be it."

Much disturbed by her encounter with her mother and the impending loss of Roger's company, Eleanor sought out her half-brother for comfort. In spite of Lady Mary's hatred, he resided in a cupola cut into the heavy wall of Gilbert's chamber, and Eleanor thought to find him there. As she rounded the final steps, she could hear the voices of strangers. Probably someone was waiting to see her father.

"Demoiselle!" It was a startled Prince Henry that spun to face her. The Old Conqueror sat wet-headed on a low bench by the fire as he struggled with his heavy boots.

"Eh? The Demoiselle, you say?"

Eleanor mistook his surprise for irritation. Stammering out an explanation even as she swept a hasty curtsy, she managed, "Y-your pardon, Your Grace, b-but I thought to find my b-brother here." She gulped for control of her thudding heart. She had intruded at an awkward time at best. Lamely she explained, "He lives there," as she pointed to the tiny alcove.

"Come here, child." Even as he commanded her, William rose and strode toward her. "Let me look at you again." His fingers lifted her chin, allowing her freshly combed hair to fall back like a parting silk curtain. Her clear brown eyes stared unwavering back at him. She was neither cowed nor overly bold. Finally the old duke threw back his head and laughed aloud, to her puzzlement.

"God's teeth, but you are a rare find, Demoiselle. Warriors cringe when I look upon them—yet you look back." He stepped back and dropped his hand as his eyes traveled to the slight swelling of young breasts. Abruptly he asked, "Have you had your courses yet?"

An embarrassed flush crept to her cheeks and she lowered her eyes. Prince Henry sought to intervene by protesting, "Really, Papa—" but William continued to wait for an answer.

Finally she nodded her head. "Aye. Once."

"Papa—"

"Be still, Henry. I would get to know the child." With his black eyes still on Eleanor, he continued his questioning. "How soon will you reach your thirteenth year?"

"September."

"You have such beauty, little one." William's raspy voice softened. "But only time can tell if it is God's gift or nature's curse."

"Nay, only God could create such perfection. When she is grown, there will be none fairer in Christendom." Henry moved behind his father's shoulder. "Pay my father no heed, Demoiselle—'tis not his intent to frighten you."

"She is not frightened—she knows I would not harm her." William continued his inspection. "Art delicately boned and small. Such a one was my Mathilda—she came but to here on me." He indicated a place on his chest that made Eleanor think the late duchess must have been very small indeed. "She gave me three living sons and five daughters, God rest her soul." With a gentle nudge to Eleanor, William nodded toward Henry. "What think you of my son?"

Eleanor frowned in puzzlement at the strange line of questioning. Raising her eyes to look at the prince, she found him smiling reassurance at her. In response, her own face broke into a soft smile as she answered his father, "I think you have a prince to be proud of, Sire."

William roared at her answer, puzzling her even more. "God's teeth, Henry! We have found us a diplomat!" He gave her head a paternal pat. "Well, don't stand there gaping—help her find that brother of hers." As Eleanor made her obeisance before leaving, the old man added, "And tonight, Demoiselle, you sup with us."

She followed Henry down the steep and narrow stone steps and into the courtyard. At the last step, the prince turned to tuck her hand in the fold of his elbow. The eyes of the curious followed them, Normandy's son and Nantes' daughter, across the open yard. The prince appeared at his most charming and her laughter could be heard floating upward to where William watched. At the lean-to that housed Nantes armory, Henry paused.

"You'll find him within, Demoiselle. My father would have him fitted with a good set of mail and helm ere we leave. And your father has commissioned a well-padded gambeson and sword for him. When he wears Normandy's leopards, he will be as well-equipped as the rest of us."

Tears sprang suddenly into the dark eyes as she nodded mutely at this reminder of Roger's leaving. Henry could have bitten his tongue for having saddened her. Reaching to brush away a tear that brimmed, he advised gently, "Patience, little Eleanor. One day you will grace Normandy's court with your brother."

Their voices had brought Roger to the doorway.

Squinting against the bright sunlight, he caught Henry's gesture and frowned at the prince's familiarity with her. Inexplicably, it made him angry.

If Henry noticed Roger's scowl, he gave no indication. "FitzGilbert"—he grinned—"I bring you your gentle sister. She was so anxious to see you whole that she invaded Normandy's chamber."

"I thought to find you in our father's room," Eleanor told Roger.

Henry waved aside any further explanation and turned away. "I leave you in safe hands, Demoiselle. But do not forget—tonight you share my trencher."

"And what was that about, Lea?" Roger glowered after the prince's retreating figure.

"I don't know. I am commanded to sup with the duke tonight." She reached out impulsively and caught Roger's hand. "Only fancy—I have met and conversed with an anointed king—and am bade to sup with him!"

"I can fancy a lot of things, Lea, and I like not any of them." He winced as he stooped slightly to pat one of Gilbert's wolfhounds. "Walk with me a pace else I grow stiff from the blows I've taken today."

He drew her along the curtain wall, wandering aimlessly, with him pushing his aching body and her lost in thought. Neither seemed to notice as they passed beneath the indulgent scrutiny of the sentries and out into the field beyond. They followed the road down toward the city until it forked between town and forest. It was warm for the season and shade trees beckoned. There, beneath the very shadow of a huge stone fortress, and above the bustle of a city teeming with revelers, the world was strangely peaceful and beautiful.

Roger stopped in the shadow of his favorite oak and stripped his sweat-soaked shirt from his body, tossing it to the ground to make a place for Eleanor to sit. She smoothed her skirt and lowered herself to the ground. With a groan, Roger dropped to her side and rolled to lie stretched out in the lush cool grass. He pillowed his head and closed his eyes.

She was conscious that too soon he would ride out—maybe never to return to Nantes—and she sought to engrave him in her memory. In her nearly thirteen years, he had been everything to her—brother, companion, teacher, friend. From him she'd learned to ride, to hawk, to sing and to strum the lute, even to read and cipher. He'd teased and laughed with her—and he'd fought any who would hurt her feelings. But his life had been hard here—and for his sake she ought to be glad he had a chance to better himself.

With a start, she realized that she was so used to him that she'd not noticed he'd grown nearly to manhood. He was a lot taller stretched out than she'd thought. At Christmas, she'd reached his shoulder—now she reached his breast. She studied the tousled waves of cropped blond hair, the finely angled and chiseled planes of a face that already showed strength and handsomeness—so much so that the priest had chosen him to play the archangel Michael in the Christmas tableau. He had a well-defined chin, even teeth, straight nose, and a downy mustache that he hated. But most of all, he had beautiful blue eyes.

As if aware of her thoughts, he opened those eyes and rolled onto his side, the movement rippling muscles in his arms and shoulders as he came to rest on a propped elbow. Fresh bruises darkened the skin along his rib cage and swelled his upper arms. A wry smile formed at the corners of his mouth. "Lea, you've not been this quiet since you were born."

"I was thinking you could have fallen off yonder wall and not been so black and blue," she teased.

"Aye. Belesme swings his sword with a power you'd not believe. I took some of these through Walter's shield. Jesu!" He appeared to examine one particularly ugly area. "I thought he meant to kill me beneath Normandy's nose."

"He probably did. Prince Henry says he's very cruel."

"Prince Henry says," he mimicked her. "God's teeth, Lea, but you have only to meet a member of a royal house and you can do naught but speak of him."

Stung, she retorted, "I did not—I have not even mentioned him before. Roger, what ails you?"

"You sup with him tonight—share his trencher even. Have a care, Lea."

"A care for what?"

The blue eyes were serious. "Sweet sister, you are very beautiful and already show signs of ripening into a woman. Henry may be but seventeen, but he already has one bastard to his credit. When he looks on you with favor, ask yourself why—is it because you are sweet and good? Or is it because he would have you?"

"Roger!"

"Listen, Lea. I am nearly sixteen and I too feel the stirrings in my blood. He may be a prince, but he is the same as me."

She was aghast. "You make it seem so base. Roger—" Her eyes were wide as they sought his. "You do not think of me like that, do you?"

He appeared to consider his words carefully. "I love you, Lea—I always have—I always will. I would protect you whatever the cost and I would never harm you."

"And your lady wife will hate me."

His mood changed abruptly. He rolled up into a sitting position and pulled himself up with a low-hanging branch. Giving her a hand, he spoke lightly. "I doubt I have a lady wife, Lea, unless she's much like you."

She bent to retrieve his dirty shirt from the grass. The coarse feel of it reminded her that soon he and all of his things would be gone from Nantes. Her resolve to show him a brave face crumbled.

"Oh, Roger! I cannot bear to see you go," she wailed as she threw herself against him. I swear I cannot stand it!"

"Would you have me stay?" he asked softly as he enveloped her in his aching arms.

"N-no," came the muffled reply before she broke into sobbing.

"Shhh . . . shhh," he murmured as he stroked the thick dark hair. "Lea, I would I never had to leave you—that it could always be just us—but there's no help for it. Here I am nothing, just another lord's by-blow—there I have a chance. Duke William fights

a war, Lea—think on it. Even a bastard with no inheritance can be knighted and rewarded on the battlefield. With all of England, Normandy, and Maine to
choose from, I can surely win something of him if I
prove myself."

"The Duke grows old," she whispered against the
hardness of his chest.

"Aye—and leaves three snarling sons to fight for all
he has won. If William lives not to care for me, one of
his sons will." He held her back a little, speaking
earnestly and searching the tearstained face for understanding. "Lea, look at me! Behold a bastard too lowly
to be a lord and too good to be a stableboy. Is that
what you would have me?"

With a heavy sigh, she looked away. "Nay. It is
wrong of me to tear at your heart for what you must
do."

His hands slid down her arms to possess hers, pulling her close again. "When I am gone from you, I am
still your champion. Once knighted, I will not hesitate
to wield my sword in your behalf and to hold for you
that which is yours. When Gilbert dies, you may have
need of someone to hold for you and yours against
those who would despoil your inheritance."

"It seems so very far away and such a long time."

"Aye. And one day you may not even need me.
You will be wed to a lord someday, who may be
strong enough to hold Nantes."

"I don't *want* to marry!" she cried with unaccustomed force.

"Lea, you will have no choice. God knows, I don't
want you given to just any lord."

"If I wed, I will be as accursed as my mother!"

Roger held her closer. "Nay, Lea, any man would
love you." Abruptly he released her. "We'd best get
back. By now, I should be lucky to be the tenth fellow
in the bathwater."

"Ugh."

"I am not so highborn as you, Eleanor of Nantes.
While servants labor to drag heated water to you, I
take my turn in the same tub with all but the scullery."

"Well, when you are become a great lord, I will see you have hot water and fresh towels, and I will bathe you myself," she promised.

The castle was crowded and everywhere she turned, Eleanor encountered strangers come to share the Maying with Gilbert. She picked her way along the covered walkway to the banquet hall with her skirts held above her ankles to avoid any spittle on the floor. She was dressed unusually fine even for a festival. Upon her return, her father had summoned her with unwonted joviality and presented her with a choice of her mother's jewelry to wear. Moreover, he'd given her an exquisitely embroidered surcoat which she wore now over a silver-threaded gown of ruby samite. The sleeves of her dress were fitted at her wrists with tiny silver bows, an unusual decoration created by Glynis. Even Herleva had outdone herself for her charge. Eleanor's hair had been brushed until it shone, then strands had been selected on her crown and woven with silver threads that ended in bows halfway between crown and shoulder.

Jostled by the crowd until she found a small open space, Eleanor came face-to-face with her brother's tormentor of the morning. She gave him what she hoped passed for her haughtiest look and moved to pass. He stepped directly into her path. She found herself staring straight into a fine green tunic embroidered with golden leaves. He left her little choice but to acknowledge him. She met his eyes coolly.

"Pray step aside that I may pass."

Up close, she could see that he was unbelievably handsome—tall, black-haired, with green eyes that flickered over her with calculated arrogance before he spoke. There was no warmth in them or in his voice.

"One day, Demoiselle, I will hold the fate of you and your family in my hands."

A chill ran down her spine, but she held her ground. "A brave speech for a boy, I think."

A black eyebrow rose. "I am older than Henry or the bastard you call brother. 'Tis you who are yet the

child, Eleanor of Nantes, but I can wait." With the
briefest of bows, he moved aside.

She swept past him and into the great hall. Catching
sight of her cousin, Walter de Clare, she made her
way to his side. Nearly twenty, Walter carried about
him an air of worldliness that always impressed her.
At her approach he took in her face, her form, and
her gown, murmuring appreciatively, "Sweet Jesu!
Cousin, you have grown since I last saw you." He
caught her hand gracefully and carried it to his lips.
"Were I not betrothed myself, I should apply to the
Pope for a dispensation and take you instead."

"Pooh."

She linked an arm through his and drew him aside
from his fellows. "Walter, have you seen Roger? I
would warn him to have a care for Belesme."

Her cousin frowned and shook his head. "Eleanor,
if you would aid him, leave Roger be. He has won
Normandy's favor—mayhap Henry's also—so do not
be stirring up a quarrel when he has a chance to rise.
'Tis time to part and cry Godspeed if you love him."
Walter leaned closer to whisper for her ears only,
"Have a care for yourself and your family, sweet cousin.
The rumor is that Prince Henry is besotted of you."
He paused as Belesme passed by. "Think on that,
Eleanor, and think how you can aid the family."

"How?" she asked bluntly.

"Make him ask for your hand in marriage."

"Walter"—she shook her head in asperity—"you
mistake the matter. Prince Henry and Duke William
are merely being kind to me."

"Foolish child. Neither the Old Bastard nor his spawn
is given to kindness unless it suits their policy. Look at
yourself and look at this hall—think you Gilbert hasn't
hopes of snaring a rich alliance with you?" Walter
waved his hand expansively around the room. "This
place has been scraped, whitewashed, strewn with fresh
rushes and flower petals, and decorated with new hangings. Why, he's even replaced the rushlights with candles. And look at that gown you are wearing."

"He would not dare to look so high as Normandy."

"No? He is Count of Nantes and you are his heiress. And Normandy's son pants after you already."

Just then they were spied by Roger and Henry. Both boys found their way through the crowd to Eleanor's side. Roger was freshly scrubbed and attired in a new tunic of fine-gauge blue wool. His blond hair was neatly combed and the faint mustache freshly shaved away.

"Brother, you are as fine as any lord," she teased.

"Aye"—he grinned back—"and I've acquired a new dagger." He fingered a jeweled scabbard that hung at his belt. "Prince Henry gave it to me."

Walter gave her a knowing look as if to say, "See?" With a flourish, he bowed over her hand. "Sweet cousin, Your Grace, Roger—I see a promising wench over there."

"Walter, you are betrothed!"

"Aye," he agreed amiably. "But Helene is at Gerberoi and I am here."

He had scarce turned his back to leave when William's attendants appeared. Wearing rich robes and carrying staffs and censers, they parted the crowd before them with cries of "Make way! Make way, good people!" As a path cleared, another man wearing Normandy's livery called out, "Stand aside for William, by grace of God, King of England, and Duke of Normandy!"

The duke himself followed immediately, his thick, graying hair circled with golden leaves, his stocky body clad in a long robe of fine red silk girded at the waist with a gold chain. He clinked as he walked, for beneath his finery he wore mail shirt, boots, and spurs. Behind him, another servant carried his battle sword. In all of his years of fighting to hold his inheritance, William had learned to stay wary of an assassin's hand.

He was met before he reached the high dais by Count Gilbert and Lady Mary. Both knelt in obeisance at his feet. Gilbert was lifted up and kissed ceremoniously on both cheeks, while Mary had to rely on a retainer to raise her. And if she thought to receive the signal honor of mounting the dais on William's arm, she was sorely disappointed. His gaze swept the assembled nobility until it settled on Eleanor.

"Come sup with us, Demoiselle, and bring that son of mine with you. God's teeth, but I grow weak waiting for my food!" His voice was rough but incredibly he was smiling.

Henry offered his elbow and led her forward while whispering, "Head high, Demoiselle—I'll not let you stumble."

She was thankful that she was spared the close company of her mother and father, they being seated to the Duke's left while she and Prince Henry were placed on his right. This meal at least she would be spared her mother's gibes.

Trenchers were placed on the tables, with two people to each one except for the duke, who had his all to himself. Once the cooks began the traditional parade of food, the hall lapsed into near-silence as people fell to the task of dividing roast pig, mutton, game birds, meat pies, stewed onions and peas, honey pots, rice, dates, and cheeses. At the high table, there was a servant for each couple and William's own squire served him with great ceremony.

Eleanor washed her hands carefully in a silver bowl and dried them on a fine linen towel held for her by a servant. As dishes were passed, Prince Henry carefully placed some of each at both ends of the trencher, serving Eleanor first with the finest portions. Then he took a spoon and stirred honey into the wine cup they would share, explaining, "I find so much of this too sour to drink, so I save myself the first tasting anymore." He proffered the cup to her. "Try it."

There was mischief in her dark eyes as she took it. "So I am to take the first sip, and if I make a hideous face, you will add more before you try it."

"Mayhap—or mayhap I want to see if you like it."

She sipped and nodded, "Ummm—it is better."

To her embarrassment, her partner took the cup, examined it, and deliberately turned it to where her lips had been, taking care to drink from the same place. "I drink to the fairest lady in Christendom—nay, the fairest in the world," he amended extravagantly.

Walter de Clare shared a trencher with Robert of Belesme, an unhappy distinction caused by his lateness in seeking the table. From where they sat, they had an excellent view of Eleanor and Prince Henry. Walter could even see Henry cut Eleanor's meat up into dainty pieces for her, and his spirits soared. Surely a betrothal would come of the attention and the de Clares would share in William's favor. Without thinking, he poked Belesme.

"My young cousin seems to have caught Prince Henry's fancy."

"Aye," Robert of Belesme agreed amiably enough.

"A pity it is not Rufus, though, for she grows beautiful enough to be a queen."

Robert gave a derisive snort. "Art a fool, de Clare. William Rufus will never wed, I promise you. Holy Church does not sanction the liaisons he prefers." Robert dipped his greasy fingers in the water bowl and rinsed them. "And do not be pinning much hope on Henry, either. A twelve-year-old he cannot bed will not hold him in thrall for long. He'll be panting after a new wench at the next town."

Walter didn't like the tone Belesme used. "My cousin is no wench to be tumbled and Henry knows it."

"Ah, de Clare, they are all alike enough under their clothes." Robert speared a sugared date with his knife before fixing Walter with those strange green eyes. "And for all *her* airs and tempers, the time will come when your fair cousin lies beneath me, moaning and panting for my seed."

Walter's hand went to the dagger he carried in his sleeve. "You forget you are speaking of my kinswoman," he warned.

"Nay, I forget nothing—ever." Robert's hand snaked out and grasped Walter's wrist, carrying it to the table. "I would not draw a blade on me, de Clare, else I wanted my lights carved out." His fingers were like a vise as they pressed Walter's palm open. The small poniard fell to the floor as Belesme abruptly released his grip.

"Roger will stand against you."

"The bastard?" Robert's lips curved scornfully as he considered Eleanor's half-brother. "Nay. You and the Demoiselle put too much faith in him. He will have too much honor to do what must be done. I, on the other hand, let nothing stand in my way."

Suddenly there was a commotion at the high table as Lady Mary rose clutching her stomach and screaming at her husband, "You foul beast—you've poisoned me!" Her face had gone white even as she cried, "A curse on you and all of your house!"

"You daft woman!" Gilbert half-knocked over the table as he tried to reach her. " 'Tis your own issue you would condemn."

She pitched forward, striking the already disturbed table and falling under it. Moans and screams intermingled as she writhed in the rushes as though possessed. Gilbert stood over her with both fists clenched. "I warned you, Mary—I said I'd put you aside, and by God, I shall!"

Gasps of horror spread through the crowd. Roger pushed his way to the front of the hall even as Prince Henry moved between Gilbert and his fallen wife. Many around them crossed themselves and craned for a better look. William stayed his host with a firm hand on the shoulder.

"Stand back that she may be ministered to. Henry, look to Lady Mary." William caught sight of Roger and motioned him forward. "Can you lift her?"

"Aye."

Henry knelt before the moaning woman and pried her mouth open, forcing some wine between her teeth. She gagged and then vomited. He nodded to Roger. "Let us lift her to a bench so that we may better see—and someone fetch the leech."

Gilbert mastered his anger as he came to the realization that his wife was indeed extremely ill. "Mary . . . Mary . . . what ails you?"

Roger pushed him back. "Let others tend her. As it is, all present saw you eat of the same food and drink of the same cup. If she dies, it is most likely that something has burst within her. Give no truth to her accusations."

"But . . . Mary . . ." Gilbert's face seemed to crumple. "Oh, God . . . Mary!"

Roger and Henry picked up Lady Mary and laid her on a bench. She was breathing heavily and sweat poured profusely from her forehead. As the prince pressed a towel against her damp face, he called, "Where is the lady's chaplain?"

Menservants cleared the way and carried her on the bench past the stunned and horrified guests. William nodded to Gilbert. "I'll come with you for witness."

Eleanor paced the floor of her father's chamber in anguish. One by one, her sisters, her mother's relatives, even her mother's tiring women had been summoned to bid farewell to her. Yet none had come for Eleanor. Even as dawn began to creep rosily across the dimly lit chamber, she still waited. Old Herleva dozed by the brazier and left the girl alone with her thoughts. That Mary could not be brought to love her daughter did not mean the daughter did not love her. Guilt for her very existence weighed heavily on Eleanor.

"Lea." Roger stood at the top of the stairs.

"Is she . . . ?"

He shook his head. "Soon, I think. Would you go to chapel with me?"

"You don't think Papa will send for me? No—I suppose not," she sighed. "Aye. Mayhap I should pray."

"Don't wake Herleva," he advised in a whisper as he reached to take her hand. He half-led her down the narrow, steep stairs in the semidarkness. At one turn, she lost her footing on a closed bowman's slit and pitched forward. From there to the bottom, Roger carried her. The passage below was deserted and pitch dark where the heavy iron torchholders had not been replenished during the night.

"Lea . . ." Roger drew her against him and wrapped his arms about her, whispering softly, "It is not your fault, lovey, that she could not accept what God gave her. Whatever happens to you, to Gilbert, or to anyone else in this household, you are not to blame."

It was so like Roger to know her thoughts and to bring them out into the open. With a wrenching cry, she buried herself against him and began to sob. He held her quietly for a long time, allowing her to vent her hurt and anguish. Then rocking her against him, he began to whisper over and over, "Cry until you can cry no more, little one."

Slowly the racking sobs subsided into gulping hiccups and then into wet sniffs. "Roger," she managed at last, "what will I do without you now?"

He stepped back a little bit, but could not see her face in the darkness. He groped for words to explain what would happen to her, to soothe the blow of Lady Mary's final revenge on her unwanted daughter. He took a deep breath and exhaled slowly, uncertain how to tell her and unwilling to have her hear from Gilbert.

"Lea . . ." It was no use—she'd take his news pitifully no matter what he said. Finally he reached again for her hand and began walking to the empty chapel. "Come pray with me, Lea."

Although neither Gilbert nor Mary was particularly religious, they had made great show of their devotion to Holy Church and no place reflected this outward display more than the chapel at Nantes. As though to tempt God to send him a legitimate son, Gilbert had spared no expense. Cloth of gold and crimson velvet paneled the narrow walls and draped the altar, while Italian windows of extraordinary beauty arched their stained-glass scenes to the sky. Rings of spring flowers decorated the backs of chairs carved and fitted into the wall. And behind the altar, a gilded statue of Christ, flanked by statues of the Virgin Mary and St. Catherine, was illuminated by purest wax candles. And in the base of Christ's statue, a special chamber held a reliquary of a saint.

The dawn filtered softly through the many-colored windows, casting strange and beautiful images on the flagstone floor. Eleanor knelt on the cold floor and began to pray for her mother's soul. Roger knelt be-

side her and tried to compose his thoughts for the task
facing him. Eleanor half-turned and was awed by the
halo effect of the light on his blond head. Surely this
must be how a man looked when he was purified for
knighthood. He looked up, caught her awestruck expression, and looked away.

"Roger, something troubles you—something more
than Maman or than your leaving Nantes." She took
his hand and held it to her cheek. "Is it Glynis?"

"My mother leaves Nantes. We escort her as far as
Abbeville, where she will join the sisters there."

"My father sends her away to salve his conscience
over Maman," Eleanor muttered bitterly.

"Nay—she chose to leave."

"Roger, nobody goes to a convent who does not
have to."

He took another deep breath and shook his head.
"Lea, I would tell you this only because I know Gilbert will do it and I'd rather you heard from one who
at least loves you."

"Heard what? Roger, what is it that is so terrible
that you cannot speak to me of it?"

"Well, because of what he thinks everyone is saying,
Gilbert wishes to appear devoted to your mother.
What she could not get out of him in life, she will get
in death."

"I don't understand."

"She is having you sent away. She has demanded
that Gilbert make a gesture of penance—something
that will aid her soul—and that gesture is you." He
paused and stared at the girl so soon to be a beautiful
woman. "You will be dedicated to Holy Church."

Eleanor sat stunned. It could not be. She who had a
future perhaps even as a prince's bride—she was to be
a nun. She who practiced her religion by rote and who
let her attention wander at Mass? Nay, it could not be.

"Look at me." Roger turned her face toward his.
"Soon you will be summoned to hear Gilbert tell you
what I have just said. Try to appear to accept it."

"What choice do I have?" she asked bitterly. "I am
as much an outcast in this family as you are. Oh,

Roger, I could bear it as a child because of you, but now I will not have even that."

"Nay, Lea, you'll always have me. I will always be your champion." He saw the hurt and confusion mirrored in her face and sought to explain. "I have not the resource nor the strength to do anything for you now, but the time will come when I will free you from wherever Gilbert sends you. There are things I cannot tell you—things I dare not tell you now—that may change everything for you and me, Lea. Trust me, and remember that I will come for you when I can."

"When? Days? Months? Years? Oh, Roger, I cannot bear it—I will grow old and die there."

"Listen, Lea, I have told you I'll get you out—and I will." Roger sought for some means to convince her that all was not hopeless. "Here . . ." He pulled her after him behind the altar. Reaching into the base of Christ's statue, he drew out the small gold casket. "In this box lies a relic of a saint—Saint Catherine, I think." He knelt on the flagstone in front of Eleanor and placed the box between his hands. "I, Roger, called FitzGilbert, do swear on this sacred relic that I will be Eleanor of Nantes' man, to champion her causes and give her justice, yea, even to the end of my life."

"Roger! You cannot! You must not! 'Tis blasphemy to swear that which you cannot keep!"

"Nay, Lea, I have done it, and I will keep my oath to you."

"But you are bound to me by such an oath!"

"Aye. I will have liege lords and swear to my sovereign, but my first allegiance will be to you." He took the small metal box and replaced it into its niche beneath the statue. "Now—it is important that you do not become a nun. They will be at you, badgering and praying, until you take your vows. Do not take them even if you are punished for refusing. It will be hard, Lea, but as long as you are a layperson, you will have the freedom to leave one day if Gilbert or your guardian orders it."

"And if I cannot?"

"Nay, Lea, you will."

She nodded slowly, a glimmer of hope somewhere in the dark future to light her way. "Roger," she said quietly, "I'll take an oath to you."

He smiled as he rose and dusted off his knees. "Not yet. You are too young to know your own mind, and I would not have you promise that which you might not want to do. When you are older, I'll tell you more and let you decide." He examined her face and rubbed at a tearstain on her cheek. "There. We'd best be getting back before Gilbert sends for you."

Lady Mary was laid to rest beneath the floor of the chapel. Given the strange circumstances of her death, her funeral had been a hasty affair with barely time allowed for an artisan to wax-cast her effigy. Most of the nobility that had gathered for the festival had left immediately upon her death. A few of her more vocal kinsmen had asked for a ducal inquiry and William had stayed long enough to conduct it. Now she was interred and he had ruled her death due to illness rather than poison.

Privately, Roger confided to Eleanor that he felt William's willingness to remain was tied to his desire to pry fresh troops for the French war out of Gilbert. And he had done just that.

As soon as the workmen began relaying the stones in the chapel floor, Duke William and his retinue were ready to ride. Eleanor watched sadly from a corner in the courtyard as Roger prepared to depart. A bitterly disappointed Prince Henry made his way to the back of the assembled mesnes for his own farewell to her. Like his father, he wore a shirt of chain mail, a short tunic of fine red English wool, and a plain brown surcoat. Unlike his father, he was bareheaded, his brown hair ruffling in the wind.

"Demoiselle." He glanced to where Roger sat mounted above her. "I would walk apart with you ere I go."

She nodded and followed him away from the others. He drew her around the corner of the armorer's, placing both her hands in his. There was genuine sympathy and regret in his brown eyes.

"I have much to say, Demoiselle, and little time to say it. 'Twas my intent to ask your father for you in marriage before your mother died. Now my father says that I will have to wait and you are safe enough where you are going that I need not worry. You are very young, Lady Eleanor, and I should not be speaking thus, but I shall not forget you. I still have hopes that your father can be brought to take you back into his household someday."

Eleanor stared in astonishment. He'd just confirmed that she could have been his bride—bride to the best of Normandy's sons.

Henry's face was grave, his voice serious as he continued, "If you do not take your vows as Christ's bride, you may yet wed a mortal man."

"Henry!" The Conqueror's voice called for his son.

"May I take a token to carry with me, Demoiselle? Something to remind me of your sweetness and your beauty?"

She loosed the jeweled pin that held back her hair. "I have nothing else on me, Your Grace. 'Tis a poor token at best, but all I have."

"Henry! God's teeth, boy! It grows late!"

"Can you read?"

"Aye."

"Good—I'll write and send them with Roger's messages." He tucked her hairpin into his scabbard. "Godspeed, Eleanor."

Roger rode around the corner as Henry departed. Leaning as far down as he dared, he reached for her. She caught his hand and stepped up into the stirrup to reach his face for a final kiss. He turned just as she brushed his cheek and instead they brushed lips.

"Godspeed, Lea."

1092

3

Eleanor shivered as her feet sought her slippers on the cold stone floor. It was still dark and the bells had not even sounded, yet she was summoned to the abbess' apartments with orders not to tarry along the way. Resentment and rebellion seethed in her breast as she made her way across the empty courtyard. Her heavy wooden crucifix dangled loosely over her chest, thumping at her sore ribs as she walked.

As she lifted the heavy iron ring to knock, she was surprised to hear the sound of a man's voice from within. A premonition of something terrible caught at her heart—a messenger for her at this hour could only mean death. Eleanor's first thought was of Roger. The oak door swung open to admit her into the dimly lit room. The abbess' eyes were red-rimmed and she appeared to have been on the verge of crying.

"It took you long enough," she greeted sourly.

Eleanor sketched a hasty obeisance before retorting, "I was asleep, Reverend Mother. Would you have me appear naked and unkempt?"

The old woman's hand caught her at the side of her face with a resounding slap. "Insolent child! I know not how your mother dared to mark you for Christ's bride!"

Eleanor heard a harsh laugh from the shadows and turned to see a tall knight half-concealed by the dimness of the room. Only the metal links of his mail caught the flickering firelight from the small brazier that burned in one corner of the room. He gestured dismissal to Mathilde with one hand while the other rested on the hilt of his broadsword.

"Leave us," he ordered the abbess curtly.

"My lord—" Mathilde hesitated, strangely unsure of herself. She cared little for the independent Eleanor, but she felt compelled to support her in the presence of a man she considered equal to the Devil himself.

"My business is with the girl." He half-emerged from the shadows to repeat, "Leave us."

"You!" Eleanor's throat constricted even as she recognized him.

The old abbess struggled between fright and duty. Finally she dropped her eyes in capitulation, muttering, "Very well, my lord, but have done before matins. It is unseemly that she be alone with you."

"Old she-wolf," he muttered as she left. "Well, Demoiselle"—he turned his attention back to Eleanor— "much has passed since last I saw you at Nantes."

"Aye." She licked her lips in fear. In those intervening years, his reputation for cruelty and depravity had grown until tales were even told of him in the abbey. She found herself staring. The eerie glow of the small fire only served to enhance the impression of coldness and arrogance in spite of the handsomeness of his face. He still wore that thick black hair cut straight across above those icy green eyes. His obvious cruelty set his face against its own attractiveness. The metal rings of his mail and the iron rowels of his spurs clinked as he moved forward for a better look. A faint smile lurked at the corners of a sensuous mouth.

"Art more beautiful than I remember even." His voice softened as he half-whispered the words more to himself than to her.

"My lord of Belesme," she found her voice and asked coldly, "what business have you with me? Had I known 'twas you, I should have kept to my bed."

He ignored the false bravado as he continued to stare at the perfection of her face. Finally he collected himself enough to answer, "I am come to see what my sword has bought me." He waited for his words to sink in, then nodded as the color drained from her face. "Aye."

Dull fear gripped her insides. "What your sword has bought you?" she echoed foolishly.

"Your craven father thought it a small price for his miserable skin." He sneered contemptuously. "I would have had it all—Nantes and you—but Curthose would play the peacemaker, asking what I would have to leave Gilbert be." Robert of Belesme waited, pausing in his explanation and savoring the telling, until Eleanor could stand it no more.

"Nay! It cannot be."

"Aye. I sent word to Curthose that I would cry peace with Gilbert if my son would rule Nantes. And thus you come to me."

"Nay! Roger—"

"The bastard busies himself at the Condes. Curthose thought it better not to tell him until the arrangements are made. Not even one who grows as fat in favor as the bastard has will dare to complain. I'll warrant he'll be content enough to accept the gift of a small fief or two from the Duke." Belesme moved a step closer. "After all," he pointed out, "he's risked nothing to save Gilbert."

She licked her lips nervously. "He had naught of Gilbert, so why should he fight?" She took a half-step backward. "Nay! I'll not do it! I'll not have you!" She caught the strange expression in those green eyes as he advanced on her. "Wed with me, my lord," she cried out even as he touched her, "and I'll fill your house with bastards!"

His hand hung suspended in mid-air for the briefest of moments before he raised it and then delivered a sound blow to her jaw that sent her crashing in a heap to the floor. "Play me false, Eleanor of Nantes"—he stood towering above her, his legs slightly apart, his fists clenched, his voice low—"and you shall watch your lover die broken bone by bone before I give you the same fate. I have fought too many years to claim you—I'll not share your favors with another." _ pulled her up roughly and held her at arm's length. "Now I would truly see what my sword has bought me."

Even before he touched the shoulder of her rough woolen robe, she knew his intent and instinctively shrank back. "Nay!"

"Aye."

One of his hands found the cord at her waist and yanked it loose while the other pushed at the material at her neck. "Take it off lest I ruin it."

"I'll scream!"

"And who dares to come? The old crone? A fat priest? I think not." He gave her gown another tug. "Take off your robe, Demoiselle, that I may look at you."

Her face flushed uncomfortably as she had to own the truth of his words. To resist him would be to provoke him to further violence. Her hand crept to her swelling jaw. In the unlikely confines of Fontaine-bleau Abbey, she was going to be ravished by her family's bitterest enemy. Slowly her hands crept to grasp the shoulders of her robe and to pull it upward over her head. Shivering from both fear and cold, she stood in undershift and slippers with her robe dangling from nearly nerveless fingers.

He nodded. "The chemise."

"You dishonor me!"

A harsh laugh escaped him. "Demoiselle, I wear mail and have little time. Nay, I would but look at you."

Her eyes met the cold green ones and wavered. Taking a deep breath, she quickly pulled off the undershift and stood naked save her slippers. "There. Look and leave."

Instead, to her horror, he reached to touch her bare skin, placing both hands at her waist and then splaying his fingers downward to her buttocks. "Art small and slightly formed for bearing," he observed, "but you are perfectly made and I'll warrant much pleasure lies within you." His hands slid upward across the slight ridge of her rib cage to touch her breasts. He cupped one, massaging the nipple between thumb and forefinger until it tautened. Slowly, leisurely, he bent his mouth there as though to taste it. "Sweet," he murmured even as he curved his tongue around the button that formed. The cold feel of steel links meshed against her skin.

It seemed that all of Eleanor's flesh tingled from the strangeness of his touch. She closed her eyes to hide from him. "Please," she whispered.

"Please what?" he whispered back. "Would you give what I would take of you?" An arm slipped around her and bent her slightly back even as he dropped his other hand lower, tracing a line along the curve of her hipbone downward to the softness between her thighs.

"Nay!" She stiffened and pushed at him. "I'll not lie willing for any man until I am wed. Force me now and I'll not wed with you!"

His eyes darkened, his breath heavy, and his pulses racing, he released her. "Aye," he muttered as he struggled to control desire, "they'll not hang out clean sheets the morning after I take you to wife." He bent to retrieve her chemise and handed it to her. His manner changed abruptly as he picked up his heavy gloves. "I am for the Vexin on Curthose's business—part of the price I pay for you—and I would have your pledge before I leave."

"Nay!" She clutched the undershift to her. "I'll not do it!"

Ignoring her, he grasped one of her wrists and pulled it away from her, possessing himself of the hand. "I, Robert, Count of Belesme, take thee, Eleanor of Nantes, for my betrothed wife. I so swear." His green eyes met hers in warning. "Now, you will make the same pledge to me."

"I will not!"

While still holding her hand, he cuffed her with his free one. The blow caught her in the temple and would have felled her had it not been for the hold he had on her other hand. As it was, she staggered and nearly fell clutching against him. "Now, give me your pledge."

She shook her head stubbornly.

"Lady Eleanor, it was not my intent to beat your vow out of you, but I will if I have to." He raised his hand to strike her again. This time, he delivered an openhanded slap across her face that sent her reeling into the wall, where her fall was broken only by the rending of an exquisite hanging. She landed in a tangle of tapestry.

This time, she would not wait meekly. She came up with her fingers curved like claws and flew at his face. Her nails dug into his skin and drew blood in their wake. He barely had time to shield his eyes.

"She-devil! You would blind me!" He managed to catch both wrists and hold her. Incredibly, he was laughing. Transferring both of her wrists into one hand, he wiped a bleeding cheek. "God's teeth, but you draw more blood than mine enemies." He took in her panting and her disheveled hair, her naked body, and the discarded chemise. Releasing her, he again handed her the undergarment. "Put this on before you tempt me further."

With a wary eye on him, Eleanor slipped the chemise over her head. She longed to rub her swelling jaw and her bruised face, but she would not give him the satisfaction of knowing just how much he hurt her.

"Old William was right," he told her, "when he said you were fit to be a warrior's bride. You will be betrothed at Rouen under Curthose's nose the first of June." He gingerly touched the red areas of her face, drawing his finger along her aching jaw. " 'Twas not my intent to harm you, Demoiselle. Learn to be the obedient wife and I will mayhap learn to curb my accursed temper." He appeared to want to say more, but thought better of it. In a few quick strides, he was by the door. "Farewell, Eleanor, until Rouen." Even as he opened the heavy door, the abbess stood ready to enter her apartment.

"But I cannot wed with you," Eleanor whispered desperately. "I cannot."

Her words were lost in the gasps of the indignant abbess. "My child—what has he done to you? Sit you down, Demoiselle, whilst I get aid for you." The old woman took in Eleanor's battered appearance and her discarded robe and reached the obvious conclusion.

"My poor child! Would that you had given your oath to Christ rather than to that devil!" She called loudly, "Sister Therese! Sister Agnes!" Returning to Eleanor's side, she soothed as best she was able, "I'll have you bathed and put to bed in a trice. Oh, I knew I should not leave you alone with that foul beast! The bishop shall hear of this!" Her old bosom fairly seethed with indignation.

Eleanor sank to her knees and began to weep. When Mathilde sought to raise her up, Eleanor lifted her tearstained face to whisper, "Truly I am accursed!" Her words echoed hollowly in her aching throat.

4

"Jesu!" muttered young Aubery de Valence. "I've served him two years and more—and I've never seen him like this."

"Aye," groused his companion. "I've known him since he was naught but a bastard whelp, and I've never seen his temper so foul. God's teeth! He would ride us all to our graves. And for what, I ask you? To visit his sister, he says. I've half a dozen of 'em, and not a one could drag me out like this."

"Not just any sister," Aubery reminded, "but the Demoiselle of Nantes. Many remark her beauty—e'en my lord Henry. 'Tis said the Conqueror marked her for a royal bride, but her lady mother marked her for the Church."

"E'en so, Lord Roger carries on about her more like a lovesick swain than a brother." Hugh de Searcy cleared his throat and spat upon the ground. "God's teeth! Look at him—'tis scarce minutes since we've rested, and he's ready to ride on."

If he heard the grumblings of his squire and man-at-arms, Roger FitzGilbert gave no sign. Instead, he impatiently checked and tightened the girth of his saddle. Without so much as a word, he swung up and jerked the bridle so savagely that his horse reared. De Searcy, de Valence, and the others chosen to accompany him scrambled for their own mounts, only to find themselves already left behind.

"I've a mind to let him ride unattended all the way to Fontainebleau with naught but that curst temper for company," Sir Hugh told all who could hear him even as he eased his aching bones into his own saddle.

"Nay, Hugh—'tis little enough he directs at us, my lord. 'Tis himself he pushes the hardest of all." Jean Merville pushed back his thick rust-colored hair and jammed his conical helmet on his head, pausing to adjust the nasal over his nose. "And if he pushes us, he must have his reasons. I for one follow him whither he goes—I am so sworn." Using a stirrup for leverage, he swung his thick-set mail-clad body onto his horse. "Nine hundred and ninety-nine times out of a thousand, he's the best lord a man could have."

Roger rode on, seemingly oblivious of the fact that his entire retinue was falling farther behind him. In the two days since Henry had arrived at the Condes with the news that Robert of Belesme had demanded and been promised Eleanor of Nantes in marriage, Roger had thought of naught else. With scarce a thank-you for the prince's effort, he'd ridden out, leaving Henry to entertain himself out of the Condes' larder. And in the space of those two days, the shock and horror had not abated. He still could not think of Eleanor and Belesme together without becoming violently, physically ill. Lea—she haunted his dreams and gave him no peace, anyway. Lea—beautiful Lea—so small, so delicate, so finely made. His free hand gripped the pommel of his saddle as he fought another wave of nausea. Nay, she could not go to the Devil when she belonged to Roger. He closed his eyes as the very world seemed to sway with revulsion.

He'd had no sleep. That first night, he and Henry had sat up until even the rushlights were gutted. They'd argued and they'd schemed until they'd convinced themselves it was yet possible to save Eleanor. And now it was up to him to convince her that all was not lost. He goaded his horse to yet a faster pace. Through pain and exhaustion, he could only focus on the fact that this night he would see Lea and renew his pledge to her. Her face seemed to float before him. "Nay, Lea," he spoke aloud, "I am still your man even to the end of my life."

"My lord! My lord!" Aubery's spurs dug unmercifully into his own mount as he sought to catch his master. "My lord! If you care not for us, have a care for that beast you ride!" The squire was breathless from yelling as he caught up to Roger. "By all the saints, my lord, but he'll not carry you much further." Aubery was gulping for air even as Roger became aware of him.

"I would reach Fontainebleau before sunset."

"Which day?" Young Aubery reached over and caught at the reins. "If we are reduced to riding double, I doubt we can make it before the morrow."

Roger looked down and saw the wet stains seeping through the embroidered trappings. Heavy lather glossed the powerful flanks and shoulders of his prized horse and flecks of foam spotted his own surcoat. He nodded. "Aye. We will slow to a walk, but we do not stop."

"My lord—" Aubery spoke with the ease of one whose relationship with his lord was secure—"is there aught you would have me know? Is your sister gravely ill?"

"She is well enough for now."

"Then what ails you?"

"I am afraid."

Aubery's eyes widened at the words. In the years since Roger had been taken into the Old Conqueror's service, his reputation for bravery and fighting skill was nearly unsurpassed. Nay, there was none better— save maybe Belesme. "Afraid, my lord?"

"Aye. I am afraid to see all of my dreams crumble when I do not know if I have the power to save them."

Aubery stared at Roger. It was obvious that the man had passed the point of exhaustion and suffered confusion. Roger's usually well-tanned face seemed pale and drawn and his brilliant blue eyes were ringed with darkened hollows. Fatigue etched and deepened every line on his face.

"My lord, can we not rest?" Aubery reasoned quietly. "You are no good to her in whatever her distress if you cannot sit your saddle."

"Aubery, how old are you?"

"Seventeen, my lord, and well you know it."

"And full of reason, Sir Squire," Roger told him tiredly. "Well, I suppose I knight you before you leave Fontainebleau."

"And you, Sir Roger," Aubery retorted, "make no sense. I have years left in your service ere I am knighted."

But Roger had ceased to attend. Ahead lay the ford that crossed onto the abbey's lands. Before nightfall, he could have his bed and see Lea. The ache that lingered beneath his shoulder blades seemed to lessen slightly as he nudged his horse toward the water. "Come—we are nearly there."

The bells sounded at the approach of mounted horsemen, slowly at first and then increasing in intensity as Roger's standard was recognized. Mother Mathilde hastily completed her prayers and rushed to the courtyard as quickly as her old bones would carry her.

"My lord!"

He swung down from the saddle and took a couple of unsteady steps. Half a dozen of his men sprang to his aid, but he pushed them aside. "Nay, leave me be—I am all right."

"My lord—" Mathilde was alarmed at his appearance.

"Mother." He half-stumbled as he knelt. "I am come to see the Lady Eleanor."

"Roger!"

He used his broadsword for balance as he pulled himself up. Even as he regained his footing, she was in his arms. Tears were streaming down her cheeks as she nuzzled a cheek against the roughness of woolen surcoat over chain mail. "Oh, brother, I knew you would come," she half-whispered into the folds she clutched.

Mother Mathilde did not know whether to be glad or exasperated at his sudden arrival. She'd been certain that Eleanor was on the verge of giving herself to Christ rather than the Count of Belesme. Surely, Roger FitzGilbert could see that it was the girl's only hope. Yet as she watched the two of them swaying in the

courtyard, oblivious of all but each other, the old
woman felt a sense of unease.

"Roger—" Eleanor looked up into his face. "Roger,
you are half-dead with fatigue. Aubery . . ." she called
out to the squire, "Sir Hugh . . . Jean—look to your
lord. Really, Roger, you are nigh to swooning on
me."

"Nay, Lea. A bath, a little bread, and a bed—and
I'll be right enough on the morrow."

Her eyes narrowed. "When did you leave the
Condes?"

"I don't know—yesterday—the day before—I think."

"And you let him do this to himself?" She turned
incredulously on Sir Hugh. "I know he sometimes
lacks sense, sir, but you?"

"I tried, Demoiselle, but he would not listen."

"Reverend Mother, have I your permission to attend my brother?" It was a question in form only—not
even a direct refusal could have stopped her.

Mathilde nodded. Long ago, in the first year or so
that Eleanor of Nantes had lived in the abbey, the
abbess had realized that there was a bond between
brother and sister that neither separation nor authority
could break. Well, let the girl have the comfort of her
brother—soon enough, as Belesme's bride, there'd be
no comfort on earth for her.

Roger made it to the guest chamber assigned him
under his own power. Waving aside help from any of
his men, he chose instead to lean only on Eleanor, a
leaning that was more spiritual than physical. He could
still give her a foot in height and nearly six stone in
weight even without the benefit of some thirty-five
pounds of hauberk and mail. She eased him onto a
low bench and ordered the others to fetch a washtub
from the kitchens.

"Tell . . . no, *ask* Sister Margretta for heated water,
Aubery. And, Hugh, get linens of Sister Alice. You,
Jean, help me get all of this off him. 'Tis no wonder
he's tired." She turned to Merville and noticed for the
first time the fatigue lines on his face. "Jean, you look

nigh to death yourself. Well, if you can but draw off his boots, I can do the rest."

"Nay!" Roger's eyes flew open. "You aren't a servant. Besides, 'tis unseemly."

"I am your sister," she stated flatly. "Can you not see these men are as tired as you are? I, on the other hand, have little to do here but rest and pray." To emphasize her seriousness, she grasped the base of his helmet and removed it with a great deal of effort. It was well-fitted and did not want to come off, but finally succumbed to several twists and jerks.

"By the saints, Lea, but you are rough! Aubery has the hands of a child in comparison!"

"And I'll warrant Aubery has had more experience in such things," she agreed cheerfully. "I had no idea that it was so tight."

" 'Twould do little good if it weren't. If a blow can dislodge it easily, then I would be looking through the nasal or through the side."

"Oh."

She unlaced the sides of his plain surcoat, frowning as she did so. "You have not put your arms on here yet."

"Nay. I rise so fast in the world that I know not what to use there. I once thought to use the white hare, but Henry says I remind him more of a falcon than a hare."

"I should hope so. A hare sounds cowardly." She pulled the garment over his head and discarded it on the floor.

"A device is what one makes of it. I rather like the hare—quick, defensively colored."

"I am for Henry in this. From bastard of Nantes to Lord of Condes sounds like you have soared as the falcon, brother."

"Mayhap only to run like the rabbit, Lea." He closed his eyes to avoid her questioning look.

His mail shirt was of the new style, complete with coif to cover his neck and head. She loosened the fastenings at the shoulder and tried to draw it off. He raised his hands obediently to help.

"Careful. I have sweat so much that Aubery needs to polish it before it rusts."

"I know." She wrinkled her nose in distaste. "In fact, you stink."

Hugh and Jean and a retainer she did not know dragged in a heavy oversized copper caldron from the scullery. It was already partially filled with steaming water. The men eyed Eleanor with a mixture of amusement and embarrassment. They had little doubt that she'd never even seen a naked man before and were waiting for her reaction. As Hugh and Jean exchanged suggestive looks, Roger caught them and frowned.

"Leave us."

"But, my lord—"

"Take to your own pallets. Lea would have it that I've nearly run all of you to death today."

"But—"

"And I've not a doubt in my mind that her hands are gentler than yours, Hugh. Go on with you, but draw lots for who sleeps by the door."

Aubery hesitated, uncertain whether to suggest impropriety or not. Roger sensed his thoughts. "Nay, as she will tell you often enough, she is my sister. Besides, I have much to discuss with her."

Even as they drew lots for the watch, Eleanor continued divesting Roger of armor and clothing. Beneath the mail shirt he wore a stiffened leather hauberk, and beneath that, a heavily quilted gambeson. As she laid aside that last garment, she shook her head. "I should thank God that it is not July, Roger, else I could not stay in the same room with you. As it is, you are sweat-soaked enough. Look at your undertunic—'tis stuck to the hairs on your chest." The brilliant blue eyes were closed again, but he dutifully raised his arms to help her rid him of the shirt. He was bare to the waist. She stared in fascination—there were more muscles than when he had been fifteen—a lot more. The upper body strength required to wield broadsword, battleax, and shield corded his arms and shoulders with muscles. A jagged scar barely healed lay between a shoulder blade and his spine. She traced it gently with fingertips before bending to brush it lightly with her lips. An involuntary shiver coursed through him.

"How came you by this?" she asked innocently.

"Belesme. On the one occasion that I had to go to Gilbert's aid, I met him on the field."

"But this is your back, Roger."

"Aye," he agreed grimly. "Robert cares not how he gets me so long as the deed is done."

Belesme. The mutually hated name hung in the air between them, with each reluctant to acknowledge its presence. Finally she nodded. "He was here last week."

"Prince Henry told me."

Her voice dropped to a near-mumble. "He means to wed with me, Roger. I . . . I cannot do it! I do not think myself cowardly, brother, but I cannot wed with such as he."

He clasped her hand reassuringly and would have drawn her down next to him, but he looked into those dark eyes ready to brim with tears and he had to look away. The time was not yet. "Lea—Henry and I will see that you do not have to. But for now," he changed the subject, "I would have my bath."

"Nay"—she shook her head even as she knelt to unwrap his cross-garters. "I have thought much on it, Roger, and I am decided that I would prefer the Church to marriage with the Devil."

"Nay! Lea, it will not come to that. Let me rest but a little and I will tell you what we must do." Her head was bent beneath him so that he could look upon the shining dark crown of her hair. By the saints, but she was beautiful. With an effort, he tore himself away and tried to study the hanging on the wall. It depicted Satan tempting Christ. Her hands were cool and light to the touch, but they seemed to burn him wherever they brushed against his bare skin. He'd had his share of wenches—none lasting more than a day or two—but none had ever affected him like Lea. Why was it that that which is most unattainable is most desirable? All he knew was that ever since the day when she'd brought him to the Conqueror's notice, the same day he found out they shared no common blood between them, he'd yearned for her with something that went beyond mere desire. In his saddle, in his bed, on the battlefield even, she was never completely out of his thoughts. But now that Curthose had allowed her to be given to Belesme, it was time to act. And later, sometime when she was safe, he would tell her how he felt—tell her what he wanted most in this world—and he would hope against hope that it would be what she wanted also. But for now, he dared not risk telling her he was not her brother.

"Roger?" She had finished the cross-garters and was peering anxiously at him. "Are you all right?"

"Aye."

"Well, you will have to stand if I am to finish this. I cannot remove your braichs with you sitting."

He rose self-consciously while she undid the waist and let them slip to the floor. And there he stood naked before her.

"But you are beautiful. Roger, I never imagined a man to be beautiful."

He reddened uncomfortably, both pleased she'd found him pleasing and embarrassed by his own growing reaction. He had to get into the water. He turned away to hide himself and eased his body into the tub. Water sloshed over the sides and splashed against the stone floor.

"Where do I start?"

"Nay. You sit over there and talk to me and I'll wash myself."

"Nay, you are too tired." She picked up the soap and wet his hair, then worked her fingers through the thick, tousled blond waves. Unlike most Normans, his hair did not lie flat and straight across his forehead. He looked like she imagined angels looked except for the two days' growth of pale stubble on cheeks and chin. When she satisfied herself that she'd gotten it clean, she began to rinse the hair, first with the bath water itself and then with a pitcher of clear water set beside the tub. While she located a dry cloth for his head, he finished lathering his body. She filled the pitcher again from a larger one and started pouring it over his shoulders. His head was leaned back and his eyes closed again. Without thinking, she leaned forward and brushed his lips. His eyes flew open and he ducked his head.

"God's teeth, Lea! Do not do that!"

"Why? You are my brother."

"I am a man."

Stung, she set aside the pitcher and turned away. "I am sorry, Roger—I didn't mean it like that—I saw little enough harm." The dark eyes were brimming again with unshed tears as she fought against a lump that formed in her throat. "I would not offend you." She clasped her hands behind her back and walked toward the door.

With a sigh, Roger heaved himself out of the water and caught up with her. "Nay, Lea, you offend me not. 'Tis that you are such an innocent you know not what you do." Her placed a wet hand on her shoulder. "I am not all you think me, and I would not betray your trust in me. Indeed, I would live up to that trust and keep my faith with you." His attention was suddenly drawn to the yellow-purple mark along her jawline. "How did this happen, Lea?"

"Belesme."

He felt sick again. He could not bear the thought of Robert's touching her at all. "I swear I'll make him pay—I swear it!"

"Nay, if I can but be safe from him, I will consider he's paid."

"Henry and I are decided—I will take you to England as soon as I can make some arrangements for the disposal of my lands."

"England? The disposal of your lands? Roger, what are you saying?"

He dropped his hand. "Lea, I am too weary to tell all tonight."

"But what of your lands?" she persisted.

"I'll get them back when all's done," he answered aloud even while thinking he would if he lived to the end of his plans.

"When all's done?"

"Lea, leave me be! I tell you I am too weary to discuss it."

"Roger, I cannot let you do anything that would cost you your lands. I know too well the price you have paid for them with your sword and your blood." She walked behind him and touched again the ugly scar still forming on his back. "You have risked your life in other men's causes to get where you are."

That burning touch again. He jerked away in guilt. "Lea, I stand here naked and freezing whilst you would talk of land. Fetch me a tunic out of my roll."

"Roger, are you angry with me?" She unrolled the pack and smoothed out a white linen shirt. " 'Tis unlike you to be so cross."

He reached for the shirt and shrugged it over his head. "Angry? Nay, I tell you I am tired." Water spots formed on the garment as it absorbed the last vestiges of bathwater from his skin. He drew back his blanket and flopped onto the narrow cot. "Leave me be."

"You haven't eaten."

"I cannot." He closed his eyes and cradled his head. He could hear her move away. "Where are you going?"

"I am leaving you be," she answered simply.

"Nay, I meant it not like that. Sit with me."

With a sigh, she pulled up a falstool and sat down. He reached for her hand and held it tightly against his cheek. The bluish rings that hollowed his eyes seemed even more pronounced in the faint light. She would have leaned over and smoothed back the damp hair from his face, but thought better of it. Instead, she had to content herself with sitting quietly as his breathing evened out. Slowly his grip on her hand relaxed and he slipped into sleep. Only then did she dare brush back the rumpled hair from his temple.

"Oh, Roger," she whispered, "I would that I knew what ails you."

"Lea, trust me!" Roger's voice was low and intense as they walked within the walled garden.

"But I cannot do it!" Lea's voice rose in an anguished whisper. "Last night, you came and offered me hope. Today, you tell me I am to wed Belesme!"

"Nay, you mistake my words, Lea. I said you are to appear to accept the marriage. I must have you out of here if I am to succeed. Once you are in Rouen, you will escape and I will smuggle you out of Normandy."

"And if you cannot—I am wed to the Devil incarnate."

"I will—I swear. Lea, I do this for myself as well as for you."

"Because of your vow to me."

"Aye. That and other reasons."

"What if he forces himself on me before I can escape?"

"He won't." Roger fingered the dagger at his belt grimly. "I will see you are not alone with him if I have to make my peace with Gilbert to do it."

Eleanor stopped and studied Roger. She wanted to believe him—indeed, in all of their years, she'd never had cause to doubt anything he'd ever told her. In the years since his vow to her at Nantes, he had been faithful to his promises, visiting often and writing with such regularity that even the scullery had come to recognize his messengers by name. But this was a new and strange Roger that had come this time, an intense, irritable, almost desperate man intent on keeping his childhood vow to her. Oh, the brilliant blue eyes, the well-defined strong face, the tall, muscular body—all were as she knew him—yet there was something indefinably different. There was a grimness that had never been there before. She lowered her eyes to the ground.

"Aye—I trust you."

He seemed relieved. "Good. 'Twill be easier if I do not have to take you away against your will. You know I love you too well to let you go to Belesme or to let you rot here any longer. I am overlong enough as it is in keeping my promise."

"But what will happen to us?" She began to pace aimlessly again. "Have you considered that this course will destroy all you have—all that you have made for

yourself. Curthose will surely hold the Condes forfeit—
and he may even demand your life for this."

"So be it, then. Lea, 'tis not as bad as you would
make it." He touched her lightly on the chin. "I expect Rufus to welcome us if for no reason other than
to spite his brother. There's no love lost between
them, believe me."

"And if he does not?"

"Nay—he will. But even if he does not, we are not
done. I visited my mother at Abbeville and was told I
have a powerful relative of mine own in England."

"But what if none will stand with us?"

"Then I will offer my sword to Byzantium and take
you with me. I can fight Turks as well as anyone, Lea.

"And me? What of me?"

"I expect to find you a better husband than Robert
of Belesme."

"Nay. I would rather go with you than become wife
to some stranger."

"Well, mayhap by that time he will not be a stranger
to you."

"Roger," she asked impulsively, "have you ever
loved somebody?"

"I love you."

"I know, but that is different. I mean, have you
ever *loved* a lady?"

He stopped abruptly. "Aye."

For some inexplicable reason, Eleanor felt her heart
drop to her stomach. And why should he not? she
rebuked herself. He is, after all, a man as well as your
brother. "This lady—would I like her?" she asked
casually.

"Sometimes. I know I find her enchanting, beautiful, kindhearted, and spirited."

"I see. Well, have you asked for her yet?"

"Lea, I have not had the means. Lowborn bastards
cannot always love where they would choose." He
plucked a flower and handed it to her. "My lady could
have a prince if she chose. I doubt she would fancy
me."

"Nay—any lady would be proud to call you husband, brother."

"I hope you are right."

Eleanor was torn between an intense dislike for an unknown lady and a curiosity to know more of a woman who could capture the heart of a man like Roger. "You are the Lord of the Condes now. Can you not ask as such?"

"I cannot. I have not the means yet."

"And you would lose everything for me." Eleanor shook her head sadly. "Nay, Roger, I cannot let you do it. You deserve happiness with your lady and I am safe enough here."

"I am your man, Lea."

"A foolish childhood vow, Roger. God will forgive you if you cannot keep it."

"Possibly, but I could not forgive myself. I have waited overlong to keep my promise to you as it is. But we speak of love," he chided lightly, "when we should be making plans. When does Gilbert come for you? Or does Robert come himself?"

"My father. I am to be in Rouen by the first of June."

Roger whistled softly. "So soon? The bridegroom must be impatient."

"Aye." Eleanor felt her mouth go dry even as she remembered the look on Belesme's face when he had undressed her. Involuntarily her hand crept to her still-discolored jaw.

"Well, it is not much time, but we shall be there. Here is what I would have you do. You will write to Robert and tell him . . ."

5

Robert of Belesme dismounted stiffly and forced his aching legs to walk the fifty paces across the uneven cobblestones of the courtyard at Belesme. Stiff, tired, and sore, it seemed that everything ached at once—legs, back, and head—from the ride in from the Vexin. Yet, for a man of uneven temper, his spirits were remarkably good. Things had gone well in the past weeks and he'd been able to push Philip back a little. He ought to be well-rewarded for his efforts. He stopped by the cistern and removed his own green-plumed helmet and pushed back the mail coil from his damp black hair. A page hastened to draw him a cup of water, which Robert used first to slake his thirst and then to wash the dust and sweat from his face.

Drying himself with a corner of his green surcoat, he straightened up to look above at his mother's solar windows. He caught the movement of green gown there as she turned away. It was odd that she had not come down to meet him after so long a separation. Even as he began to climb to the solar, he felt a sense of unease that he refused to acknowledge.

She still stood at the edge of the tall, narrow window slit. Poets wrote of her fiery red hair and her green eyes that were supposed to tempt men's souls, but there was little enchantment in Mabille's eyes as she turned to face her son.

"Nantes!" she spat out without greeting. "Robert, how could you?"

"Ah—'twould seem you received my message, Mother." He stepped into the open area and kicked the door shut behind him. "I tired of fighting Gilbert and came home."

"Aye. In a month's time, and by way of the Vexin."

"There are advantages to the marriage, Mabille. My son will rule Nantes."

"Your son? Nay, Robert, *you* could have had it for yourself. There is more to it than that."

His memory flashed to Eleanor, remembering her as he'd last seen her standing nearly naked in the abbess' chamber. "Aye." His mouth curved into a slow smile as he recalled her. "I would have the girl."

"Daughter to Gilbert and sister to your sworn enemy, Robert. Are you daft, boy? Grind Nantes beneath your heel, and take the girl if you will, but do not marry her." Mabille's voice rose and fell in the cadence of reasoning, but he knew there was more to her objections than her words would betray. She was lovely, his mother, and she was evil.

"A man must have sons, Mabille, and I will get mine of her."

"A convent-bred girl, my son?" Mabille's mouth twisted into a sneer. "Tell me, Robert, does she know what you would have of her? Has she felt the fury of your body, or borne the mark of your teeth in her flesh as I have? Nay, she cannot be a match for you."

"She will be my wife and my lady, Mother, and how I use her concerns you not." He reached out and cupped Mabille's chin, meeting her eyes until they wavered. "She is very beautiful—the most beautiful girl I have ever seen."

"Robert, don't tease me." Mabille's face changed as she put her hand on her son's arm. " 'Tis not like you to have a care for a pretty face."

"She is so beautiful," he persisted cruelly, "that I have carried her image in my mind since I was eighteen, and so I will carry it as long as I breathe."

They were not alone in the solar. A couple of the young men Mabille always kept around her hovered on stools near a low brazier. Oblivious of them, she twined her arms around her son's neck and put on her most seductive smile. "Ah, Robert, what need have you of another woman when you have me?"

Robert looked across the room at a boy hardly sixteen and read the message of jealousy and sorrow on the young face. It was so like Mabille to flaunt one lover in front of another. She pressed her body suggestively against him, molding the contours of her body to his. "Art an even better lover than your father," she murmured softly.

He knew he should have sent her to dower lands long before. There was that about her that sickened even the Devil of Belesme. Roughly he jerked her hands down. "I doubt you even can remember my father, Mabille, for 'tis so long since you gave him poison that you've had a thousand others since." He nodded to the pathetic boy. "If you have need of service, call on him—I've no taste for it anymore."

She came at him then, her fingers curled like talons, scratching and clawing. He tried to fend her off by catching her hands before resorting to a blow that sent her reeling. She gained her balance and came at him again, gasping, and raking at his face with her nails. He caught her easily about the waist and carried her to the bed, dropping her like a sack into its midsts. She lay there waiting.

"Don't ever do that again," he growled as he straightened up. "I've done with your tricks and your wiles—'tis a wife I need, and not some old woman crawling into my bed," he taunted her.

"You'll come to me when you tire of her, Robert—you always have. And she cannot keep you with her convent ways," Mabille panted. "You won't be able to beat her, else you'll have that brother of hers on your back. You'll sicken her with the way you would touch her and the things you would do to her."

"Sometimes I sicken myself, Mother, because I am your spawn." His green eyes lost some of their harshness as he thought of Eleanor. "Nay, I would use her gently to get what I would have of her."

"Robert . . ." Her voice was a plaintive whine. "Can we not . . . ?"

Her meaning angered him as he drew back from her outstretched arms. "Nay, Mabille, can we not be as mother and son? You've enough boars to play to your sow without me. You, fellow!" he called out to the boy he'd been watching. "How old are you?"

"Sixteen," was the sullen reply.

"Sixteen. And you share her favors with a dozen others, I'll warrant." He turned back to his mother. "Where do you get them? What fools send their sons to you to be schooled? Poor knights with too many mouths to feed—bastards not too nice in their tastes? Art a witch, Mabelle."

"A witch that spawned the Devil," she reminded him. "And what of you—art so pure, my son?"

"I am your son," he answered bitterly.

She rose from the bed with a sigh. "I suppose we cannot help that which we are—I fear the blood is bad."

"Aye. And I would not have it touch my wife or my children." He reached out and gripped her shoulder painfully. "You will be courteous to Lady Eleanor if you see her, and you will hide your foulness from her—do you understand?"

"You are hurting me!"

"Aye. 'Tis my intent to do so." His fingers tightened until he felt he could almost snap the bones beneath the flesh. "If you ever tell her what I have been to you, I swear by the blood that flows in my veins, I will kill you with my own hands." He released her and flung her away from him, watching as she lost her balance and fell on all fours to the stone floor. "Be the dog you are when you are out of my sight." He towered over her, his fists clenched to control his anger. "But if you meet the Lady Eleanor, you will be pleased to be *Lady* Mabille."

"Robert—"

"And if you cannot do as I ask, I'll lock you up. Do you attend me, Mother?"

His tone frightened even Mabille. She half-crouched, watching him warily. Finally she nodded in acquiescence. He backed away, his body still tense from the confrontation. A heavy sigh escaped him.

"I am weary, Mother. I would have a bath and a meal before I press on to Rouen at daybreak." He passed a hand over his forehead, brushing back the thick black hair that hung almost to his brows. "Three days on the road leave me saddle-weary."

The boy helped her up, his hand resting challengingly on his poniard. Mabille knocked his hand away and shook her head. "Nay, Piers, he would carve your liver from your body while yet you live and then stand to watch your lifeblood drench the rushes. Go instead and get him supper."

Robert watched him leave before sinking to a bench near the slitted window. Mabille walked over and began to massage his neck and shoulders as though nothing had just passed between them. He leaned forward to rest his elbows on his knees and cup his chin with his hands.

"Is she really so very beautiful?"

He nodded. "Aye—I have never seen her like. She is smaller than you, with a dark, silken curtain of hair that hangs down her back, and great dark eyes that are like deep pools. Her skin is as fair and perfect as any I've ever seen."

"And you are besotted." Mabille's fingers worked up his neck. "She is still the daughter of your enemy."

"Mine enemies change as it suits me. I would cry peace with Gilbert—yea, even with the FitzGilbert—to get her."

"Ah—the FitzGilbert—what did he say to this marriage?"

"I know not *what* he said, as 'twas done secretly, but I know he stands against it." Robert stretched his neck to ease his aching head. "But he grows strong on his own. Unlike his father, he loses nothing that comes into his hands. For now, I would have him as ally."

Mabille changed the subject back to Eleanor. "This girl—were it not for . . . for this thing between us— would I like her?"

Robert ducked his head away from her hands. "When have you liked another woman, Mother?"

"Never."

"There is your answer."

"Will you bring her to see me?"

"Nay. And I would not have you at Rouen, either, for too many have spoken of us, Mabille, to let the tales die. I would not have it come to her ears." He could sense his mother's disappointment, but he shook his head. "Nay, send her a few ells of velvet or something, if you will, but do not go see her."

"You cannot hide me forever, Robert. She will come home to Belesme, after all."

"Aye—but you will not be here. You will retire to your dower lands, where you can continue your sick sports."

"You would cast me out?" Mabille's voice rose in incredulous shock. "Nay, Robert, you would not! You dare not!" She bent to wrap her arms around him, but he pushed her away and stood. "Robert, think of what we are—what we have been to each other."

"What are we, Mabille? Witch and Devil, as men say, or mother and son?"

"We are much alike."

"Aye, but I would not have it that way. Sometimes I curse the blood that flows in this body because of what I am."

"If I have ever loved anything, Robert, I have loved you." Mabille let her voice drop to a near-whisper. "And well you know it."

The boy called Piers returned with a tray and waited. Robert sat heavily down at a low table and began to eat even as Piers watched him. With the intensity of youth, the boy believed himself in love with the beautiful Mabille, and her cruelty hurt. Always before she'd reassured him that the other boys she lay with meant nothing to her, but the encounter with her son was an enlightening experience. It was obvious that Mabille now told the truth—if she loved anyone, it was her own son—a revelation that sickened Piers. Had he thought it possible, he would have driven his dagger into both of them.

Belesme seemed to become aware of his presence and turned his attention toward the boy. "Do you have a name?" he asked casually between mouthfuls.

"Aye. Piers de Sols."

"Your father?"

"A knight in the service of my lord Humphrey de Granville."

"You should be learning war, boy, instead of playing the rutting boar. 'Tis your sword arm and not your privates that will put bread in your mouth." Robert appeared to study Piers. "You look able enough to wield a sword—what would you say if I sent you to one of my vassals for useful training?"

"I wouldn't go!" The boy was alarmed. What if the Devil of Belesme intended to get him away from Mabille and have him murdered?

Robert's face turned cold and cruel instantly. "You'll do what you are told unless you would be flayed for your insolence. I've done worse for less," he reminded grimly. He pointed at Mabille and added, " 'Tis time you were weaned from her and repented of your sins."

"What care you about sins?" Piers cried out hotly. "Are you so pure you can judge others? I've heard you lie with both men and women, my lord!"

Robert came crashing to his feet, sending food and trencher scattering to the floor. With knotted fist he cuffed Piers against the side of the head. The boy's neck seemed to grow longer and then his whole body collapsed in a pile at Robert's feet. The count stood over him with a face contorted with fury, distorted into a mask of evil. He gave the boy a hard kick in the ribs with his boot. It was a sickening sound as the wind was knocked out of the slender body.

"Where had you the story?" Robert demanded. When he received no answer, he kicked again. "Where?"

"Have done!" Mabille screamed. "You'll kill him!"

Robert reached down and pulled up the retching Piers, shaking him like a sack of bones as he did so. "*Where* had you the story?"

"Y-you s-served with R-Rufus," the terrified boy managed before he brought up the contents of his stomach.

"So have half the men in Normandy!" Robert shouted. "Yet they've not such a taint!" His fingers closed about Piers' throat in a vise of fury. "By the blood of Belesme, I swear I have done many foul things, but I've never lain with another man!"

Piers' eyes bulged and his face took on a bluish, purplish hue. Alarmed, Mabille grabbed her son's arm and tried to break his grip. "Robert! Don't!" Tears were streaming down her beautiful face. "He knew not what he said! Please, Robert," she pleaded, "do not kill an innocent child."

"Child!" He spat out the word as he dropped the choking boy to the floor. "An innocent child! God's teeth! That's a wonder for you to say, Mother!"

Mabille sank to her knees and cradled the unconscious form of her youthful lover, crooning to him softly and trying to rub life back into his face. "You've killed him! D'ye hear? You've killed him!" She bent to kiss unresponsive lips. "Oh, Robert . . . why?"

Belesme looked at her strangely, the heat and anger fading from his body. "Nay, he's not dead, Mabille, for all he should be. Give him time to come around." He laughed harshly, his voice sounding odd even to his own ears. "Nay, I've tortured enough men to know the limits of life." He reached down and engaged in a tug-of-war over the inert body. "Give him up and I'll show you." He pulled Piers up and laid him across bended knee, giving the boy several sharp blows to the back. The youth coughed and began drooling mucus from his mouth. Slowly, color crept back into the pallid face. With that demonstration of life, Robert let him slip back to the rushes. "When he rouses, tell him he is to move his pallet to my chamber, and that he will serve me and none other in this household. If he runs, I *will* kill him."

"You will kill him anyway, will you not?" Mabille's voice was flat and toneless in defeat.

"Nay, I will train him in something more useful than

lying with an old woman." He bent and picked up the remnants of his supper, placing them on the low table. That done, he fastidiously washed his hands in a small basin and wiped them on a linen towel. His eyes caught sight of the other boy cowering, terrified and speechless, in the corner. "Clean up this mess," he ordered curtly, "and be quick at it—I cannot abide disorder." When the boy did not move, Robert walked toward him. "I care not from whence you came or of whose blood you are—you will join my service or you will be returned to your home. My mother has no further need of you."

"Robert!" Mabille fairly screeched out his name. "Nay!"

"Aye." he nodded grimly. "I'll not support this foulness further, Mother. Tomorrow I ride for Rouen to prepare for the betrothal. When I return, I expect to find you have retired to your dower lands." His eyes met hers and locked. "If I would see you, I have a horse." When at last she wavered and looked away, he pulled open the heavy oak door and left.

Mabille could hear the sound of boots and spurs on the narrow rock steps as he descended into the yard below. Piers moaned softly at her feet while the other boy sat as still as stone. In all of her forty years, she had never doubted her power over her son until this.

"Nay—she'll never take my place," she half-whispered.

6

After leaving Fontainebleau, Roger cut southward toward Abbeville, forming his plans as he went. The success of the venture depended both on its boldness and on his ability to at least temporarily confuse Belesme as to where he was taking Eleanor. To that end, Roger prepared a number of letters to various acquaintances to suggest he might visit them sometime in June, and these he dispatched to France, Lombardy, Aquitaine, and Flanders to confuse the pursuit. And, as he rode, he confided only the briefest details of his plans to Aubery, Hugh, and Jean Merville, giving them the choice of following or of safely distancing themselves from his plotting. To a man, they chose to stand with him despite Belesme's awful reputation for vengeance.

At Abbeville, he knelt and asked his mother's blessing after telling her what he meant to do. It was not an easy task to confide that he meant to take Eleanor to Harlowe, even if he had to. He knew it grieved Glynis to open the old heart wounds, but he had to know everything possible about his father before he showed up on his drawbridge with Belesme's fugitive bride. She had cried, then begged and cried some more, asking him not to reveal himself to the earl, but in the end, Roger had made her see the reality—aside from William Rufus, his father was his only potential ally in England. Besides, Harlowe would be an unlikely place to look for them and would possibly prove a haven away from the crudity and immorality of Rufus' court. He didn't relish going to Rufus anyway, for despite what Henry said, Roger did not like the way Rufus looked at him. But so much depended on the Earl of Harlowe and his willingness to accept his bastard son.

From Abbeville, Roger moved on to Poix, where he met Prince Henry. There, in the faint illumination of rushlight in Hubert of Poix's wood-and-stone pile, he executed the agreement whereby he gave Henry the wardship of the Condes for an unspecified length of time in return for the loan of five hundred English marks. Both reasoned that Curthose would be more reluctant to take possession from his brother than from Roger, for he too relied heavily on Henry for money. There was an added purpose to the agreement— Belesme might hesitate to march on the Condes for fear that Robert Curthose would support Henry's wardship. It was a masterful stroke that would ensure that Roger would not lose the Condes outright.

Henry sanded the document to dry the ink and then shook the sand back into a leather pouch. Passing the vellum to Roger to read, he waited expectantly. "Well, can you see anything that we have missed? Do you think I have provided you with sufficient guarantee?"

Roger scanned it briefly and shook his head. "I think you have been overgenerous, my lord prince."

"Nonsense. You will need money if you are to keep the Demoiselle as befits her station. And you will find a woman is damned expensive, I can tell you."

"Henry . . ." Roger had to know. "Why do you do this for me?"

"For you?" Henry half-smiled and shook his head. "Nay, I do it for her."

"For her, then. Why?"

The prince fingered the chain that hung at his neck, feeling again the pendant he'd had made from Eleanor's hairpin. "I could have loved your sister, Roger—I know I could have. She is not like the others of her sex, but just how she is different, I cannot tell you. None other has ever affected me so." His voice dropped and his eyes took on a faraway expression as he remembered Eleanor of Nantes the way he favored her as a young girl. "She touched my heart, Roger. Had things turned out differently then," he mused softly,

"I would have her to wive and a lawful son or two by now."

Roger fought back a stab of jealousy. "Nay, you would not have suited. She would have demanded constancy and you have not that in you. You would have quarreled with her over your wenching."

"Nay." Henry was positive. "You mistake the matter. Had I Eleanor of Nantes in my bed, I'd need no other."

Roger felt a sense of unease at the prince's confession and pressed for Henry's intent. "I will not stand back and let her be any man's leman, prince or no," he warned quietly.

"Believe me . . ." Henry's brown eyes were serious, his face sober in spite of the wine he'd drunk. "Believe me when I say I mean your sister no disgrace. I would not take her else I could wed with her, and that time has passed me by." He gave a heavy sigh of regret and met Roger's curious gaze. "Aye. Rufus names me his heir in England and Curthose will fight me for it, well you know. Nay—I must wed where 'tis most politic, Roger, and your pardon for saying it, but I cannot afford Gilbert for a father-in-law. When I raise my standard, I have to know who will come." He fingered the pendant again. "I have not the luxury of wedding where I would now, if I want to wear England's crown, my friend. But oh how I shall envy the man who weds your sister—and I will do everything in my power to see that 'tis not Belesme." Abruptly he rose and walked to a shuttered window. "I grow maudlin from the wine, Roger," he murmured as he unhooked the shutters and opened them. "What I need is a warm wench to lift my spirits. So do you. Hubert says there are some passable ones to be had in the village. What say you—shall we find them?"

"You go on, my lord—'tis sleep I need," Roger lied. He felt taut as a bowstring whenever he discussed Eleanor.

Henry peered at Roger closely for the first time since they'd been at the Condes. Deep bluish circles ringed tired blue eyes, and fatigue lined the handsome

face. He nodded. Roger was the closest person he had
for a friend since the Old Conqueror had taught him
that princes do not have friends. It disturbed him to
see Roger stretch himself to such limits. "Aye," he
said aloud, "you look as though you had not slept for
a week."

" 'Tis but ten days since you came to the Condes to
warn me about Belesme's plans for Lea, but it seems
like a year. I have thought of little else since."

"Well, if you have no care for yourself, you will be
of little use to her when the time comes." Henry
walked over to where Roger sat and clasped him on
the shoulder to squeeze reassurance. "But 'twill all
work out if we can but get her out of Rouen."

"If it does not, I will have to kill Belesme. Jesu, but
I do not know if I can do it. Face-to-face, I have never
bested him."

"It won't come to that. We'll get her out of Rouen
and you'll get her to England. There's little enough
love lost between the Count of Belesme and my brother
Rufus—you can count on sanctuary there until you
can decide what to do with your sister." Henry paused
at that—nothing had been said about what ought to be
done with her. "She'll have to have a husband, you
know. I can write to Rufus and see if he can arrange
something.

"No!"

"All right, I won't mention it, but it is the only
answer, Roger. Think on it—even Robert of Belesme
cannot claim another man's wife." He released the
shoulder that had suddenly gone stiff beneath his fingers. "You take to your bed and I'll look over the
wenches in this place."

When Henry had left, Roger refilled his goblet with
honeyed wine and made his way to the bed he'd share
with the prince later. Stripping down to nothing but a
shirt, he downed the last of the wine and climbed into
the depths of the curtained bed. The mattress was
feather rather than straw and seemed luxurious after
his nights on the road. As he eased his body into its
softness, it seemed that every muscle cried out for

rest. He rolled up one of the silk-covered cushions and cradled his head against it.

But sleep would not come. Once his eyes were closed, visions of Lea floated in his memory. He could remember the feel of her hands as she'd undressed him for his bath, her touch on his bare skin, the feel of her lips as she'd kissed him when he sat in the bathing tub. He could smell the clean scent of her and see the shiny silken hair that had hung over him. And most of all, his body could feel the firm, round contours of hers as he had held her last at Fontainebleau. His tongue grew dry with desire and his pulse raced as he allowed his mind free rein to imagine her there as he'd done so many times before. In his half-dreams, she came to him as a wife, a lover eager to please her lord, smiling, caressing, and opening her body to him. Now every fiber of his body cried out for ease from this overwhelming desire.

He threw back the curtains and flung himself out of bed. He could not sleep like this. Wine—some more wine, he decided, and he could pursue sleep more readily. He drew on his braichs and did not bother to cross-wrap them or to put on his boots. With a rush-light taken from an iron ring in the passageway, he lighted his way back to the hall.

The place was deserted now except for an occasional servant removing the last vestiges of supper. A few men slept on pallets placed along the walls. Roger walked silently around checking wineskins and jugs until he found one with enough left to bother with.

Aaaiiiieeee!" Someone emitted a high-pitched shriek behind him. He swung the rushlight around and faced a girl he'd startled. Her hands were laden with empty pitchers that she clasped tightly to her breasts. Her eyes were luminous and large in the flickering light.

"Milord! You frightened me—I thought everyone asleep."

"So you came to get some extra wine for yourself?"

She shook her head. "I came to finish clearing the tables after all the louts were asleep."

"Oh." He eyed her with interest. Her eyes were

dark and her hair was long and dark also. The small-
ness of her stature reminded him of Eleanor. "How
old are you?"

"Fifteen."

"Are you a virgin?" he asked foolishly, knowing
that it was unlikely.

She looked at the rushes while answering. He could
have sworn she reddened at the question, but perhaps
it was the firelight. "Nay," she answered finally in a
low voice. "I am not."

"Would you like to share my wine?" He could not
bring himself to ask her the obvious, but she understood his meaning.

She took in his half-dressed appearance before lifting her gaze to his face, where she could see the blue
eyes, the tousled blond hair, the well-defined face. He
was far handsomer than any she'd lain with before.
She placed her pitchers on the nearest trestle table and
nodded. "Aye."

Once back in the chamber he shared with Henry,
Roger stopped and kissed the girl. It was a gentle kiss
at first that deepened as he closed his eyes and thought
of Eleanor. Heat flooded his body as he imagined that
he held Lea in his arms as a lover rather than a sister.
Slowly, almost languorously, he wooed her with soft
kisses and caresses, undressing her as though they had
all the time in the world to experience the pleasure of
each other. The girl was confused by his gentleness at
first, but soon began to respond wholeheartedly to
him. Roger cradled and caressed until she thought she
would go mad before he took her. And when at last he
straddled her and entered her, she cried out with
floods of pleasure that came again and again until he
drove himself to release. "Lea . . . Lea . . . I love you
so much," he whispered brokenly as he came within
her. And for one brief moment in her life, the girl felt
loved instead of used. He rolled off her and lay back
with his eyes closed, swallowing to get his breath. She
crept closer to rest her head against his shoulder as his
breathing evened out. He put an arm around her and
held her against him while he drifted off to sleep. She

lay awake a long time wishing fervently that she were some unknown lady called Lea.

"God's teeth! Roger, have you got a wench in there with you?" Prince Henry pulled back the bed curtains and peered within. His voice was thicker than usual with drink. "So the old dog found a bitch to lay after all." He looked even closer as Roger tried to drag himself awake. "Leave it to you to find a comely one, too, whilst all I've had were fat with greasy hair."

The girl tried to cover herself from Henry's leering gaze. Roger rolled away and reached for his discarded shirt. "Here." He handed her his shirt even as he sat up on the side of the bed. "You'd best be going."

She hastily pulled on the shirt and scampered out of the bed past the prince. Before he could reach out to her, she had achieved the safety of the door. She looked back at Roger and smiled. "My thanks, milord."

"You hear that, Roger? The wench *thanked* you for giving her a tumble." Henry rubbed the stubble on his chin and shook his head. "I'll be damned if I've had any thank me."

But Roger wasn't attending him. He was thinking that he'd find the girl on the morrow and give her some money. Remorse already flooded over him as he thought he might have unwittingly loosed another bastard to suffer for his sins. And long ago he'd vowed that he would not be responsible for bringing another bastard child into the world. Well, he'd give her his direction and see what happened. His body felt good—a lot better than it had in months. If only it could have been Lea there as his lady wife.

"Roger, have you heard anything I've said?" Henry asked querulously. "What ails you?"

"I hope she doesn't drop a bastard."

Henry eyed him in disgust. "Trouble with you, Roger, is that you don't lay enough of them. I mean, what's a man to do when he's unwed? Burn? If they don't lie with you, they lie with some other lout. If they drop bastards, ten to one they don't know whose it is."

"Then why do you keep your bastards?"

"Because I'm the only man that has lain with the mother. With a serving wench, it's a different matter. A brat'd have to look like me before I'd acknowledge it then." He looked around the room for some more wine. "Don't tell me you've swilled it all."

"All."

"Go on back to bed. I'll go find myself some more."

Roger waited while Henry walked unsteadily out the door. Then he lay back down and thought of Lea. Somehow it seemed that he'd betrayed her—a foolish thought, since she had no idea how he really felt about her. How would she react if she knew? he wondered. Would she recoil in horror? Or would she return the love he felt for her? He ought to tell her before they left Rouen, but he doubted that he would. He could not chance that she might not go with him. It seemed he puzzled it a long time, wavering on how to tell Lea the truth about himself.

"Well . . ." Henry wobbled in the door carrying a pitcher of wine that he sloshed on the floor. "Your conscience can be clear, my friend. If she has a bastard from this night's work, she's more apt to blame me than you." He set the wine down on a low table. "And you don't have to pay her, either—I gave her plenty enough for both of us."

Roger curled up and felt sick.

7

Eleanor sat pensively in the high-walled garden at Nantes, her thoughts wandering from those around her. In the background, her sister Margaret's still-sharp tongue could be heard in gossip with her sister Adelicia. But she was not attending what they were disputing. Old Herleva, now half-blind and more than a little deaf, sat in a corner on a low bench, working her needle with a deftness born of feel rather than sight.

It seemed strange to be sitting there after so many years had passed. To Eleanor, there was an aura of unreality to the scene—it was as though all that had passed since had happened to someone else. Her thoughts turned to that day when she'd been so frustrated with her stitching just before she'd heard the fight. Her ears harkened for a sound of it even now. And the Old Conqueror—she and Roger had met him that day—a day that had indeed proven fateful for both of them in more ways than one. Well, Roger had prospered since, and if men dared to call him "the Bastard," it was with the respect they'd used with "the Conqueror." Even Belesme seemed to have a measure of respect for Roger. He'd made sure that her brother was absent from court when he'd asked for her.

Belesme. A shudder passed through her at the thought of him. In the weeks since she'd agreed to Roger's mad scheme, she'd tried very hard to blot out any thoughts of the Count of Belesme. Now, outside the walls of Fontainebleau, she felt exposed and un-protected. Indeed, in the absence of Roger and in the frantic preparations for her trip to Rouen, Eleanor felt

herself being pushed into a maelstrom from which
there was no real escape. Everywhere she was surrounded by signs of preparations for a marriage that
she fervently prayed would never take place. Belesme
had written a stiffly worded letter and sent her a large
heavy necklace set with round green stones, a pretty,
expensive necklace that she likened to a slave yoke
when she tried it on. Margaret, in her envy, had
voiced Eleanor's fears by deciding aloud that it must've
come from the neck of a dead woman somewhere.
And Mabille, Count Robert's mother, had written her
a letter couched in such sweet words that it was repulsive. Welcoming her "dear daughter Eleanor," the
countess had sent ells of a rich new fabric that the
French dubbed "Flames of Fire" for its shimmering
iridescence. It was truly beautiful, but Margaret had
managed to dampen Eleanor's spirits about that, too,
pronouncing it "probably poisoned—she poisons everything, you know."

As for Gilbert—her father had all but avoided her
since she'd returned to Nantes. While he would spare
no expense on her marriage, he wanted little enough
to do with his eldest daughter. Perhaps it was because
he felt some pang of guilt when he looked on her, or
perhaps he wished to avoid any reproach over his
selling her to save his own skin. Not even the convent
walls had obscured the gossip about how Belesme had
backed him into desperation, how he'd pushed Gilbert
off first one piece of land and then another until there
was naught left but the city of Nantes itself. Cornered,
with no place left to run to, Gilbert had clutched at
Curthose's offer of mediation with the feeblest of hopes,
only to be relieved to find that Belesme would settle
for Eleanor and leave him in peace. When reminded
that she had been given to God, Gilbert offered first
Margaret then Adelicia, but Belesme was adamant—
he'd have Eleanor and none other—or he'd hang Gilbert's head from the gates of Nantes. Not that her
father was not still afraid of his future son-in-law. In a
moment of rare conversation with Eleanor, he'd confided that he'd sent for Roger to accompany them to

Rouen. He still feared to cross land held by the count's allies—particularly since the impending betrothal had been kept quiet on both sides to prevent vassals from feeling betrayed by this meek settling of a long and violent quarrel. "But with Roger at my side," Gilbert had gloated, "none will dare touch me. And when Robert of Belesme is bound to me by blood, none will dare gainsay me."

"Really, Papa?" she had responded. "And when I am wed to him, I wonder just how safe you are. He does not appear to be a man overgiven to waiting to rule."

She could tell that she'd given him food for thought there, but she had no real hope of his standing up to the count. Her thoughts turned yet again to Roger. Where was he? What was he doing? Did he think to arrive only in time to take her to Rouen? Had he changed his mind about saving her from Belesme? No—not Roger, she reassured herself for the hundredth time. He would stand firm when all else failed. He'd not given his word lightly, and he meant to keep it, she was positive. But too often she awoke from nightmares where he lay, his blood drenching the dust beneath him, while a laughing Belesme stood over him, calling him a bastard. Ah, if he would only come, surely everything would be all right.

"Sister!" Margaret's sharp voice betrayed her annoyance. "Really, Eleanor, but you ought to have the manners to listen when someone speaks to you."

Eleanor flushed guiltily. "Your pardon—I wasn't attending."

"Well," Margaret conceded with mock graciousness, "I suppose we can forgive you for thinking of your bridegroom. Were he mine, I should be worrying also."

"If you must know, Maggie, I was wondering about our brother. I cannot understand how it is that we have not heard from him."

"I care not if we ever hear from him," Margaret sniffed, "for 'tis little enough help he gave Papa when Belesme sat at out very gates. We could hear the

screams of the peasants being tortured until we could
not sleep."

"He came once, Maggie," Eleanor answered as
evenly as she could, "and Papa left him to fight the
battle alone. He came in Papa's defense, and Papa
ran, Maggie. Whatever you would say of our brother,
he is no fool. He had no land of our father, but he
came that once. Why should he have come again?"
Her voice dropped lower to avoid disturbing the now-
dozing Herleva. "He lost thirty good men whilst Papa
saved himself. No, Maggie, Roger has no shame for
what Papa brought on himself."

" 'Tis our father you fault," Maggie sniffed, much
as she had done as a child.

" 'Tis our brother you fault, Margaret."

"Half-brother. Son of a Saxon whore." Margaret
would not leave the subject be. "And if he had come
to our defense, Belesme would have been routed.
Much as I dislike him, I have heard what men say of
him. If he can fight for Curthose and for Prince Henry,
he can fight for his father. Then we should not have
come to this pass, sister, and Papa would not have to
squander what we have left on a dowry and marriage
goods for you. *I* could have a husband, Eleanor, were
it not for your precious Roger."

"Well, if it rankles you to be unmarried, Maggie,
you may have Belesme and *all* my dowry. I shall be
happy to stand aside for you."

"Nay. He didn't ask for me—and I'd not wed with
him if he did."

"Then shut your evil mouth, Margaret." All eyes
turned to Herleva, who had roused herself enough to
follow the conversation. "If you've no husband, look
to your father."

They were interrupted by the sound of a rather
large retinue clattering into the courtyard beyond the
interior wall of the garden. Eleanor lifted her skirts
and stepped to a low bench to reach a dip in the
crenellated wall. The men riding in wore surcoats of
soft blue and carried a blue-and-gray standard. The
leader was unmistakable to her. "Roger!" she squeaked

in excitement even before she stepped down. "He's here!" she shouted to everyone as she made for the gate.

"Aye," Margaret muttered nastily, "go after him like a wolfhound bitch in season."

"Margaret"—Eleanor paused in mid-step,—"you have an evil mind to match your evil tongue. 'Tis a pity you are not marrying Count Robert, because I think you would be well-matched."

Without waiting for a rejoinder, she fairly ran into the courtyard where the men were dismounting. Roger just had time to hand Aubery his helmet and his gloves before she was in his arms. Purposefully he set her back from him a step and bent to kiss her gently on both cheeks, his lips barely brushing her skin. His blue eyes warned her even as he drew away.

"What . . . ?" She was confused and disappointed. This was a different Roger even from Fontainebleau.

"You look well, sister."

She licked her lips nervously, not liking this grim stranger who stood before her. "I am well, my lord brother. And you?"

"Well enough." He glanced up to where Gilbert had descended the narrow tower steps. "I never thought to return here again."

"I suppose not."

"My son!" Gilbert enveloped the stiff stranger in a bear hug, kissing him warmly on both cheeks and then on the mouth. "How left you the Condes? Is it as rich a fief as I have heard?"

"Rich enough." Roger's eyes surveyed the gathering crowd until they lit on old Herleva. For her he reserved the warmest greeting. He smiled and hugged and kissed the old woman until she fairly glowed from the attention.

"Put me down!" she squealed in delight as he lifted her and swung her around a couple of times. "These old bones break easily, boy!"

"Ah, Herleva, you never change." He grinned down on the rotund little woman. "What greeting is that for

the boy who wanted to grow up and wed with you?"
he teased.

"I grew old."

"Does this mean you won't consider my suit?" he
asked in mock injury.

"Nay, you need a flesh-and-blood woman to warm
your bones at night, my young lord. If you wed with
me, you'd be complaining you had to warm mine."
Unbelievably, the old woman was bantering back like
a simpering young girl.

Margaret watched the scene with interest. It had
been seven years since she'd seen Roger, and she was
unprepared for the way he looked now. In the flesh at
nearly twenty-three, he was incredibly handsome. He
had grown and filled out to where he must strike
desire in all but the dullest of females. She sucked in
her breath as he noticed her at last.

"Ah—Margaret. Come give a brother a welcoming
kiss."

Eleanor was stunned to watch him greet Maggie
with more warmth than he had her. She had to turn
away to hide her hurt and her jealousy. Something
was very wrong with this Roger who rode into Nantes.

"Ahem." Eleanor turned to face a still-mounted
rider. He wore no device, but she would have recognized him anywhere.

"My lord prince." She dropped a hasty curtsy to the
ground beneath his horse.

"Fashion dictates that I raise you, Demoiselle, but
you will have to be patient whilst I dismount. Think
you to keep your head to the ground that long?" He
grinned even as he swung himself out of the saddle
and unsteadily balanced ride-weary legs on the ground.
She raised herself just as he stood over her. His breath
caught in his chest as he faced Eleanor in the flesh.
Jesu, but she could stir a man. Small wonder that
Belesme wanted her.

Gilbert pushed his way forward. "The prince, you
say! How came you to ride behind my boy, Your
Grace? 'Tis unseemly."

"I would have his homecoming more private, Count

Gilbert. I did but ride this way with him for company. I am meeting my brother at Rennes and decided to come this far that I might see the Demoiselle of Nantes again. She is as I remember her." He drew her hand to his lips and kissed each finger lightly. Both Roger and Gilbert frowned at the gesture. Henry pulled the necklace he wore from beneath his plain surcoat. "See, fair Eleanor, I still have it."

"A trifling token, Your Grace."

"I value it highly and wear it for luck."

"Pay him no heed, Lea," Roger advised, "for he says pleasing things to all the ladies." It was the first time he'd used his special name for her since he'd arrived.

"Surely he does not wear a token for each one," she pointed out.

"Nay, if he did, he would not be able to raise his neck from the earth."

"Pay *him* no heed, Demoiselle. I may flirt with the ladies, but I have you in my heart."

"Enough of this prattle," Margaret asserted herself. "Brother, pray present me and Adelicia to the prince."

Presentations were made around and Gilbert shepherded Roger and his royal guest off to the bathhouse. Usually the lady of the household performed such a task, but Gilbert was having none of that—especially since Eleanor was the ranking female at Nantes and Prince Henry had such a reputation for dallying with ladies of noble as well as indeterminate birth. And it would be folly to send Eleanor to Belesme as anything but a virgin.

The rest of the morning passed, and much of the afternoon. Torn by doubt and confused by Roger's strange behavior, Eleanor paced the length and breadth of the solar anxiously. Could the brother who stayed so faithful during those long years of her confinement mean to abandon her now? Nay, he would not—he could not—he *must* not. But he was at Nantes and, except for that brief greeting, she'd not seen him.

He'd missed the midday meal and there was no sign of him.

Fourteen-year-old Adelicia came up the narrow stairs, bright-eyed and breathless, her chestnut hair wind-tangled. Catching sight of Eleanor, she hastened to share her excitement.

"I have been with Roger and the prince, sister, and have seen where you and he played beyond the walls when your were children! His favorite oak still stands as he left it. Oh—he is the best of brothers, Eleanor! He has offered to dower me so that I may wed."

"You've been with Roger?"

The younger girl nodded. "Aye, and with Prince Henry. He could talk of little else but you."

"Roger?" Eleanor asked foolishly.

"Nay." Adelicia shook her head in exasperation. "The prince, silly goose—'twas the prince who would talk of you."

"Oh."

Eleanor felt unreasonable pangs of jealousy as she faced her younger sister. In justice, she told herself, it should be Roger who angered her rather than Lissy. He'd shared her memories with others and had not bothered to take her with him.

"Where did you leave him?" she asked as casually as she could.

"Prince Henry or my brother?"

"Both."

"In the courtyard below, but I'll warrant they've gone by now."

Eleanor moved to the long, slitted window and looked down. The yard bustled with the activity of a great castle, but there was no sign of either man.

"Art uncommonly foul-tempered, sister," Adelicia told her from behind.

"Aye," Eleanor sighed. "Oh Lissy, leave me be—'tis not your fault."

Just then she spied Roger's squire crossing to the cistern. Without a word, she strode purposefully to the stairs and made her way down.

Adelicia shook her head over her sister's strange

behavior until a new thought occurred to her. It came suddenly that perhaps Eleanor still cherished memories of Prince Henry. Though she had been only seven at the time, she could still remember that there was much talk of a match between them before Eleanor had been sent away. And now her poor sister had been promised to that awful Belesme. Adelicia crossed herself three times even as she thought of the hated name.

Beneath the window, she could see Eleanor catch up with Aubery, and she watched with interest. Already she had taken a fancy to the handsome young squire. She could see him drop to one knee in obeisance to her sister, his gilded head bent low.

"Lady Eleanor." Even as he knelt, he mumbled, "Art a vision or flesh, lady?" No sooner had the words escaped his mouth than he felt like an idiot for saying them. In his years of service with Roger, he had never been able to face her without feeling like a fool. Indeed, there was something about her that seemed to make all men fools—even her own brother.

Her laughter above him was pleasant. "Today, Aubery, I am more nightmare than vision. Look to yourself—'tis you who are as fresh-scrubbed as an angel. I'll warrant every maid in this pile of stone envies me my speech with you."

Relieved, he rose and faced her. "How may I serve you, Demoiselle?" he asked respectfully.

"I would have Roger's direction." Impulsively she laid a hand on his arm. "Tell me—is there something wrong with him? Does he seem different to you?"

"Aye." Aubery looked at his feet, uncertain as to whether to discuss his master with her. "Aye. He is like a man obsessed—and so he has been since Fontainebleau." When she did not say anything, he blurted out, "He would have you safe, Demoiselle—I fear he thinks of little else."

"Where is he now?"

"The chapel."

"My thanks, Aubery." She lifted her skirts and picked her way across the uneven cobblestones in the direction of the chapel. The squire looked after her and shook his head. They were an odd pair, his master and the Lady Eleanor.

She found him alone. Apparently his prayers were nearly done, because she could hear only the last words as he whispered, "And deny not this hungry heart, O Lord," before she slipped down to her knees beside him. He looked up in surprise and then looked away.

"How long have you been here?" he asked quietly.

"I did but arrive."

He appeared relieved. "Lea, 'tis unseemly to intrude on a man at his prayers," he chided. But he was smiling with those brilliant blue eyes as he was used to do. Her spirits rose. "Did any see you come here?" he asked.

"Nay—I don't think so. Why?"

He looked around to make sure they were alone before answering, "We must be as other brothers and sisters, Lea, until this thing is done. We cannot be in each other's company as we would like—else how am I to convince Gilbert and Curthose that I will let you go to Belesme?" He searched her face for a sign of understanding. "No man who loves you as I do could possibly let him have you, Lea."

"But you've scarce spoken to me," she protested.

"Aye. You need to remember that most brothers and sisters barely tolerate one another." He frowned at her perplexed expression and sought to explain, "Think on it. Our affection for each other is so remarked that even the duke wanted me away from his court while he negotiated this marriage. Lea, if I am to be in Rouen for your betrothal, I must appear to accept it."

"Oh."

He possessed and squeezed both her hands, smiling and pleading at the same time, "Trust me, Lea."

"Roger, as long as I know you love me, I will do as you ask."

Her fingers were warm and slender beneath his own. It was an effort not to pull her against him and tell her

the truth then and there. Instead, he looked away to
hide the intense longing he felt. "I love you too well,
Lea."

She returned to the solar in high spirits certain she
would be safe, she would be secure. Impulsively she
called for the gown the seamstress had just finished,
for its brightness suited her mood. She'd intended to
wear it in Rouen, but why waste it in a place where all
the fine ladies would be gowned as well? Nay, better
to shine as a dove among sparrows at Nantes, she
reasoned. Besides, tonight she supped with Roger and
Prince Henry, an excuse to bring out her finery. Adelicia
had confided that Henry still liked her—let them all
think she dressed for him. It was Roger she wanted to
please.

Her tiring women were surprised and more than a
little dismayed, but it did not matter. She pulled on
the gown and then sat for her maid to plait her thick
dark hair with threads of gold and then knot the braid
into a crown on the top of her head. Even as she rose,
she heard old Herleva's gasp as the woman came into
the solar. Her whole body appeared to be arrayed in
light, from the fitted undergown of cloth of gold to the
overgown sewn from the fabulous material Mabille
had sent. Mother Mathilde would have been scandal-
ized to see her now, she decided as she looked down
to where the undergown dipped into a V that almost
reached the crevice between her breasts. She turned
around, swirling the shimmering fabric with its irides-
cent reds, greens, and golds.

"Demoiselle! You wear your wedding dress!"

"Nay, I have chosen another for that—I would not
waste this on Count Robert. Besides, I dress for my
brother and the prince tonight."

Herleva drew her mouth into a thin, disapproving
line. "Be careful, little Eleanor, that you tempt not
where you would not."

"You speak in riddles, old woman," Eleanor chided.
"If you would scold me, out with it!"

"Why do you seek to rouse a man's passion when

you dare not satisfy it?" Herleva asked bluntly. "Do you wish to be another of Prince Henry's lemans? 'Twas not for that that I taught you."

"I've no wish to lie with him. Oh, leave me be! I know not what I want!"

The old woman nodded knowingly. "*I* know what you would have, Demoiselle. Who knows—mayhap it will come to pass."

"More riddles?"

"Nay—the truth." Herleva shrugged and retired to the alcove where she kept her cot.

Unwilling to face Margaret and Adelicia in her new gown, Eleanor made her way to the great hall early. As she entered the passageway between living quarters and hall, she reflected it was much as it had been those years ago when Gilbert had freshened it for that fateful May Day. She reached the place where Belesme had accosted her and stopped. There he'd foretold that he'd hold the fate of her and her family in his hands. Who could have guessed then his powers of prophecy?

"God's teeth, Lea! Where are you going dressed like that?"

She spun around to face Roger. His eyes lit up as he took in her appearance, and then he frowned. Inexplicably, his change in expression hurt and angered her. "I am going to sup, brother," she retorted.

"Nay—I think not." His hand touched the bottom of her neckline. "You'll have Henry panting after you like a hound after a bitch, and I won't have it, Lea." He took her hand and pulled her back toward the solar stairs. "Wear discreet clothes when you sup with Henry, lovey, because it takes little enough to inflame his passions as it is."

She pulled back. "Roger!" she protested as she dug in her heels to stop him. "What is the matter with you? You have not the right to order my appearance."

"Not too long ago, you said you'd do as I ask. Change your gown."

"Nay. In this you sound like a jealous husband and you are wrong! I see little enough harm in dressing to please a prince. Why should I save this for the likes of Belesme?"

"Take care, Lea"—Roger lowered his voice and bent his face to within inches of hers—"that you do not take yourself where I cannot help you. Right now, Henry is full of noble intentions where you are concerned. Tempt him and he is likely to take you to his bed before he considers the consequences."

"You make him sound like a rutting beast."

"Sometimes he is. He is but a man, after all."

"Really, Roger? You are but a man, after all, too."

"Aye, and sometimes I am ruled by my passions, also."

"Roger, you told me that I would have to have a husband."

She was unprepared for his reaction. He reached out and shook her as one would a small child when one was furious. "Don't be a fool, Lea! Your chance to wed Normandy's son has passed. He would not openly defy Belesme for you, but he is not above a little dalliance before your wedding. Do you understand me?"

Hot angry tears welled in her eyes. "Aye—I understand! Now that I am out of Fontainebleau, you would rule me!"

He dropped his hands. "Rule you? Lea, I would protect you, and tonight you need protection from your own designs." He turned to stalk off.

"Roger, *Please*!" A lump formed in her throat. "Please do not quarrel with me—I cannot bear it!" She stood rooted to the floor. "Very well—I will change my clothes if it pleases you."

He stopped, but did not turn around. "Nay, Lea—I would not want to rule you," he answered tonelessly. "You are a woman grown—follow your own mind."

"Turn around and *look* at me!" she implored.

"Nay. I have said my piece."

She sat at the high table at her father's right while Roger and Prince Henry shared a trencher on his left. It seemed the most miserable meal she'd eaten in many years. Her father barely grunted acknowledgment of her efforts at conversation and Roger never seemed to look her way. Occasionally she could sense Prince Henry's eyes on her, but that provided little comfort. Her sister Margaret prattled endlessly to Adelicia. She felt small and insignificant in her plain green gown.

"Damn, girl!" her father exploded. "You've drained the cup!" He refilled the goblet and turned his attention back to Roger and the prince. Aimlessly she stirred in more honey as Henry had taught her and sipped. She didn't feel like eating, and the sweet-tasting wine seemed to soothe her hurt.

The tables were cleared and the torches doused in all but a few holders as the hastily assembled musicians struck up a tune. Beneath the still-lit candle rings, jongleurs gathered to provide the night's entertainment. Eleanor rose unsteadily to her feet, but no one seemed to notice. She suddenly felt very sick.

The room spun crazily, making her close her eyes briefly for balance. The little food she had eaten seemed to rise uncomfortably toward her throat. She put a hand to her reeling head and realized that she would have to leave or disgrace herself in front of everyone. She motioned a serving boy over and nodded toward the doorway. "Please," she whispered before she had to cover her mouth.

The boy nodded and helped her from the room. At the doorway, he sent for one of her tiring maids. Eleanor leaned her head against the cold stone of the wall as she fought rising waves of nausea. The woman called Gerda came out and together with the boy supported Eleanor to the garderobe.

Prince Henry was the first to miss her when he turned around. In the dim light, he could see her being helped from the hall. Without drawing Roger's attention, he followed. By the time he reached her, she was within the garderobe retching. He stood helplessly with the servants and waited.

Finally, when the sounds stopped, he put his head to the door and called, "Are you all right, Demoiselle?"

"Aye," came the muffled reply.

He knew in a trice what ailed her—she'd had too much to drink. He'd experienced the same feeling far too often to condemn a girl fresh out of the convent. They probably watered the wine where she'd been. What she needed was a walk in the open air, he decided.

She was white and pasty when she came out at last, but she'd managed to spare her clothing. A shred of corn husk clung to a dampened tendril of hair at her temple. Before the servants could move to her assistance, Henry stepped forward and pulled out a handkerchief, mopping her face and pulling tiny pieces of husking off. He spit on a corner of the cloth and began dabbing around her mouth much as a mother would her child. The servants stood back in uncertainty, bemused at the sight of the Conqueror's son cleaning up their mistress.

"Get me some water," he ordered curtly. Both ran to do his bidding. "What you need, Demoiselle, is air." He put an arm around her waist and supported her against him. "Are you well enough to walk now?"

"Aye." She nodded weakly.

"Then let's get out into the yard."

He managed to walk her to the cistern and drew up a bucket. There was no sign of either servant now. Pouring water over the handkerchief and wringing it out, he washed her face. "Here—drink this," he told her as he proffered a dipper of water from the bucket. When she would push it away, he insisted, "If you will not drink, then rinse your mouth—'twill help. There's naught much worse than the taste of wine when it comes back up."

She nodded gratefully and tried to swallow the water. For one awful moment it seemed as though the cold liquid would hit bottom and make her sick again. She swallowed hard.

"Nay—spit," he advised. "Swallowing only makes it worse."

Slowly the waves of nausea ceased and she nodded

gratefully. "My thanks, Your Grace. I fear I've made a fool of myself in your eyes."

"Because you were overcome with wine? Nay," he answered softly as he stared at her in the moonlight. "How can I fault you for what I have done so often myself?"

"Where's Gerda?"

"The serving wench? Gone for water, I think." He put her arm back around his shoulder and circled her waist. "Come, let us walk until your head clears, Demoiselle."

She was light in his arms, as light as a child, but there was nothing childlike about the firm, rounded breast above his hand. She was the most beautiful girl he could remember seeing, and they were alone. And she was sister to a man he considered friend. Resolutely he pointed her back toward the hall.

Her kidskin slipper caught on a loose cobblestone and she pitched against him. He caught her with his free arm and encircled her. She was warm and small and lovely. Instinctively he bent to kiss her, his lips just grazing hers at first; then, with a groan, he took possession of her mouth. As small as she was, she seemed to fit against him in all of the right places. His hands slid down her back, molding her to him even as the heat rose within his body.

Eleanor was totally unprepared for her first real kiss. Her eyes flew open in astonishment and then closed tightly as she savored the feel of a man's mouth on hers. His body was strong and warm against hers and he was making her feel giddy all over again. He still smelled of Gilbert's strong lye soap and it was a far headier smell than perfume. She allowed her hands to creep to his shoulders, feeling the muscles that lay beneath the soft material of his tunic. He was not so big as Roger, but he was a well-made man.

"My lord Henry," Roger spoke coldly from the doorway, where he seemed to loom larger than life. "I would not raise my hand against you, but, by all the saints, I will if you do not take your hands off Lea." Eleanor jumped guiltily, but Henry did not move.

Roger stepped forward with his fists clenched. "I did not bring her out of Fontainebleau to see her dishonored."

Henry stared hard for a moment at his liegeman. Finally he released Eleanor and stepped back.

"Roger—" Eleanor put out a hand to her brother.

"Go back inside. Gerda awaits you by the door."

She could tell by his tone of voice that he was extremely angry with her. "Brother," she cried out, "it was not as it seems—I was sick!"

"Aye. Go inside."

She would have tried to say more, but Henry nodded. "Leave us, Demoiselle, and I will explain to your brother."

Roger could accept everything was as Henry said it was. Gerda and the boy had confirmed just how ill Eleanor had been. Still, he had been unprepared for the way he'd felt when he'd seen her in Henry's arms. He did not doubt her innocence, but it rankled him even in reflection to watch her response to another man. For one very brief moment he'd wanted to kill his lord. And he'd wanted to tear her from Henry and drag her off to his own bed. Jesu! If she wanted to learn of a man, he wanted to be that man.

"Roger." Henry came into the small chamber they shared. He raised his hands in supplication and then dropped them. "What can I say? She is very beautiful and I have ever wanted her, but I meant her no dishonor tonight."

"I believe you," Roger answered tiredly. He sat down and pulled off his boots. "My lord prince, I am weary and I would sleep." He pulled back the curtains and eased himself into the bed without even removing the rest of his clothing.

Henry stripped and crawled into bed next to him. Like Roger, he had mixed feelings about his brief moment with Eleanor. She'd awakened old feelings within him and he felt certain sadness that she lay out of his reach. He spoke the truth when he told Roger that he meant her no dishonor—he had long known that he could not take her to wive. And she was obviously too fine a lady to be any man's leman.

Roger lay stiff and awake at his side. Henry turned away and tried to wriggle a niche for his body within the feather bed. After several attempts to get comfortable he gave up. "I cannot sleep," he muttered, "if you have to lie there like an affronted virgin, Roger." There was no answer. Finally Henry turned on his back. "I value your friendship and your service more than I want the girl." With a sigh he added, "And I'll still help you get her out of Rouen." When Roger still did not speak or move, Henry threw back the covers in exasperation. "God's teeth, man, I know not which is worse—trying to sleep with you when you toss and turn all night or when you lie awake still as stone!" The bed behind him began to shake with suppressed laughter in spite of Roger's anger. "Pray, what is so amusing?" Henry demanded in exasperation.

" 'Tis surely the first time I have ever been called an affronted virgin."

Henry lay back down, sighing. "Aye, and I am heartily sorry, my friend. Once you have your sister safe, 'twould be wise to find a husband for her. The Demoiselle is overripe for one as it is."

"I intend to—without Gilbert's blessing."

"Jesu!" Henry breathed as he remembered the feel of Eleanor in his arms. "I would that I could be the man to take her—I envy the one who does." When Roger made no comment, he sighed again. "I think I should press on to Rennes tomorrow, lest Gilbert hear of this."

"Aye, I think it best," Roger agreed. "and I think I'll go with you. The longer I am at Nantes, the greater risk of betraying my plans."

"But I thought you escorted her to Rouen."

"Let Gilbert do it—the less I am in her company before we flee, the better it is for everyone." He could sense Henry's disapproval. "Surely little enough can happen if they keep to the duke's roads."

"I don't know," the prince answered slowly, "for too many consider my brother weak, and, your pardon for saying it, I'd sooner send my sister in the company of an old woman than with Gilbert."

"Sweet Mary!" Roger swore softly. "Who dares to interfere with Belesme's intended wife?"

"Thing is—not too many know of the contract," Henry reminded him.

"Then let Gilbert tell them," Roger snapped irritably. "If you have no wish for my company, I'll ride to mine own lands, but I cannot stay here."

"Please yourself." Henry shrugged. "Ten to one, I am an old man for worrying, and you are right. Certes, you are welcome enough to ride with me."

Considering the subject closed, the prince rolled over on his side and went to sleep easily. Roger lay staring into the darkness for a long time, thinking of Eleanor and trying to sort out his troubled thoughts. All of his hopes were dependent on his ability to get Eleanor safely out of Rouen, and he dared not chance betraying himself or her. Yet the more he found himself in her company, the harder it was not to give himself away. The scheme was mad enough as it was without the risk of further complications, and so much depended on its success. Slowly he slipped into that half-conscious state where the mind wanders at will. Eleanor came to him there, her dark eyes laughing, her dark hair spreading over him like a silken curtain shimmering against his bare skin. Her mouth curved into a soft smile as she bent for his kiss, and her skin was warm to his touch. With a groan, he forced himself awake. If all went as he planned, soon enough Lea would be with him in the flesh, and they would have a lifetime together.

"I will not fail thee, Lea, I swear," he half-whispered in the stillness of the night.

Eleanor climbed to her father's solar, drawn by the sound of quarreling voices. Her heart pounded uncomfortably as she realized Gilbert and Roger argued over Roger's accompanying her to Rouen.

"Aye—leave me again—desert me!" Gilbert shouted. "What use are you to me when I dare not depend on you?" Red-faced, he turned away, muttering, "I acknowledged you, yet you serve me not."

"Nay," Roger answered coldly, "you forget—'twas you who deserted me at Ancennes, and left me and my men to die in your cause. Thirty of my best perished while you ran, Gilbert. Talk not to me of desertion."

Both men became aware of the white-faced girl at the same time. Gilbert gestured at Roger while speaking to her. "He leaves us—the whore's son leaves us!"

Ignoring him, Roger moved to Eleanor, his blue eyes softening perceptibly. "I have to go, Lea, but I will see you again in Rouen. Nothing has changed except that I ride with Henry now."

"Aye—he cares more for his highborn prince than for me!"

"Lea, you understand my meaning, don't you?"

"Aye—nay—" She shook her head in disbelief. "Nay, I cannot face Rouen or Belesme alone."

"Lea . . ." He possessed her hand. "I cannot speak here—come down with me ere I leave."

Behind him, Gilbert continued venting his anger, gibing, "I give you and that Saxon whore a home and this is how I am repaid—she takes herself to a convent and you give me naught!" When he realized that his words were having little effect, he raised his hand to strike. "Listen when I speak!"

Roger dodged as he spun around. "Hit me, Gilbert of Nantes, and, afore God, you can feel the weight of my hand."

"Bastard!" Gilbert spat out.

"Aye," Roger agreed calmly, "and all I have become I owe to myself and Lea. Do not cry to me of what you have done for me."

"Lea—'tis always Lea," Gilbert growled. "Did you come this time because I asked or did you come for her?"

"For Lea."

"Art a fool." Gilbert sneered. "For once she goes to Belesme, I doubt you'll ever see her again."

"What kind of father are you?" Roger's voice was low and contemptuous.

"And what kind of brother are you? Aye—think you I have no eyes, boy?"

"Gilbert—" Roger frowned warningly.

"Oh, aye, I know—I was blind till now, but now I can see," Gilbert growled. "You would lie with your own sister."

Behind them, Eleanor gasped at her father's accusation. Roger whitened, his jaw twitching with the effort of controlling himself. His fist clenched involuntarily and he stepped toward Gilbert.

Thinking he and her father meant to come to blows, Eleanor pushed between them. Slowly Roger mastered his temper and lowered his hands.

"Pay him no heed, brother," she pleaded, "for he knows not what he says."

"I know," Gilbert persisted. "Aye, I know."

"Lea, I cannot stay here now even if I would. You can see it will not serve. I ride with Henry as far as Rennes, then I am for mine own lands. I will see you again in Rouen"—his eyes met Gilbert's over her head—"before the betrothal."

"Roger . . . please!"

"Nay, Lea—do you come down with me or not?"

She knew defeat. Whatever he and Gilbert had quarreled about before she'd come up, it had decided him. Nothing she could say would change his leaving Nantes. Bitterly she turned on her father. "Papa, I would have not believed your mind so foul—see what you do?" Roger was already on his way down the steps. "Papa, you sicken me."

"Ask him what he would have of you, daughter—ask why he plays the fool for you."

"Because I am his sister," she answered over her shoulder as she went after Roger.

"Art the bigger fool, Eleanor, an you believe that."

"Roger, wait!"

She found him standing at the bottom of the winding tower stairs, his handsome face creased in concern.

She reached for him only to be clasped firmly by the elbows and set back.

"Brother, do not leave me! I cannot face Count Robert alone!"

"Lea, I have to." His grip on her elbows was almost painful.

"Is it because of last night? I swear we were both innocent, Roger, and naught else has happened."

"Nay, 'twas not that—though I am glad Henry leaves."

"Then . . . ?"

He looked at her upturned face with her dark eyes glistening with unshed tears and was nearly unnerved. She was beautiful, loving, and trusting—and God willing, she'd be his one day.

"You heard Gilbert," he answered finally.

"But—"

His hands slid down to her hands. "Lea, I am still your man, bound to you by oath, and nothing ever changes that. I swear I will not let you go to Belesme as long as there is breath in my body." His blue eyes searched her face for understanding. "I still meet you in Rouen and we will escape from there, but so much depends on the secrecy of our plans. Robert would not hesitate to destroy me if he even suspected—you know that."

"Aye," she sighed heavily, "and you risk much for me."

"And for myself, Lea." He released her hands and bent to quickly brush her lips with his. "Let us look forward to an adventure together."

8

Eleanor sat her saddle uneasily, weary from the plodding step of the horse beneath her as her party made its slow progress toward Rouen. Each passing mile lowered her already faltering spirits as she drew nearer her inevitable meeting with Belesme. At her side, Margaret chattered incessantly while Adelicia gamely tried to follow her conversation. Behind them, some thirty sumpter horses carried Eleanor's bride-things, a treasure of clothing, jewelry, plate, and furniture that had nearly beggared the people of Nantes. Gilbert might care little for his eldest daughter, but he'd give Belesme no cause for complaint.

Given Roger's still puzzling departure from Nantes, Gilbert had wanted to send to Belesme for an additional contingent of men-at-arms to guard them across Maine and Normandy, but Eleanor had managed to dissuade him. She feared that the hated count might take it upon himself to come in person to escort her to Normandy's capital.

Roger—something clearly ailed him, but she was unable to determine to her satisfaction just what it was. She'd seen his anger that night in the courtyard, and that anger still stung. He'd been right, she supposed, about Prince Henry, but it hadn't seemed so at the time. She knew she should not have let him kiss her, and she must have looked wanton to both men. Unconsciously she hugged herself as she remembered the feel of Henry's arms about her and the strange sensation of his mouth on hers. It had not been an unpleasant experience—in fact, she rather liked it. Idly she wondered if Roger had ever kissed anyone

like that. Fool, she chided herself, he must have, for
he was nearly three-and-twenty and a man, after all.

A lone rider approached ahead and then veered off
without exchanging the customary greetings. Since they
were about three miles from Mayenne, Gilbert observed him anxiously before signaling to Bernard de
Moray, his captain, to intercept the intruder. They
neared Fuld Nevers' stronghold and Gilbert had no
wish to draw his attention. The stupid and savage Fuld
had allied himself with Belesme during the recent quarrels with Nantes, and his savagery was well-remembered
by the people of that city. Cursing Roger for his absence, Gilbert watched his men pursue and lose their
prey. Nervously he ordered his scanty column to draw
more closely together.

A cloud of dust formed on the horizon shortly after
de Moray returned. An early count by the sharp-eyed
captain confirmed Gilbert's worst fears—at least forty
armed men lay in wait ahead. And above them the
hated red-and-black pennon of Nevers waved in the
wind. Panic seized Gilbert.

"Sound retreat!" he called out even as he whirled
his own mount and made for the ford they'd crossed
less than a mile before.

It was the last thing de Moray wanted to do. Pro-
tecting a fleeing pack train was nearly impossible, and
flight would be the sign of weakness that whetted
Fuld's blood lust. Like Belesme, Fuld preferred to
chase and corner rather than to stand and fight. De
Moray watched with sinking heart the movement of
the men on the horizon—Gilbert's flight was bringing
them forward.

"Cut loose the pack animals!" De Moray yelled to
his men. To Gilbert he called out, "The Demoiselle!
We must save the Demoiselle!"

"Nay—let Belesme come for her," were Gilbert's
parting words. "She'll be his soon enough, anyway."

Gamely the captain attempted to draw his men behind the now-fleeing girls. "Mayhap the pack animals
will satisfy them!" he told Eleanor as he urged her to
speed.

It was a futile hope. Seeing the sumpter horses abandoned, Fuld accounted them his already, and his attention was devoted to securing Gilbert's head now. He signaled his men to go for the retreating escort.

Knowing his case hopeless, de Moray had the choice of standing to fight with his men in disarray or surrendering to almost certain death at the hands of the violent and unpredictable Fuld. But to fight could result in death to the Demoiselle and her sisters. Cursing the fate that gave him a craven master, he made his decision.

Suspecting Belesme's possible complicity in the attack, de Moray shouted to Aymer de Clare, Eleanor's young cousin, "Ride for the FitzGilbert! If you find him not at Rennes, seek him until you do."

It was an awesome responsibility for the boy scarcely into his teens, but Aymer nodded. He rode Fireleaper, a gift from his brother Walter, and the horse was by far the swiftest there. If any of them could outrun Fuld's men, it would be Aymer. He cut away and dug his spurs in the big black. The horse reared and took off as though pursued by the Devil.

To Eleanor's complete horror, de Moray then dismounted and awaited Fuld's approach with his sword extended hilt-first in a gesture of surrender. When the other men of Nantes would follow him, she tried to stop them.

"Nay, let us fight!" she cried to rally them. One by one they followed their captain's example. When she could see it was no use, she spurred her own horse and prepared to flee alone. Old Erlen, a household knight since her childhood, caught her bridle and held on in spite of her raised whip. "Art cowards all!" she screamed in frustration.

Erlen winced but did not release her horse. "Nay lady"—he shook his head sadly—"we die to save you."

In the weeks that followed her capture, Eleanor learned to pray for survival. Bestial, cruel, stupid, and capricious, Fuld Nevers terrorized her with threats of ravishment and death, while at the same time he sent to Gilbert his demand for one thousand marks, ransom. In the first three days, most of her men had succumbed to his torturing and their heads now hung over Fuld's gate—old Erlen, Giles de Searcy, William Perichal, Stephen de Perigny, to name but a few. But thus far she had not seen Bernard de Moray alive or dead.

The workings of Fuld's tortured mind made it impossible to reason with him. From the first, when she'd tried to make him understand that she was to be betrothed to his overlord, he'd refused to believe her, and he'd beaten her severely for lying to him.

Fuld's greed seemed to know no bounds, either. He'd confiscated all of her bridethings and strutted around wearing much of her jewelry himself, while his slatternly wife, Blanche, squeezed her filthy body into Eleanor's gowns. That they were inches too tight and inches too short seemed to make little difference to the indolent Blanche. As an afterthought and a sop to his liege lord, Fuld had sent the ever weeping Margaret and the still-defiant Adelicia to Robert of Belesme for ransom. He reasoned it was cheaper than parting with any of Eleanor's treasure; and besides, Gilbert was slow to ransom his girls. With his limited powers of reasoning, Fuld expected his lord to be pleased with the offering. Belesme was not, and his message enraged Fuld.

Eleanor had feared for her life when she had read Belesme's message to him. It had been an effort to say the words aloud, but since she was literally the only person who could read and write in the whole of Nevers' stronghold, it had fallen on her to decipher the words for her captor. It was tersely worded, Belesme's message, but it was to the point: Release the Demoiselle of Nantes and all of her belongings to Belesme or be forsworn. Fuld had beaten her again after the reading, first saying she was lying, and then saying she was a witch who would come between him and Belesme. Finally he came to curse Belesme for what he perceived to be greed—the count meant to steal his ransom, he reasoned. Eleanor gave up any further attempt at explaining anything to Fuld. And Fuld, from the safety of a stone-walled fortress, decided to defy his liege lord.

Days had turned into weeks without any word from her father, and Fuld grew surlier than before as he waited. He felt the ransom was due him, and it rankled that the girl's family had not chosen to pay. With each passing day he increased her humiliation, forcing her to serve Blanche in her chamber and him at his table like a village girl, and making her sleep in a narrow closetlike room cut into his chamber wall. Eleanor reflected bitterly that the lowliest servant at Nantes was better-treated than she. Yet, despite the frequent beatings and the threats, she survived. Sometimes she felt that only the rigors of Fontainebleau could have prepared her for this.

It was hot and damp the third week of June, and the air lay over the keep like the steam that rose from the kitchen kettles. Eleanor wearily brushed back a damp strand of straggling hair that escaped her braids and set about straightening her corner of Fuld's chamber. It was a nearly impossible task, given the housekeeping of the whole place. The entire castle needed freshening, she decided as she wrinkled her nose at the smell of the room. Winter rushes, strewn about to give warmth against a stone floor, still lay rotting in summer's heat, and the musty odor of them commingled with the malodorous mound of Fuld's unwashed clothing to give the place a nauseating closeness. In contrast, the rush carpets at Nantes had long since been removed and the floors swept clean and rinsed with limewater in preparation for warm weather. And certainly the clothing there was kept washed and repaired and neatly stored away.

She turned her attention to her cot and its age-yellowed sheets. It was a disgrace to expect anyone to sleep in such filth, she muttered to herself, but how could she expect to get anything better when Fuld and his lady slept on dirty bedding themselves? It was a wonder they were not overrun with vermin. The whole fortress was a pigsty as far as she had been able to tell—about the only thing that did not stink was, oddly enough, the garderobe. Fuld Nevers must surely have the only keep where the air was cleaner in the privy than in the courtyard or the family's quarters.

Someone yelled from the vicinity of the outer wall, and curiosity compelled her to look out the slender arrow slit that served for both light and ventilation. Men could be seen running up the steep cut out steps in the wall to look where a sentry pointed. Before long, even the loathsome Fuld joined them. She could not see what they saw, but she could tell by Fuld's gestures that he had unwelcome company. He lumbered down, shouting out orders, and made his way across the open yard toward the tower where she stood. Too soon, she could hear him coming up the stairs.

He lumbered into his chamber, effectively blocking any way out. Spitting into the filthy rushes at her feet, he came to a halt less than a foot away. He gestured toward the arrow slit where she'd watched.

His face broke into a hideous grin, his blackened teeth showing against sallow lips. "The Bastard," he announced succinctly.

"Wh . . . Roger?" She could not believe her ears—her brother came to her aid.

"Aye, FitzGilbert camps across the river. My men have recognized his standard, and outriders have seen him."

She could not say anything for a moment as his news sank in. Roger had come—Roger lay less than a mile away. She tried to hide her elation and waited.

Abruptly Fuld moved away to rummage through the contents of an old chest. Without looking up, he asked, "You can read—can you write enough that any can understand it?"

"Aye." Her mouth went dry. Did Fuld mean to treat with her brother for her release? Her hopes were shattered with his next words.

"You will write to Belesme for me and offer him the FitzGilbert's head for the taking. Then mayhap my lord will forget his petty quarrel with me." He rubbed his hands together in anticipation of solving all of his problems at once. "Aye, many's the time I've heard him say he wanted the Bastard's head on his gate."

"You think to make him attack Roger?" she asked incredulously. "Nay, he would not dare!"

"Fool!" Fuld spat again as he turned back around. "My lord of Belesme dares anything! He knows no fear," he boasted.

"Nay, he would not attack my brother when he expects to wed with me."

"Lying slut!" Fuld slapped her across the mouth. "I listen to no more of your lies."

" 'Tis the truth!"

"You read his message," Fuld growled, "and he said nothing of any betrothal. I am his vassal, and I would know of it. You lie, Demoiselle. Besides, Belesme would not have Gilbert's blood in his sons."

She winced at the painful reminder of her father's well-known cowardice. To her, it seemed that all men must call Gilbert of Nantes craven and without honor. "Mayhap Count Robert wants the wealth of Nantes for his sons," she countered.

"Pfaugh! 'Tis his for the taking anyway." Fuld appeared to have found what he searched for. "We waste time, Demoiselle—today you write Belesme as I tell you."

And if I do not?"

"Then your head will hang over my gate with the rest."

It was a persuasive argument. It did her little good to defy Fuld if she did not survive to see her brother again. She nodded.

There was no ink or vellum to be found, but Fuld managed to come up with some poorly sharpened pens. "Does no one even keep household accounts here?" she asked incredulously when he presented them.

"Nay. My steward sickened and died from eating rotten eels, and I sent the puling priest away long ago."

When he finally assembled everything to his satisfaction, she did not know whether to laugh or cry—he provided cloth dye and a piece of smooth wood. She almost wished she could be present to watch Belesme read it.

Fuld stood over her and gave her his message, repeating it several times until he was satisfied with the sound of it. And when she'd finished writing it, he'd made her point out each word to ensure she'd done as told. Finally satisfied, he'd dispatched his messenger to Belesme.

Robert sent no written reply to Nevers, but Fuld did not worry. Confident that Belesme would not pass up this chance to take Roger FitzGilbert, Fuld continued preparation for the squeeze maneuver. He and Count Robert would come at the Bastard from both sides, with Belesme cutting off any avenue of retreat at the river. Together they would crush him—then Gilbert would have to ransom Eleanor.

Roger appeared unhurried in his siege preparations. His catapults and mangonels were rolled near Fuld's walls and positioned, pitch vats were built, and large rocks were collected, but little else was done. Fuld watched the leisurely preparations with glee. "The fool thinks he has all summer!" he joked to his captains.

Outside, Roger directed the digging of a drainage ditch to be connected at the last to Fuld's, and did his best to keep his men busy enough to prevent their fighting among themselves. Occasionally he let them lay waste to the rich fields that surrounded Nevers' stronghold, but he kept them away from the villages that lay below the castle. And, like Fuld, he waited. The castle was stone and nearly impregnable, with thick walls and solid towers, a rare fortress for the area. If it were to be taken, it would either be a long and slow process of gradual starvation, or a weakness would have to be found. The best thing Roger had going for him was Fuld's unpredictability—the man's vanity could well lead him to make mistakes.

Finally he received the word he had been waiting for, and he ordered the pitch vats heated. Fuld watched

from his walls with new confidence. Both men had
received the same reports—Robert of Belesme was on
the move and lay with his army less than three miles
away. When Fuld received the count at some four
hundred men, he was disappointed. The Bastard lay
below with nearly twice that number. But Belesme
was Belesme—he never lost—and Fuld did not expect
him to do so now.

Fuld spent most of his daylight hours on the wall,
watching and waiting for the moment when Roger
FitzGilbert became aware that Belesme lay behind
him. Fuld's messenger slipped out to Robert's camp,
but never came back. Finally, on July 2, new and
frenzied activity could be noted in the encampment
below. Standards of Roger's vassals were raised to
wave in the summer breeze, and men put on their
emblazoned surcoats to identify their houses. A raft
was put to on the river and a party floated across.
Beneath him, Fuld could see a bareheaded Robert of
Belesme step ashore, unmistakable with that black
hair and green surcoat. The blond-headed Bastard
moved to greet him, and together they walked up the
bank to Roger's tent, followed by several lords from
both parties. That they did not exchange the customary kiss of peace was small comfort to Fuld Nevers.

Inside his tent, Roger faced the man he hated most
in the world. Even for the sake of Eleanor's release, it
was difficult to treat with Robert of Belesme, and he knew
the count felt much the same way about him. But they
each had something to lend to the operation that was
invaluable to the other—Roger had men, while most
of Robert's levies were still occupied fighting Curthose's
war in the Vexin; Robert, on the other hand, had the
reputation that struck dread in men's souls. And both
wanted Eleanor safely out of Fuld's hands. Roger
hoped against hope that a siege would prove unnecessary—that somehow Robert's appearance would strike
enough fear in Fuld's weak mind that he would release
her. Robert dashed any such hopes.

"Nay," he replied to the suggestion, "he will fight
to the death now. He knows what I will do to him."

His green eyes glittered in anticipation, and his sensuous mouth curved into his strange half-smile. "And so I will."

"I would have my sister safe," Roger reminded him grimly.

"Think you I want her dead?" Robert demanded harshly. "Dead bones make a poor wife. Nay, I would have her whole, also."

"Then what's to be done? He'll kill her before he's killed." Roger ran his fingers through his blond hair in distraction. "Is there no way?"

"Complete war. We cannot breach the walls—they are too thick—but we can rain fire over them and we can cut out all supplies. If we are fortunate and fire the granaries and the stables, we can cut their will to resist."

"And burn Lea in her bed. Nay, my lord, 'tis too risky."

Belesme eyed him with disgust. "If I had not seen you in battle, FitzGilbert, I should think you your father's son. War is no May game to be played on the hillside." He walked outside the tent and picked up a stick. "Here." He drew a large oval that flattened out on one side in the dirt. Inside it, he traced the outline of Fuld's castle, and then he drew circles for the three main towers. "Fuld's apartments are here." He made a large cross over the tower as he pointed to it. "The granaries are about as far away as they can be within the walls. The stables are here." He stood up and moved back to give Roger a clearer view. "Because of her value to him, I would expect Fuld to keep Eleanor near him."

"In his tower?"

Belesme nodded. "As yet, the other towers are largely unfinished. Fuld's father started building the structure the same year the Conqueror sailed for England. He knew what he was doing and laid the groundworks for a formidable fortress." Belesme dropped the stick and brushed his hands against his green tunic. "Alas, Fuld lacked the brains to finish it. He has a stone curtain and stone towers—and that is all."

Roger turned his eyes toward Fuld's walls. "It looks like enough."

"It may be, FitzGilbert, but I think it can be taken. Every fortress has a weakness. For some it is a flaw in the structure. For others, it is a flaw in the men behind the walls."

"Fuld."

"Aye."

"What if he kills her?"

"If she is dead, no man comes out of there alive. But I expect he will first decide to fight in defiance. If we can destroy much of his food, he will try to treat with you, FitzGilbert. He is not fool enough to expect to treat with me. When that happens, we can decide what to do." Robert of Belesme turned his green eyes toward the siege machines. "You have placed them well for not knowing your target. And I see you already have plans to dry out his ditch. Small work for so many men, though. I propose we loose our forces on the countryside to keep them busy."

"Nay." Roger stared levelly at Belesme. "I did not bring my men to burn and rape, my lord."

Belesme shrugged. "Then keep them in line however you will. My men are used to taking what lies in their path." Abruptly he changed the subject. "Can your pitch vats be ready by morning? I am for raining fire as soon as we can."

"Aye. My men will wrap the torches tonight."

"FitzGilbert . . ."

Roger met the strange green eyes. "What?"

"Fuld is mine to take. If he survives to the end, he is mine to kill."

A chill descended down Roger's spine. Belesme's meaning was clear—he would torture Fuld Nevers slowly to death. Roger took a deep breath before answering. "Aye."

"He is forsworn."

"You owe me no explanation, my lord. My only concern is that Eleanor of Nantes comes out of there alive."

"Aye." Belesme frowned. "It may be difficult to

recognize your sister at first, FitzGilbert. Fuld has a heavy hand."

Roger felt sick—Belesme was putting into words what he dared not even think. He nodded. "Then I cannot promise you Fuld."

"Aye—you can"—Robert spoke softly—"for I know better than you the limits of life. He'll pay for each and every mark he has put on her."

The acrid smell of smoke and burning flesh assailed her nose and irritated her eyes as Eleanor awoke to more cries of "Tend the buckets!" It was apparent that yet another pitch torch had found its mark within Fuld's walls. His boasts of the invincibility of stone might prove right, but Roger and Belesme were taking a heavy toll of thatched roofs and livestock within the stronghold. Rock and pitch rained down day and night with devastating results. Eleanor herself had formed part of the human chain that had labored in vain to save the stables and the frightened animals inside. The memory of their stamping and whinnying came flooding back to her as she opened her eyes and recollected her surroundings.

Sitting up and rubbing smoke-reddened eyes with a sooty hand, she groped for the water pitcher by her cot. Her hand stopped in mid-reach—there was no water for washing now. Ruefully she pulled a corner of dirty sheet up and rubbed at her face. She winced as she did so—Fuld's hands had left many bruises. Ah, if those who had acclaimed her beautiful could but see her now. If Robert of Belesme faced her like this, would he still want to wed with her? And what of Roger? Nay, he would still love her—Roger was always Roger. She just hoped he would get the chance to avenge all her hurts and all the insults she'd borne.

Wearily she dragged herself to an arrow slit that served for her window and peered to the courtyard below to see what new damage had been done. Across the way, the few timbers that remained of the stable still smoldered. And in the distance, between inner bailey and curtain wall, the granaries flared orange in

the morning light. One of Fuld's men looked up and
spat when he saw her. Most of them now barely con-
cealed their hatred of her, too often blaming their
predicament on "that witch of Nantes" rather than on
their lord. Beside him, men labored to pile rubble and
charred carcasses into a central mound from whence
carts could be loaded and the bodies of men and
animals could be moved outside the bailey wall for
burial. Eleanor turned away from the sight and the
smell.

So intent had she been on the scene below her that
she failed to hear Fuld come into the room behind
her. His ugly face was even more repulsive with its red
eyes and soot-streaked cheeks.

"What do you want?" she asked tiredly.

"You are to get me safe passage out of here."

She almost laughed. "Had I the means, my lord, I
should have been gone myself." She indicated the window slit. "My brother's pitch finds its way closer and
closer."

"Aye," Fuld agreed grimly, "and I won't be here to
be fried in my bed or to starve."

"I thought this place invincible."

"It is—the walls will stand." He grabbed her hair
and pulled her back to the window. "Look down, fool,
and see what the Bastard and Belesme have done to
the livestock. In two days' time and in this heat, all
that will be rotting—then what will happen?" Without
waiting for her answer, he flung her savagely away
from him. She had to catch herself against the uneven
rocks of the wall. "Well, Fuld won't be here to suffer—
you buy my way to safety. Aye, you write to the
Bastard and tell him I am willing to treat for a safe
conduct. If he can hold Belesme until I am away, I will
release you at Dieppe."

"I don't believe you!"

Fuld's open hand struck her across the mouth. "Fool!
I care not what you believe! It only matters that the
FitzGilbert believe it!" he exploded. "Now, you will
write—else your head joins the others on the pikes."

*   *   *

Fuld Nevers' messenger rode out under flag of truce to deliver Eleanor's letter. Roger had him detained while he sent for Belesme. While he was waiting for the count to come, he reread it several times, trying to decide if it were a trick. The tent flap parted, and Robert of Belesme ducked his head to gain admittance. Roger handed him the letter.

Belesme took his time before commenting, "It could be a ruse, but I doubt Fuld has the intelligence to think up something like this. The Demoiselle—is she able to understand what she asks?"

"She is no fool. I trust Lea as much as I trust any man."

"She is a woman."

"Mabille is a woman," Roger retorted, "and you have left her in command of Belesme often enough."

"Leave Mabille out of this!" Belesme responded with such a flash of anger that they were both taken aback. Finally Robert took a deep breath and nodded. "All right, FitzGilbert, we go in if you believe what she writes, but I warn you—I have no wish to die at Fuld's hands. If this is a trick, I will have my sword at your back."

"Isn't that its usual place?" Roger shot back sarcastically.

Belesme's green eyes flashed momentarily. "Bastard, there is little liking between us, but soon we are to be joined by a bond of blood. If I can stomach Gilbert, I can stomach anything. And you are cut from far different cloth than he is."

Roger relaxed slightly. "Then you want to go in with me?"

"Aye, I know the place—and Fuld is mine." Belesme moved to the center of the tent, where he could better stand straight. Flexing his shoulders by clasping his hands behind him and stretching, he offered his own plans.

"When we clear the garderobe, we are one level below Fuld's quarters. We'll have to get up the stairs and into his chamber before he realizes we are in."

"What if she isn't there?"

"She'll be where Fuld is. If they aren't in his quarters, she'll be dead before we can find her."

Roger crossed himself and murmured a quick prayer for her safety. Belesme eyed him with disgust. "Trust your sword, FitzGilbert—'twill serve you better."

Roger's mouth was dry, his stomach heavy. "If she is safe, it will be enough for me."

"When do you want to go in?"

"Tonight."

Belesme nodded. "I'll give orders to break camp and pull back immediately. Then, under cover of darkness, I'll ride back in and we'll look for the old ditch."

"All right."

Belesme moved toward the flap. "If we are successful, FitzGilbert, you will need to take the Demoiselle and press on to Rouen before I deal with Fuld. I doubt either of you has the stomach for it."

Once he saw that Belesme's troops were pulling back to higher ground, Fuld's spirits improved. Impulsively he ordered that any salvageable meat be served at his supper table along with whatever else his cooks could provide. Feeling his escape imminent, he ate and drank liberally. Behind him, Eleanor kept his cup refilled with its sour wine until at last he lurched from his chair and made his way to his bed.

Eleanor retired when Fuld and Blanche did. For a long time she lay listening to the sounds of the castle as it settled down for the night. She could hear Fuld's clumsy attempts at lovemaking, and Blanche's guttural moans as the ropes of the bed creaked and strained. Fuld heaved and grunted until he found release, and then all was quiet. Eleanor shuddered in disgust and wondered if all men sounded like that. Somehow, she couldn't imagine either Roger or Robert of Belesme making such noises.

She rose and crept back to the arrow slit, peering anxiously into the darkness for some sign of activity. Fires flickered in the distance, but she could detect no movement. Had Roger received her letter? And would he trust what she said? She fervently prayed he would, for she had no wish to flee in the company of Fuld Nevers. Finally she slipped back into her bed and waited.

In spite of her best efforts to remain awake, she found her eyes growing heavy. Even thoughts of Roger could not hold her attention while her weary body demanded rest.

She could not hazard a guess as to how long she slept before she woke to the sounds of scraping on the stairs and of sleepy men groping for their arms. She came fully awake when Fuld loomed across the opening to her tiny cut-out chamber. He was barefoot, and He'd managed to pull on mail over his bare skin, and he held his sword in his hand. She knew terror—there could be no escape past him. For one awful minute she could envision her head over his gate.

"Lying witch!" he snarled. "Your brother betrays me!" He lurched toward her in semidarkness. "Well, when I go down, you go with me!"

Eleanor rolled out of her cot to the opposite side and ducked away from him, her only thought for the door behind him. Her eyes never left his hideous face as he advanced toward her, until she judged it safe to move. Torchlights appeared behind him, illuminating his outline against the doorway. He reached for her like a bear making a swipe with a great paw.

"Demoiselle!"

She could recognize Robert of Belesme's voice. Fuld hesitated momentarily, his face paling with fear. Eleanor used the distraction to push the cot at him and to run toward the door. Fuld grasped for her and came up empty-handed.

Belesme pushed his body between her and Fuld, forcing her into another knight's arms. Her protector drew her back a pace and sheltered her with his body.

"Take her to safety," commanded Robert of Belesme as he faced Fuld. With deadly deliberation he raised his broadsword and moved into the tiny cut-out chamber.

Eleanor stood transfixed watching the most feared man in Normandy and Maine advance on Nevers.

Fuld lunged for better position, hoping to force Belesme back out into the larger chamber, where he would at least have room to maneuver against Belesme's greater height and longer reach. From the moment that he'd realized whom he faced, Fuld knew it would be no match, but he was intent now on fighting for the means of his dying. If he could not win, he had no wish to be taken alive into Belesme's terrible hands.

Surprisingly, Count Robert yielded enough room for Fuld to pass into the larger chamber, but his strange half-smile dispelled any thoughts of weakness. Fuld himself knew it was a game now—that Robert meant to toy with him, to terrorize him, and to take him slowly. Fuld swung wildly, moving forward as his sword arced wide of its mark. Belesme's blade touched him lightly on the chest before it was drawn back.

"You would skewer yourself like a fat pig," Belesme murmured as he yielded yet more room. He caught another blow with the side of his blade and broke contact. The smile seemed graven on his face now.

Terror and a night of excesses rendered Fuld clumsy and inept. Gone was the swaggering savage Eleanor knew and despised. The man who faced Belesme seemed to have shrunk measurably. He made so many mistakes and defended himself so poorly that it was obvious even to her that Robert could finish him at will. The fight for Fuld Nevers' life amounted to little more than the clanging of his sword against the count's green-and-white buckler.

It seemed that the encounter went on forever, when in fact it lasted but a few minutes. Belesme teased, taunted, and flaunted his superior skill with the broadsword until Fuld could stand it no longer. As Belesme moved back yet again, Fuld lunged wildly, taking a wide cut with his blade. He caught only air, but the effort staggered him and cost him his balance. The count decided he'd played enough—he swung a heavybooted foot to kick Fuld's legs out from under him. Then he threw his own weapon away and stepped on Fuld's sword arm, releasing Fuld's grip. With another kick he sent the blade sliding across the floor.

"Jesu!" Roger breathed to break the spell that held everyone in the room. Only then was Eleanor even aware that she stood within her half-brother's arms. Freed finally from Fuld, she could give vent to her emotions, and she began to cry and talk at the same time.

"Oh, Roger . . . I was so afraid I'd never see you again," she choked. "I thought I'd come here to die." Tears streamed down her bruised face. "I feared you would not understand my message."

He closed protectively around her and murmured soothingly while stroking her hair. "Lea . . . Lea, you are safe enough now," he reassured her over and over again through his own tears.

Convulsively she clutched the blue material of his surcoat, burying her head in it. Metal links pressed into her skin. Somewhere above her head he spoke softly. "I thought I'd lost you, Lea—I thought my foolishness at Nantes had lost you . . . Sweet Jesu, but I could have killed him with my hands, Lea!" His gloves dug into her shoulders. "I have been out of my mind, Lea."

The sickening sound of Belesme's boot repeatedly coming down on Fuld's now inert body brought them back to a realization of their surroundings. The count seemed intent on kicking his vassal to death. When it became apparent even to him that Fuld had lapsed into unconsciousness, he gave one last blow. Eleanor winced and let out an audible "Oh."

Robert of Belesme turned to her as though suddenly reminded of her presence. Pulling off his conical helmet with its telltale green plumes, he smoothed back his sweat-damped hair. His high cheekbones bore the imprint of the helmet nasal and his face seemed tired. Walking over to where she stood in the safety of Roger's arms, he removed his glove and touched a bruise that discolored her jaw. His touch was light.

"He will pay for every mark he has placed on you, Demoiselle, I swear. I intend to show everyone what happens to those who would interfere with what is mine." His voice was harsh with anger. His green eyes narrowed as they rested on her scratches and bruises. "He did you no other harm?"

"Nay."

"Your face will heal and men will again remark your beauty, but I am thankful that it will take FitzGilbert several days to get you to Rouen." He watched her eyes widen. "Aye, we still go there. Curthose will yet witness our betrothal."

"But . . . 'tis July," she protested lamely.

"Still so eager, I see," he gibed. "Make the best of it, Eleanor of Nantes, for I have not marched to your aid for nothing."

She could feel Roger tense against her, and she instinctively sought to protect him. "Nay, my lord, you mistake the matter," she told Belesme. "I am but surprised, that is all."

"I take her to Rouen, Robert," Roger spoke coldly, "and after that, I return to my own lands."

"Aye." Belesme's green eyes flickered over both of them. "I think it best if you leave at first light on the morrow." He turned to leave, and then stopped. "What made you write such a letter, Demoiselle?"

"Fuld said he meant to take me as far as Dieppe before he released me," she answered simply, "and I was sure he intended to kill me as an act of defiance to you."

"Probably so. Still, what made you think to direct us to the garderobe pit?"

"I could see daylight at the bottom, and by the smell of it, the pit was but newly dug. Also, 'twould put you within quick reach of Fuld's chamber," she explained.

"Well, 'tis the first time I ever took a castle by climbing through the privy"—Roger grinned happily—"but I am most glad it worked."

Even Belesme was forced to smile. "Aye. Strange that a man of Fuld's filth should be betrayed by a clean garderobe."

Belesme walked to an arrow slit and checked the courtyard below. In the rosy light of dawn, he could see men in Belesme green and Condes blue rounding up prisoners. Roger's squire and Jean Merville were counting and listing them according to rank. In the grassy area between the bailey and curtain walls, others added a few bodies to the open pits. Directly beneath him, Hugh and his captain argued over several prisoners' arms. He leaned forward to order that mail and weapons were to be divided equally between the camps.

Behind him, Fuld Nevers stirred undetected, and bided his time. Hatred and terror commingled—he would not lie tamely waiting for the revenge Belesme would take. Now conscious, he watched his lord from beneath half-closed lids. His fingers inched toward the dagger he wore in his belt.

Eleanor was the first to see him move when he used his strength to rise to a crouch. Even as she screamed out, "My lord, watch him!" Fuld lunged at Belesme's back, his dagger raised and targeted for the unprotected neck. Both Eleanor and Roger acted instinctively. She grabbed at a bed hanging and threw it over Fuld. Enraged, he struck at her wildly. Roger caught his wrist as the dagger cut through her sleeve, and twisted it painfully until Fuld released his grip on the weapon. It slid harmlessly to the floor. Roger delivered a heavy blow to Fuld's stomach, doubling him over. Belesme stepped on his hand and ground the bones into the stone floor.

"Mother of God!" Fuld cried out. "Kill me and be done."

"In due time," Belesme answered as he stood over him, tall and cold, his face set in arrogant cruelty. "You pay, Fuld Nevers, for what you would do to me and mine." Without looking at Eleanor, he murmured, "My thanks, Demoiselle. Are you hurt?"

"Nay, he cut my sleeve, but he drew no blood."

"Demoiselle . . ." Fuld spoke hoarsely through swollen lips. "Your mercy."

Her hand crept unconsciously to her own battered face and she turned away. "Nay," she half-whispered, "I will pray for your soul, but I can do no more."

"FitzGilbert . . ." Fuld's eyes moved with effort to Roger.

Roger shook his head. "I gave my word—you are his to do with as he will."

"Roger." Eleanor laid her hand on his shoulder. "By the looks of it, someone has opened your old wound. Blood seeps through your mail and stains your tunic."

" 'Tis nothing."

"Nay," she persisted, "it must be tended to, brother. Let me find Blanche and get something for it." When he did not move, she pushed him toward the stairs. "Come, let us find a place where I may bathe you and tend your shoulder. 'Twill fester, otherwise."

Roger was torn between a desire to be alone with her and a fear that he might somehow betray himself to her. The thought of her hands on his bare skin was tantalizing. Finally he compromised with himself.

"All right, Lea, but I bathe myself—I am better at it. You can salve whatever wounds I have taken."

As they left Fuld's chamber, they could hear Fuld pleading with Robert of Belesme. "My lord, I served you well," he cried, "and answered every call. I am your liegeman."

"In this you served me ill," Belesme answered coldly, "and for that you pay."

"Roger, sit you still whilst I get these last few scrapes."

He winced under her touch as she applied ointment to his back. She dipped her fingers again into the container and then resalved his old shoulder wound.

"I was mistaken," she murmured. "Whoever gave you this blow did not open the other one. It at least is healing well."

He ducked his head and turned to look at the container of ointment. "What is this stuff, anyway?"

"I don't know," she answered truthfully. "I had it of Fuld's steward, who said 'twas good for healing horses. Blanche said they had nothing else."

"Are you sure you had it right?" He sniffed it and

made a face at her. "Mayhap he said it was made of horse dung. God's teeth, but it smells bad enough. Lea, I cannot go down to eat like this."

She had to smile in spite of the soreness of her face. "It does smell rather strong, doesn't it? But it does not smell like manure to me—'tis more like some kind of grease that has sat overlong." She wiped her hands on a piece of linen and stepped back to survey her handiwork. "Aye—I got them all."

He stood and flexed his bare arms, rippling the muscles in his shoulders. "There were not many this time—I am more sore than cut." He reached for a clean tunic from his roll and pulled it over his head. "At least I have had a bath, though I doubt any will be able to tell."

"They can tell—you no longer smell like Fuld's privy."

"Aye. Lea, I would that you could have seen Belesme scaling the inside of the walls with his sword strapped to his back and his hands bare to hold the scaling hooks. He is ever so careful of his appearance that I had to force myself not to laugh." He sobered, frowning. "But I give him one thing, Lea—he was first up. Jesu, but the man knows no fear."

She came to stand in front of him and reached to place her hands against the sides of his face. "And you were right behind him." She grew serious as she stared up into the brilliant blue eyes. "You cannot know how proud you make me, brother, to know we share the same blood. Sometimes I could die of shame for my father, but you more than make up for his cowardice." She dropped her hands and looked away. "But sometimes I fear I have the taint."

"You, Lea? Nay, you have as much courage as any man. Remember what the Conqueror said of you? That you were the only man amongst us that day?" He spoke lightly until he could see that something really troubled her. "Lea, what ails you?"

"Oh, Roger, all my life I have been afraid of things—that you would leave me, that I would grow old and die at Fontainebleau, that I would be forced to wed with Belesme—I have feared so many things." She swallowed hard for composure. "But these last weeks were the worst of all. I was so frightened that I would not live to see you again."

"Lea . . . Lea . . ." he murmured as he enveloped her in strong arms.

"But what if I am like my father?"

" 'Tis no cowardice, Lea, to know fear. I have gone into battle many times, and each and every time, I have faced my enemy with my heart pounding and my stomach in my throat," he told her gently. "Yet no man calls me coward. It is right to fear, but wrong to run." He stepped back slightly while still holding her with one arm. He ran a fingertip along her discolored jaw and shook his head. "And it would seem you had much reason to fear." He became aware as he studied her face that she had many small bruises on her neck and larger ones on her face. She also had several small cuts around her mouth and a swollen upper lip. Abruptly he released her and reached for the salve. "Sit you down, Lea, and let me take care of you."

"Nay, I am all right now," she protested even as he pushed her gently down on the bench. Her hands touched where he had already begun applying the ointment. "I must look awful to you."

He stopped dabbing and shook his head. "On my honor, Lea, you never looked more beautiful to me than when Belesme shoved you into my arms this morning." His hands were gentle as he smoothed the balm over cuts and bruises. "We should have tended you first, I think. I did not realize that he'd cut you."

"He spoke only with his hand, brother. He was too stupid to do otherwise." She sighed heavily. "What will Belesme do to him?"

"Kill him."

"Then I pray he does it quickly."

"He won't." He stepped back and placed the salve container on a low table. "Tell me," he asked casually, "why did you warn Robert today?"

"Belesme fought for me."

"Nay, Lea. He fought for himself and for his wounded

pride." He turned away and shook his head. "Fuld could have killed Robert."

"You stopped him also."

"Aye. I could not see him struck from behind." He struck his palm in disgust. "We could have been rid of him, Lea."

"With a stain on our honor."

"In my heart, I know you are right, but my mind tells me that we should have let Fuld take him."

"Roger, how came you to join with Belesme, anyway?"

"Believe it or not, he came to me, Lea, because he would punish Fuld and he had not the men. His troops still fight in the Vexin for Curthose under de Mortain's command. And, to be truthful, I have to admit I was glad enough to see him." Roger's mouth drew into a wry smile. "Aye, his very reputation gives him an edge in battle."

"Fuld thought he'd come to make an end to you, and I was afraid that between them, they'd kill you." She shook her head at the memory. "But when Fuld saw you parley with Count Robert, I think he knew he could not survive."

Roger came behind her and put his hands on her shoulders. With his thumbs he began massaging above her shoulder blades. She relaxed under his touch, leaning forward and closing her eyes.

"Let us speak no more of Fuld or Robert, Lea. We leave this accursed place in the morning, and move on to Rouen. Once there, I can send my messengers out to people I have positioned along the way of our escape. God willing, we shall be in England by August, and we can put Belesme and all of this behind us."

"I pray he does not hunt us down like rabbits, Roger."

He stopped working on her shoulders. "I am not without resources, Lea, once we are in England. And Henry will ever stand our friend."

"Sweet Jesu, I hope so."

By noon, the castle was secured, and many of its inhabitants slept to make up for a short night. It was peaceful inside due to both Roger's and Count Robert's forbidding any further looting, destruction, or killing of prisoners. But in the town below, it was a different case—Belesme's men fell upon the citizenry with a vengeance, robbing, raping, and killing. Finally, Aubery woke Roger to tell him.

"My lord . . ." He shook him. "My lord, there is pillaging in the town."

"Unnnnh?" Roger tried to rouse from a deep sleep, but it was too much effort. He rolled over and pillowed his head with his arm. "Ummmmm."

"My lord!" Aubery shook him more insistently. "Wake up, my lord!"

Roger finally pulled himself to a sitting position on his pallet and eyed his squire irritably. "Well?"

"My lord, Belesme has let his men loose on the town! They ravish and kill at will, and we are powerless to stop them without engaging them in combat."

"What?" Roger was fully awake now. "By all saints, 'twas agreed to spare the people, for they provisioned us whilst we waited to take Fuld." Roger pulled himself up and reached for his tunic. "Damn his green eyes to hell! Cannot he keep his word one day?" He shrugged on his tunic and pulled on his chausses, wrapping them so hastily with his cross-garters that they bagged at the knees. Briefly he considered the wisdom of putting on his mail, but decided that Belesme would probably be unarmed and in bed. He contented himself with picking up his broadsword.

"Where did he quarter?"

Aubery pointed above the hall where they billeted. "He took Fuld's chamber as his own."

"Jesu! And where does he expect Lea to sleep? Nay—don't answer."

"He didn't say, but surely he would not dishonor your sister with you here."

"Robert would do anything," Roger reminded his squire grimly. "He would not have harmed the townspeople, either, or so he said. Spawn of devil and

witch, he has the Talvas taint! Sweet Jesu! And Gilbert would give Lea to him!''

Aubery's eyes widened as Roger purposefully buck-
led his scabbard belt. "What will you do, my lord?"

"Confront him!" Roger snapped. "God's teeth! What
did you expect me to do when you awakened me?
Well, do you come to witness, Sir Squire—or are you
as afraid of him as the rest?"

Stung, Aubery retorted, "I go where you go, my
lord."

Roger found the Count of Belesme fully awake and
engaged in going over the list of Eleanor's repossessed
bridethings. "Your father is most generous," he murmured even as Roger cleared the last step. It was
uncanny that he recognized his visitor without seeing
him.

Roger came straight to the point. "My lord, the
townspeople have claimed my protection, and I have
given it, yet your men are there now looting and
raping those who helped us."

"I wondered how long it would take you to come
up." Belesme turned around and allowed his green
eyes to flicker over Roger. With an exaggerated shrug
he seemed to dismiss the complaint. "My men have
sat overlong, FitzGilbert, and the means of taking this
stronghold has deprived them of the means to slake
their blood lust. You would not have them put the
garrison to sword because your sister is here, would
you?" He turned back to his list. "Until they are
satisfied, I can do nothing with them."

"You lie!" Roger placed his hand on his sword hilt.

Belesme spun around. His eyes flashed anger and
then veiled themselves. He noted the sword and raised
an eyebrow. "You find me unarmed, FitzGilbert."

"That can be remedied, my lord," Roger replied
with an edge to his voice. "Unlike many around you, I
am not afraid to face you."

"Then you are the greater fool in this room."

"Nay, my lord." Roger advanced a few steps to
stand directly in front of Belesme. "Order your men
back, or I will."

"And how do you propose to enforce such an order?" Belesme asked contemptuously.

"I have the greater force here," Roger reminded him, "and I will not hesitate to give the command that they enforce my promised protection by the sword if need be." He stared hard at Robert of Belesme, his face set and unyielding.

"Art soft as a woman," Belesme taunted before backing down.

"Justice is not softness, my lord, nor is cruelty strength."

The count walked to the arrow slit and called down to the courtyard, "To me! To me! To Belesme!"

The response was swift. Half a dozen men ran up the winding stone stairs to their master. For a brief moment Roger's neck hairs stiffened, but he held his ground. He drew his sword and waited. If Belesme meant to have him taken, he would take out the count first.

"Sheathe your sword, Bastard," Belesme ordered curtly before motioning one of his men forward. "Ralph, pass the word, death to murderers and ravishers." When the man looked at him in stunned silence, he snapped, "Aye, you heard me aright—I hang those who break FitzGilbert's peace. Go into the town and bring back those who pillage, and bring whatever villagers will testify against them."

"But—"

"Nay." Belesme waved aside any protest. "You heard me." Turning again to Roger, he spoke softly now. "You wanted justice, my lord—well, you can witness Belesme justice."

Roger felt sick as he observed that strange half-smile and realized the Belesme had his own blood lust to satisfy. And he would enjoy even the execution of some of his own men.

"You sicken me, Robert." Roger sheathed his sword and strode to the stairwell. "Lea pallets with me tonight for her own protection."

"Sometimes, FitzGilbert"—Robert's voice followed

him on the stairs—"I wonder which of you is convent-
bred."

Once he was clear of the steps, Roger's concern was
finding a place for Eleanor. It was one thing to tell
Belesme that she would pallet with him, but it was
quite another to even consider her bedding down in
the company of rough men-at-arms. In his mind he
could see the effect she would have on soldiers who
had no women of their own. Nay, it was better to
preserve that distance, that chasm between great lady
and commoner, than to let any see they had fought for
a flesh-and-blood woman. On reflection, he reluctantly
concluded she would have to stay in the cut-out chamber one last night, and that he would have to pallet
between her and Belesme.

Unaware of the contretemps between Roger and the
count, Eleanor finished ministering to the wounded of
both men, washing and stitching ugly gashes received
in the final taking of the stronghold, and then found
clean linens for her cot. She came up the stairs unattended, her arms laden with the fresh sheets, and
found Robert of Belesme. For an awful moment her
heart seemed to have stopped. In spite of his earlier
defense of her, she was still very much afraid of him.
Her eyes widened in horror, betraying her as she
stared at him, before she could recover her composure.

"My lord! Y-you startled me! I . . . I did not think
to see you here."

He noted her fear of him and it angered him. "Don't
look at me like that!" he snapped.

"Like what, my lord?" she asked as innocently as
she could.

He dropped his eyes and looked away, lowering his
voice until she could scarce hear him. "As though I
would as soon take your head as your maidenhead."

"My lord," she spoke slowly and carefully to avoid
angering him, "if I cannot conceal my fear of you,
mayhap 'tis because of what has passed between us.
When I was a child, you sought to kill my brother;
when you came to the abbey, you laid heavy hands on
me." Her heart raced at the expression in the strange

green eyes as he turned back to her, and she involuntarily raised the linens to shield her chest. "Give me time, my lord," she offered, "and mayhap I will cease to fear you."

"Aye." He stared at her intently. She was composed now and her dark eyes did not waver under his direct gaze. His breath caught—despite her cuts and bruises, she still claimed great beauty, and she was soon to be his. The Old Conqueror's words echoed in his ears and fed his pride. "Eleanor . . ." He reached to touch her temple where an older bruise had yellowed, his fingers brushing back the errant strands of dark hair, and sought to convince her. "I am not a gentle man—I can be no FitzGilbert—but I would not harm you. Come to me, Eleanor, and give me sons of my body, and I will treat you as well as may be."

There was unmistakable warmth in the usually cold eyes. For a brief moment the handsome face dropped its guard and let her see a man beneath the cruelty. Had he been another, it would have been a heady feeling to know he wanted her for herself, but this was Belesme.

"My lord, if I am wed to you, and if 'tis the will of God, I will have no choice in the matter," she answered finally.

"I care not for God's will, Eleanor—'tis you I would have."

His voice dropped again, but this time there was a husky, intimate quality to it. His hand left her face and moved to her shoulder, lightly tracing the bones beneath her gown. Fighting the urge to recoil from his touch, she kept her eyes on his face while clutching the linens even closer to her breasts. Stepping back half a pace, she drew his attention to the sheets. "I brought these up," she murmured lamely.

"I already ordered the beds changed—I bring my own, Demoiselle." His hand made a contemptuous sweep of the room and a black eyebrow lifted as he noted the bed newly hung with green-and-gold brocade. "Aye—I would not sleep with Fuld's vermin."

"Oh." Her gaze traveled from the bed to the tiny chamber off to the side. "Then where . . . ?"

"Your brother makes provision for you—though I doubt he can find any place safer. If he is so intent on preserving your maidenhead, he can sleep with me, but 'tis not likely he will."

Obvious relief flooded over her, irritating him again. Would her life always be tied so closely to Roger FitzGilbert's? Even as he sought to control the anger he felt, she slipped past him to place the folded linens at the foot of the cot. His body stirred as he watched her move about, her small, lithe body graceful and perfect. He sat on a low bench and kept his eyes on her while she stripped the filthy rags from the cot, dropped them into a pile on the floor, and began repacking the straw mattress. She was a joy to watch and she was going to be his.

"I would have you tend me."

The hairs at the back of her neck prickled in warning as she turned slowly around. "What?"

"I would have you tend me," he repeated.

"But you have already bathed . . . and Blanche—"

"Think you I would have her filthy hands on me?" he demanded harshly. "Nay—you tended FitzGilbert, did you not? Aye, I have bathed, but my shoulder pains me, Demoiselle. I would have you see to it."

"Your squire—"

"Is not here just now," he finished for her.

It was a simple enough request, one that was not uncommon, but she was loath to touch him. Even seated, he seemed large, overwhelming, and dangerous. Unconsciously she wet her lips and dried her damp palms against the skirt of her gown. She had no grounds for refusal—he'd offered her no violence this time—indeed, he'd fought Fuld Nevers to save her. Finally she nodded. "I'll get the unguent, my lord."

"If you mean that foul-smelling stuff they use here, I won't have it. Nay, my mother is skilled in the simples. You'll find hers on that table." He watched as her gaze traveled to where he indicated. "It won't hurt you to use it," he offered as an afterthought.

"Aye."

She moved to pick up the salve pot and then stood behind him uncertainly. "Which shoulder is it?"

"Above my sword arm."

"I did not think Fuld landed a blow."

"He did not, but I wrenched it pulling myself up the wall, and it pains me now." He leaned forward and pulled his tunic over his head, exposing a well-muscled torso. He was bigger, more powerfully constructed than she would have imagined from seeing him clothed. "Can you see anything?" he asked, his voice muffled by his tunic.

"Aye, you have bruised yourself, my lord." Eleanor dipped her fingers in the balm and prepared to touch her worst enemy.

"Wait—let me take this off." He finished pulling the tunic down over his arms and dropped it to the floor. "There."

She gingerly dabbed at the bruise, barely touching the discolored muscle until he urged, "Rub it in." Gradually losing her fear of him, she did as he asked, letting her fingers massage the oily substance across the shoulder. For a fleeting moment it occurred to her that he had skin like everyone else, and then she chided herself for thinking he would not—he was a man, after all. The stuff smelled good—it had the aroma of cooked cloves.

"There's another place in the front—must've scraped it."

"It surprises me that you would admit to pain," she murmured as she leaned to inspect the reddened area.

"Mayhap I wanted to feel your touch. It pleases me, Eleanor." Before she could pull back, he reached to grasp her nearest braid. With an almost painful jerk he brought her face even with his own. She dropped the salve pot and it rolled away on the floor as his other arm encircled her and pulled her onto his lap. She tried to lurch away in disgust, but found herself trapped. She ceased struggling and sat docilely while biding her time to catch him off his guard. And despite her outward calm, her pulses pounded and her stomach knotted in fear. "Pray release me, my lord," she managed in a cold voice.

"Nay, Eleanor—you are mine now. Twice my sword has bought you." His voice was soft, but there was nothing soft about the body that held her. His arms were like iron bands and his green eyes glittered with a strange light as his fingers twined in her braid and pulled her head back. Hungrily he bent his mouth to hers, and unlike Henry's first tentative brushing of lips, Robert of Belesme took full possession of her mouth, crushing her bruised lips until he forced her teeth open. His tongue slid along the edges, teasing and then taking. She was suffocating, she was drowning, and yet she was powerless to stop him. His hand brushed over her breasts and then cupped one, squeezing it and pinching at the nipple with strong fingers even while his mouth still possessed hers. She stiffened in shock and tried to wrench away in spite of the strange new sensations she was experiencing.

When at last he released her bruised lips to trail hot, breathless kisses to her ear, her flesh was alive with awareness of him. The nipples of her breasts strained against the cloth of her gown. His hands moved over her, touching and caressing roughly with almost hypnotic effect. His warm breath sent shivers down her spine and raised gooseflesh on her arms. Conflicting emotions flooded over her as her traitorous body softened under her despised enemy's touch, and yet she felt far from helpless now. Somewhere in the barely lucid reaches of her mind, her thoughts echoed the warning that she played a dangerous game.

His mouth explored along her neck and into the hollow of her throat and then back to her ear. His breath came like hot flames licking at her as he whispered, "Art fire, Eleanor of Nantes," and still she felt a sense of power over him. He was wanting, he was needing what she could give him.

Abruptly he stood, tumbling her off his lap and breaking the spell. She staggered but did not fall as his hand clasped her wrist so tightly that her fingers went numb. His manner had changed, his eyes were glittering with lust, and there was not gentleness, no tenderness in him. He was breathing rapidly, panting even, and he stood before her thoroughly aroused. She shrank back from his expression and cried out, "Nay! Nay—I will not!"

"Aye—you will! Art mine to take, Eleanor," he croaked as he pulled her toward the great tapestried bed.

"Stop! Nay!"

He flung her down on the feather mattress and blocked her escape while he began untying his chausses. "Aye, years I've dreamed of naught else," he panted as he freed himself from the restraining clothing.

"I'll scream!"

"Nay, you will not." He leaned over her and whispered hoarsely, "I would see all of you again, Eleanor—undo your gown for me."

Bargaining for time, she nodded. Very slowly her hands crept to the shoulder of her gown and began working it downward while he watched. Edging up to sit on the side of the feather bed, she let her feet touch the floor. His eyes never left the neckline of her gown while she eased it off one shoulder to reveal the curve of her breast. Then, appearing to stand to take off the garment, she suddenly bolted for the door, screaming at the top of her lungs, "To me! To me! Nantes! To Nantes! Sweet Mary, help me!"

Belesme caught her before she could secure the door and clamped his hand over her mouth to silence her. She bit down on a finger, but that had no effect on him. He stood holding her against him for what seemed an eternity until he was sure none had heard her; then he turned her around. "Now, Eleanor," he mocked her, "I would see all of you."

"Nay!"

His fingers reached for the shoulder of her gown, and with a great wrenching motion he tore the fabric to expose a white breast. Then, deliberately, he bent to suck the nipple. She writhed and twisted away from him until he pinned her against the wall with his body.

"Please, my lord, let me go . . . please."

"I cannot. I've waited too long for you, Eleanor, as it is." Slowly, deliberately, he stifled her protest with his mouth. She closed her eyes and twisted her head away while trying to kick free of him. Suddenly she felt him stiffen against her and his hold slackened.

"Release her." Roger spoke curtly from behind Belesme. Eleanor opened her eyes to see his blade resting against the count's neck vein. "Now—take your hands off her." The muscles in Roger's jaw twitched with the effort he made to control his anger. "*Now*, Robert."

Belesme dropped his hands and stepped back, his ardor cooled by the cold steel. Roger's eyes took in the torn dress and his mouth went dry at the sight of her bare breast. He stared, his own heart racing, his own body acutely aware of her. With an effort, he ordered, "Cover yourself, Lea."

Her face flaming under his gaze, she hastily pinned the shoulder of the torn gown with a brooch repossessed from Blanche. Backing away from Belesme, she made a wide arc around him until she put Roger between her and the count.

Roger held the sword steady. "You know, Robert, I ought to kill you here and now for what you would have done to Lea." For emphasis, he let the Damascus blade nick into Belesme's flesh until a fine trickle of blood ran down his neck.

Belesme did not even flinch as he taunted, "Nay, you will not. She comes to me, anyway."

Roger lowered his blade but did not lay it down. "Nay. Unlike you, I have never murdered an unarmed man, and I've no wish for the bloodletting that would follow. Are you all right, Lea?"

"Aye, I am all right."

"The day will come when you will pay for this, FitzGilbert," Belesme promised coldly.

"Do you challenge me, my lord?" Roger murmured softly. "For if you do, I am more than ready."

Belesme shook his head. "Why should I fight you now, FitzGilbert, when soon enough I can lie with her when and where I will?"

Roger took a step forward, but Eleanor caught his arm. "Sweet Mary—nay! I am not worth dying for, brother." Her hand closed over his on the hilt. "The blame is mine also."

"Nay, Lea—if any shares the blame, 'tis I, for I left you alone in this accursed place. Come on." He sheathed his weapon and pulled her after him. He walked quickly with her in tow. Twice she nearly stumbled on the stairs, and she had to follow at a half-trot to keep up as they crossed the courtyard. She could tell he was angry, but she was uncertain as to whether his anger was directed at her or Robert of Belesme. When he stopped abruptly at the bailey wall, she nearly collided with him.

"God's teeth, Lea!" he exploded. "Are you so like the rest that you think him able to kill me when he is not even armed? Sweet Jesu! He is but a man who wraps his chausses and walks on two legs like me. Aye—you even saw him bleed! He is bad, but he is not invincible."

"I'm sorry."

"For what? For thinking me incapable of taking Belesme?"

"Nay, I feared I had shamed you, Roger. First I let Prince Henry kiss me, and now Count Robert."

"Foolish girl. I could see you struggling to free yourself, Lea, and I heard your cries. As for Henry, he is easy to like. Neither was your fault."

He began to walk along the wall, his thoughts troubled by what he'd seen. If she only knew what he thought when he looked on her, he was certain she would consider him little better than the others. Beside him, she sorted out her own conflicting emotions. "Roger, I fear there is something wrong with me," she finally blurted out.

He stopped short and waited. "What?"

"Well . . ." She hesitated, reddening and looking at the ground. "The sisters taught it a sin, but . . ." She groped helplessly for words to express her shame and then plunged on, "Oh, Roger, I . . . I must be wanton or something. I—that is . . . well, I did not *mind* being kissed by the prince, or by Belesme even—not at first." When he said nothing, she threw up her hands and cried out, "Well, is something the matter with me?"

"Nay, Lea, there is not," he answered finally. "A woman is supposed to want a man. Why else did God make both? Without the wanting, there is little joy in the union between them. I would not have a woman who lay like stone in my bed."

Intrigued by this glimpse of his feelings about women, she ventured to ask, "Have you lain with many women, Roger?"

"What kind of a question is that?" he asked defensively. "I am not a monk."

"Have you?"

"How many is many?"

"Ten . . . twenty—I don't know. Roger, I have little knowledge of such things."

He relented. She was an innocent in such matters, and none had bothered to instruct her—not Lady Mary, Herleva, or any of the other women she knew. "Aye—probably."

"Don't you know?" she asked incredulously.

"God's teeth, Lea! I have not kept records, if that is what you ask." He studied her closely. "What *do* you want to know?"

"I want to know how men regard women." Her expression was grave, her dark eyes suddenly intent on him. "Did you love any of them?"

"Nay."

"Yet you once told me you loved a lady."

"Aye." he eyed her warily, wondering where she was leading him. "I have never had her, if that is what you would know."

"Why not?"

"Because she is a lady. I am not an animal, Lea, who takes what he would have. And she is no serving wench to be tumbled at will."

"But it is not fair, brother. You are Lord of the Condes, more handsome than Belesme, and a hundred times kinder. Were I her father, I'd give her to you."

"When you are safe, I will have her."

"Aye—that's it, isn't it? Roger, you cannot put my safety above your happiness—'tis wrong." She laid a hand on his forearm. "I cannot ask it of you—it was wrong to think I could. I'm going back to Fontaine-bleau—once I take my vows, I am safe enough from Count Robert."

"Jesu! What is this madness, Lea? In one breath you confess to the desires of the flesh, and in the next you would go back to a convent. Mother of God, girl! You are flesh-and-blood woman!"

"But what if we fail? What if Belesme hunts you down and kills you like he will kill Fuld? I could not bear it! You deserve happiness!"

"Stop it, Lea!" He grabbed her shoulders and shook her. "Do not speak such nonsense to me. I am your knight, sworn to you above all things. I cannot take you back to Fontainebleau."

" 'Tis not the same, Roger—you are my brother. I cannot give you children of your body, heirs to your lands. Seek your happiness with this lady."

"Lea," he exploded, "you are my lady! I mean to keep you safe."

"But—"

"Nay—no buts.' He placed a finger over her lips. "We are for England."

Eleanor lay awake far into the night, unable to sleep for the unearthly high-pitched screams that seemed to reverberate through the castle before tapering off into prolonged periods of silence. It was easy to imagine that the screams came from the death throes of Fuld Nevers and that the man would not die quickly. It was easy to think in the darkness that the silences came from those times he fainted and had to be revived. At first, Eleanor tried to hide the sounds with her pillow, but could not. Finally she sought out Roger. He and Hugh and the others had lugged their pallets into Fuld's chamber and placed them between her and the

bed Belesme had taken as his. But as she rose from
her cot, she could see where a slice of moonlight from
the arrow slit fell across the pallets, and they were
empty.

Barefoot, she made her way carefully into the outer
room and found it totally unoccupied. And when she
looked down into the courtyard below, it was deserted
also. A knot of fear formed in her stomach. What if
Belesme in his anger from earlier had managed by
some trick to arrest Roger and his attendants whilst
she slept? Certainly he was not a man to forgive at all,
and Roger had drawn steel on him. Suddenly it was of
utmost importance to find her brother.

One last terrified scream cut through the darkness
with such intensity that the hairs on her neck stood
and her skin crawled. Nay, she chided herself, Roger
could never be reduced to such a terror-stricken thing.
It was possible, but not likely, that he and the others
had gone to watch Fuld die. But even as a child,
Roger had never enjoyed the suffering of anything and
had preferred to dispatch it quickly and mercifully.

Loosing a rushlight from a holder near the door, she
held it in front of her to light her way down the
treacherous steps. As she reached the bottom and
stepped out to cross the courtyard, a sentry appeared
from the deep shadows and halted her. Startled, she
dropped the torch to the cobbled stones. The fellow
bent to retrieve it, and when he stood up, she could
see by the flickering light that he wore Belesme green.
If he recognized her, he gave no sign.

She licked dry lips and managed a tentative smile.
"Pray let me pass, sir." When he did not move, she
felt compelled to explain herself. "I am Eleanor of
Nantes, and I am looking for my brother, Roger,
called FitzGilbert."

The man held the torch closer to study her curiously
for a moment. Apparently satisfied that she spoke the
truth, he stepped back respectfully. "Nay, lady, I have
not seen him." When she moved to pass, he barred
the way. "You cannot go further, Demoiselle, under
orders from my lord of Belesme."

"I would find my brother."

"He is not here."

She drew in a sharp breath. Given his encounter with Robert of Belesme, he could well be in grave danger. She shook her head. "Then I would see Count Robert."

The guard seemed taken aback by the request. In his years of service with Belesme, he could remember no lady willingly seeking him out. But then, this was the one they'd just been to war for. He hesitated, unwilling to offend her and unable to allow her to go any further. "You'd best go back, Demoiselle. When he comes up, I will tell him you seek him."

"Nay," she persisted stubbornly. "I would see my brother, or I would see my lord of Belesme."

It was silent in the depths of the castle now. Belesme's man wavered—there seemed little enough harm in letting Count Robert know she was in the courtyard. Finally he nodded acquiescence. "Aye, I'll tell him you wait." He put his fingers to his mouth and made a shrill whistle that brought other guards out into the open. He pointed at Eleanor. "Guard her well," he ordered, "for 'tis the Demoiselle herself. And do not think to touch her, for my lord would not want your hands on his countess." With that, he left her to disappear into the darkness. A cellar door could be heard creaking on its hinges somewhere in the direction he went, and then all was silent again.

It seemed that she stood a long time waiting. None of the men spoke at all, and most eyed her warily. When it began to appear that Belesme would not see her, she turned to go back to Fuld's tower, but a man moved to block her way.

"Nay, Demoiselle," one man spoke while keeping his eyes respectfully on the ground. "You wait for my lord."

"I tire of waiting—I would seek my brother."

"The Bastard?" The fellow seemed to spit out the words. "Nay . . ." His mouth curved scornfully. "He is not here. He has not the stomach to watch."

He spoke so matter-of-factly about Fuld's fate that

Eleanor shivered involuntarily. And his placid acceptance of the horror made her wish she'd never ventured down. She'd no real wish to see Belesme—it was Roger she sought.

The trapdoor creaked, then slammed, and booted footsteps could be heard crunching on loose cobblestones. And then he emerged from the shadows. He walked to the cistern and washed his hands before coming to her.

Even in the torchlight she could see his fancy tunic was blood-spattered, but the usually fastidious Belesme seemed unconcerned. His mouth curved into a slight smile as he faced her.

"Demoiselle," he acknowledged. "How may I serve you?"

One look at the tunic was enough for Eleanor—she knew she had no business there. She twisted her hands in the folds of her gown and looked away.

"You sent for me," he prompted impatiently. "Surely you must want something."

"I . . . I wanted to see my brother."

He frowned. "My man said 'twas me you asked for."

"I did," she admitted uncomfortably under that strange green-eyed gaze. "My lord, what have you down with my brother?"

"FitzGilbert?" He raised a quizzical eyebrow. "I supposed him fast asleep at your feet, guarding you like the faithful hound." He could see she was unconvinced. "All I can tell you, Eleanor, is that he was with me for a while, but his stomach betrayed his disgust of the task. I thought he left to go to bed."

"You are certain?"

"Demoiselle"—his voice grew deadly soft—"I do not lie to you."

"Your pardon, my lord, I should not have come," she managed finally.

"Nay, you should not. In the future, you will not go about unescorted, Lady Eleanor, for I've far too many in my service who would take first and repent later."

"Like yourself?"

"Nay, I never have to repent."

A captain emerged from the shadows, carrying a bloody towel with something fairly small wrapped in it. Belesme frowned at the intrusion before ordering curtly, "Burn it."

"What is it?" she asked before she thought. Instantly she regretted the question.

"Nothing of importance," Belesme answered. "Suffice it to say that Fuld Nevers will never again curse me." He took in her bare feet and her loose shift. " 'Tis no place for you. Demoiselle—you'd best seek your bed. You and FitzGilbert leave at first light." He motioned to the guard nearest her. "Take the lady to her quarters and remain outside until either I or the Bastard comes up."

It was with a sense of relief that she followed the Belesme man back up the tower stairs. Behind her she could hear Robert of Belesme tell someone, "We are not done—I would bring him around again." She mumbled a prayer for Fuld Nevers' soul.

Once back in her cot, she lay awake waiting for Roger. He finally came up and pulled his pallet across her doorway. She rose and padded to where he unrolled his blanket.

"Roger, where have you been?" she demanded. "I could not sleep for the sound of Belesme's vengeance, and I feared for you."

"Well, as you can see, I am all right." His voice sounded strange to her.

"Are you sure, brother?" She peered anxiously in the semidarkness.

"Aye. Leave me be, Lea, and let me sleep. Tomorrow we leave this accursed place."

Aubery and Jean Merville came up dragging their pallets with them. Jean saw her and explained cheerfully, " 'Tis crowded in the hall below, and I doubt many will want to sleep here." He glanced at Roger and added, "Though Belesme did offer to share the bed with him."

"I'd sooner sleep with a viper."

"By the looks of it, Count Robert will be up most of

the night," Aubery observed. "I think I'd take the bed."

"I thought Fuld was dead," Eleanor spoke. "He cries out no more."

"Nay," Roger answered grimly. "If he is silent now, 'tis because he has no tongue." He struck his palm angrily. "Robert's blood lust is too great—he promised to wait until we left."

"Fuld has no tongue, Roger?" she echoed foolishly. "Sweet Jesu!"

"Nay, nor eyes either, Lea. And Robert means to skin him like an animal before he is dead." Roger's face was grayish and waxy in the faint light.

"He said you weren't there."

"Who?"

"Belesme."

"Mother of God! Lea, you did not go down there? 'Tis no fit place for a lady—nor for anyone else."

She nodded. "I couldn't find you," she answered simply.

"Well, I was there for a while, but Belesme's means sickened me. I dispatch mine enemies in battle, or I hang them." He looked away. "I walked the curtain wall until I was sick no more, Lea." He bent to turn back the blanket. "Get you to bed so that we may undress and get some sleep."

"Aye." She moved back into the cut-out chamber and lay down. In the outer room she could hear the rustling of clothes being discarded. One by one, the men crawled into their pallets. "God guard you, Roger," she whispered softly into the darkness.

9

Ahead lay Rouen, Normandy's capital, the Romanesque spires of the Conqueror's cathedral dominating its city walls. Roger reined in his horse and signaled a halt to the armed escort behind him. Before Aubery could assist him, he dismounted and made his way to Eleanor.

His blond hair gleamed in the sunlight as he spoke up to her, "We stop here." He reached up to help her down while explaining, "It grows late, and I would not deprive Curthose of his welcome. We can ride into the city in the morning with his full escort, and play to his love of ceremony."

"Aye," she agreed as his strong hands grasped her waist and set her on the ground. Her legs were tired and aching from hours in the saddle. She took an unsteady step and caught at Roger's arm for balance. "Jesu, but I am weary."

"Walk a pace—'twill ease the stiffness, I promise." In a low undervoice he reminded her, " 'Tis best to get used to it, Lea, for by the end of the week we'll have to ride for our lives."

"So soon?"

"Aye." He squinted into the sun. "Once betrothed, you are his."

She sighed and nodded. "Oh, Roger, sometimes I allow myself to forget why I am here. I have so enjoyed your company since Mayenne that I willed the journey not to end. I would we could always be like this, laughing, jesting, with no thought of Belesme."

"We can."

She shook her head. "Nay, he will always be behind us, seeking vengeance for the insult we offer."

"He has to find us first, Lea, and I doubt he can know where I mean to take you."

"England is not unknown to him, brother. You would forget he holds lands there also." They were away from the rest and she felt free to speak her mind. She traced aimless circles in soft dirt with the toe of her shoe. "What I would say is that he will come for us—England is no proof against discovery."

"I know that. But by the time he finds us, I hope to have secured a powerful ally of mine own." He frowned thoughtfully into the sun. "and if I have not, we will flee to Byzantium like I told you."

"And then you would give up forever any hope of reclaiming your lands! Nay, I cannot let you do it!"

"Lea—" Over her head he could see the interested glances of his men-at-arms. He put an arm about her shoulder and turned her away from them, lowering his voice again as he did so. "Lea, let me worry about my lands. I trust Henry to hold them for me. Come," he coaxed, "let us talk no more of Robert of Belesme tonight."

"But I fear for us!" She would have turned into his arms, but he moved away.

"Do you doubt my ability to protect you?"

"Nay . . . yea . . . I don't know—'tis no light thing we do to defy Church, state, and family, Roger. 'Twill not be just Belesme—the world will be against us."

"And that frightens you."

"Aye."

He put both hands on her shoulders and studied her face. "Tell me, and tell me true, Lea—is it for me or for you that you fear?"

She looked away. "For both of us."

"Nay, Lea, 'tis not so. Look at me and answer."

"All right," she answered low, "I fear for you."

"You think me no match for Belesme." His blue eyes were intent and serious. "And you are wrong. Besides, now there is no other way."

"Nay, I could wed with Belesme," she half-whispered.

"Did I hear you aright, Lea? You did not say that."

"Aye." She nodded. "Now that we are here, I see no other course. 'Tis folly to think we can escape him."

"Lea." He touched her nearly healed bruises lightly with a fingertip. "Remember the beatings you took of Fuld? Well, Robert can be ten times worse—I have served with him in William's train and I know the man. The first time he is displeased with dinner or with your gown, he is like to beat you to death."

"If I give him sons . . ." Her voice trailed off in uncertainty.

"What if you do not? Your mother bore no sons," he reminded her gently. "Robert is no Gilbert—he might kill you to wed another."

"But there is naught else for me!" she cried out. "I can take my vows as a nun and rot at Fontainebleau or I can wed with Robert Talvas and rot at Belesme!"

"Nay. I can promise you a better life in England, if you will but trust me. Lea—you do trust me, do you not?"

"Aye."

"Then let me hear no more of these foolish fears. We leave from Rouen as soon as my riders report all is ready." He turned and yelled back at the milling men, "Put up the tents! We camp here until my sister enters Rouen under Curthose's escort!"

The Duke of Normandy, resplendent in crimson satin and cloth of gold, rode out in person to greet her. As he dismounted and walked over for the presentation, Eleanor found it easy to understand why he was called Curthose. He had little of Prince Henry's good looks, and certainly none of his height. She remembered the Conqueror telling her how small the Duchess Mathilde had been and she surmised that their eldest son favored his mother. Moreover, his legs were disproportionately short. But his manner was bluff and friendly to a fault.

"Demoiselle," he called out before he reached her.

"Art even comelier than Henry said—if such is possible."

She sank to her knees in obeisance, murmuring, "Your Grace is most kind."

"We bid you welcome to Normandy's court," he announced as he raised her himself, then turned to a lord at his side, saying openly, " 'Tis no wonder Robert would have her and none other."

"Demoiselle." Eleanor spun around at the sound of Prince Henry's voice, and found her hands clasped warmly in both of his. "You gave us a fright when we heard that Fuld Nevers held you."

"Aye, Lady Eleanor," Curthose agreed, "but when we knew FitzGilbert and Robert came to your aid, we were sure you would be all right."

"I never thought so," Henry reminded him.

"Aye, you would have called up an army and marched yourself—if you but had an army to call. As it was, you badgered me to release some from Bec to you. Praise God, it proved unnecessary." He motioned some well-dressed courtiers forward, saying, "Allow me, dear child, to present the counts of Blois, Artois, Champagne, and also Rannulf of Coutances, William de Egremont, Henry of Avranches, and Geoffrey de Monthermer." Each man acknowledged her with a deferential bow. "My duchess and the ladies of her court would have come also, but she nears her time, and the physicians advise against riding." He glanced up at an imperious woman who still sat astride her horse and nodded. "My sister Adela comes in her stead to bid you welcome." Adela inclined her head slightly.

Eleanor could not help but remember Henry telling her long ago that his sister Adela had the temper of a viper. One look at the haughty lady who sat above her made Eleanor think he'd not exaggerated. Nonetheless, she was the Conqueror's daughter, and Eleanor sank in a curtsy next to her horse.

"Rise you, Demoiselle, that we may ride back in. The sun grows high and hot." Adela leaned across her pommel. "Ah, FitzGilbert, your return to my brother's court is a most welcome diversion. Marie already pastes and powders her face in anticipation of your arrival."

Roger reddened. "The lady of Coutances has little need of artifice," he answered smoothly in spite of his blush.

"Aye." Adela cast a significant look at Rannulf de Coutances. "But her brother would have for her a higher-born lover."

Henry leaned closer to whisper to Eleanor. "They speak of Marie de Coutances, Demoiselle, for 'twas well known she cast sheep's eyes at your brother."

"Is she very beautiful?" Eleanor asked without even thinking.

"Very." Henry flashed his winning smile at Eleanor. "But not nearly so much so as you. I'll warrant you'll set Normandy's court on its ears. Long have I wanted to bring you here to show its conceited ladies a rarer beauty. I just wish you had come under different circumstances."

But Eleanor was barely attending. She had conceived a real desire to meet and know Lady Marie, for she had to determine if Marie were Roger's unnamed love.

"Demoiselle"—Henry still smiled—"I pay you lavish praise, and you do not attend me. Had I less conceit, you would destroy me."

"Oh . . . your pardon—I was thinking of why I am here, I suppose."

"Enough to make any maid absentminded, I'll warrant. Here, let me put you up." He indicated the palfrey that Aubrey had brought forward. "My gift to you, Demoiselle, for your betrothal—a fast-paced goer," he added significantly. His brown eyes met her darker ones and his gaze was warm with the intimacy of conspiracy. He cupped his hand and bent to allow her to step into it.

"How left you the Count of Belesme?" Curthose asked Roger behind her. "When can we expect him in Rouen?"

"I left him well enough, and I expect him within the

next day or two—however long it took Fuld Nevers to die will be the length of his delay."

Robert of Normandy hastily signed the cross over his breast. "God aid his troubled soul," he murmured.

"Robert's or Fuld's?" asked his brother-in-law, the Count of Blois. "If you speak of Belesme's, you waste your breath, for I doubt he has one."

"You forget why we are here." Robert Curthose frowned with a furtive nod toward Eleanor. "No doubt the maid's skittish enough as it is."

Stephen I of Blois shook his head. "The girl's a beauty and I pity her for what you and her father would do to her."

"We make her a countess."

"Queen of Hell, you mean." Stephen's gaze rested on Eleanor as she sat talking down to Prince Henry. "The girl will stir men, and Belesme in his jealousy will either kill her or them."

"My sister watches you," Curthose warned.

"Let her." Stephen shrugged. "I grow tired of her coldness in my bed, and I have my heir in my namesake."

"Well, I would not look to Belesme's betrothed."

"Nay, I am no fool." He leaned in front of the duke and addressed Roger. "Speaking of the fair Marie, FitzGilbert, what interest have you in that quarter?" He spoke low enough that neither Eleanor or Henry could hear.

"None at all, my lord."

Stephen appeared relieved. "I thought not, but I was not sure. I would hate to lose you to Rannulf's fury. He guards her well."

"Then take care yourself, my lord count," Roger retorted.

"FitzGilbert gives wise counsel." Curthose nodded. "And Adela will brook no dalliance with a lady of the court." He looked around and noted that both Fitz-Gilbert's and his own escort were mounted and ready for Eleanor of Nantes' official entry into Rouen. He motioned to his herald, who blew the approach signal, and the columns fell in, moving slowly and sedately toward the open city gates.

Built by the Romans some seven centuries earlier, Rouen was a large and ancient city. Even Eleanor was caught in the excitement of being in the provincial capital as their retinue wended its way through narrow streets lined with tall row houses. In honor of her arrival, Curthose had ordered bunting hung from windows, and great banners combining the gold of Nantes with the green of Belesme waved from specially raised flagpoles. The curious citizenry leaned from windows and balconies to view the girl chosen to be Robert of Belesme's bride. Earlier, festivities had been planned for the week of June 1, but Fuld Nevers had caused a postponement that necessitated a paring down of plans—food that could not be kept had been consumed at the time. Now Curthose had to content himself with more show and less substance.

Eleanor waved until her shoulder ached from the effort, and the town seemed to take her to its heart. The sight of the beautiful girl so soon to be condemned to a life with Robert Talvas of Belesme touched them and they made up for what they could not do by cheering hoarsely as she passed. About halfway through the city, someone noted the blond-headed knight, resplendent in polished mail and flowing surcoat of blue and gray, who rode at her side. Cries of "Demoiselle! Demoiselle!" were joined by the chant "FitzGilbert! FitzGilbert!"

Henry, who rode on her other side, yelled above the crowd to tell her, "They remember your brother for his defense of my father at Mantes."

Ahead of them, Curthose frowned and ceased waving. It was one thing for the town to open its heart to a girl on her way to Belesme, but it was another to watch his people cheering the baseborn Roger FitzGilbert. He spurred his horse and moved faster toward the ducal palace. The entire entourage picked up speed until it raced the last quarter-mile.

Once inside the palace yard, Duke Robert threw down his reins and dismounted quickly. Brushing Henry and Roger aside, he reached to help Eleanor down. As he set her on the ground, he smiled, tight-lipped, and told her, "You cannot say all of Normandy does not love you, Demoiselle."

I wish you would not pace like a chained animal, Demoiselle," the Duchess of Normandy reproved mildly, "for the bridegroom will come whether you will it or not." She jabbed at a hanging she was working and pulled the silken thread through, expertly knotting it and breaking it off. " 'Tis the lot of a woman to take what her father gives her."

Eleanor moved back from the open casement and sighed. Less than an hour before, the duchess' page had scurried in with the news that Robert of Belesme approached the city and would be there before nightfall. The duchess' ladies viewed her with a mixture of pity and amusement. Marie de Coutances moved to her side and laid a timid hand on her arm.

"We could play at chess, or we could walk the garden if you like."

"I care not which," Eleanor sighed.

Marie went to get the pieces from a low chest in a corner of the duchess' bower. She returned and set up the game on a small table, positioned silk cushions on the well-swept floor, and motioned the restless Eleanor over. Both girls took their places and began their play.

Usually a decent player, Eleanor let her attention stray too often and her game suffered. Finally Marie pushed the board away. "Lady Eleanor, 'twould be unfair to continue. Come—let us go to the garden."

Try as she would, Eleanor found it impossible to dislike the fair Marie. Younger than herself by at least three years, the girl possessed a good mind and a gentle disposition. Her main folly seemed to be her open admiration of Roger FitzGilbert, a passion that made her the object of gibes and jests from some of the other ladies. It was obvious that she was not alone in her affection for him, but she was less able to conceal her feelings than the others were. And, Elea-

nor suspected, some of the barbs reflected jealousy of
the girl's beauty. With long silky hair of pale gold,
large blue eyes, delicately translucent skin, and almost
regal carriage, Marie de Coutances was much admired
by the men of the court. Eleanor nodded at the taller
girl. "Aye, I could use the walk."

"The FitzGilbert will not be there." The much older
Adela spoke from a seat by the duchess. "He rode out
with my brother Henry somewhere this morning."

"Pay her no heed," Eleanor whispered as she followed Marie from the bower. "He will be back before
supper."

"Nay, I do not care what she says. She enjoys
making people uncomfortable, and even her brothers
do not like her. I can scarce wait until she and Count
Stephen return to Blois and take their pack of brats
with them."

"Stephen is a handsome man to be wed to such a
sharp face," Eleanor commented.

"Aye, but he thinks himself far handsomer than he
is. Myself, I do not like dark men."

"I own I do not like him much either, but I barely
know the man."

They traversed a long rock-walled corridor to a door
that opened out into the spacious garden where flowers and bushes formed geometric patterns between
flagstone walks, and where the castle's herbs grew in a
brick-marked bed in the center. The July air was hot
and heavy with the intermingled fragrances of flowers.

"Would you walk, or would you sit?" Marie asked.

"Let us sit for a while." Eleanor found a stone
bench and sat down, spreading her skirts while making
room for the other girl. "Jesu, but 'tis hot."

Neither girl spoke of Belesme's arrival for some
time. Marie valiantly tried to carry the conversation
everywhere but there, but Eleanor's mind was troubled by a decision she struggled to make. She turned
impulsively to Marie.

"Do you know Count Robert?"

Startled by the directness, Marie hesitated. "Only
by sight and reputation," she answered slowly. "When

he comes to court, most of the ladies avoid him. My eyes tell me he is an exceedingly handsome man, but my mind tells me he is exceedingly vain. He dresses in only the finest jewels and clothing, and he is very careful of his appearance. Unlike others, his hair is always trimmed, his face always shaven, his nails always pared, and he is always clean. But"—she frowned thoughtfully—"I think him harsh and cruel. It says something of a man when he has no friends." She looked up and her blue eyes were grave. "Your pardon, Lady Eleanor, I should not speak so freely of the man you are to wed."

"Nay, I can see all of the things you tell me, anyway. But—you have been long at court—does he not have any interest in the ladies?"

"If you would ask does he lie with any of the bolder ones, the answer would be no. Most would not lie with him because of what is said of him."

"What?" Eleanor asked bluntly.

" 'Tis just rumor," Marie evaded.

"What is just rumor?" Eleanor persisted. "I would know what is said of him."

"Mayhap you should ask Lord Roger," the younger girl answered uncomfortably.

"Nay—Roger hates him and Belesme hates Roger. I would ask you."

"Lady Eleanor, I would just be repeating malicious gossip," Marie protested. "I know not the man."

"But you know what is said of him. What have you heard?"

"Little." Marie sighed. "Countess Adela says often enough that the reason Belesme does not flirt with the ladies is that he has strange appetites. She says that he finds Mabille such a woman that any other pales in comparison."

"I heard something like that from Prince Henry long ago, but I find it hard to credit. Mabille is his mother, and she must be fairly old."

"Have you seen her?"

"Nay. You forget, I have spent years in confinement at Fontainebleau."

"Well"—Marie gestured expansively—"I have seen her once within the past two years. She may be old enough to have borne him, but Mabille of Belesme is still beautiful. She has the face and form of a twenty-year-old woman. Men say she is a witch because she does not seem to grow older."

"I thought they called her witch for other things."

"Aye, they say she murdered William Talvas to secure her son's inheritance. By all accounts, he was an evil man, but I'll warrant he died of bad food rather than poison."

"Sweet Jesu!" Eleanor breathed. "And this is the family my father would give me." Abruptly she changed the subject to Marie herself. "Tell me, Demoiselle, do you love my brother?"

The girl was taken aback by the direct question. She seemed to fix her gaze on the flagstones beneath her feet. "Aye," she finally answered low. "I would be given to him if I had the choice."

"Why?" Eleanor leaned closer. "Why do you think you love him?"

Marie colored, the rosiness that spread across her face diffused through her cheeks, enhancing her beauty.

It was Eleanor's turn to look away. "I would know."

"Because he is kind and good, because he can laugh and tease without hurting, because he is a most puissant lord."

It spoke well of the girl that she tied her affection to qualities in the man rather than to appearances. Surprised, Eleanor asked, "But do you not think him handsome?"

"Oh, aye. Roger FitzGilbert is the most handsome man I have ever seen, and most of the other ladies here think so also. In truth, you were made most welcome, Demoiselle, because your brother is so admired at court." She smiled ingeniously and added, "In truth, most would know you in hopes of knowing your brother better."

"And you, Marie?"

"I am like all the rest, Lady Eleanor."

The girl's beauty and candor won Eleanor's admiration. If this were the love that Roger denied, she would not be the one to stand in his way. She swallowed her jealousy and nodded. "I would welcome you as a sister, Lady Marie."

Eleanor did not have to wait until supper to see Robert of Belesme. Soon after she and Marie returned to the duchess' bower, a ducal page appeared to announce his arrival and seek permission for him to speak with Eleanor. The women around her recoiled at the thought he might actually appear in the duchess' apartment. The young Countess of Evreux went so far as to protest, "Madam, to allow him up could mark your unborn child."

"Nonsense." Adela, Countess of Blois, dismissed the idea with a word. "Let him come. I for one am not afraid of the Count of Belesme. What harm can he do surrounded by all of us?"

The duchess crossed herself before venturing timidly, "Perhaps I should rather send the Demoiselle down to him."

"Alone?" Adela scoffed. "Nay—and who is to go down with her?" She turned imperiously to the page and ordered, "You may tell my lord of Belesme that she awaits him here."

It was actually some time before he made his appearance. Apparently he'd chosen to bathe and shave before coming to the ladies' bower, for when he arrived, he was clean and smelled faintly of rosewater. Once he made his obeisance to the Duchess of Normandy, the duchess withdrew tactfully to a corner of the room and took her ladies with her.

Even without battle dress, he was forbidding, from the tip of his soft leather shoes to the top of his green-and-gold tunic. Eleanor met his eyes squarely with thudding heart and wondered if she could ever face him unafraid.

"Demoiselle," he acknowledged. "You had a pleasant journey, I trust?"

"Aye." She wet her dry lips with the tip of her tongue. "And you, my lord?"

" 'Twas hot. I stewed in my own sweat most of the way."

"Oh." If she were going to live with him, Eleanor supposed she would have to learn to talk to him. "You look well," she ventured lamely.

He favored her with that strange half-smile. "I am never ill, Demoiselle."

"Nay, I suppose you are not. Well, my lord," she tried again, "how left you Mayenne?"

"It still stands."

"Jesu!" Eleanor threw up her hands in disgust. "How are we to live together, my lord, if we cannot even speak to one another?"

"What would you have me say?"

"Anything, my lord, but I would have some speech with you."

The green eyes warmed slightly. "You will have years at Belesme in which to talk with me, Eleanor. For now, I have little time and there is much to do. We pledge ourselves before the archbishop tomorrow so that Curthose may witness. His quarrel with Philip goes ill again and he is for the Vexin as soon as may be." He watched her startled expression and his eyes narrowed. "Aye, tomorrow. We wed on Monday—even the Church agrees there is no need to wait."

"But—"

"Your father arrives sometime today, Demoiselle, so all is ready."

"When do we go to Belesme, my lord?" she asked hopelessly.

"Tuesday." Again, that half-smile. "We deplete Curthose's larder. You will be pleased to know that once I have taken you to Belesme, I go to join Curthose."

"So soon?"

He raised a black eyebrow. "Does it matter to you?"

"Nay." She twisted her hands nervously in the folds of her gown. " 'Tis only that I shall know no one in a strange place. I have never been to Belesme before."

"Belesme is a fortress, Eleanor, a great stone keep well-constructed against siege and ill-suited to comfort.

As soon as I negotiated for you, I began the building of a hall and larger living quarters, but it will not be finished until late autumn. Until then, you will have to make your home in one of the towers."

She closed her eyes briefly to hide her panic. "But I will know no one there."

"Gilbert sends an old woman and some maids. He offered your sister Margaret for company, but I had enough of her weeping when Fuld sent her to me. If there is another you would bring, do so." His eyes swept the women at the other end of the bower. "Though I doubt you can find any eager to come."

Herleva, Eleanor thought to herself. I ought to have known she would come with me. Aloud she managed, "Nay, there is no one I would take."

He seemed relieved. " 'Tis as well—my men are unused to women." he reached for her hands and possessed them. "Let us hope your body is warmer than your fingers, Demoiselle." She thought he meant to draw a hand to his lips, but instead he leaned forward and brushed her cheek, murmuring low by her ear, "But I remember fire, Eleanor, and would know it again." He straightened up before she could reply. "Until the morrow, Demoiselle."

He left abruptly without so much as a nod to the duchess or any of the ladies. Marie hurried over to Eleanor and took her hand.

"Sweet Mary! What did he want?"

"I am betrothed tomorrow and wed Monday."

"Mother of God! Does your brother know?"

Eleanor drew in a deep breath and shook her head. "Nay, but I will tell him."

At Hugh's direction, Eleanor found Roger in the palace chapel. This time, he prayed silently if at all. She slipped down beside him at the altar rail, thinking it a fit place for her to sunder his vow to her. Timidly she reached out to touch his shoulder. When he turned around, she stared silently for a moment to stamp him on her memory.

"Roger, I love you," she whispered softly. When he

would reach for her, she shook her head. "Nay, 'tis
because of that that I would speak to you, brother."
She took a deep breath and looked away. "As a lord
to his vassal, I release you from your childhood vow to
me, Roger."

"Lea, what in God's name are you talking about?"

"I have decided to wed with Belesme."

"Nay!"

"Aye. Roger, do not look at me like that! I have
thought and thought and I have decided. 'Twas folly
to think it could be any other way."

"Lea, listen to me—you know not what you would
say! You know not what manner of man you would
wed!"

"I know," she whispered, "but perhaps he will be
different to me if I am his own."

"Lea, listen! I am no maid—I am a soldier used to
the battlefield. I have seen men broken open, their
entrails spilling out onto the ground, and I have listened to their dying cries. But I saw what he intended
with Fuld Nevers and it sickened me so that I vomited.
Lea, before he killed him, Robert blinded and cas-
trated Fuld, cut out his tongue, and skinned him like a
rabbit. Aye—well you can look like that! And the
thing that repelled me the most, Lea, was that 'twas
not for vengeance that he did those things. He enjoyed it!"

She closed her eyes and swallowed hard. "I know
these things, Roger, but it can make no difference."

Roger reached out and shook her hard. "Do you
want to wed with Belesme?" he asked harshly.

"N-nay."

"Jesu! Then why—?"

"Think you I want to see your life ended like Fuld's?"
she cried out. "Nay, I will not let you die in my cause,
brother." She searched his face for some hint of understanding. "Roger, wed with your lady and take
what happiness you can—there is little enough in this
life."

"You are my happiness!"

"Nay, 'tis not the same. What we have will always

be—in spite of Belesme, in spite of your lady—but we just will not see each other."

"Lea," he reasoned patiently, " 'tis a noble sacrifice you would make, but it will not happen. We are leaving Rouen. We are going to England. Think you I could live knowing that you were at Robert of Belesme's mercy night and day?"

"Roger, you yourself said I must wed someday."

"Not to Belesme!"

"Roger, don't go on with this," she pleaded desperately. "My father gives me to Count Robert, the Church blesses the union, and the Duke of Normandy orders it. We cannot stand against that. You have lands now, you can win your lady and get your heirs of her—you can found a great family, brother. Do not lose it all for me."

Roger could feel his world collapsing. Obviously Eleanor did not believe he had the strength to carry out his plans, and she expected him to lose in the ultimate struggle with Robert of Belesme. Well, he would not—his whole future was tied up in Eleanor of Nantes and he could not let her go. "We'll talk more of this later, Lea," he managed finally.

"Nay—let us take what time we have and be happy."

"Mayhap Henry can speak more sense to you."

There was no sign of Count Robert at supper. Several of the ladies remarked his absence to her, but Eleanor neither knew where he was nor did she care. She was thankful for one last night without him. But Roger's anger marred whatever pleasure she could take in Belesme's absence. He sat several seats below her and seemed to pay no attention to her at all. Marie and her brother Rannulf sat across from him, and from time to time Eleanor could hear Marie's soft laugh. It pained her deeply to part from him like this.

She picked at her food until even her father showed concern. He cut a piece of meat from his end of the trencher and moved it down to hers.

"God's teeth, girl! You'll faint in church in the morning if you do not eat!"

"I am not hungry, Papa."

"Eat anyway," he advised, "for you need your strength. You've lost weight since you left Nantes."

"If I have, 'twas because Fuld starved me."

He winced at the reference to her captivity and changed the subject. "How is it that Robert sups not?"

"I don't know—mayhap he drinks blood and bays at the moon—the moon is full."

Gilbert unconsciously crossed himself before retorting, "I pray he never hears you talk like that."

"What will he do—beat me to death?"

"Eleanor, the man is hot to have you."

"For now." She suddenly felt ill. The interview with Belesme, her quarrel with Roger, the crowd in the hall—all combined to make her stomach seem like a painful knot in her midriff. "Pray excuse me, Papa." She half-rose to leave, but Gilbert caught at her and pulled her back down.

"What nonsense is this? You cannot just leave Duke Robert's table."

"I'll shame you more if I stay—I am unwell."

Gilbert knew he should go with her or else call for a servant, but he was irritated by her sullenness. "I pray you do not disturb the duke by your leaving," he muttered.

Eleanor gained the outer corridor and leaned her head against the cool stone of the wall. The air inside Curthose's hall had been hot and heavy, and the odors of the food and people combined had seemed unbearable. She pressed against the knot in her stomach. She was not really ill, she decided, but rather she just needed to be alone.

"Demoiselle, are you all right?" she heard Prince Henry say behind her.

"Aye. 'Twas to hot in there."

"What you need is air—if you trust me to walk outside with you again."

"Aren't you afraid to be seen conversing with Belesme's bride?" she asked before she could bite back the words.

"Nay—my birth protects me, Demoiselle." He came

closer. "You seem uncommonly cross—is anything amiss?"

"Nay. Oh . . . aye. I quarrel with Roger, my lord."

"He told me. You know, I agree with him—'tis folly to wed with Robert of Belesme, Demoiselle. He could kill you in one of his black moods and repent of it later."

"Must everyone remind me? Can no one comfort me?" she cried out.

"Your pardon. The future must seem grim enough without the reminding."

He drew her down unfamiliar stairs and along a passage that seemed to lead toward the kitchens. She stopped and looked around the deserted passageway. The torches that hung in iron rings were spaced far apart and barely lit the way.

"Where are we, my lord?"

"You forget"—he smiled—"that I lived here as a child. There are many ways outside, Demoiselle. Would you have us discovered?"

"Nay."

"I thought not."

"But this seems to lead to the scullery."

"It does. They remove the covers now, and the jongleurs and mummers take their places, so most have gone up for a glimpse of the entertainment."

Something moved in the passage ahead of them and Eleanor drew back. Henry seemed unconcerned and gently took her elbow. " 'Tis nothing, he reassured her.

'My thanks." Roger stepped out and looked behind them. "Did any see you with her? I would not have him accuse you."

"Nay, the place is deserted. Gilbert, fool that he is, let her leave unattended."

"Roger, what are you doing here?"

"I saw you leave, so Henry and I thought now was as good a time as any to make our escape."

"Nay—Roger, I will not."

"Believe me, Demoiselle," Henry whispered, " 'tis the only way."

"Lea, if you come not willingly, I will muzzle you and carry you out anyway." Roger moved forward. "I do not want to hurt you, but I will if I must."

"Cry out now, and you seal his fate," Henry warned her.

"But I cannot go with you!"

"You can—you will!" Roger turned to Henry. "Is everything ready?"

"Aye, and we waste precious time. Come on."

Roger grabbed Eleanor's hand and pulled her after them into the depths of the scullery. Just as Henry had said, it was deserted except for Aubery. He stood waiting with what appeared to be an armful of clothes. When he saw them, he wrinkled his nose in disgust.

"I got them, my lord," he addressed Roger, "of one of the kitchen wenches. I pray she had no vermin." He extended the clothing to Eleanor. "Your pardon, Demoiselle, but 'twas what my lord requested. I hope they fit—the girl was bigger than you." He shook his head at Roger and added, "There were none as small as the demoiselle in the kitchens."

Roger took the clothes and turned to Eleanor. "Do you go behind the door and put these on, or do I strip you and put them on for you?"

This was a new and different brother that stood before her. His face was set with determination and there was none of the gentleness she was used to. She blinked at his tone and reached for the dirty clothing. "I will dress myself, Roger."

"Be quick—there's no telling how soon you may be missed." He spoke low to Henry, "You'd best be getting back, my lord. I would not have his wrath on your head."

"Nay, why should he suspect? He rode out earlier, telling my brother that he had business at Caudebec but would return by morning."

"I wonder what it was," Roger mused half to himself. "No matter—time is short. Lea, are you dressed yet?"

She came out from behind the door, her head hanging in embarrassment. Aubery had been right—the dress came from a larger girl. The neck opening hung precariously low over Eleanor's breasts, half-exposing them. She pulled the coarse material back in vain, frustrated that she could not walk holding her shoulders without drawing attention. And certainly she could not go out bare-chested without even more notice. Both Prince Henry and Aubery stared appreciatively at her. Her temples pounded as the blood rushed to her head, and she had to look down in embarrassment. "Sweet Jesu, Roger! I cannot go anywhere like this," she whispered, mortified.

"Nay, Lea. 'Twill do for its purpose." Roger turned around and stopped still as his eyes took in what the others saw. His own blood rushed and he could barely conceal the hunger he felt. He turned her away from them and pulled her close to cover her. "Just hide your face in my shoulder when we leave, and pay no heed to what I have to say."

"Here's the ale, my lord." Aubery stepped forward with a cup and handed it to Roger. " 'Tis foul stuff," he warned even as Roger slopped it down the front of the rough gown.

"Ugh!" She recoiled. "it smells rank."

"Aye—the ranker the better, Lea. Common wenches smell far different from gentle ladies, I can tell you, and this will make it easier to get you out without arousing suspicion amongst the guards." He looked over her shoulder at his squire. "Is there anyone in the passageway, Aubery?"

The younger man went to the door and cracked it to peer out cautiously. "Nay, there is not one."

"Well, gentle sister," Roger asked Eleanor the last time, "do you come quietly, or do I render you unconscious until we are safe?"

All three men stared at her and the tension in the room mounted. If she screamed or drew attention to them, explanations to the duke and Belesme would be awkward, if not impossible. "Please, Roger," she tried one last time, "let me go back."

"Nay, I cannot. My mind is decided, Lea—the only question is how you go."

She capitulated. "Quietly then."

"Then we are ready." He took a full purse and a scrap of parchment from Prince Henry and nodded to Aubery. "My thanks to you both—few men are blessed with better friends."

"Wait." Henry cut in front of them and opened the door. "I'll go first and call out if I see anyone."

They followed him into the empty passageway and up a narrow backstairs to the yard. It too was deserted. Henry stopped before they reached the sentry gate and waited for them to catch up. "God grant you success," he whispered. Motioning to Aubery, he hissed, "You come with me, and if any asks, we have been wenching together." His hand touched Eleanor's shoulder in the darkness. "Godspeed, Demoiselle, until we meet again in England." With that, he and Aubery faded into the blackness. Behind them, Eleanor could hear the door creak as they disappeared.

"Come on," Roger urged her, " 'tis now."

Before she could know what he intended, he grasped her about the waist and hoisted her over his shoulder like a sack of grain on a peasant's back. With his free hand he pushed her dress up to expose her bare legs, while the hand that steadied her on his shoulder rested suggestively on her buttocks.

"Nay . . . Roger!" she hissed in shock.

"Shhhh—put your head against me and hide your face."

"But—"

"Just do it, Lea."

"Aye." She buried her head in the softness of his tunic while he moved toward the gate. He began to weave unevenly and to sing a ribald tune she'd never heard before. His voice grew louder the closer he got to the sentries.

"Hold! Who goes there?" A soldier in Normandy's colors stepped forward to challenge them. Eleanor sucked in her breath and waited.

"FitzGilbert," Roger answered thickly. "Leave us be."

"My lord." The sentry nodded in recognition.

Roger seemed to stagger under Eleanor's weight and she had to clutch at him. "Itsh hot in there," he slurred, "and I'd lay a fine wench." He gave a drunken giggle and raised her skirt higher. "See for yourself."

The guard moved closer and laid a hand on her white thigh, stroking the smooth flesh while Eleanor tried not to flinch. "Aye, she's a young one—mayhap a virgin," he noted.

"Nay—she lays like a whore who knows her business, but I would have her to myself." Roger winked broadly at the soldier. "And the grass is soft."

"Aye, my lord." The fellow laughed and slapped Eleanor's thigh hard. "I wish you joy of the wench. If you wear yourself out, you can pass her on to me."

"Aye," Roger muttered thickly.

He adjusted her on his shoulder and carried her past the other guard. He belched loudly as he passed through the gate and began to sing again about some Bertha whose pit was deep and tight. Mortified, Eleanor could hear the sentries laughing behind her.

Instead of going into the woods, he kept to the wall and made his way down to the road into town. He stopped and set her down, apologizing as he pulled her skirt back over her legs, "I am sorry, Lea, but was the only plausible way I could think to get you out."

"I think men are disgusting," she muttered with feeling as she rubbed the place where the sentry had struck her. "Is this what you do with your wenches, Roger?"

"It is not." He reached for her hand and squeezed reassurance. "We made it thus far, Lea. We walk into Rouen and change clothes where Aubery has arranged it. From there, I am a mere knight, Richard of Clemence, and you are my lady wife, called Joan. 'Twill be uncomfortable for you, and I am sorry for it, but we decided that the best way to hide your small stature would be if you were heavy with child."

"What!"

"Aye—none will look for it. My armorer at the Condes has made a device to be strapped double around you so that it will not slip. 'Tis straw and horsehair

encased in several layers of fine linen to soften it, but
'twill be hot, I know. Henry has arranged documents
for us so that we may cross at Saint Valéry—we are
going to pray for your safe delivery of a son at the
tomb of the Confessor in London. But we waste time
talking—come on.''

10

The innyard was neither deserted nor crowded as they approached. Ostlers led away a couple of horses while travelers visited lazily at tethering posts or on wooden benches positioned by the inn itself. The few who did look up saw nothing extraordinary about the couple coming in, an impoverished knight and his pregnant wife. Any who bothered to note them could plainly see he was at best a mercenary, a probable younger son, because the packhorse behind them carried the tools of his trade, a plain shield, a broadsword, a lance, a serviceable suit of mail, and a helmet, in addition to a couple of packs that probably contained most of their clothing. He was shabbily dressed in a brocaded tunic whose colors had long since faded, a pair of plain brown chausses wrapped with leather garters, and heavy but worn boots, while she wore a plain gown of dull blue cloth untied at the waist to allow for her swollen belly. The only remarkable thing about them to any interested observer was that they were obviously besotted with each other.

He dismounted and turned to lift her from her horse as carefully as if she had been a basket of uncooked eggs. His hands lingered at her thickening waist possessively before he stepped back to straighten her gown. Then, slipping a protective arm about her shoulders, he leaned closer and whispered something for her ears alone. Her laughter floated through the courtyard. She seemed quite young, probably with child for the first time, judging from her small stature and a certain aura of innocence about her face. She was a beautiful girl even with her hair braided and severely pulled back into a roll at the back of her head. Had she not been so heavy with her husband's heir, she would have stirred any man. Closer inspection by a few curious eyes revealed that the knight, though impoverished, was not so unremarkable after all. He stood head and shoulders above his lady, a well-built young man with softly waving blond hair and bright blue eyes that sparkled with good humor. A couple of men watched them and shook their heads at the vagaries of a fortune that made some great lords and others merely younger sons.

Roger's blue eyes were warm with approbation as he teased Eleanor aloud, "Art beautiful even near your time, Joan."

"Nay, Richard, your eyesight fails you," she teased back, "for I am ugly and ungainly—only my lord could love me like this."

"Your lord loves you right well, lady, even if he cannot show it until you are delivered. But it grows late and, by the looks of the yard, room will be scarce. Wait here with the horses while I bespeak a bed, Joan."

He walked casually into the inn and scanned the dining travelers for a sign of his man. Across the room in a nearly secluded corner sat Jean Merville eating alone. Roger nodded almost imperceptibly before seeking out the innkeeper, a stout, hearty fellow whose pocketed apron marked his trade.

"I need a bed for myself and my lady."

The man took in his faded tunic and shook his head regretfully. "As you can see, we are most crowded." He gestured around the taproom with a broad sweep of his hand. "Nay—a common pallet with three or four others could be found for you, but I've no space suitable for your lady."

Roger reached into the bag at his belt and drew out a small purse of coins. "I have money." He weighed the purse in his hand before extending it to the landlord. "Here—count it for yourself. My wife is with child and nears her time—she cannot go further tonight."

"Well . . ." The fellow rubbed his chin thoughtfully before reaching for the money. " 'Tis not much, but here is the loft over the horses, sir. Gundrade can spread you a clean pallet there."

"So be it then." Roger nodded in agreement. "We need supper also, and water for washing."

"There's a well in the yard—you can draw from it. Gundrade!" the man called out to a pleasantly rounded apple-cheeked woman who came in from the kitchens. "Get this man a drying cloth for himself and his lady, and make up a pallet for them in the loft."

"Aye."

"And fetch some of the pigeon pie." The innkeeper judged the weight of the purse he held. "Aye—and a little of the wine."

"The wine, Gerbod?"

"Aye," he answered gruffly. "His lady nears her time, Gundrade—would you have her drink the stout?"

"Nay." The woman smiled at Roger. "Bring her in, sir, and I will clear a place for her away from the others."

Roger returned to the yard with the coarse linen squares and tossed a coin to the ostler, saying, "Put up the horses and guard our things well—there's another coin for you on the morrow if everything is still there." Turning to Eleanor, he grinned. "We are fortunate, Joan, to get a bed and a meal here. I had so little notion of the advantage of traveling with a big-bellied woman." He handed her one of the rough cloths and pointed toward the well. "We wash there."

"There?" Eleanor raised a skeptical eyebrow until she caught Roger's warning eye. "Oh . . . I see." It had never occurred to her before that the lower orders of the nobility did not enjoy the same privileges she had had even in the convent. Apparently they waited on themselves.

He drew up a bucket of cool water and proffered a dipper for her. It was hot and the air was heavy with unshed moisture. She took the dipper without question and drank deeply, draining it, and then waited for him to do the same. He poured another cup or so on one of the pieces of cloth and gave it to her, saying, " 'Twill at least take the dust and sweat off your face, Joan, before we eat."

"Aye." She rubbed the cool wetness over her face, savoring the feeling of temporary freshness it gave. "Do they have baths here, Richard?" she asked hopefully.

"Aye." He pointed to a shed behind the inn itself where buckets hung suspended over open cubicles. "But I doubt you would want to use them."

"Oh." Daunted, she had to content herself with pushing back her wide sleeve and thrusting the wet cloth deep within it to wash her arm and what portion of her body she could decently reach. It might not be a bath, but it was better than living with the sticky-damp feel of one's sweat. She rinsed the cloth and repeated the process on the other side, furtively scratching at the belt beneath her gown. Roger shed his tunic and the wet linen undertunic, tied the undertunic around his waist to catch excess water, and then poured several dippers of cool water over his head while she watched in fascination as the water trickled down over his shoulders and his upper torso. She looked at the wet hair on his chest with open envy. "Jesu, but I wish I were a man," she told him with feeling.

"Do you now?" He rubbed his head vigorously with a dry strip of linen and grinned at her. "You'd not find it nearly so exciting as you imagine, Joan, for your life would be spent fighting other men's wars and wondering each time if it is your turn to fall. It is endless days on horseback in heat and cold, clad in heavy leather and steel, with mostly cold biscuits and stale ale to keep you alive. Nay, you would not like it."

"Is that truly how it is, R-Richard?" she asked, fascinated by this glimpse into the life of a fighting man.

"Aye—and 'tis little better for any from soldier to king. Did you never wonder why the Old Conqueror was so grizzled or so wary? He sat at the same camp-fires and ate of the same food as the rest of us most of the time."

"Well, it could not be worse than a convent."

"Shhhh," he cautioned her low. "Do not forget yourself."

"Aye." She stood back and waited for him to finish drying himself off. "At least you can bare your chest and cool off."

"And if you did the same, lovey"—he grinned—"I could not defend you by myself." He pulled on his overtunic and left his undertunic to dry on the bucket post. "Let us go eat—I am famished, my lady."

Jean Merville, clad in Prince Henry's colors now, rose and hailed them as they entered the inn. "Richard—Richard of Clemence!" he called out loudly. "Lady Joan! Over here!"

Roger appeared startled and then recognized his man slowly as one who had just seen an old and seldom-met acquaintance. He furrowed his brow thoughtfully before snapping his fingers and grinning. "Merville, is it not? I thought you at the Condes."

"I am for there, Richard, but I serve my lord Henry now."

"How is that?"

" 'Tis a long tale—I'll tell you after I have supped. Do you and your lady stay here the night?"

"Aye."

Merville looked at Eleanor curiously. "God's teeth, Richard! Should she be traveling like that? She looks ready to drop twins."

"Ah, Sir Merville," Eleanor joined, " 'tis always thus—I get huge early on."

"Aye," Roger laughed, "One day it can scarcely be noted, the next she looks ready to lie in."

"Well, would you and the Lady Joan join me? The place clears out now."

"Aye." Roger looked around the room to make sure there were no familiar faces before seating Eleanor and himself at Merville's trestle table. Jean leaned across to murmur low, "All hell came down after you left, my lord."

Roger frowned a warning. "I am most anxious to

hear of it, but not here. We have the loft—you can pallet with us and tell us then."

Gunrade produced the promised pigeon pie and wine. Roger smiled his thanks, winning for them an extra dish of fruit and cheeses. When she had left, Jean Merville poked Eleanor as an equal and asked. "Did you see that, my lady? 'Tis always the same—he but smiles at a woman to get whatever he would have."

"Really?" She turned her dark eyes mischievously to Roger. "And just *what* do you usually get for your smiles?"

"Jean—" Roger seemed less than pleased. "Cease this, else you'll have her appearing as the jealous wife."

"Leave him be. I was but teasing you."

To avoid further embarrassing conversation, Roger dug into his share of the pigeon pie with gusto. Eleanor, on the other hand, found that the heat had robbed her of much of her appetite. She merely picked at the pie and then munched slowly on an apple. Gundrade reappeared to clear the covers and noted Eleanor's still-full trencher. She left to bring back a fresh fruit tart, still warm from the ovens.

"Gentle lady," she addressed Eleanor, "you must eat for your strength. Pray try one of these—they are fresh for the morrow's meals."

Merville and Roger exchanged glances after she returned to the kitchen. "Now, Jean, you can see 'tis more advantage to travel with a lady near her time than with a smiling fellow. Look who got the best of the meal."

"Nay." Eleanor pushed the tart toward them. "You divide it between you—I am too hot to eat."

Roger eyed her anxiously. "You are not getting sick, are you?"

"Nay, 'tis the heat."

Roger rose and reached for her. "Let us walk outside where it is cooler then. Jean, you may have the sweet." He looked out an unshuttered window and noted, "It grows dark outside—we'll meet you in the loft later."

"Aye." Merville weighed the wineskin and nodded. "There's some left here, anyway."

He watched them leave curiously. He genuinely liked the Demoiselle, but he still could not reason out the strange hold she had on Roger FitzGilbert. Were the girl not of his blood, it would be easier to understand, but still not fully comprehensible. There was no woman on earth who could move Jean the way Eleanor of Nantes did Roger FitzGilbert.

The innyard was empty now, its occupants having gone in to sup or having already sought their beds. The still nearly full moon peacefully illuminated the open space while night insects hummed their summer songs in the distance.

"I hate the way I look now," Eleanor murmured as she clutched Roger's arm and walked toward a deserted bench.

"Nay—you are beautiful."

"Tell me truly, brother—could you love a lady who looked as I do now?"

He stopped walking and looked down for a long moment. Soberly he replied, "Aye—doubly so were it my child she carried."

"Your son," she corrected.

"Nay"—he shook his head emphatically—"my child."

"You cannot deny that all men demand sons."

"Only God chooses what a man gets in this life, Lea. Not all men are Gilberts and you would do well to remember that. There are those of us who would love first the wife, and then the children, if they come."

"And if they do not? Roger, my father's love for my mother turned to hate when she had no son."

"Lea, I repeat what I said—not all men are Gilberts."

"Well, I still think it will be different when you are wed, brother. Then it will be a matter of your heir."

He shrugged. "Think what you will, but I really do not care that much about building dynasties. If my wife proves barren even, 'twould be a source of sadness for us both, but I would not reproach her for what she could not help. Besides, the fault could be mine—I've long thought your mother bore no sons because Gilbert planted none."

"Marie is most fortunate," Eleanor murmured softly.

"Marie?" Roger looked at her sharply and then recovered himself. So Eleanor thought Marie de Coutances to be the lady he sought. Well, he reasoned, it did no harm to let her think so for the moment. "Oh . . . aye."

Eleanor felt a stab of jealousy and tried to focus on Roger's gain rather than her own loss to ease the pain. "She is very beautiful, brother," she managed.

"She is that," he agreed. He began again to move toward the bench. "Come on—sit down and rest yourself."

"If I sit down, I sit on that which is the most tired after two days of riding."

"Then stand while I sit."

She followed him to the bench and waited while he dusted it off with his hand. With a rueful sigh she adjusted the heavy padding at her waist and sat anyway. "The next time I run away, Roger, I will choose mine own disguise."

"And be what?"

"A nun or a squire—or anything except a fat lady."

"You are not fat." He eyed her appreciatively. "Truly, Lea, you are still the most beautiful lady I've seen."

They heard the inn door bang open and saw the ostlers make their way out for one last inspection of the stable. Roger slid closer to Eleanor and laid an arm about her shoulders while whispering, "Do not forget and call me 'Roger' or 'brother' when we can be heard."

"I would not." She eyed the loft window above them and sighed. "I suppose they sleep in the stable below us."

"Mayhap, but I doubt it. 'Tis hot and close inside, so they are more like to pull their pallets out into the grass of the yard."

"Well, I wish we had stayed at a priory."

"As do I, but we could not chance it. I am too

well-recognized in most, and besides, while Roger FitzGilbert can command a clean bed, Richard of Clemence would fare not better there than here."

"Richard!" Jean Merville emerged from the inn and called out. "Do not keep Lady Joan out in this night air—'tis unhealthy! And I am for my bed."

The stable boys began dragging out straw-filled pallets and placed them at the side of the building. Roger stood and pulled Eleanor up after him. "Come—they'll bar the door soon."

"Do we have to? 'Twill be like a baker's oven up there."

"Aye, but as soon as the candle is doused, you can strip down to nothing and lie on top of your sheet."

"And have you and Jean stare when you wake in the morning? Nay, I think not."

"Well, by tomorrow night we'll be on a vessel bound for England, and I've heard 'tis cooler there. Until then, get what rest you can."

"Your pardon, Richard." Eleanor leaned closer and lowered her voice for him alone. "I am unbearably cross, I know, and 'tis wrong when you do what you do for me."

"Hush—the heat is enough to try any temper."

"Richard! D'ye hear me?" Merville called.

"Aye, Jean—we come."

They crossed the yard to the stable, where Jean waited with a candle sent by the innkeeper's wife. He handed the light to Roger and nodded. "Here—you go on up and just call down when she is ready."

"My thanks, sir." Eleanor smiled at his consideration.

" 'Tis nothing, my lady. Now that we are equals, I will try my best to treat you as a sister."

Roger held the candle to light the ladder and waited for Eleanor to make the climb. He followed, pulling himself up one-handed until he cleared the top.

"Here."

Eleanor reached out and took the light to allow him to heave himself up to the loft floor. She placed the flickering candle on a low bench near the freshly spread pallets. Roger moved behind her to open the shutters at each end of the long narrow room.

"There's a little breeze tonight that may cool us somewhat."

"Aye." Eleanor turned away and lifted her long skirts to undo the bundle strapped at her waist. She let it fall with a sigh of relief. "Sweet Mary, but that thing is hot to wear."

"Once we are ashore in England, you may watch me burn it," Roger promised. "Here—I'll turn my back and you can strip off your clothes. Dry sheets are bound to be better than what you wear."

She hesitated and then compromised by taking off her gown and leaving only her undershift on before rolling gratefully into the pallet. Pulling her sheet up to her chin, she told him, "You can call Jean up now."

No sooner had she spoken than Merville's russet-haired head appeared above the loft opening. He pulled himself up and surveyed the loft with a quick sweep of hazel eyes. "Well, my lord, I've seen better and I've seen worse."

"At least it's clean and away from the crowd. Last night, Lea and I shared the common room at a place where there were at least a dozen others. She did not complain, but I thought she'd burrow under my backside until she rolled me over."

Eleanor reddened at the reminder and retorted, "I did not like the way some of them looked at me, brother, and neither did you."

"No one there would ravish a woman as far gone as you," he laughed. "But 'twas all right. I did not really mind."

"Well, I had not thought that men were so disgusting until I got to Rouen. Men did not look at me in such a way at Fontainebleau." She turned her attention to Merville, saying, "Jean, you would have blushed to hear what Roger said to those guards at Rouen—I hope I never have to see any of them again. Ugh!"

"Enough, Lea," Roger laughed. "Besides, I would hear from him of what happened after we left."

Merville sat down cross-legged on the other pallet

and frowned wryly at the memory. " 'Twas not pleasant, my lord, I can tell you. Curthose was furious,
fuming and shouting at any and all who crossed his
path; Gilbert was frightened half out of his wits; and
Belesme was furious enough that he lost that coldness
that controls his temper. He cursed and raged until
none would come near him. Gilbert bore most of the
blame from Curthose because he did not miss the
Demoiselle until he was ready to go up to his own
bed. He excused himself by saying he thought her
unwell and was certain she'd gone to the ladies' bower."
Merville's frown lightened to a grin. "Aye—'twasn't
until he sent a page to inquire of her and found her
not there that he became anxious. He went to Curthose,
who was already at his prayers, and told him she was
missing. A cry was raised throughout the place and
everyone was roused to search for the Demoiselle
before they sent for Belesme. I would you could have
seen it—half-drunk men and sleepy servants collided
in dark corridors everywhere to ask if any had seen
the Lady Eleanor. Finally, in the middle of the night,
'twas decided to send for Belesme. I think they wished
to give him time to vent his anger before they faced
him. Anyway, a messenger went to Caudebec, where
Count Robert had gone to confront Mabille, who
stopped there on her way to Rouen. It seems he did
not want her present at his betrothal to the Demoiselle. I have heard he was in the Devil's temper over
her defiance, and it needed but Curthose's news to set
him off. 'Twas said only Normandy's livery saved the
poor man who carried the message to him."

"Jesu, but I'll warrant he frightened the fellow nigh
to death."

"Aye, and while they waited for Belesme, Curthose
and Gilbert planned what they could say, but each
only accused the other of failing to protect Lady Eleanor. Both breathed easier when they found Count
Robert laid all the blame at your feet, my lord, and
swore you'd abducted her against her will. He demanded that Curthose hold your lands forfeit, but
Prince Henry and Gilbert held against it, saying 'twas

not proved you were guilty. Besides, Henry would
have it that he held the Condes as security for a loan.
After much arguing, Curthose confirmed Henry as
guardian of your lands until you could be found to
answer Belesme's accusations." Merville paused to catch
his breath.

"Gilbert held for me?"

"Aye—he was afraid they'd suspect him if you were
involved."

"Nay—they know him for too much a coward to
stand against them even in secret."

"Well, Belesme then turned on my lord Henry and
accused him of stealing her for his mistress. He demanded the prince account for his whereabouts during
the night. For once, the prince was as ill-tempered as
Belesme, at first refusing to reply, and then at Curthose's
urging, producing Aubery and two wenches they claimed
to have lain with together. Thwarted, Count Robert
turned those cold green eyes on me and Hugh, demanding to know what we'd done that night. The
duchess spoke up for us, saying that we had entertained her ladies in the bower after supper. I can tell
you that for once I was glad to have been asked to sing
and play my lute."

"But Belesme was appeased?"

"Barely. Curthose gave in to his demands to conduct a search in Normandy's name. Until you are
found, my lord, all your men serve Prince Henry—we
wear his badge for protection." He pointed to the red
chevron that was sewn to the left shoulder of his tunic.

"God aid Prince Henry for his loyalty to me." Roger
nodded. "I knew I could depend on him."

"Aye—he and Aubery lied like 'twas the truth, my
lord."

"What of Curthose? Does he still go to the Vexin
without Robert?"

"Aye, he left early. None wanted to stay around
Belesme for fear of his turning on them." Merville
stopped and frowned. "There is one other thing you
should know, my lord—Belesme offers five hundred
silver marks to any who can deliver you alive to him."

"Mother Mary!" Eleanor's hands flew to cover her mouth. "Nay!"

"He has to take me first, Lea. We'll be at Saint Valéry tomorrow and out of Normandy soon after. Let him cross the sea for us."

"But what if he closes the port?" she asked practically.

"Then we press on to Boulogne. The coast is full of ports." He caught her skeptical expression and added, "Or we can take to the country until the cry dies down. Not even Robert of Belesme can be everywhere and he cannot sustain a search indefinitely when Curthose expects him to lead his own levies in the Vexin." He stood abruptly and stretched his long frame until he could touch the cross rafters. Yawning widely, he announced, "We have leagues to travel in the morning so we'd best get our sleep. Jean, are you ready for me to put out the light?"

"Aye."

Roger picked up the candle and blew out the flame, sending the loft into moonlit shadows. He waited a minute or so and then pinched the end of the wick to make sure it would not spark when set among the hay.

Eleanor lay back and listened to the rustling sounds of men undressing and sliding between sheets. She kicked off her own sticky covers with relief and turned over to attempt sleep. Eventually one of the men settled into a rest punctuated by the rumbling sounds of snoring. Jean and Roger might be amused by Belesme's reaction to her disappearance, but she found herself still afraid. The knowledge that he searched for them was disquieting, for she, like most others, believed Robert of Belesme capable of nearly anything. Her mind tumbled with fear and kept her awake long into the night. She finally attempted prayer to find comfort.

"Mother Mary, Blessed Virgin, deliver us," she prayed aloud softly into the night.

"Lea, you are not asleep yet?" Roger spoke across the loft.

"Nay—the place is strange."

He rose and came to her, dropping down next to her and rolling against her back. "You are safe enough, Lea," he whispered softly as he pulled her closer and threw an arm over her. "I will protect you, I swear." She would have turned toward him, but he held her too tightly. "Be still and sleep."

"But—"

"Nay—hush."

She settled back against him with a sigh. "I am such a burden to you, brother."

"Lea, do not speak nonsense to me in the middle of the night." He yawned behind her ear and wrapped her closer.

Eleanor found it strange but comforting to lie within a man's arms, and she relaxed. Even Merville's sonorous breathing seemed to lull her now with its rhythm. Slowly she let go of her fears and slipped into sleep.

Roger felt the easing of her tense body and heard her breathing slowly even out. Afraid to move and disturb her, he lay quietly for a time. Her small body nested against him, the rounded curve of her hip pressed against his stomach. Slowly he drew his leg up until she fit perfectly into the hollow created between his belly and his thigh. He felt an overwhelming sense of protectiveness with her in his arms. His hand crept to smooth back her hair. He could feel her soft breath against the palm of his hand when it brushed across her face. Moonlight flooded in from the open window and bathed her in silver. She was so delicate, so fine-boned, and so perfectly made that even after years of knowing her, he still could not look on her without experiencing an odd catch in his chest.

He moved slightly to ease out the arm he lay on and then he cradled her again. His free arm circled her waist and rested beneath her breasts. Still seeking a comfortable position for himself, he shifted again and brushed his hand into the hollow between them, touching the full, rounded mound of one. He drew back as though burned, his entire body suddenly and acutely aware of hers. Her thin undertunic and his shirt seem now to provide little barrier between them as heat and desire flooded through him. He knew that since she slept, he should move back to the pallet he shared with Merville, but he could not. After years of dreaming of her in his bed, he held her now in the flesh and she was as soft and well-made as he'd imagined.

She stirred slightly and sighed in her sleep. Her undershift was damp from the heat of two bodies in a July night. He moved back a little and eased the sticky material away from the back of her thighs—it was a wonder to him that she could sleep in the shift. His fingertips touched the satin of her bare skin and gently moved upward to trace the curve of her hip. Unwilling to stop himself, he moved back a little more to give him more room to work up the shift. He found the flat plain of her belly and splayed his hand across it with concern—there did not seem to be enough width for her to carry a child within. And whether he wanted a child or not, it was possible that if she lay with him, she'd conceive of him. Too many women died in childbirth, and it frightened him. But then, the Old Conqueror's duchess was said to have been much smaller than Eleanor and she'd borne nine or ten children for him. Roger's hand moved upward past the hollow below her ribs and touched a bare breast. He remembered how it looked—firm, rounded, white and pink. His mouth went dry as he thought of seeing her, of her coming to him willingly, her body naked and open for him. He left her breast and let his hand drift to the soft, almost downy area between her legs. She was warm and moist to his touch.

"Unnnnnhhhhhh . . ." She stirred and turned against his hand.

He drew back and held his breath. She settled again and cradled her cheek in the palm of her hand. Jesu, he thought, but she is perfect. He longed to turn her over, to lie facing her, to wake her with his mouth and tongue, and to satisfy his need for her. Instead, he tore himself away with a groan and pulled her shift down to cover her hips. Leaning forward to brush the crown of her head with his lips, he whispered, "Sweet Mary, but I love you, Lea."

She sighed in her sleep and turned over toward him. Reluctantly he rolled away and sat up. It was neither the time nor the place to reveal himself. The soft, silvery light provided a clear view of her face as she slept innocent of his desire. He felt a sense of shame, as though he'd violated her by touching her body with his hands, and the heat ebbed from his own. He rose to seek the other pallet. Stripping his wet shirt from his shoulders, he threw it into a corner and lay down to press his naked body against cool, clean sheets. It was long before he slept.

And when he finally did manage to sleep, it seemed not to last long. Sometime, in the stillness of night, she cried out with several piercing, terrified shrieks. Both he and Jean Merville sat bolt upright and reached for weapons. Roger gained his dagger first and lunged to where Eleanor lay. Her eyes were closed and her hands held out as though to fend off someone. Otherwise, the three of them were alone.

"Lea! Lea!" He shook her awake with his free hand. "What is it?"

Her eyes flew open and she began to shake uncontrollably before covering her face with her hands. Heedless of his nakedness, he dropped his knife and knelt beside her. She clutched at him convulsively and began to sob. Roger began to croon softly. "Shhhhh . . . hush, Lea . . . shhhh . . . 'tis all right."

"What ails her, my lord?" Merville asked anxiously behind him.

"A dream, I think."

Jean crossed himself superstitiously and bent closer. "Demoiselle, are you all right?"

"Aye," Roger answered for her, "but she is frightened. Lea . . . Lea, what is it you fear?"

Eleanor swallowed and caught her breath without releasing her grip on him. " 'Twas Belesme, Roger—I saw him as clearly as if he stood in this very room. He came at me."

"Well, he is not here, as you can see. 'Twas but a dream. I am here and I have you safe."

"Roger . . ." She clutched him even more tightly

and swallowed hard. "I saw you lying in blood at his feet."

"Jesu! God's teeth, Lea, but you are a comfort to a man! Listen, it was but a dream. Here . . ." He turned to Merville and ordered, "Give me my tunic—I am as naked as I was born."

Slowly Eleanor mastered herself, and the terror of a dream too real began to fade. Though the sun was not yet rising, the loft was fairly light and she could see there were only the three of them. She released Roger self-consciously and hung her head in embarrassment.

"I am sorry, brother—I did not mean to wake either of you."

"Nay, Lea, 'tis all right." He looked to his bare shoulders, where her fingernails had dug in and left ugly red marks. "Jesu, but you are strong for such a little maid." He pulled on his tunic and lay back down beside her.

Below, the footsteps of men running could be heard. Someone stood on a lower rung of the ladder and called up, "Is it your lady's time? Should we call Gundrade?"

"Nay, 'twas a bad dream," Roger called back down. "She is all right now."

One by one, the curious left and the stable settled again into silence. The three of them lay without speaking, each uncertain as to the significance of her dream. It seemed that it was still enough to hear time slipping by like the sands in a glass. Finally Eleanor could stand it no longer and sat up.

"What is it this time?" Roger asked quietly.

"Nothing—I cannot sleep."

Reluctantly he sat up also. "Jean, are you awake?"

"I could scarce be anything else, my lord."

"Aye." Roger rose and went to the window at the end of the room. "Well, I think the sun comes up soon—'twill be light by the time we break our fast. You have a long ride to the Condes and we can reach Saint Valéry early."

Merville heaved his stocky body up heavily and reached for his brown chausses. Eleanor reddened and turned her back while both men dressed. When it came her turn, Roger assured her they had no intention of watching. Reluctantly she got up and fastened the thick bundle at her waist before straightening her shift and pulling the dull blue gown over it.

"Jesu, but she looks small to be with child, Roger," Merville noticed.

"Sweet Mary, if I hear one more time how little I am, Jean, I shall box your ears myself."

"Nay, Demoiselle," Merville apologized, "that was not my meaning. God knows our Duchess Mathilde made you look like a warhorse."

"Did you ever see her?"

"Aye—I was seven or eight at the time, and I came eye-to-eye with her. Now, there was a tiny woman." He sat to pull on his boots. "She had the bones of a child herself, yet she was safely delivered nine or more times, by all counts."

"Was she very pretty?"

"Not then, but I think she once was. Nay—she must have been, for 'twas said the Old Conqueror never strayed once from her bed."

"Aye," Roger joined in soberly, "we bastards are loath to get bastards."

11

"Jesu!" Eleanor clutched at Roger's arm as they made their way to the pier. "Brother, turn round and walk across the grass toward the steps. Nay, do not look up."

"Joan, what ails thee?" Roger asked aloud before whispering in an undervoice, "Where do you think you are going, Lea?"

"Belesme!" she hissed back.

"God's teeth, but you imagine him everywhere."

"Nay, he is here—I just saw him on the pier."

Roger stopped in his tracks and barely turned back for a quick look. There, boarding the deck of the *Sea Wolf*, was indeed Robert of Belesme, his tall frame unmistakable in its telltale green clothing. At dockside, several men wearing his colors waited.

"We are betrayed, brother," Eleanor whispered as she walked slowly across the steep hillside that sloped down to the harbor.

"Nay—Henry would not, and only he knew which ship we took. 'Tis but ill luck that brings Belesme here." He put an arm easily about Eleanor's shoulders and cautioned. "Do not do anything rash, Lea, for we are not yet noted. We are but a poor knight and his lady come to look at the ships. Walk leisurely over to watch the one coming in, but keep you face away from view."

"Aye." She kept her face on his as though intent on conversation. "But what do we do now?"

"First, we leave Saint Valéry and seek another port. If that proves unfeasible, we take to the woods and wait for the soldiers to leave. Once he is satisfied we

190

are not in the area, Robert will move on to another place."

To Eleanor it seemed the casual stroll up the hill was the longest walk of her life. Her legs ached as though from walking a league or more, and her neck hurt from the tension of holding her head studiously away from Belesme's line of vision.

No sooner had they reached their horses than a new contingent of green-shirted soldiers arrived and dismounted. The leader hailed Roger, "Halt, sir—where go you and your lady?"

Eleanor's heart thumped painfully in her chest as she tightened her grip on Roger. Had they come this far to be taken? Roger turned cheerfully to the captain and saluted his greeting. The man walked over to talk and Eleanor held her breath.

"What goes here?" Roger asked with the air of the most casual observer. "Joan and I are wont to watch the ships, but the place is overrun with men-at-arms."

"Aye." The captain squinted into the full sun at them and nodded. "We seek two runaways, a man and a woman, for my lord of Belesme."

Roger crossed himself as though struck by the dreaded name. Eleanor saw and did the same, a gesture not unnoticed by the man. "Nay, 'tis only those two we want—Count Robert has no need of a woman in her condition." He laughed at his own humor. "But you, sir—you bear the look of a mercenary."

"Aye. I serve in Alan of Brittany's train, but am released to take Joan, my wife, to her relatives before she is brought to bed with the child."

The captain squinted again in Eleanor's direction and shook his head. "Well, were she mine, she'd not be in camp anyway. 'Tis a fine-looking lady you have."

"These two you seek—what have they done?" Eleanor asked innocently.

"Think you Belesme tells the likes of us? Nay, we are but told to find Roger FitzGilbert and Eleanor of Nantes. A fool's chase, if you ask me, for I doubt the FitzGilbert would seek a port. From all I've heard of the man, he's as shrewd as Count Robert. Nay—by now, I'd say he and the lady were safe in France." He turned again to Roger. "Sir, if you should mark a wealthy lord and an heiress on the road, seek out the authority in any village—'tis worth five hundred silver marks to you."

"Five hundred marks! Jesu, but he must want them," Roger breathed as though he contemplated a fortune.

"Aye—'tis a lifetime of fighting for you and me to see a quarter of that, isn't it?" The captain nodded to the wharf and pointed out Robert of Belesme. "There's my lord himself—he awaits us. Well, I suppose we'll have to go down and tell him the search is fruitless."

"What then?"

The man shrugged. " 'Tis a thankless task, what with merchants and townsmen protesting, but I suppose we'll close some more ports and not let any board without a pass from Normandy's officials."

"Well, I wish you good fortune in your search, but I have to get Joan back on the road else the babe will be born ere we get there."

"Where are you bound?"

"Humphrey de Granville's keep—he is my wife's kinsman."

"Well, I am not from the area, so I have no knowledge of the man, but I wish you a safe journey, sir. And to you, lady, a safe lying-in."

"My thanks," Eleanor murmured, grateful that the man gave signs of moving away at last.

When the men had passed and were making their way down the steep wooden steps to the quay, Eleanor turned to Roger, asking, "What now, brother?"

"We take to the woods and pray I can feed us," he answered with a new grimness. "Nay, we are not done yet, Lea—let him close the ports. There is still a way out if we can but last until he moves to another place." He patted the hand that clutched his arm. "Come, we've got to get out of here before we are recognized."

He led her leisurely to the horses and put her up before checking the packs on the sumpter horse. Then, mounting his own big bay, he clicked the reins and set a slow, easy pace out of town. It wasn't until the city gates were far behind them that he spurred into a gallop.

"Where are we bound?" Eleanor shouted after him as she applied the whip to her own horse.

"You'll see soon enough!" he yelled back. " 'Tis not far."

Eleanor surveyed the pallets she'd laid within the walls of an abandoned church and sighed. It was not Nantes or Rouen, to be sure—it was not even Fontaine-bleau—but it was well off the main road. In fact, the old road that had led to the church had been abandoned and allowed to grow up with weeds. She walked around the broken-shell walls and inspected the place. A field mouse scampered from a pile of unsalvageable wood in one corner and ran to hide again beneath rubble where the apse had stood. The place was roof-less now, but in July it mattered little. Tonight they would sleep under a starry sky, anyway. She moved to where Christ's altar had stood and imagined how the place must have been once. It could not have been demolished too long ago—the wind and rain and sun had not managed to destroy the marks on the floor where altar and statues had been.

She did not hear Roger return until his boots sounded on the stone-paved floor and he startled her. Grasping the jewel-hilted dagger he'd left her, she spun around. He stood there grinning, holding a dead rabbit and a scarf full of weeds.

"You frightened me!"

"So I see." He held up his catch for inspection. "I robbed some poor poacher's trap, Lea, but 'twas the best I could do. A knight's arms are of little use when hunting small game, I can tell you."

She had to giggle in spite of herself. "Aye, I'll warrant that is so." She eyed the rabbit curiously. "How do we cook it?"

"Well, my lady, do you favor it boiled or roasted? There are these to boil also."

"Weeds?"

"Aye, but they can be eaten with a little salt, Lea,

and will help fill our stomachs." He turned to leave, but she stopped him with a hand on his arm. "Nay—I go but to clean them—unless you want the task."

"Oh. If that be the case, go with my blessing, brother," she laughed.

"See if you can manage a fire while I am gone."

She gathered dry grass and small, broken twigs from the churchyard and piled them in the middle of a bare place she cleared on the ground. Using Roger's fire stones from his saddlebags, she struck them again and again until they sparked and a small red spot glowed on the dried grass. She bent closer and blew gently until it caught and then flamed. Satisfied, she piled some larger sticks over the grass and twigs and waited until they too caught.

Roger returned and set up a crude spit, speared the skinned and cleaned rabbit with a green stick, and set it to roast. Removing the leather strapping from Richard of Clemence's old-fashioned pot-helmet, he filled it with water from a skin bag and dumped the leaves into it. "Put this on the fire while I get the salt, Lea," he ordered.

"Aye."

He went to the packs and searched for his chunk of salt and a small knife. Returning, he pared some into the pot-helmet and set the block aside. "Now, Lea, all we have to do is wait."

"How did you learn to do this, Roger?" she asked in fascination.

"I told you—a soldier's life is not all you think, Lea. An army travels on its stomach, and all too often, supply carts are lost. I learned much of it from Old William's knights." He stretched out on a grassy spot and pillowed his head. "Turn it when it gets brown and crusted, will you? 'Twill need to be turned at least four times to make sure it is done."

She gave the spitted rabbit a dubious look, but nodded. "If your supper burns, 'tis not my fault—I have little knowledge of such things."

"Then 'tis time you learned, Lady Joan."

She moved to drop down beside him. "Ah, Roger,

you've no notion how much cooler it is without that thing tied to my middle. Here—you cannot be comfortable like that—I am softer than the ground." She scooted behind his head and lifted it into her lap. "There—'tis better, is it not?"

"Aye."

"Roger . . ." She picked bits of grass from the blond hair. "How is it that they destroyed this beautiful church?"

"Old William's orders. 'Twas done to make a hunting forest for him."

"I thought he built churches like the one at Caen."

"Aye—and he replaced this one, too, but he wanted to reserve large pieces of forest for his own use. Any who poach here stand to lose a hand if caught. Nay, do not start, Lea. If we are taken, poaching is the least of our concerns." He settled his head more comfortably against the fullness of her skirt and closed his eyes.

He looked tired—blue hollows formed beneath his eyes and fatigue lines were set at the corners of his mouth. She began massaging his forehead and temples to ease him, and then let her fingers wander to the thick blond waves that lay tousled above. He relaxed and the lines seemed to soften until his breathing slipped into the deep, even pattern of sleep. Sweet Jesu, she thought as she traced the profile of his face, but he is twice the man Belesme is.

"Sweet Mary!" She jumped up with a start and let him roll off her lap. "The food!"

"What? Huh?" He came awake groping for his knife.

" 'Tis nothing, brother," she told him. "I did but nearly burn the rabbit." She moved to turn the spit and to inspect the damage. "Little enough harm done," she decided aloud.

"If you do not consider my poor head. God's teeth, Lea, but you gave me another fright!"

"Your pardon, brother, but would you rather be rudely awakened or would you prefer burnt meat?"

"Burnt meat."

"You would not!"

"Well, come back and let me have your lap again, Lea, so that I may better decide."

"Nay, I will spoil you, Roger, and Marie may not want to indulge your lazy habits."

He rolled to his side and propped his head on an elbow. "What makes you think of Marie?"

"I don't know—I was watching you sleep, brother, and I just thought of how much you give up for me. You should have stayed in Rouen and worked to win your love."

"You seem to have an uncommon interest in the state of my heart, Lea," he told her quietly. "What would you say if I told you that I expect to be wed soon—mayhap before the leaves turn again?"

"I . . . I'd be pleased, Roger." She flushed under his unwavering stare and looked away. "Nay, I lie, brother—I am sorry . . . 'tis just I fear she will come between you and me. You see, I have no one else to turn to." She looked up and met his sober gaze. " 'Tis wrong of me, I know, and I will try to be happy for your sake."

"I hope you will." He rose and came to stand behind her. "God knows, Lea, I will try to please you."

"Nay! Not in this!" She drew away and turned to face him. "Nay, you must not—you cannot—give up your dreams because of my foolish fears, Roger. Take your lady, and let me be content to hold your children when they come."

"I expect you will." He would have stepped closer, but she whirled suddenly and sniffed the air. "Sweet Mary, I've done it again! If I forget one more time, you'll have to steal us another rabbit!"

"Here, let me turn it. You stir the potage."

Roger cursed himself for a fool and bent to the task of watching the meat cook. He'd almost revealed himself, and it was not yet time—he needed more days and a safe distance from Belesme before he dared to tell her. She'd just admitted jealousy of the fair Marie, but that did not mean she cared for him like a lover. Nay, to her he was but a brother, a trusted friend.

"I think 'tis done."

"Huh? Oh . . . the leaves? Aye, they probably are."

"Do we eat them like this?" she asked dubiously. "I mean, they are but a soggy mess."

"They always are, Lea, but we eat them anyway." He turned the rabbit one last time. "You can get the plates from the bags."

It wasn't until he'd divided the rabbit into pieces and placed it on the plates beside the stringy green potage that she realized just how hungry she really was. She took hers to a nearby wall and made herself comfortable against it. He picked his up and followed.

"Mmmm—I had not tasted it prepared like this, brother, but 'tis not as bad as I expected," she managed as she chewed the meat.

"Do not be sure until you have tried the other"—he grinned— "for it has almost nothing to recommend it except it takes room in the stomach."

They finished eating and she set about to clear away the mess, rinsing the plates with water from the skin, and then stamping out the fire. It was, after all, July, and there was no need of any extra heat. When she finished and turned her attention back to Roger, he was asleep propped up against the wall, his head resting on his knees. She thought about trying to ease him to a more comfortable position but decided against it. If he were tired enough to sleep sitting up, he did not need to be moved.

The sky above was bright and cloudless and the heat was oppressive. She fanned her skirts to cool her legs and mopped her sweaty face with the sleeve of her gown. How Roger could sleep in the heat was beyond her comprehension. She stopped and dropped her skirt, listening now for the sound of distant hoofbeats.

"Roger. Roger." She shook him frantically, hissing, "Riders come."

"Unnnnh? Jesu, Lea, what is it that makes you unable to let a man sleep?"

"I said riders are coming, Roger. They can smell the fire."

He was fully awake in an instant and listening. "God's

teeth! The road is overgrown and unused." He sprang to his feet and grabbed her hand. "We've got to get to the horses!"

They ran for the woods where the animals had been hidden, clearing the first heavy overgrowth and plunging into a short, narrow ditch. Roger pushed Eleanor down ahead of him and then covered her with his body. They lay listening as mounted riders thundered down the old road and passed without stopping.

"Sweet Mary!" Eleanor breathed to break their silence. "I thought they came looking for us."

"Nay—they could smell the fire, Lea. If they'd searched, they'd have stopped to see whether we were poachers or Belesme's quarry." He released her reluctantly and heaved himself up. She crawled out after him and began picking grass and dead leaves off her clothing and out of her hair. There had been some stagnant water in the ditch and it had soaked the front of her gown with a foul-smelling stain. She lifted the wet material away from her and wrinkled her nose in disgust. "Ugh, brother, but I smell as bad as the drainage pond at Nantes. I'll have to use the water left in the skins to wash myself and I'll have to change my clothes."

She was a mess and, in spite of her predicament, Roger found it difficult not to laugh at her bedraggled appearance. She noted the twitch at the corners of his mouth and managed a rueful grin. "Aye, if we were discovered this instant, none would mark me for Eleanor of Nantes. I look more the barnyard wench than the heiress."

A slow smile spread across his face. "You don't have to wash with a rag and a cup of water, Lea. There's a stream across the road and I've brought some of Gilbert's soap." He watched her expression brighten and nodded. "Aye, 'tis hot and we both stink, and the water's cool—what say you to a bath?"

"There's a stream?" She turned on him, rounding indignantly. "Had I known there was extra water, I'd have bathed before I ate. There I stood complaining of the heat and the smell of me, and you never told me there was water."

"I thought you could guess," he defended, "for I filled the skins and we ate and cooked with it."

"I thought 'twas a well you found." Her mood changed abruptly and she began unplaiting her hair and combing it with her fingers. She let it fall loose about her shoulders as she picked up her skirts above her ankles and began to run playfully toward the road. "Do not stand there like a dolt, brother," she called back.

He watched her run like a young colt, her hair streaming wildly after her. "Aye! do not forget to stop for the soap!" he yelled after her as he began to run also. She cut across the open area to the church and stopped to rummage quickly for a chunk of her father's strong tallow soap. With it in her hand, she raced for the road.

"Wait!"

She turned, laughing, and shook her head. "Nay, 'tis up to you to catch me, Roger!"

He took the challenge and tried to catch her. For a time, she zigzagged out of his reach, but she was no match for his longer legs. He finally lunged and caught her from behind and they collapsed, giggling and shrieking like children, in a heap at the top of the hill that overlooked the stream bank. She was out of breath. He pulled a seed stem of wild grass and tickled the end of her nose. She pushed it away and rolled to sit up. "Ugh! I don't see how you can stand to be this close to me, brother, for I cannot stand myself." Using his shoulder for balance, she pushed herself up and surveyed the scene below. "Look—there's a fall! Is the pool deep?"

"Nay." Reluctantly he pulled himself up and followed her line of vision. "But I warn you, Lea, the water's not warm like you are used to." He pulled off his boots and stripped his tunic, throwing it down the hillside toward the water. When he bent to unfasten the leather strips that held his chausses, she eyed him curiously.

"What are you doing?" she asked.

"Stripping myself." He looked up and met her dark eyes staring in fascination. "Wet clothes are heavy, Lea. You'd best take yours off too."

She reddened and shook her head. "What if somebody came?"

"There's none but me to see you." His mouth was dry as he waited for her decision.

"Nay, I cannot." She unfastened her gown at the waist and pulled it over her head, revealing a plain white undershift now stained with muddy water. "I can wade in this and 'twill cool my body."

"As you please." He shrugged to hide his disappointment. "But it would not be the first time I've seen you bare."

"When?"

"Well . . . you could not have been above three or four—but I have seen you."

" 'Tis not the same." She gathered her dress and started down the hill ahead of him. "Bring your clothes and we'll wash them."

He finished removing his clothing and collected it. She stood on the bank and slipped off her slippers while trying to suppress a mischievous grin. When he caught up, she pointed toward the fall. "Look there." He turned to see what she saw and was rewarded with a playful push that sent him headlong into the water. Instead of splashing and coming up indignantly, he kept his head down and lay motionless.

"Roger? Roger!" Anxiously she slid into the water and made her way to him. "Sweet Mary! Did you strike your head?" He still did not move when she reached to pull his head out of the water. As she grasped his hair, his hand shot out and caught her leg and tipped her over. She came up sputtering and squealing. " 'Twas *most* unfair, brother."

"Oh . . . aye." He grinned. "And 'twas most honorable to send your champion head first into a pool when you did not even know the depth."

"I could see the bottom," she answered. Cold water streamed in rivulets down her face as she pushed the

wet hair back. She tried to wade in the waist-deep
water and found her movement hampered by the wet
shift. She looked down in disgust and then blushed in
embarrassment—the white fabric clung like plaster,
outlining the swell of her breasts, and its wetness gave
it a transparency that revealed the darker circles of her
nipples. He noted the flush in her cheeks and followed
her downward gaze to where the offending nipples
stood like hard little knobs against the clinging shift.
He looked away and moved to the bank to reach for
the soap. "Here . . ." His voice sounded strange in his
own ears as he turned back. "Let me help you wash
your hair."

"Nay," she choked as she covered her chest with
crossed arms, "I can do it myself."

"And keep me from seeing you? Lea, you might as
well just take off your shift and wash it with the rest of
the clothes." He moved closer, but she just shook her
head stubbornly. "Here, then . . ." He reached out
and caught her shoulder. "I will soap your head for
you while you cover yourself, and then you can duck
your head under the water to rinse it." He made a
weak lather, combing and smoothing as he went, to
avoid any unnecessary tangling. Her back was to him
and he could feel her relax slightly. It was an effort
not to just reach around her and cup a full, rounded
breast in his hand, but he cautioned himself not to
frighten her. "There." He gave her a light push and
told her, "Rinse it."

She held her breath and lowered her head beneath
the surface. Her hair fanned out around her in the
water. Pushing it back with both hands, she stood up
and let it fall straight down over her shoulders. "That
feels so good, Roger, that I could do it again, but I
fear I'd never get the tangles out. Here—turn yourself
around and squat down—I'll wash yours for you."

The water was cold but not unbearable and soon
they finished bathing and began to play like children.
She lost her self-consciousness over the transparency
of her shift and splashed about happily, sending palmfuls
of water his direction and squealing when he sent

sprays back. She sloshed over to him and twined her
arms about his neck in an effort to dunk him underwater. He could feel her taut nipples against his skin
unconsciously enticing him. He broke her hold and
pushed away. "Come, Lea, 'tis getting late and we
haven't done the clothes. If they are to dry, they'll
have to be spread out while there's still sun."

"Aye," she agreed reluctantly, "but 'tis so cool and
peaceful I could stay right here forever."

"You already grow wrinkled," he teased while he
reached for his tunic and chausses. "Here—start pounding these on the rocks while I get your gown."

She did as he asked, working soap into the dirty
garments and then pounding them with a small rock
against a large flat one to work in the suds. Some of
the stains would be impossible, she decided, but at
least the smell of sweat and horses would come out.
She looked up to see him standing on the bank above
her, his tall, well-muscled body still unclad. She blushed
furiously and turned away, amusing him. "Here," he
called as he tossed down her gown. She nodded and
rinsed his clothes. "Here yourself," she answered when
she was done. "Spread them out to dry."

"Is this the best you can wring, Lea?" he teased as
he squeezed out rivulets of water from his tunic. "They'll
not dry by the morrow."

"Washing was not one of the tasks I was taught,"
she shot back with a grin. "Great ladies do not do
their own washing, and well you know it."

"Ah, so you *do* aspire to be a lady, after all. I can
see you in my mind with keys at your waist, ordering
the running of your husband's keep, seeing to his
comfort, sewing fine things— "

"Stop it!" she laughed, her eyes lit with amusement
at his vision of her domesticity. "You see no such
thing, Roger FitzGilbert! You know full well I have no
skill in such things!"

"Nay, Lea," he persisted in teasing, "after seeing
you labor over my clothes, I agree with Henry—'tis
time you took a husband." His eyes traveled to the
wet, clinging shift, taking in the full curve of rosy-

tipped breasts pushing at the almost transparent material. "Aye," he murmured half to himself, " 'tis overlong, I think." Sliding back into the water, he reached to take the gown she'd been washing.

She waited until he turned to wring it out, and then came up behind him to give him one last playful ducking. He stood like a rock while she pushed with all her might; then he reached around to pull her down. She fell back, flailing and sputtering, and sank under the water.

" 'Twas not fair!" she cried as she came up, spitting and pushing at her tangled hair. "You are strong and I am weak!"

"Nay, we are as God made us, Lea—each for a purpose."

He'd stopped laughing and stood there soberly staring at her with an odd, arrested expression on his face. There was something in those blue eyes that she'd never seen before, something that made her breath catch and her throat constrict. Guiltily she looked away, muttering, "Ah, we'd best get out, brother."

"Aye." He reluctantly heaved himself up on the bank and set to laying out their wet clothing. "There's naught to dry with," he spoke over his shoulder, "but the sun's warm after the cold water."

Without waiting for him, she dropped to the ground and stretched out on her stomach to embrace the warmth of the soft grass. Cradling her head in the crook of an elbow, she closed her eyes and inhaled deeply of the earth's smell. " 'Tis so good to be clean, Roger," she murmured.

Behind her, he finished spreading and shaping her dress and his tunic in the full sun before stooping to pick up and shake out his wet chausses. Pulling them on, he tied them at his waist, shivering despite the summer heat. Without bothering to wrap them, he stood over her for a moment, his whole body alive with its acute awareness of her. Finally he lowered his tall frame down beside her, rolled over, and propped himself up on his elbow to study her. He let his eyes roam over the wet, tangled mass of dark hair, the black fringe of still-wet lashes, the gentle curve of fair cheek, and down to the slender white neck. The minstrels could sing of Edith Swan-Neck, Saxon Harold's leman, but Roger would hazard all he possessed that she could not have begun to compare with Eleanor of Nantes. Nay, there could be none more beautiful than his Lea.

Thinking her asleep, he allowed himself the luxury of looking lower to where her breasts swelled against the ground, and he remembered how they looked that day Belesme had ripped her gown. The image of her standing there uncovered flooded his mind, almost crowding out rational thought, and gave him that familiar dryness of mouth. His blood raced, pounding in his temples, warming him, and he thought he would burst with longing. His loins tautened, filling him with an aching that he no longer wanted to deny. It was as though every fiber of his being demanded more than the sight of her. He reached to touch where the wet shift still clung to her damp skin, tantalizing him with what it would hide. His fingers, sensitive with his desire, smoothed the wet linen over her shoulder and down to her narrow waist.

Eleanor held her breath and lay very still beneath his touch and tried to deny the inner trembling that threatened possession of her body. Then an involuntary shiver of excitement coursed through her when he moved closer. His fingers against her back were light as they smoothed and stroked the wrinkles of her shift, but there was nothing soothing about the way they made her feel. She waited, afraid he would roll away from her and afraid he wouldn't.

He traced downward to the curve of her hip, drawing his fingertips gently over the outer round of the bone to brush along her thigh. She swallowed hard, but did not recoil from his touch. Above his hand, the division of her hips was revealed through the wet fabric.

"Sweet Jesu, Lea," he croaked, "I love you."

Drawn by the strangeness of his voice, she half-rolled to face him and was unprepared for the sudden

violent rush she felt at the open desire in his eyes. Her
heart beat wildly and her eyes widened as he lowered
his head to hers and sought her lips hungrily. His
hands came up to cradle her head and hold it still
while he kissed her with the fervor of a yearning too
long denied.

Fire raced through her veins, sending a tremor of
delight that shook her to the very core of her being.
"Hold me, Lea," he mumbled thickly, and for answer
she slid her arms around him tightly. Without reason,
without thought, she clung to him as he laid her on her
back. She was floating breathlessly while his lips traveled softly, reverently over her closed eyelids, her
temples, and on to her earlobe. His warm breath
against her ear raised gooseflesh on her arms and sent
shivers down her spine, but she was feeling far from
cold. His tongue darted and teased and his teeth nib-
bled, bringing her alive with desire.

"Sweet," he whispered as he lifted his head to return to her mouth for a long, searching kiss. Her
fingers restlessly traced the length of his strong, muscular back, and then dug into his shoulders when his
mouth sought the sensitive hollow of her throat. The
heat and strength of his body diffused into hers, overwhelming her with a mindless need for closeness. Rational thought ceased as her body eagerly responded
to his.

"I've loved you for so long, Lea," he breathed when
at last he lifted his head to search her face. Her eyes
were still closed, but the low moan that escaped as she
moved restlessly beneath him told him that her passion matched his own. Her hands crept to caress the
thick blond hair and to draw him back to her mouth.
Instinctively her lips parted, allowing him full possession of the warm, moist depths. His tongue edged her
teeth, exploring the sharp edges, before plunging to
discover the taste of her. Her body was alive beneath
him, twisting and rubbing against his aching manhood.

This time, when he left her mouth, it was to move
lower, tracing hotly along her neck and throat, and
then down over her collarbone to the soft, velvety

flesh just above the rounded neckline of her undershift. Murmuring incoherently, she tried to draw him again to her lips. His hand pushed the shift off one shoulder to reveal the perfectly mounded breast. Cupping it, he bent his head lower to taste, to lick, to tease, until the rosy nipple hardened into a button. She gasped at the strange, wonderful sensation that flooded over her when he began to suck, and arched her back beneath his weight to demand more.

Roger's heart, body, and soul urged—nay, *demanded*—the union of his dreams. Experience and instinct told him she wanted to yield—to receive him and give him what he wanted now. He grasped the shift and began working it up from her knees. Laying his head on her breast, his ear over her pounding heart, he delighted in the revealing of her body. She was even more perfect in the flesh than he'd imagined. His hand caressed the soft silk of her skin along her thigh as he eased his body away just enough to get her shift out of the way. She moaned softly as his fingers brushed along the inside of her leg upward to the soft hair. Her leg splayed outward, opening to him, and her breath came in great harsh rushes.

Her whole body shuddered when he touched the wet down, and she rocked against him instinctively, striving for an unknown but promised ecstasy. She could not draw back from the indescribable pleasure of his touch—every inch of her body cried out for him.

With his free hand he pulled at his chausses until the ties loosened and gave way. He rolled over her to press himself against where his fingers had caressed her, and clasped her hips beneath his.

She gasped and stiffened with shock at the feel of him. With a heavy groan he rolled off her and fought to control his raging need. Gulping for air, he rasped, "Sweet Jesu, but I want you, Lea, but 'tis not the time."

She blinked in bewilderment and then was overcome with shame and humiliation. As she stared at his aroused body, the realization that she'd nearly played the harlot filled her with conflict, anger, and self-

loathing. Roger, shaken to the core with his own painful emotions, reached out to her. She pushed him
away frantically, her eyes dilated in horror, and scrambled wildly on her hands and knees away from him. In
agony he lurched to his feet and stumbled after her.

"Mother Mary!" she panted as she gained her balance and turned away to pull down the shift. "Jesu,
brother!" Her face flamed and her whole body shook
uncontrollably.

"Lea—" He reached to grasp her shoulder, but she
jerked free of him and spun around.

She stared hard for a moment, remembering her
reaction to him, and then burst into tears. "Nay, do
not come closer!" she cried. "Sweet Mary, but you
would have taken me! And . . . and I would have let
you—nay, I *wanted* you to!"

"Lea—" He tried to catch her again, but she backed
away from him blindly. "Lea, 'tis not what you think!"

"Stay away from me!" The tears streamed down her
face unchecked. "Brother, we would have sinned!"
With a wrenching sob she turned and would have run
back toward the abandoned church.

"Nay, Lea!" He caught her and held her while she
kicked and sobbed hysterically to get away from him.
" 'Tis not as you think—I share no blood of yours!"
When she would have jerked free, he held fast. "Turn
around and look at me, Lea! 'Tis the truth—Gilbert is
not my father!" He turned her around by her shoulders and held her there, willing her to look at him. For
a few moments she was silent and his words seemed to
hang between them in the air. The color drained from
her face and she raised her eyes to stare numbly at the
man she'd loved all her life as her brother. Roger felt
as though his heart had stopped beating. "Aye," he
told her simply, "you are not my sister, Lea."

"Then everything has been a lie," she mumbled
tonelessly.

"Nay." He searched her face soberly and sighed.
"That day that William came to Nantes, Lea—'twas
that day my mother told me. I was ashamed to be a
coward's son, and she said 'twas not so—that I had no

shame for the blood in my veins, that Gilbert was not my father." He dropped his hands and stepped back to retie his chausses. "I wanted to tell you then, Lea, but my mother would not have it—she loved you and did not want you to think her a whore. Then when Lady Mary died and I knew you were going to the convent, I couldn't tell you."

"And all we have lived since than has been a lie," she repeated dully.

"I have never lied about loving you, Lea."

"But all those years you let me think—"

"Aye, but 'twas the only way. Think on it, Lea— think you that I could have ever seen you again had it been known that I was not your brother?" He reached to lift her chin gently. "Look at me, Lea. Ever have I loved you, I swear. I gave you my heart that morning when I swore my oath to you in the chapel at Nantes. Remember that? Aye, I knew we were not related then and I was glad—glad that maybe someday the lord that came for you would be me. It was ever my intent to make my way with my sword—to rise high enough that I could ask for you."

"But Belesme—"

"But Belesme came first and then I had not the time. I could wait no longer, Lea, for if you went to Belesme, there was naught for me. I love you—I would wed with you and keep you safe all the days of my life. Lea, you have ever said you loved me."

"Aye," she whispered finally from the hollow ache in her throat, "but not like this, Roger. I have loved you as my brother."

"Have you?" When she dropped her eyes and was silent, he forced her chin up again. "Nay, love, I think you want me too—I know it. Had I not stopped just now, we would have lain together." He watched her redden again and whisper, "We would have sinned," and he shook his head. "Nay—not if we love each other and are wed. 'Tis not an easy thing, I know, to defy Belesme and Curthose and Gilbert, but we can do it."

"Nay, I . . . I cannot—oh, Roger, I am so confused! 'Tis not right!"

He wrapped his arms around her and pulled her close, holding her against his bare shoulder. "It is right, Lea, if you love me." His hand smoothed the wet tangles that still dripped down her back.

"Roger, I cannot wed with you—I cannot!" she wrung out. With a sob, she turned her head against his flesh and clung miserably to him.

His own emotions strained nearly to the breaking point, he held her closer and let her cry until he could stand it no longer. Resolutely he set her back enough to look at her. "I can wait, Lea, as long as I know you love me."

"Roger—"

"Do you?"

"Aye, but not—"

Before she realized what he meant to do, he drew her into his arms again and bent to brush his lips against her. One of his hands twined in her hair and the other slid lightly down her back and over the curve of her hip. She knew he could feel the tremor that ran through her. His breath was warm, alive, and inviting. When he finally released her, her knees wanted to buckle and she had to clutch at him for balance.

"You never could lie to me, Lea," he told her bluntly.

"You don't understand!"

"Nay, I do not. Can it be that my bastardy stands between us? Mayhap 'tis fine to have a bastard for brother but not for husband." He shook free of her and started back toward the church.

"Nay!" She stood rooted to the ground for a moment and then ran after him, catching his arm and holding it to stop him. " 'Tis unfair, Roger! 'Twas I that defended you all those years! You have naught to be ashamed of for bastardy. Men look up to you and call you Bastard like they did the Conqueror—they say 'How stands the Bastard?' like 'tis a title." She hugged his arm against her body and looked up, her face pleading for understanding.

"All right," he sighed finally, "I've waited seven years, Lea—another few months cannot make that much difference."

They walked back across the road in silence, each sorting out his own inner turmoil. For Roger, it was bittersweet relief to finally have his feeling for Eleanor out in the open. He'd not meant for her to discover it like that and he'd not meant to get carried away with his own desire. Nay, he could not just take her and live with the consequences—not when he knew not how it all would end with Belesme. Years ago, when he was still but a boy at Nantes, he'd promised himself that none should suffer as he and his mother had over his own illegitimate birth. Nay, when he took Lea, it would be honorably and the marriage would be witnessed first.

For Eleanor, the confusion was almost unbearable. All those years, her savior, her champion, her one link with the rest of the world, had deceived her. He'd given her a pride in her blood that had been false—she was Gilbert's daughter and not Roger's sister. Aye— all those times that his exploits on the battlefield and his rise in fortune had brought her status among the nuns, she had not really shared in his glory after all, for they were not of the same blood. She'd loved him so. Her thoughts turned toward those moments just past in the spring and in the grass, and her face flushed in humiliation. The way he'd made her feel . . . the places he'd touched—

"Ah, Lea," he broke into her thoughts and put a reassuring arm about her shoulder, " 'tis all right. 'Twill all come about—you'll see."

"Roger, what happens to us now?" she choked out, unable to bear her loss.

"Nothing has changed—we still have to escape Belesme."

"But the Condes . . . your other lands—I have no right—"

"They mean nothing to me without you, Lea," he cut in soberly. "It isn't just Robert, either. Once I tried to convince myself that I could bear it if you went to

Henry, but I couldn't. When I saw you in his arms at
Nantes, I wanted to kill him. For me, it is you or
none—but I am willing to wait."

"And Marie—"

" 'Twas only you who spoke of Marie," he reminded
her. "I spoke only of you." He dropped his arm and
searched in the packs, pulling out a clean undershift
and a faded green gown. "Here—you can go behind
the wall and put these on. When you are done, I'll
help you work your hair."

She took the clothing and walked to where he'd
pointed. Out of his sight, she slowly took off the wet
shift and looked down at her body as though seeing it
for the first time. Her fingertips traced the nipples of
her breasts while she remembered the feel of his mouth.
Her whole body tensed and tautened at the memory of
his kisses, his touch, his body against hers. He was
right—she'd wanted him like she'd never wanted anything before. She closed her eyes and tried to imagine
what it wouldn've been like if he had not come to his
senses and stopped. She could still see how he looked
standing there, his body ready, and that gave her pause
as she wondered if he would have hurt her. She'd
heard the serving wenches talking when she was a
child at Nantes, and some claimed to loathe it when
they were taken to bed by the men of the castle. But
she'd wanted it to happen. If only she were not Mary
de Clare's daughter and accursed.

"Lea, are you dressed?"

Roger came around the corner and stopped, staring
for a moment and then dropping his eyes. "Your
pardon, Lea, but you'd been here long enough that I
thought . . ." His voice trailed off.

"I was looking at myself, Roger." Her face flamed
even as she admitted it. "I wanted to see what it was
that made you and Belesme look at me like that."

He kept his eyes on the ground and drew in his
breath sharply. "Jesu, Lea!"

"What is it?"

"I don't know, Lea. I've looked at many women's
bodies, and all I can tell you is that when I look on

you, naked or clothed, it is different." He turned his
back and took another deep breath for control. "Jesu,
why do you do this to me? Do you want to punish me
for what I would have?"

"No"—she shook her head—"but I would know."
She hastily picked up her clean shift and pulled it over
her head. Coming up behind him, she laid a timid
hand on his shoulder, burning him. "I did not mean to
anger you."

He jerked away from her touch. "I am not angry,
Lea, but I am just a man, after all, and not a saint."

"Roger—" Her pulse raced and her body felt the
nearness of his. "If . . . if it is what you truly want—if
it means so much to you . . ." She took a deep breath
and moved closer. "I mean . . ." Her voice dropped
to a near-whisper as she touched him again. "If you
want, I will lie with you."

In spite of the lowness of her voice, every word
burned into his consciousness. He spun around to face
her. She bit her lip nervously and waited, watching
him with enormous dark eyes. "Aye"—she nodded
under his questioning gaze.

It was a long time before he could bring himself to
answer her. "Nay," he answered finally, " 'tis not the
time."

"Roger—"

"Lea, why do you think I stopped out there? I want
to wed with you in Holy Church with witnesses so
none can say 'tisn't so. I was a fool out there. What if
you were to conceive and something happened to me?
'Twould be said you were my leman and the child a
bastard—I could not bear that. I saw what happened
to my mother and to me. Nay, Lea, if you will but
pledge to wed with me, I can wait."

She shook her head. "I cannot."

"Jesu, Lea, you can lie with me but not wed with
me? God's teeth, girl! 'Tis nonsense!"

"But out there—"

"Aye, and 'twas the heat of my body that spoke.
You cannot think I would rather have you for a leman
than a wife, surely."

"Nay, but I cannot wed with anyone," she persisted stubbornly.

"Jesu!" He threw up his hands in disgust. "Here—raise your arms," he ordered, "and get into this." he picked up the green gown and pulled it over her shoulders with unusual roughness. "I'll get the comb."

By the time he returned, his anger had abated. She sat obediently on the remains of an upended bench and let him work through the mass of tangles. His fingers painstakingly separated the strands and worked out the matted clumps before he even tried to drag the comb through it. It was a slow process, but he was patient and gentle—more so than most tiring women—and the tangles finally yielded to his efforts. "You hair is beautiful, Lea," he told her, "but it makes me glad I wear mine short. 'Tis a wonder that you have not cried out from the pain."

"I am used to it."

"Do you want one braid or two?"

"I don't care, but you don't have to do that."

"One's easier," he decided for her as he plaited the thick hair into a single braid that hung down her back almost to her waist. Stepping back to admire his handiwork, he nodded. "Aye, 'twill do until we get to Walter's."

"Walter's?"

"Aye, 'tis what we should have done in the first place. Walter is lord of the port of Dieppe, and he is fond of you, and he hates Robert of Belesme."

"He is a de Clare, Lea, and your kinsman. His family is powerful both here and in England. He would dare."

"We still go to England then?"

"Aye." he raised a surprised eyebrow. "I am still sworn to you—did you think I meant to leave you with Walter? Nay, we go as planned."

"But if I am not your sister—"

"You still have to escape Belesme, Lea. Once you are safe, we can decide what to do." He looked up to the sky and frowned. "The sun is lowering already, and I've not got our supper. You turn the clothes over and fill the skins while I rob the poacher's traps."

"Shall I make another fire?"

"Aye—we'll try for a stew this time. God knows I shall be tired of rabbit any way 'tis prepared before we reach Walter's." He undid the dagger that he wore at his belt and proffered it hilt-first. "Remember this? Henry gave it to me that day at Nantes. You take it for protection, and if you see or hear anything untoward, hide yourself in the trees until I get back."

"Can I not come with you?" she asked as she noted the lowering sun.

"Nay. 'Tis possible I might meet friend poacher and he might not welcome the theft of his dinner." He flashed a brief smile and shook his head. "I'd not want to have to kill a man in front of you."

She watched him disappear softly into the woods and waited. She had plenty of time before he returned in which to do as he'd asked, so she sat on a broken piece of wall and tried to collect her tumbled and troubled thoughts into some semblance of order and good sense. At first, her mind seemed incapable of thinking, echoing only his words: "I share no blood of yours!" and "Aye, you are not my sister . . . I am not your brother," over and over again.

To compensate for the overwhelming sense of loss she felt, she tried to concentrate on what she must've meant to him for him to give up all he owned in a daring scheme to save her from Belesme. Aye, she reminded herself, and even before that, he'd been the single constant thing in her life. She recollected the letters, the visits, the constancy over the years, and marveled at his steadiness of purpose. And what they'd been to each other, she shook her head in remembrance, blushing even now for the things she'd been able to talk of with him. Roger was never offended nor was he shocked by any of her innermost thoughts. She sighed regretfully with the realization that never again would she be able to speak to him of love and life, of men and women—and all because they'd lived a lie once and now knew the truth.

The truth. Glynis must have told Roger that very day that William the Conqueror had intervened against Robert of Belesme. Looking back, she could see now just how subtle the change had been, and she knew for certain he'd known when he promised to be her champion. He'd warned her then about what men would have of her, and yet, years later, it was what he would have of her also.

She drew her legs up on the broken wall and hugged her knees to her. Well, she sighed sadly to herself, one thing was certain—they could not go back to the way there were no matter what he'd said. She'd seen the way he looked at her and she'd felt his body against hers, and she would never forget the passion he'd aroused in her. Nay, things would never be the same.

It would be so easy to love him as he wanted. She chewed reflectively on a thumbnail and let her mind wander to imagine really lying with him. Aye, he loved her now and life would be sweet—for a time. So it had been with her parents. By all accounts, Gilbert had been besotted of Mary de Clare when she came to him, and yet there was little but dislike—aye, hate even—between them when she died. And Eleanor had been the start of it by reason of her birth. Nay, it would be better to strive to maintain what she and Roger had once had rather than to wed with him and chance letting love turn to hatred.

A hunting horn sounded in the distance, drawing her back to reality. She held her breath and waited for it again. Her hand instinctively sought Roger's dagger and closed over it, while her eyes turned toward the woods where she would seek refuge if any came closer. The horn sounded again and, from the sound of it, it came from yet further away. She relaxed and turned her attention toward the tasks Roger had assigned her.

12

Eleanor and Roger sat within the great tapestried hall of Walter de Clare's manor house and waited. It was a luxuriously appointed room in a building that sat in the middle of what was once an extensive courtyard surrounded by high, towered walls. Walter, a shipping merchant as well as a lord, had taken much of what he'd seen of English manors and constructed one of his own within the protection of his fortress. The place was furnished with things collected in his travels to Italy, Spain, Portugal, the emperor's court at Byzantium, and the Holy Land itself.

"I tell you I know of no Richard of Clemence!" Walter's voice carried from somewhere outside.

"My lord, he desires speech with you," his steward urged, "and I could not turn them away, for his lady is near her time."

"A landless knight, you say! God's teeth, but what am I supposed to do with them? I've enough levy to satisfy mine obligations."

"My lord, he said if you were unconvinced, I was to give you this."

"Jesu! Mother of God!"

Roger smiled at Walter's reaction to Henry's ring. Henry had been right—it could well gain him an audience where his appearance could not. He could hear footsteps now in the corridor outside the hall. Eleanor shrank against him, uncertain of her welcome as a runaway from parent, liege, and bridegroom. Roger clasped her hand tightly and waited for the door to burst open.

"I will speak to them alone," Walter ordered from

the entrance as he dismissed his steward. He stepped in and banged the door shut behind him. When he first saw Roger and Eleanor, he regretted his decision to talk to the visitors, for, by appearances, he faced naught but a poor knight and a distressed lady. He frowned and stepped closer. Roger stood and pulled Eleanor up with him.

"Mother of God! It *is* you! Can you not know they comb all of Normandy looking for you?" Any uncertainty they'd had of his welcome was dispelled as he enveloped Eleanor in a tight hug and then turned to bestow the kiss of peace on both of Roger's cheeks. "Sweet Mary, but I've worried about you since I heard!" He stepped back and patted Eleanor's padded abdomen, laughing. "Ho! And what's this, fair cousin?"

"Roger thought none would look for a plain knight and a fat lady," she laughed. "And he was right. We passed under the very noses of Belesme's men, and not as far as from here to your gate from Belesme himself."

"Where were you? Or should I ask where you have been this past week or more?"

"Three days on the road to Saint Valéry, two days in the woods near there, and three days here."

"Saint Valéry! Jesu, but you were fortunate. Belesme stopped on his way there and demanded quartering for the night. He came to tell me my ships would not sail until you were found."

"Aye, he's closed the port."

"And everywhere else in Normandy, Roger." Walter rubbed his chin and frowned thoughtfully. "You are safe enough here, of course, though you'll have to remain this Richard of Clemence. I will, however, get you a bed on the pretense of your lady's imminent confinement."

Eleanor looked at Roger in dismay and he reddened even as he nodded agreement, "Aye, 'twould be remarked if we were separated in a strange place."

"And she cannot sleep with the women without betraying her disguise," Walter mused aloud. " 'Twill have to be a cut-out chamber in the old castle walls if it is to go unremarked. You can spread your pallet there."

"Helene?" Eleanor could not but venture a question about Walter's wife, a highborn lady with connections to Curthose himself.

"I'll tell her nothing while you are here—you are the Lady Joan and nothing more. If she discovers the truth after you have gone, what can she do? Tell Curthose and have his wrath come down on her husband?" Walter's face broke into a broad grin. "Nay, she likes the life I give her here—'twould be uncomfortable if I were taken away." He turned back to Roger, asking, "And what are your plans now? You may stay here, and well you know it, but 'twill not do to stay overlong. I am Eleanor's kinsman and I expect Belesme to come back."

'Aye—we are for England."

"With the ports closed? Jesu, but the man ruins me, and so I told him when he was here."

"You control Dieppe, Walter. Can you not sail from there?"

"Not without letting Belesme inspect my cargo, Roger. When I told him I would sail whether or no, he gave me that strange smile of his and said, "Aye, but my agents will check your shipping bill against your cargo."

"Then we will have to be shipped goods."

"I am mostly a cloth merchant, Roger."

"How does it go?" Eleanor asked. "I mean—is it crated, in trunks, or baled?"

"All ways, I suppose, but mostly just baled." Walter eyed her suspiciously and waited.

"Well, why could Roger and I not be a trunk of cloth?"

"And Belesme will have every one of them opened when he hears I would sail, cousin. Nay, 'tis too risky for you and for me."

"Walter, how much sits on the wharves that will be bound for England? Enough to fill a ship?"

Walter rubbed his chin again while he thought. "More

than that—there's enough to stock six or eight merchant ships ready. Why do you ask?"

"Lea's right. Let us be trunks of cloth and send so much that they will tire of opening them. And do it boldly—apply openly to both Curthose and Belesme for a permit to leave. Aye, invite them to inspect your cargo, saying you must sail or be ruined by the losses you suffer."

"Much Robert of Belesme would care about that," Walter snorted. "An admission like that would guarantee that he would stop us."

"Nay, your lady is of Curthose's blood on the Flemish side, is she not? Can she write? Have her apply to Curthose by messenger."

"What if you are taken?"

Eleanor sucked in her breath as Walter asked the question she dreaded most. Roger shook his head. "Nay, Lea it will not happen. But if you are afraid, we can get word to Henry. He travels to England often enough that I might be able to persuade him to sail with us."

"Aye." Walter warmed to the plan. "One of you could go in his trunks—not even Robert of Belesme would dare to open them without permission."

"Roger, we cannot ask it. Prince Henry has done so much already that he risks Curthose's anger. He has no land and is dependent on his brothers."

"He has the Condes now," Roger reminded her. "And he would do it to see you safe, Lea."

"He still thinks he loves her?" Walter asked, fascinated. "I'd supposed he'd forgotten her long ago, judging by how well he's consoled himself."

" 'Love' is a strong word for what Henry feels," Roger answered, "but he still cares for her."

Walter's lips pursed into a low whistle. "So it *was* true. Jesu, sweet cousin, have a care around him then. I've no desire to see a kinswoman of mine made a royal mistress."

"Nay, he is not like that," Eleanor defended.

"Humph," Walter snorted derisively. "You have

been too long in a convent, cousin. Henry usually takes what he wants if he wants it badly enough."

"Henry is Rufus' heir, and it is not likely Rufus will wed,' Roger pointed out. "If Henry is to sit England's throne, he will have need of men like you and me. He would not risk our support even to have Lea in his bed. If naught else can be said of him. Henry is a practical man."

"Aye. Write to him, then, and I will send it by my rider today with orders it is for his hands only." Walter held up the prince's ring to the light. "And if we send this, he is bound to know it comes from you."

"Aye. 'Tis better if you write, and only in the vaguest terms, in case it falls into Belesme's hands. The ring will be enough to bring Henry."

"Walter," Eleanor asked suddenly, "could I have a bath and a bed? I am tired and dirty and I've not slept much these two days past."

Both men looked at her and frowned. Her disguise would be difficult enough to maintain in a busy household without exposing her to the scrutiny of servants. Besides, as wife to an itinerant knight, she would be accorded no such privileges. But as Walter looked on her tired face with its hollows and shadows, he relented. "Aye," he answered finally, "but you will have to bathe yourself. I will tell Helene it is a courtesy because of your condition."

"Thank you, Walter."

De Clare went to the door and called out to a passing servant, "Ask my lady to come down—we have visitors."

Eleanor luxuriated alone in her bath, soaping herself and rinsing again and again with pitchers of fresh warm water. The door was closed and the privacy was welcome. The room itself was larger than she'd expected and better appointed, but then, her cousin was a wealthy lord. She had to smile at Helene's condescending way of bringing her up and carefully explaining that these used to be the family's quarters before the new house was built in the courtyard. Obviously, Walter's wife took much pride in her husband's wealth.

She leaned her head back and thought of how much had changed in her life since Robert of Belesme had come to her at Fontainebleau—of Fuld Nevers, of Rouen, of Henry, and of Roger. Jesu, what a mess other people had made of her life while she moved through it. She stretched her neck back and yawned, wondering what else would come her way before all was done. It was getting harder to think rationally.

Nearly an hour later, Roger tapped gently at the door, but she did not hear him, as she'd slipped into sleep. He tried again and received no answer. Finally he lifted the iron handle and pulled. At first glance, the room was empty when the heavy door swung inward to reveal the silk-hung bed, woven floor mats, cushioned benches, a table, and finally a bathtub that had been dragged into the corner. There was no sign of Eleanor. Alarmed, he entered the chamber and saw her discarded clothing on a bench. Turning to pull back the bed hangings, he was surprised to find the bed empty also. Then he saw her.

Her head was tilted back against the rim of the oaken tub, her profile outlined perfectly in shadows against the wall. Her lips were parted slightly as she breathed and her hair cascaded in unbound ripples to the floor. He ought to shout at her to wake her up, he knew, but he was inexorably drawn to stand over the tub. He could not help staring at her with that old familiar hunger. The memory of the feel of her beneath him flooded over him for the thousandth time since it had happened, as he allowed his gaze to follow the smooth line of her neck down to her shoulders and below to the swell of her perfect breasts. Her knees were drawn up to accommodate her body in the confines of the tub. He reached down and dipped his fingers in the cool water. A dull soap film sat like oil over the top of it. Sweet Mary, but she must have been tired to have gone to sleep like that.

Reluctantly he bent to shake her gently, but she only groaned and shifted slightly. He swallowed con-

vulsively to combat the awful yearning that tightened
his loins and quickened his heart.

"Lea! Lea!" He shook her again more insistently
and watched her rouse unwillingly. A folded sheet of
linen lay beside the tub. He picked it up and shook it
out. "Come on, Lea, you've soaked yourself so long
you are wrinkled like an old woman. Come on," he
coaxed, "stand up and I'll cover you."

She yawned wide and murmured sleepily, "Leave
me be—I am too tired." Her eyes were still closed.

"Nay, you'll sleep better in bed. Here . . ." He
bent over and slid his hands under her arms, lifting her
to a standing position. Water showered off her and
spotted his tunic. She lurched and weaved before she
could get her balance. "Jesu, Lea, but I've had more
help from a drunken soldier than you give me. Come
on—step over the side."

She still fought being wakened, but she managed to
follow his guide and stepped out. Her legs were cramped
from being folded in the tub and threatened not to
support her. She swayed slightly while he slipped the
linen around her. "Mother of God," she muttered,
"but all of me aches."

"Aye, 'twas a long ride, Lea, but we are at Walter's
—remember?"

She yawned and stretched, leaning against him for
support. "Ummmm . . . I remember. Walter's," she
repeated.

Not trusting himself to rub her dry, he blotted the
linen quickly and told her, " 'Tis nigh to supper—you've
got to get dressed."

"I am too tired to eat—I cannot."

"Aye, love—let me get you to bed. I'll bring you
something up later when I come back." He slipped an
arm beneath hers and walked her across the room.
The linen fell away as he half-bent to pick up the clean
undershift she'd laid out. His eyes traveled upward
from the flat plane of her white belly to the crevice
between her breasts. "Sweet Mary, Lea, do not do
this to me," he groaned, "for I cannot stand it. Oh,
God . . ." He pulled her against him, savoring the feel

of her bare skin as his hands roamed freely over her
bare hips. She was soft and pliant in his arms. For an
instant she snuggled closer, laying her head against his
shoulder, and his whole body blazed with rekindled
passion.

"Sir Richard! Lady Joan!"

He could hear a woman's voice calling from the
tower stairs. Muttering a soft curse under his breath,
he pushed Eleanor away and hung the now-wrinkled
undershift over her head. "Aye," he called back, "Joan
is abed!" Working the garment down over her damp
body, he half-lifted her and guided her toward the
bed, thrusting her between the curtains. Just as Walter's wife reached the doorway, he saw Eleanor's padding lying in full view. He lunged for it and kicked it
beneath the bed.

"Ah, Sir Richard—I came to look to your lady"
—Lady Helene smiled—"for Walter tells me she nears
her time."

"Aye, but she is very tired and could not stay awake."

"Poor child," Helene sympathized. "Walter tells me
she is very young—is it her first?"

"Aye."

"I came to tell her that if her time comes whilst she
is here, we have a woman skilled in simples." Helene
de Clare moved closer and extended a bundle she
carried in her arms. "Here—when she wakes, give
her these." Roger took the pile of folded cloths curiously. "Swaddling clothes," she explained.

"Our thanks, my lady—'tis very kind of you."

As soon as she left, he turned back to Eleanor. She
had half-rolled into the feather mattress and cradled
her head on a white arm. Her chest rose and fell
rhythmically in sleep.

"Clemence!" Walter called from the high table to
where Roger sat. "You are Breton, are you not? Aye—
come to my chamber and tell me of how Count Alan
does."

"Aye, my lord," Roger managed respectfully. He
was tired himself now, but still welcomed more time

and more wine before he sought his bed. He'd been surprised when Walter had put him and Eleanor in the same chamber, but then realized that there was little else that could be done without explanation. A few hours of drinking with Walter might possibly ease the tension of sharing a room again with her.

Strange how the revelation of his birth and his desire for her had changed things between them. He could sense her inner turmoil when he watched her, and he knew part of her regretted the loss of a brother while another part was intrigued with him as a man. It would take time, but he was confident now that he could win her if he had the patience. He'd promised to go back to what they'd always been, but both knew it for a false promise. He'd seen her body, felt her response to his, and knew her capable of loving him with a passion that could match his own. If he could but wait a few more weeks, she would be his.

"Richard." He felt Walter's hand on his shoulder and realized that he'd not been paying attention to his host. He nodded and rose to follow de Clare to his chamber.

"All's done as you asked," Walter told him after the door was closed. "Helene has begged Curthose to save me from financial disaster, I have applied for a permit to leave my own port, and I have written to Henry. Now all we can do is wait." He took a seat at a low table and motioned Roger to sit while he poured two cups of sweet Aquitaine wine. "My cousin—how does she fare?"

"She's tired but well enough, I think."

"Have you thought what you are going to do with her when you reach England? 'Twould be better to take her back to Fontainebleau."

"She was miserable there, Walter. I would not do that to her again."

"But what happens in England? Do you want to be tied to your sister for the rest of your life? Belesme will come for you, and well you know it."

"'Tis my intent to find her a husband."

Walter raised a skeptical eyebrow. "At Rufus' court?

Without Gilbert's blessing? Nay—who's to have her
when 'tis known Belesme wants her?" He leaned forward and stared at Roger. "You can tell me—would
Prince Henry still wed with her?"

"Mayhap he would."

"Jesu!" Walter breathed. "She could be Queen of
England."

"Nay, I think in the end he will realize that the risks
are too great. He'd have to stand against Belesme to
take her, and she cannot bring him anything now.
Besides, he truly likes her—he knows she could not be
happy surrounded by his bastards. Constancy is not in
him, Walter."

"I know. 'Tis said he's got FitzAlan's daughter with
child this time."

"So I have heard."

"We wander," Walter reminded him as he poured
yet two more cups of wine. "The question is, what
happens to my cousin?"

"She will marry."

"But whom?" Walter persisted. "One of Rufus' courtiers? Most of them fawn on *him*."

"I am thinking of taking her to Harlowe."

"De Brione's keep? To what end, Roger?" Walter
fixed him with a slightly befuddled gaze. "You've never
been much out of Normandy, have you? I did not
know you knew the man."

"I've been to England before, but only to London
with Henry."

"Harlowe's old—too old to take a young wife,
anyway."

"Do you know him?"

"Aye, we deal together sometimes. He's rich and
powerful—he has the wardship of several ports. He's
kind enough, I suppose, but hardly a man I'd apply to
for protection of a girl. He's a widower and, by all
accounts, he's not interested in another wife."

"My mother's family is from there."

"Oh. Aye—I see—you have hopes of help from
them." Walter rested his chin in his palm and studied

the dregs of his wine. "Have you thought that Saxons are not strong in their own land?"

"Leave it to me. If you can but get us across to England, I can take care of Lea."

"You know, Roger, one would think you and my cousin shared the womb before you were born, the way you stay together." Walter drained his cup and leaned back. "Aye, I can remember visiting Nantes when she could barely trip behind you in the courtyard. Is it always to be like that?"

"Always." Roger smiled.

"A pity you two are related by blood," Walter mused aloud, "for you have the strength to hold her. Aye, she could do worse."

"You forget I am bastard-born."

"So was the Conqueror. You have done well for yourself with the Condes and a few other rewards from Old William's family. Men look up to you, Roger FitzGilbert."

Roger emptied the contents of his cup and rose unsteadily. "We are drunk, you and I, Walter, and we talk nonsense. Let us seek our beds."

"Well, we've naught to do until we get answers, and you are too closemouthed even when drunk to tell me your plans." Walter lurched to his feet and clapped Roger on the shoulder. "I meant what I said—I should not be ashamed to be related to you."

The rushlights that lit the tower stairs sputtered and smoked as Roger made his way carefully up the narrow, winding steps. No one was about, since even the servants had relocated once Walter and his family had moved to his manor house. Carrying bread, cheese, and a skin of Walter's best wine in his arms, he had to push the handle with his elbow and kick the door open with his foot.

The room was dark except for a sliver of light that followed him through the door. He set down the food and stepped back to the top step to loose a light from its ring. Using it to ignite a branch of candles on an iron stand, he then threw the rush torch into an empty brazier, where it popped and crackled in the grate. Eleanor still slept undisturbed, her head cradled the same as when he'd left her. Her hair lay dark against a silk pillow. Jesu, but she was beautiful!

He unrolled his pallet and spread it near the door before moving to a bench to remove his boots. Apparently the light disturbed her because he could hear her change positions. In spite of the silence in the room, he was intensely aware of her presence, and he wondered if there were enough wine in the world to make him oblivious of her. He untied his chausses and let them drop to the garters that held them before he bent to the task of unwrapping the finely stamped leather bands. He stood to pull off his long tunic and his shirt and laid them aside on a bench. It was hot and he was tempted to sleep as he was used to, without clothing, but the thought that she might get up stopped him. Instead, he shrugged into a clean, dry shirt from his pack. It came to mid-thigh and made him feel ridiculous, but he wore it as proof of his good intentions.

"Roger?" Eleanor sat up sleepily and peered across the dimly lit room. "Is that you?"

"And just how many men come creeping to your chamber at night, Lady Eleanor?" he asked with mock severity.

"None—and you should not either."

"Are you afraid of me now? Jesu, Lea, but we've shared pallets in inns and in the woods. Look, I have already laid my pallet over here."

" 'Tis not that—'Tis just . . . just if it became known we are not of the same blood, 'twill be said I am your harlot. Aye—Walter would force you to wed with me."

"Then let us shout it from the tower—the Demoiselle and FitzGilbert are not of the same blood!"

"Shhhhhh—Roger, are you more than a little drunk?"

"More than a little—aye, you could say that."

"Do not jest with me!" She flung back the covers and slid her bare feet to the floor.

"Lea . . ." He caught her shoulders and forced her to face him. "I am not jesting with you. Walter put us here because he hides us as Sir Richard and his lady. We cannot risk discovery now."

"I cannot share a chamber with you!"

"God's teeth!" He gave her a disgusted shake. "Two days ago you stood naked in a church and offered to lie with me, Eleanor of Nantes. Jesu, woman! You give me no peace!"

"Roger, *Henry* comes—what is he to think?"

"Henry—Henry comes," he mimicked. "Henry will pay no attention, I swear, but if you want, I can confess the whole to Walter and ask him to witness a marriage between us."

"Nay!" She seemed to recoil in alarm. "Roger, I cannot wed with you! Nay—nor with anyone else! I am accursed, brother. You were there—you saw it."

"What in Mary's name do you speak of, Lea? Mayhap you should go back to sleep and wake again."

"I don't know," she evaded miserably. "Roger, I know not what ails me. I am sorry for being so cross." She moved to the window and peered out into the starless night. A cool breeze now blew in, bearing the scent of fresh rain. Her thin shift billowed out from her body.

"I know what ails you, little one," he spoke softly from behind her. "And I would help you."

"Men! 'Tis as Adela says—you have the same answer to a woman's problems."

He could see the faint outline of her body through the thin material and his resolve to be noble was fast deserting him. His fingers touched the back of her shoulders, sending a rush of shivers down her spine. "I would not listen to Adela, love," he whispered as he dropped a light kiss on her neck. She jerked away as though burned, and spun to face him.

"Don't do that!"

"Why?"

"I don't know!"

"Lea, you make it hard on a man when your body tells him his touch sets you on fire and your mouth tells him to stay away." He moved closer and reached for her. "You cannot forget, can you?"

She could not meet his eyes and looked away. "Aye, I've thought of little else since then." His hands touched the side of her face, his thumbs pressed into her cheekbones as he deliberately tilted her head back and lowered his mouth to hers. She closed her eyes. "Please . . ." It was little more than a whisper.

"Shhhhhhhh."

Fire seemed to course through her veins and warm every part of her body when their lips touched. Arms that used to hold and soothe now inflamed with their strength. A low moan rose in her throat as he pressed against her. Abruptly he released her and stood staring with eyes that glittered in the moonlight. She caught at his arms for support and exhaled to master her emotions.

"Wed with me, Lea."

"I cannot—you know not what you ask!"

" 'Tis the last time I ask." He dropped his hands and pulled away from her. "I thought you loved me."

"I do—I always have, Roger—but not like that!" She watched him reach for and draw on his discarded chausses. "Where are you going?"

"To sleep with the other poor knights in the common room."

"Roger, please do not be so angry with me! Please do not leave me!" Her face crumpled and her hands clenched as she lost control. "Please—you are all I have—do not leave me!" Sobs began to rack her body and words came pouring out in gasps. "I am afraid! Can you not understand? What if we came to hate each other one day? My father hated my mother and would have put her away! Mayhap he poisoned her! Roger, what if I cannot bear sons for you? What if I cannot bear at all?"

"Lea, I am no Gilbert, and I resent your lack of faith in what I feel for you." He sat to pull on his boots. "I have reached the point where I cannot be hugged one minute and pushed away the next."

"And I have not done so! Brother—Roger—it has been but three days! Can you not let me get used to the idea that we are not related before you ask for more?"

"Aye," he sighed. "I have waited years, but now I push too fast. I am sorry, Lea." He stood and pointed to a table near the bed. "I brought you food and wine—drink some to calm yourself. I shall be back in the morning." He managed a wry smile. "I can give it out that we have quarreled as most couples are wont to do."

"Nay—listen to me! Roger, I'd give you what you ask if I thought I could make you happy!"

"I am easy to make happy." He stooped to roll up his pallet.

"Wait!" She caught up to him and clutched his arm. "You do not understand! I've loved you all my life!"

"I am not going far, Eleanor—I'll be back early." He picked up the bedroll and pushed past her for the stairs. Behind him, he could hear her crying so hard that she could not catch her breath now. By the time he cleared the first landing, the sobs were coming in great whoops that tore at him. He stopped and sat to clear his head.

It was not fair, what he'd done, and well he knew it. In wanting her, in pressing her, he stood to lose what he wanted most. Lying with her was important, but so was having her safe. What if she refused to go to England now? She needed time to accept him as a lover. Cursing himself for a fool, he heaved himself up and made his way back.

Henry sent no messenger, choosing instead to arrive in person at Walter de Clare's fortress outside Dieppe. A string of red-draped packhorses followed him through the gates and drew up in Walter's courtyard. Eleanor jumped to the window with unusual agility and then turned back guiltily to where Helene sat cradling her second daughter. If Helene had seen anything amiss, she gave no sign.

"Lady, Prince Henry comes!" Eleanor announced excitedly.

"Walter was expecting him." Helene handed the

babe back to a nurse and smiled at Eleanor. "Would you come down with me, Joan, and greet him for yourself?"

At first, Eleanor had not liked the quiet Helene, but in the week and a half since her arrival, she had found the lady to be rather sweet-tempered and gentle. In fact, Helene had bade Eleanor to attend her, and had given her many of her own clothes she'd worn when carrying her daughters. Walter himself had been up earlier to visit his wife and play with their baby girl. He seemed to have a real affection for Helene in spite of the fact she'd borne him no sons, and he obviously loved his daughters.

Surprisingly, Lady Helene made little or no mention of Lady Joan's apparently imminent lying-in, and treated the girl nearly as an equal. Only at dinner, when seating was determined by rigid custom, was Lady Joan separated from the lady of the castle. And even then, it seemed that the fare at the lower table was little different from that on the dais.

Eleanor followed Helene out into the courtyard and watched the lady make her obeisance to the prince. After he greeted the rest of the assembled officials of Walter's well-run keep, Henry turned to Eleanor and took both her hands in his.

"Ah . . . Lady Joan." Henry smiled and leaned forward to kiss her cheek. She drew back red-faced and managed a hasty curtsy. Henry took in her huge belly and his smile broadened. "It has been some time since last we met, lady, and you've changed much. You are well, I trust?"

"Aye, Your Grace."

"And where's that husband of yours? He served Alan with me at Avranches and I would see him again." He turned around and called out, "Richard! Richard of Clemence!"

"Aye, my lord?" Roger stepped forward diffidently and was immediately embraced and kissed. "Henry, you forget yourself," he hissed under his breath.

"Nay," Henry hissed back. "Your Joan looks over-due, Richard."

"She has some time left, I think."

"Only if she drops twins."

"Nay," Roger laughed. "Have done, Your Grace. Poor Joan must last all the way to Westminster."

"Ah, you cross the sea. 'Tis not without problems at this time."

"Well I know." Roger surveyed the pack animals. "God's teeth, but you would sink the ship! Do you go yourself?"

"Not this time. I am but shipping goods across the Channel." Henry patted a packet that hung from his belt, and added significantly, "I have the papers approving my cargo from my brother."

"Thank you, my lord Henry," Roger managed gratefully under his breath.

"Do not thank me too soon," Henry murmured low for Roger's ears alone, "for I do but send goods from the Condes with you."

"God's teeth! You must have gutted the place."

"Aye, but you may need it." Henry turned back to Walter and asked aloud, "Is all set for the morrow? I would see my goods safe on the water before the wind changes."

"Aye. Well, barring trouble with Count Robert, there should be no problem," Walter answered. "Does Your Grace come as far as Dieppe to see to the loading of your goods?"

"Aye. There are some delicate things I send my brother Rufus, and I would not have them broken carelessly."

"My men will carry them gently and load them carefully," Walter promised.

The men walked off in the direction of Henry's train with Henry in the middle, his arms draped casually over both Roger and Walter. Helene turned to Eleanor with a smile. "It would seem we are not needed, Lady Joan. Would you care to pick herbs with me? I dry fennel for headaches and make a pomade to whiten my skin from some of the other things I grow."

"Herleva was wont to give us fennel at Nantes."

"Herleva?"

"My nurse."

"Oh—aye. I grow pennyroyal, too, and give it to the scullery maids to ensure their courses."

"Does it work?"

"I don't know," Helene admitted freely, "but we are not overrun with bastards here." She stopped to open a gate in the walled garden. "I doubt this can compare to Nantes, Demoiselle, but I have worked to make it meet our needs."

Eleanor stopped in mid-step and realized she'd given herself away by her reference to Herleva and Nantes. She whitened and wondered what she ought to do to retrieve the situation. Helene turned back and laughed. "Do not look so stricken, Eleanor. I have known since the second day you were here. 'Tis not like Walter to take in poor knights."

"But—"

"Nay, you are safe enough here—you are Walter's kinswoman and we will aid you. Besides, I'd not give a dog to Belesme."

"Who else knows?"

"None save Walter and myself, though I am glad Prince Henry comes to distract some of our more curious retainers. 'Tis well you leave on the morrow because Count Robert comes back soon." Helene leaned down and plucked some of her herbs and gathered them in the skirt of her gown. Eleanor moved to a well-trimmed row of rosebushes. Helene looked up and nodded. "Pluck some if you want. We can make rosewater for you to take with you so that you can scent your hair in England. If they did not teach you in Fontainebleau how 'tis done, I can show you."

"I should like to learn."

"Does FitzGilbert favor rosewater? We can make him some also." Helene straightened up and knotted her overskirt to hold her herbs. "You are fortunate to have the Bastard to look after you, Demoiselle."

Eleanor looked at her sharply for a sign of spite and found none. "I suppose I am," she admitted. "Nay—I *know* I am."

"Walter says 'tis a pity you share the same father,

Demoiselle, for he thinks Roger FitzGilbert a good match for you."

"*What?*"

"Aye, he does," Helene confided, "because you are of like minds."

"Not always." Eleanor busied herself with collecting blooms from the bushes. Jesu, was she the only one not mad anymore? she asked herself.

"Come, you have enough for our purposes and we have to get to the task if we are to be done before you have to leave." Helene took some of Eleanor's pick and added them to her skirt. "We are not of a size, Eleanor, but I would not have you go to London in rags. I have spoken to Walter and he is agreed you should have some shifts, and bliauts, overgowns, and girdles that befit your station. So while the rosewater boils, you may try on some things in my chamber."

"I cannot."

"You are Walter's kinswoman, Demoiselle, and he would not see you presented in rags where he has trade. He already gives the Bastard new garments."

"Does Walter sail with us?" Unable to deal directly with the other woman's generosity, Eleanor changed the subject. "I would not have him risk his life for me."

"You are of his blood," Helene answered simply. "Aye, he goes."

"Has . . . has Roger said what he plans in England— or do you know?"

"He told Walter he will find a husband for you so that you never have to return to your father's house."

"Sometimes I feel my life is never in mine own hands," Eleanor sighed.

Helene raised an eyebrow at the younger girl's complaint. "We are women—how can it be otherwise? I wed Walter having seen him only two times, and I am content."

13

Eleanor stood on the deck and watched the shore cliffs loom ahead. The salt breeze whipped tendrils of hair loose from her braids and bathed her face with its coolness. Her new blue gown clung to her in front and flapped about her legs. Walter de Clare stood beside her and pointed out the seaport of Dover, a mere speck in the distance. The fog had lifted and only a few clouds hung over head.

After weeks of hiding and hours spent cramped in a crate of silk, she felt suddenly free. An expanse of ocean, no matter how narrow, stood between her and Robert of Belesme and provided a sense of relief she had not felt since Roger carried her out of Rouen. She had to smile over their final escape—Henry and Walter had supervised the loading of Henry's cargo beneath the noses of Belesme's agents, allowing them to inspect as much as they wanted until the men lost interest in the later crates and left the deck. Then Walter's men had loaded those containing Eleanor and Roger into the hold. It had been hot and miserable for a short time until the lids were pried off and they were released to come up.

They'd sailed without final clearance when word spread on the docks that Belesme himself was coming. Walter's flagship, the *Triumph*, was a swift vessel, and an easy match for the boarding ship that set out to stop her. Walter had only had to stand on his deck and shout across the widening gap that he had clearance from the Duke of Normandy to sail and there was nothing Belesme or his agents could do.

"Art quiet, cousin," Walter chided.

" 'Tis a strange land," she answered.

"Aye, but overrun with Normans now, and not as strange as it once was. William Rufus had a firm hold on the country and there is peace."

"Will I like it?"

"Aye—it is a pretty place with sloping hills and farms beneath castle walls."

"And no Belesme."

"Nay—Belesme owns much land in England, Eleanor, but he is little there."

"Sweet Mary, will I never be rid of him!"

"Let your brother find you a husband to end the matter. I doubt Robert wants a wife who's lain with another in the marriage bed—he's too proud not to want to be the only man with you." Walter spied Roger coming up and hailed him, "Over here! Look at England!"

Roger came and leaned on the polished rail to let the sea spray in his face. The wind ruffled his blond hair, and sea and sky reflected in his blue eyes. There was a new air about him, a sense of freedom and adventure that did not escape Eleanor. She felt a catch in her throat as she watched him. Jesu, she thought, but a man ought not to look like that—it wasn't fair to a mortal woman. She longed to touch the tousled hair and to run her fingers over the muscles of his back. When he was around now, her whole body was aware of him, and she was conscious of a tension that made a return to their old, easy ways impossible. She tore her eyes away and concentrated on the cliffs ahead.

"When do we dock?" she heard Roger ask Walter.

"About another hour if the wind holds. We'll put the landing boats and the tow ropes down before long."

"Well, Lea"—Roger kept his eyes on the sea below while he addressed her—"another few days and we should be at Harlowe. Then you can decide what you want to do."

"Oh, aye—among strangers in a strange land," she answered with unwonted sarcasm, and could have bitten back the words even as she said them. Both men

turned to her. She hung her head and traced the grain
of the wooden rail with a fingertip to avoid their eyes.
"Your pardon—you've risked much to save me and
you deserve better from me."

"The choice is still yours, Lea."

"Well, she'll take a husband, of course," Walter
answered for her. "What else can she do?"

"I can go back to a convent," she reminded him
bitterly.

"You?" Walter eyed her strangely. "Nay, 'twould
be a waste, cousin. You should be gracing some lord's
castle, attending your household."

"And some lord's bed—is that what you mean, Walter?" Eleanor pushed herself away from the railing
and stalked off.

"Jesu! What ails *her*?"

"She thinks she escapes one prison for another, I
suppose. Pay her no heed—she is but restless," Roger
answered.

"Aye. How old is she now, anyway? Nineteen?
Twenty?"

"Nineteen—she turns twenty in September."

"By now, she should have a babe or two to calm her
down. What she needs is a man."

"Tell her that." Roger stared again into the sea and
frowned. "But she is so small—scarcely this wide . . ."
He spread his hand as far as it would stretch across.
"Women die in childbed, you know."

"And men die in battle. Neither thing keeps women
from loving nor men from fighting, does it?" Walter
eyed Roger soberly. "What you need to do is just pick
the man and present him to her without choice. Helene came to me a stranger and we are both well
satisfied. Your problem is that you worry too much
about how she feels."

"Aye, I suppose so." Roger lapsed into silence and
watched the furrowing waves below for a time. Finally
he straightened up and started to leave.

"Where are you going? We are nearly there."

"To count my money. There are things I would buy
her in London before we go to Harlowe."

*   *   *

Instead of presenting himself and Eleanor at Rufus' court as Henry had suggested, Roger took lodging in the city of London for two days and spent his time preparing to face the Earl of Harlowe. He found a tailor willing to work day and night to make two suits of clothing for himself and two new dresses for Eleanor. It would not do, he reasoned, to show up at Richard de Brione's gate like pensioners asking for succor.

The day they left London, Roger made a stop at a goldsmith's and purchased a gold filigree hair case and girdle and a silver fillet for Eleanor and tucked them away in his pack bags. He would either use them as marriage gifts or would give them to her on her birth anniversary, depending on which occasion came first. Eleanor had been as wide-eyed as a child in London, and it had pleased him to take her by barge down the Thames past the White Tower, to the open markets where all sorts of goods were hawked, and through the narrow streets. They prayed at the Confessor's tomb in Westminster and marveled at his church. It had been a pleasant time for both of them, a time much like those they'd shared before his revelation. London had been a sweet lull from a tense adventure.

They rode across England as themselves: Roger, called FitzGilbert, and Eleanor, daughter to the Count of Nantes. They broke their journey at priories along the way, staying in separate chambers and maintaining the strictest propriety. He'd meant what he'd said at Walter's—he wanted her but he would not ask her again. By day, he laughed, teased, and listened as he had done most of her life, but by night, he went his separate way.

On 3 August, 1092, they drew up beneath the shadow of Harlowe. It was an imposing fortress that loomed huge and forbidding, on an island surrounded by a lake. It was a military masterpiece, nearly inaccessible from the outside, that dominated the countryside around it. Commissioned by the Conqueror as a symbol of Norman authority in a conquered land, Harlowe stood guard over the convergence of roads linking Wales to England. To the west lay the lands of the marcher lords; to the east lay Stamford and Belvoir.

Eleanor looked upward to the high ramparts of the curtain wall and across to the corner towers that crowded water's edge. "Sweet Mary, Roger—this is where you would bring me?"

He followed her line of vision and was nearly as awestruck as she. "Aye," he managed. " 'Tis large, isn't it?"

"Large? Nay—'tis bigger than Curthose's palace at Rouen." She scanned the fortress ahead and shook her head. "Roger, are you certain we will be welcomed?"

"We shall see." He spurred his horse to the floating bridge and urged the unwilling animal across. "Follow me, Lea," he called back from the security of solid ground.

Above him, a man in the gatehouse shouted down, "By Earl Richard's authority, I ask your business here!"

Roger shaded his eyes to look up and answer, "Roger, Lord of the Condes, come to see the earl!"

"He is away!"

"We seek beds!" Roger gestured to Eleanor, who still crossed the unsteady bridge.

The face in the window above drew back. Slowly the huge iron gate creaked upward as the cogs turned the chains that held it. It stopped, suspended high enough to allow a horse and rider to pass beneath its spiked bars. Eleanor caught up and together they entered through the narrow gateway into the open area beyond. A second wall some fifty feet inward rose to form the main portion of the stronghold. Another set of corner towers dominated this wall also. Again, a heavy iron gate was lifted and guards stepped forward with shields lifted. In the center of them walked an older man wearing the symbolic key of the seneschal.

Roger nudged his horse forward until he was nearly even with them. "I have business with Earl Richard. We come from Normandy." He reached into the purse at his belt and drew out a piece of parchment bearing Henry's seal. "Here—Prince Henry vouches for me."

The old man stepped closer to study Roger. "You are Norman, then?" he asked.

"My father is Norman, my mother Saxon."

"And this lady is your wife?"

"Nay, she is Eleanor, daughter to Count Gilbert of Nantes. We are but lately arrived in England."

"I see." If the seneschal thought it odd that a well-dressed young lord came unattended with an unwed girl of noble birth, he gave no sign. Instead, his face broke into a welcoming smile as he nodded. "Aye, Lord Roger, you are welcome enough here. The earl is not now in residence due to some small trouble at Belvoir, but I will send word to him that he has visitors."

Eleanor leaned across the pommel of her saddle to address the old man. "Will he return soon?"

"I expect him to ride back as soon as he reads my message."

Surrounded by a hastily assembled group of tiring women, Eleanor surveyed herself in the steel mirror held for her. Bathed and dressed in an undertunic of cream silk with an overgown of purple samite, she had to admit even to herself that she looked unusually fine. One of the women had managed to brush her long hair until it had the sheen of fine silk and it hung free to her waist as a symbol of her maidenhood. A braided gold circlet crossed her forehead and testified to her high birth. Satisfied, she stepped back to give a maid room to fold back her wide sleeves so that the fitted cream silk could be seen on her arms. Taking a deep breath, she nodded and prepared to face supper at Harlowe. "I am ready," she announced.

Because of her rank and the dearth of noble guests, supper was a lonely affair for her. Two pages parted company before her as she walked down the corridors, and the entire company rose when she entered the earl's hall. She felt dozens of pairs of eyes on her while she mounted the two steps to the high table and took her place alone. Had the earl been in residence, he would have at least sat with her. She supposed the formality in a household full of men was necessary for her protection, but it made her feel isolated and alone in a strange place. She scanned the hall openly, looking for Roger, and encountered the admiring gaze of a number of men-at-arms and squires fostering at Harlowe. Even Roger stared from his place at the second table.

"I have never seen her like!" the fellow next to him breathed almost reverently.

"Aye, she is much remarked in Normandy also," Roger answered dryly.

"She is your kinswoman?"

"She is not of my blood, but we were reared together at Nantes like brother and sister.

"Jesu, to be alone with one like that—"

"Nay, you'd not dare touch her—she is daughter to Gilbert and heiress to Nantes."

"And I am Chester's firstborn. Aye, I'd dare. Is she betrothed?"

Roger took in the young man's eager stare and liked it not. "Aye," he answered softly, "she is soon to wed."

"A pity." The fellow reluctantly tore his eyes away from Eleanor to look at Roger. "Aye—I'd have asked my father for one such as she." His eyes narrowed and his brow furrowed as he studied his supper partner. "You are of Earl Richard's blood?"

"Aye."

"Your pardon, my lord—I am Rannulf of Chester."

"And I am Roger, lord of the Condes, by vassalage to Robert Curthose of Normandy."

"I would not speak loudly of Curthose here—we are Rufus' men."

Roger shrugged. " 'Tis of little difference to me, Rannulf of Chester—Curthose did but give me what I'd earned. I served the Old Conqueror first and was with him at Mantes ere he died."

"You look too young for such service," Rannulf pointed out skeptically.

"Aye, but I was taken into his train in eighty-five at

the age of fifteen—I saw my twenty-third birth anniversary last month."

Before the other man could ply him with questions about Old William, Roger's attention was drawn to a late arrival in the hall. A tall man dressed in an embroidered tunic over mail entered and made his way with authority to the high table where Eleanor sat. His brown hair was touched with gray but his step was that of a man still in his prime. Roger stared hard as though to will him to look down.

"Do not rise, Demoiselle," the newcomer addressed a startled Eleanor. "My apologies for the tardiness of my arrival, but I have been long on the road."

Eleanor gave a start, flushed, and then whitened. "Mother of God!" She involuntarily looked toward Roger.

"Aye, I am Richard de Brione," the earl acknowledged as he followed her gaze, "and he does have the look of me." He took a seat next to her and motioned to a servant behind them for service. "Now, Demoiselle"—he turned his attention fully to her—"you may tell me how it is that I am hosting you at Harlowe when we are unacquainted."

"I am Eleanor of Nantes," she began before pausing to take a breath, "and I do not know why I am here. I mean, my lord, that I know why I am in England, but I do not know why Roger brought me to you."

"I know who you are, Lady Eleanor"—the earl nodded—"for Brian wrote of you to me. I suppose if I would know more, I will have to ask the boy."

"He is no boy, my lord—he is three-and-twenty."

"Your pardon." Richard de Brione's mouth twitched at the corners much as Roger's did sometimes. "I am two-and-forty, you see, and he appears young to me." His blue eyes twinkled with humor and she warmed to him.

"*Your* pardon, my lord—I did not intend insolence."

"I did not think it, Demoiselle." He pushed her half-finished trencher toward her. "Here—eat your

supper and let me eat mine. I will speak to this Roger
after I have supped."

She tried to do as he told her, but she was too
stunned to taste the rest of her food. The man next to
her, a belted earl, bore a strong resemblance to Roger.
It did not make sense—she'd never even heard of
Richard de Brione until they fled Normandy. She felt
compelled to defend Roger to him, but she knew not
how to do it.

Earl Richard chewed his food thoughtfully and studied the girl next to him covertly. She was a breathtak-
ingly beautiful child or woman—she was soo small and
fine-boned he could not decide her age—and she
seemed to have some wits about her. Her quick defense of the boy spoke of an affection that disturbed
him. He had no love of Gilbert of Nantes from years
back, but he knew the girl's blood set her far above
most men. She looked up under long black lashes.

"He may be young to you, my lord, but he is not
without means or power in Normandy," she spoke up
finally. "When the Old Conqueror came to Nantes, he
recognized Roger's worth and took him into his own
household, saying bastards should stand together, and
he fostered him when my father failed to find him a
place. Roger served him well against King Philip of
France and was rewarded on the battlefield with his
spurs. William knighted him himself when Roger was
but seventeen, my lord, because my brother showed
his courage. Indeed, Roger was with him at Mantes
when he took his final blow."

"Your brother? Nay, he is not Gilbert's spawn."

"Aye—I grew up thinking him my half-brother, but
he is not. He did not tell me until after we left Rouen."
She raised her eyes to his face and spoke proudly.
"But brother or no, he is the best knight, the truest
champion I could have."

"Brian—my seneschal—wrote that your Roger called
himself Lord of the Condes," Richard prompted.

"Aye, he holds it of Curthose, and other lands as
well. Indeed, I think he has some small fiefs in this

country from the Old Conqueror, and he is Prince Henry's man also."

"A remarkable career for a bastard, I admit." The earl smiled. "And you, Demoiselle—you interest me. Are you betrothed or wed?" he asked bluntly.

"I am neither. I was dedicated to Holy Church at the age of twelve, my lord."

"I see—yet you do not wear the habit of your vocation."

"Nay, I refused to take my vows—I am unsuited."

"Well, you *are* too pretty a child to languish within cloisters, Demoiselle."

"I am nineteen, my lord, and will be twenty next month," she told him quietly. "I am but small and despair of growing taller."

Richard de Brione found it hard not to ask how she came to be unattended in the company of a strong and vigorous young man on a journey that must have lasted weeks. She was plainly no harlot—she fairly shone with innocence—and yet she sat at Harlowe with no escort and certainly without her father's blessing. The tale would bear hearing. Aloud he managed, "It would be a pity if you were taller, Lady Eleanor, for full half your beauty is in your fine bones."

"You really think so, my lord?" She seemed to brighten.

"Aye—big men protect small women."

She leaned forward impulsively and fixed him with her large dark eyes. "You are easy to like, my lord. I find you as kind as the Conqueror."

Richard nearly choked at the comparison. It was probably the first time in his memory anyone had called Old William kind. "You met the Conqueror?"

"Aye." Her eyes shone as she remembered. "He came to see my father for his levies and brought Prince Henry with him. They were to have arranged a betrothal between us, but my mother's death prevented it."

Jesu, he thought, but this girl could have been England's queen one day. Henry was Rufus' heir, and given that harsh man's unwillingness to marry, he would likely be king. Eleanor of Nantes was an extraordinary girl. "Well, Demoiselle, you will have to excuse me—I would meet your Lord of the Condes." He beckoned a servant and pointed to Roger. "Tell him I would speak with him alone in my chamber."

Roger approached the meeting with Earl Richard with mixed emotions. He'd wanted to face the man for seven years just to ask why he'd abandoned Glynis, and yet he had to ask for his aid now. He followed the page to the closed door and reached hesitantly for the handle. The boy bobbed a quick bow and disappeared, leaving him alone in the corridor. Roger took a deep breath and wrenched the door open.

The earl stood over a table studying some papers that bore official seals. He looked up as Roger walked in, and gave him a wry smile. "Well, you do not look in need of my purse, at least."

"Nay, I have money."

"The Demoiselle speaks highly of you—says you are a lord of Normandy with ties to the Conqueror and his family, knighted by William himself before he died."

"Aye."

"Why then to you come to Harlowe?" Richard de Brione was blunt and to the point.

"Because, my father, I would have your aid." Roger spoke quietly, but the words hung in the aftersilence as though they had been shouted.

The earl drew in his breath and nodded. " 'Twould be difficult to deny you, boy. Even Brian wrote that you look much as I once did."

"You are my best hope, else I would not have come."

"Your mother—who gave you life?" Richard's question was almost inaudible as he faced Roger.

"Did you have so many lemans you could not remember? Do you forget the daughter of a Saxon thane?"

"Nay! Name your mother!"

"Glynis, daughter to Aeldrid."

"You lie!"

Roger was unprepared for the vehemence of de Brione's reaction, but he stood his ground. "Aye—I am Glynis' son of your loins, my lord, born in Normandy in July 1069—your bastard, Earl Richard!"

"Nay, you cannot be! 'Tis a hoax! Name your mother!"

"Glynis!"

Richard de Brione was as white as parchment. "Nay, Roger whoever-you-are, my Glynis lies dead in the churchyard—and has these twenty-three years past! How dare you claim to be her son!"

"She said you'd repudiate me as you did her long ago!" Roger shouted back. 'Aye, you let them turn her out knowing she carried your child!"

"I tell you she is dead! I do not know what cruel trick you would play, boy, but you cannot be hers!" The earl was obviously shaken by Roger's assertion of his birth. "You may well be my son, but you are not hers!"

"And I know not who is buried in your churchyard, my lord, but it is not Aeldrid's daughter." Roger lowered his voice and spoke as reasonably as he could. "She spoke to me the day I went into the Conqueror's service, saying I need have no shame over Gilbert of Nantes—that I was not his son." He raised his eyes to the earl, his pain evident. "For fifteen years I had lived in his house, treated little better than a stableboy even though he acknowledged me, and I saw my mother despised as his leman. She did it to provide for me, my lord, and I was not his son! She did not tell me then, else I would have sought you out long ago, my lord, and I would have asked you why you let Gilbert take her. 'Twas not until a few months ago that she would tell me you were my father. And it pained her greatly to know that I would bring Lea here." He let out his breath slowly to control the anger he feltt. "I know not who is in your churchyard," he repeatetd, "but Glynis of Harlowe lives!"

Richard de Brione's hands shook and his jaw worked as he struggled to maintain his own composure. "Brian said you reminded him of Glynis," he half-whispered, "but it cannot be!"

"Dig up the grave, my lord, and you'll not find her there. My mother is in the care of the nuns of Abbeville—she went there when I went into the Conqueror's service. It pained her greatly," he repeated, "to know that I would come to you after what you did to her."

"Nay—ever did I love her! I left her in my family's care, Roger, when I went off to fight the Wake in William's cause with my father. She died ere I returned. There was naught but a grave to show me when I came home to her."

"Nay—you knew they meant to sell her to Gilbert! You were through with her!" Roger accused.

"She is dead, I tell you!"

"Dig up her grave and show me!"

" 'Tis sacrilege to disturb the dead!"

"She is not there!"

Both men were shouting again. Roger stepped back and tried again to regain his temper. He took another deep breath and let it out slowly until he could speak in an even voice. "Very well, my lord, if you fear God's retribution, give me a shovel. I am certain enough that she lives in Abbeville that I will risk my immortal soul to show you."

"So be it then! I'll not wait until morning—you can come down now and show me."

Richard de Brione spun on his heel and stalked out of his chamber into the corridor. Roger followed him silently nearly the length of the wall on one side until he stopped at the south tower. The earl stopped finally and removed a pitch torch that smoked in a ring before opening a narrow door to the outside.

"Here—you carry this and I'll show you the way."

They cut across an open space between tower and wall. Frogs could be heard from the lake beyond and the water lapped against the rock pilings where the island had been raised. Harlowe boasted a separate chapel, a small church that had been incorporated within its walls when the castle had been built, and the building stood butted against the curtain wall. Richard opened a small shed behind the church and rummaged for a shovel, cursing the darkness until he found one. He threw it out onto the grass, muttering, "There—dig!"

"Where?"

"My family lies within the church floor, but they buried her outside because she was Saxon." Richard led him around to the side of the church to what appeared to be some sort of a garden. A stone bench flanked by fragrant rosebushes sat near the center. The earl walked behind it and pointed down. "Here—she lies here."

There was a carved stone, but Roger could not read it in the darkness. Richard brushed the grass away and murmured, "This marks the very spot, Roger. I had it set when I became earl."

Uncertain as to just what he'd find, Roger crossed himself and murmured a prayer before he began to dig. The earth was soft from summer rains and gave way easily beneath the shovel. The earl held the torch off to the side and watched as Roger turned shovelful after shovelful out onto the grass. Roger's shoulders ached as he spaded out a pit some three or four feet deep and several feet wide. Finally he straightened and wiped his forehead with a dirty hand. "Are you sure you had it aright, my lord? This is the place?"

"Aye. I wept here often enough when I came home. My mother led me here and showed me the spaded earth and said, 'She died of the fever shortly after you left, Richard.'"

"Well, as you can see, she is not here. There is no box and no bones. She was sold to Gilbert of Nantes—he was to use her and then to kill her. They could not know that he would not tire of the Saxon girl and would keep her with him. She told me she wanted to die, but she knew she carried me, and then she bore me in Gilbert's stronghold and let everyone think me his."

"She still lives." Richard's voice was hollow. "Mother of God! Why did she not seek me out?"

"She did not want to. You see, she heard at Gilbert's table that you had wed."

"Aye—the girl died in childbed. My father chose a fine Norman girl for me." The earl shook his head bitterly. "And all these years Glynis lived. Jesu! I took another while my wife yet lived."

"Your *wife*?"

"Aye—did she not tell you? Her family wanted no part of my Norman blood and mine wanted no part of her Saxon blood. She was pure when she came to me, Roger, and we did not lie together until we pledged ourselves at the church door. When 'twas done, we faced the wrath of both families." He straightened up and looked off into the darkness. "Had I not gone against the Wake, things would have been very different." Slowly he turned his attention back to Roger. "You are no bastard of mine if you are her son—you are Roger de Brione."

"Jesu!"

"Aye."

"She never told me that."

"Mayhap she did not know—mayhap she thought the pledge was not binding or that I repudiated her." Richard de Brione stood up and looked at Roger awkwardly. "Right now, I feel nothing, Roger—I am unused to the idea of having a son . . . and you are a man grown."

"I had not expected this."

"You must have expected something—you came to me for aid."

"I intended to confront you as your bastard son and ask that you at least help me stand against the wrath of Robert of Belesme—mayhap the wrath of Curthose also."

"Belesme?" Richard gave a start.

"Aye. You see, I have run off with his intended bride."

It was dawn almost and the candles were nearly gutted for the third time before they sought their beds. Roger sat in Earl Richard's chamber and told the

whole story of his and Eleanor's lives at Nantes, of her
misery and his own when they were children, of his
rise in William's household, of her exile to Fontainebleau, of Prince Henry, of Robert of Belesme, of Fuld
Nevers, and of Rouen. He told of their flight from
Rouen and their escape in Walter's ship and their
subsequent journey to Harlowe. The earl listened intently and asked a question occasionally when he found
the tale too tangled to follow. The only thing Roger
could not bring himself to tell of was his intense desire
for Eleanor—that was still too personal, too close to
his soul for discussion.

When he finished, Richard de Brione leaned back
and watched his son beneath lowered lids. For a moment Roger thought he'd slipped into sleep. Finally
the earl sighed heavily and shook his head. "Aye,
there's no help for it—you'll have to marry the
Demoiselle."

"She won't wed with me," Roger told him flatly.
"She would still think of me as brother rather than
husband."

"I'll speak with her if you wish."

"Nay—'tis yet too soon."

"Roger . . ." Richard studied his son. "Does she
not realize that in our class strangers wed? It is a
matter of policy."

"I think she could accept it better if we were
strangers."

"So long as she is neither wed nor given to Christ,
Robert can lay claim to her. Her best chance is in
marriage to a strong lord. If you have no stomach for
it, I can approach Chester—his heir fostered with me
and serves me yet. The boy is but twenty, but his
father is powerful and has Rufus' ear."

"Nay! God's teeth! I did not bring her out of Normandy to give her to another man or to God."

"I thought not when you were doing the telling."

"She won't have me."

"Aye—she will."

"I will not have her unwilling." Roger stood and
walked to the window to watch the dawn break over

the horizon. "In my dreams, she comes to me with love—I could not have it otherwise."

"A man's dreams rarely turn into reality, Roger," the earl told him as he rose to stretch his long frame. "If you would indeed have her safe from Robert of Belesme, marriage is the only answer, and if you want her to wive, take her now and woo her later." His eyes swept over Roger and his face broke into a grin. "You look like a strong, healthy man capable of pleasing a maid once she is bound to you."

"I would not force her!"

"I cannot believe you would have to—she would seem to have some affection for you, from what she said to me." The earl stood, flexing tired muscles, and came to face his son. "Is she yet a virgin?"

"Aye."

"Then it is important to have witnesses to that fact."

"I won't have her humiliated! Nay—none shall look on her!"

" 'Twas not my meaning, Roger. I would counsel you that several must be ready to attest she came a virgin to you—to witness the evidence of her maiden-head when the sheets are removed from the bed."

"She is convent-bred, my lord, and ignorant of such things."

"And I have no lady suitable to speak with her. Surely she has seen animals—"

"It is not the same."

"Jesu! Well, she will survive, anyway. The sooner 'tis done, the better, if we are to face Belesme when he comes for her."

"You will stand with me then?"

" 'Tis time someone stood against him, Roger. As soon as the Demoiselle is settled, I go to Abbeville to see your mother and plead my own case." An ironic smile twisted Richard's mouth. "What I would not give to tell Gilbert that his daughter has gone to my son."

The sun rose and waxed high in the sky and Richard de Brione sat alone in his chamber. Roger's revelations gave him too much food for thought to allow him

the peace of sleep. The boy—nay, the man—was tall
and strong and well-favored . . . and he was his son. A
sigh of regret escaped him—regret that he could never
know the joy of holding the boy when small, of watching him grow and strengthen, and of seeing him rise in
men's favor. But those times were past and irretriev-
able. Richard frowned and tried to bring Glynis' image to his mind. Memories were faulty at best, but he
could swear the boy had something of Glynis in his
face. Mayhap it was the blondness of his hair or the
straightness of his nose. Jesu, but the years had robbed
them, Glynis, himself, and his son.

His son. The thought echoed in Richard's mind and
filled him with pride. He had a son of his body, an
heir to his lands—yea, a strong, fine son. And in need,
that son had turned at last to him. The boy did not
want for courage or daring, he mused. But then, one
look at the girl could tell him why. They were well-
matched, those two, and they deserved better than he
and Glynis had had.

He could tell from the way Roger spoke of her that
Eleanor of Nantes was everything to him. For the boy,
life without her would be without meaning, and Richard understood. The joy and the pain of a love nearly
eased by time but never forgotten flooded over him.
Aye, he would stand by his son—and he would give
him the Demoiselle. Well, there was no time like the
present to make a move.

Richard de Brione nodded to himself. He would
speak to the girl and make her understand. He stood,
settled his shoulders back, and strode for the stairs. It
was a long walk to what had once been his mother's
solar, but it was something he had to do before he
slept. He called out to a page that crossed in front of
him, "Run tell the Demoiselle that I would speak with
her!"

When he arrived, he found her waiting. She wore a
simple robe of smooth blue sendal caught at the waist
with a golden chain. Jesu, but it was not difficult to
see why the boy wanted her—she was perfection in the

flesh. She looked up with clear brown eyes before dropping to a deep curtsy at his feet.

"Nay, Lady Eleanor, do not kneel to me." He touched the soft crown of her hair awkwardly. "I do not expect it."

She rose gracefully and faced him. "You wished to see me?"

"Aye." He was no callow youth, but even at his age he found it difficult to look at her and speak. He cleared his throat and motioned her to a window bench. "I know why you are here, Demoiselle, and I would help you." He waited for her to sit and then took a place next to her, leaning forward to rest his elbows on his knees. "You have only three courses of action, child—you can marry, you can take the veil, or you can return to Belesme—and those are the only choices you have. I would advise you to take my Roger."

She did not look at him. Twisting the fabric of her skirt with her hands, she shook her head. "You do not understand, my lord."

"Aye—I fear I do. My son has risked everything for you—his lands, his life even—and it will all be for naught if you go back to Belesme. That leaves but the convent or marriage. You could have taken your vows long ago if that was your wish, and saved everyone much trouble, but you did not." The earl cocked his head to study her reaction to his words. "Roger would wed with you, and I think it the best way." When she made no answer, he added gently, "The boy loves you, Eleanor."

"For now." She nodded. "Aye, for now."

"And now may be the only time there is—take the advice of one who has lived with pain and sorrow for years. Death or separation can end anything at any time without warning."

"You do not understand—I can bring him nothing . . . and—and I may disappoint him."

"He is not without resources, Demoiselle."

"But I am accursed!" The words escaped before she could hold them back.

"Nay, I think not. Eleanor . . ." He reached out

and stilled her twisting hands. "He has had little happiness, you know—give him this."

"But I am like to bring him none!"

"Why?" he asked bluntly.

"My mother bore no sons and my father's love turned to hate. What if it is the same with me?" She stared miserably at the floor as she confessed her deepest fear.

"That is in the hands of God alone, child. Do not let your parents' meanness deny you happiness. If you do not dare because you fear to fail, you rob yourself of the fullness of life. Where would England be if William had not dared?" He patted the hand he touched. "Besides, my son would have you at whatever cost."

"I know."

"And you owe him his chance for happiness—he has given all for you."

"I pray I do not cost him his life, my lord. Belesme hates him and will kill him if the opportunity arises."

"Whether you wed him or not," Richard reasoned. "Aye . . . well, think on it—the choice is yours, Eleanor." He rose to leave and found himself unbelievably tired. "My son has offered marriage—I ask you to consider his offer."

"Did he send you, my lord?"

"Nay, he sleeps. We spoke until long after the sun came up this morning." He managed a rueful smile. "I have missed much in these twenty-three years and I would give all I have to live them over. Do not let that be your lament one day."

She watched him leave with troubled heart. As a girl who prided herself for her honesty, she had to admit the truth of everything the earl had said. Aye, Roger wanted her, loved her—he'd said so. And he was a desirable husband in more ways than one. She'd seen the way the women at Rouen had watched him eagerly. Moreover, there was no denying that she loved him. It had been days since she'd admitted the truth to herself, but now she realized the bond they'd shared for years was more than the affection of a

brother and sister. Aye, well she could remember her
jealousy when he'd admitted his love for the unknown
lady. And it gave her pleasure to know she'd been that
lady. As for wanting him—she could not be in his
presence without being acutely aware of him as a man
now. At night, she knew no peace alone in her bed.
Over and over again, she relived that afternoon spent
in the stream and wondered what it would have been
like if she had not stopped him. Even her memories
left her weak with desire and hungry again for his
touch.

There was much to love in him—qualities like strength
of character, steadfastness in the face of danger, physical and emotional courage, and a genuine goodness of
heart. Then too, there were things like the blue eyes
that could darken with passion, warm with pleasure,
and brighten with mischief—eyes that seemed to mirror his soul. She'd long thought the world did not hold
a handsomer man. Jesu, but he was beautiful.

What if Earl Richard were right? What if the present might be all the time there was for them? Roger
wanted her and loved her; she loved and wanted him.
Were her fears sufficient reason to deny them a chance
for happiness? She sat, she paced, she pondered. Finally she sought out Roger.

She was uncertain what she would say when she
faced him—the debate raged in her mind every step
she took. When she climbed the winding stairs and
reached the doorway, she did not knock to warn him.

Finding him still abed, she pulled open the bed
hangings and leaned over him to blurt out, "I am
come to tell you I will wed with you if you still wish
it."

Her words penetrated his consciousness and brought
him awake with a start. "*What*?"

"I said I'd wed with you if you still wished it." Her
hands were clenched at her side and her face betrayed
her fright at her decision.

"Sweet Mary!" he breathed. "If I wish it—aye, above
all things!" He sat up to look at her. The sheet fell

away from his bare shoulders and chest. "Jesu! Am I dreaming, Lea?"

"Do you want me to shout it, Roger—twice I've said I would marry you—three times now."

"When?"

"Whenever you wish."

He reached out and clasped her hand. "Tomorrow, then. You find me unready for today." He felt her stiffen and looked up in surprise. "You said whenever I wished," he reminded her.

"So be it."

In spite of her sudden decision, Roger could tell that she was still afraid of something. He released her hand and spoke lightly. "You find me unprepared for company, love. Unless you would join me here, you'll have to let me get up and get dressed. I cannot converse properly if I am lying down and you are standing."

"Aye." She moved toward the door.

" 'Twas not my meaning, Lea. Turn your back and look at the window—or look at me again, if you wish, but do not flee."

"I wasn't fleeing." She wiped her damp palms against the folds of her skirt. "I have said what I came to say."

"Nay—there is more to it than that." He thrust his feet on the floor and stood while reaching for his knee-length tunic. Hastily shrugging it over his head, he moved between her and the door. "Now, Lea, we will talk."

She was pale as parchment, her hands were nervously working against her gown, and her eyes were huge in her pale face. She chewed her lip to fight against her rising fright. She'd said she'd wed, but she was by no means certain that it was right. What if her mother's curse were real? "I . . . I . . ." she began. "Oh, Roger—help me, *please!*"

"Help you what?" he asked gently as he moved closer. "What ails you? Of what are you afraid, Lea?"

"I don't know." With a sob, she threw herself into his arms. "It was so sensible, so right when I reasoned it out," she whispered against his shoulder. "Roger, tell me it is the right thing to do."

" 'Tis the right thing, I swear to you." He held her back a little to search her face. "Are you afraid of me, Lea? Look at me—I am Roger, the same Roger you have known all your life. I have held your hand and shared your sorrows these nearly twenty years. You cannot be afraid of me."

"N-nay, 'tis not that—'tis I fear for you."

"Because of Belesme? Because of Mary de Clare? Lea, share with me. I cannot fight that which I do not know, but together we can overcome anything."

"But Belesme—"

"Has wanted my head for seven years and more and he's not got it yet. Let me worry about Belesme." He let her burrow back into his shoulder and began rubbing her back to ease her tension. "And do not be comparing me to Gilbert, love, for we are not at all alike. I might have strangled Mary de Clare for her tongue, but I'd never have put her aside for the lack of a son. That is in the hands of God and none other," he told her flatly.

"You are sure—you won't feel differently later?"

"I swear. Lea, I love *you* and you only. If you come to me barren, I am content so long as you come to me." He could feel her relax a little and he pressed his advantage. "I took my oath to you long ago in the chapel at Nantes—I swore on a sacred relic to be your champion, your man until I die. That oath has precedence over any other oath I take to king, liege, or Church, Lea. Now I would pledge my love and my body to you in marriage, and I ask the same of you."

"Aye—but tomorrow? There's not even time to cry the banns, and we are unbetrothed even."

" 'Tis simple—the Church recognizes pledges made at its doors by consenting parties. The thing to remember is that, while there is no prescribed oath for such a marriage, each of us must say we come of our free will, name our spouse, and state we take each other in marriage."

"Surely that is not all."

"Aye—that is why it was so important that you not say anything to Belesme that he could take as a promise to wed."

"Nay, I said nothing to him."

"I know." He ruffled her soft hair and fought his growing awareness of her. "Would you like to hear what I would say? You may say what you wish." Before she could answer, he caught her hand in his and began, "I, Roger de Brione, take thee, Eleanor of Nantes, to wive, to have and to love in joy and in adversity from now to the end of my life, I so swear."

"What a pretty way to say it—can I not just say the same thing?"

"Aye, if you want, but you'll probably have to practice it. I know I have for a long time."

She looked up in surprise and found him grinning down at her. "Aye, you may have known for only weeks that we could wed—I have known for years."

She laid her head back against his shoulder and felt easier than she had since Belesme came to Fontainebleau. "And just how long have you wanted to wed with me?" she asked.

"A long time. I suppose I first thought of it when William came to Nantes and there was talk of your being given to Henry. It was insane, but I kept thinking: Not Henry—*me*! And I was all of fifteen at the time!"

"Roger, my father will disown me—I can bring you nothing."

" 'Tis all right—I have enough for both of us, Lea. I am certain I can keep the Condes now." His arms tightened around her. "And you wed no bastard, Eleanor." When she looked up in surprise, he smiled broadly and nodded. "Aye—my mother and father were wed in church—the same place where we will give our vows. I am not a bastard—not Gilbert's nor Earl Richard's by-blow. Richard de Brione is my father in fact and in law."

"Sweet Mary! 'Tis wonderful, Roger!" Her face flushed with pleasure for him. "But how . . . ?"

"A long story that I'll tell you later."

" 'Tis not right that I bring you nothing then."

"Oh, so you would wed a bastard, Lea, and cavil at taking the heir to an earldom."

"And you know that is not it!"

"Ah, now you are more like my Lea. I wondered how long it would be before this weak, frightened creature gave way to your real self," he teased. "Truly, though, I doubt Gilbert has the power to disinherit his firstborn entirely. But if he does, I have enough for both of us—unless, of course, you give me so many children that I must needs conquer new lands to provide for them all."

Outside, the bells began to ring midday. Roger reluctantly loosed his hold on her and gave her a playful push toward the door. "My belly is empty and my legs are bare, love. If you would see me break my fast at all before tonight, I have to get dressed and shaved."

If dinner at noon had caused a stir with Roger sitting at the high table, supper surpassed it for drama. Eleanor entered the hall on Earl Richard's arm and Roger followed them all the way to the dais. A murmur passed through the assembled guests, retainers, and men-at-arms when Roger again sat there. And before Richard de Brione gave the signal for the cook's parade, he stood to make his announcement.

"Good friends, vassals, men of Harlowe, I make known to you Roger de Brione, my son, who is lately arrived from Normandy." He seemed almost overcome by emotion as he continued, "Through a cruel trick, knowledge of his existence was denied me until yesterday, but I mean to make up for those years we were apart. I ask your welcome, I ask your loyalty to my son," he told the stunned audience. "Aye—he is my heir. His mother and I were contracted before the Wake's rebellion, and he was conceived ere I left to fight for my king. But because his mother was Saxon, daughter to Aeldrid, my mother had her taken away." He stopped to wipe his eyes briefly before going on. "Now, as soon as may be practical, I leave for France to see my wife. I have hopes of persuading her to return here with me. Until then, I ask you to join me in celebrating the return of my son and in witnessing his marriage to the Demoiselle of Nantes." He reached down to clasp Eleanor's hand and drew her up beside him. "Aye—who could not be proud of a daughter such as this one? May she give you a future earl of my blood." Eleanor flushed beside him, but he seemed not to notice. "They pledge to each other before Mass tomorrow and ask Father Alain's blessing then." Richard then gestured Roger to rise and placed Eleanor's hand in his. "I give you your third earl, God willing, and his lady."

At first, everyone was too stunned to do anything but stare. Finally Brian de Scoville, Harlowe's seneschal, and Ralph d'Escrivet, the steward, rose and began to clap loudly. The others followed suit and the hall seemed alive with approbation. It might be a shock, most reasoned, but an earldom with an heir was more secure in Rufus' England than one whose succession was at the king's mercy. A traveler who knew of Roger FitzGilbert hastened to tell all who would listen of Roger's remarkable abilities as a soldier. Those around listened and tried to take pride in the fact that the heir had something to recommend him.

"Roger de Brione—it sounds strange to my ears," Eleanor whispered as she took her seat again.

"Aye—to mine too, but I like the sound of it," Roger whispered back. His hand sought hers in her lap. "A new name, a new land, a new wife—how could I ask for more?"

Her fingers tightened around his. It was the end of one portion of her life also. The man beside her offered her a new beginning far from Belesme, far from Gilbert, far from Fontainebleau. Her brother, the FitzGilbert, lived no more; her husband, Roger de Brione, would build her a future free from fear. She would wed with him and try to give him an heir of his body.

*   *   *

Eleanor spent much of her wedding day being bathed, having her hair washed and dried and scented with honeysuckle. She wore a simple gown of her favorite purple samite with Roger's bride gifts of girdle and golden circlet. In her hands she carried a pearl-and-gold chaplet for her prayers.

A maid answered a tap at the door and admitted the earl after a brief conference. He stepped in and surveyed Eleanor appreciatively before handing her a parchment that bore his seal. She looked up in surprise before turning her attention to the document. Richard de Brione watched her flush with pleasure as she read.

"I don't understand . . ." she began when she'd finished reading.

" 'Tis plain enough." He smiled. "You were worried to come to your husband with nothing, Eleanor, so I have dowered you myself."

"But—"

"Hush, child. Before you and Roger came to Harlowe, I had naught but land and wealth. Now I have an heir of my body." He leaned forward to plant a chaste kiss on her cheek. "Now I have a son and a daughter, Eleanor." He moved away to stare down from the window to the peaceful lake that lapped the castle's very foundation. "God willing, I hope to regain my wife after so many years. I pray she can be persuaded to return with me." He straightened his shoulders as though he lifted a weight off them. "Aye, once you and Roger are pledged, I leave for London to present proof of my own marriage and to ask Rufus' recognition of my heir. That done, I am for Abbeville to see Glynis."

"I pray she comes also, my lord," Eleanor told him, "for I loved her dearly as a child and I love her still. Will you tell her that for me, please?"

"I will." There were a dozen questions Richard wanted to ask the girl before him, but could not bring himself to put them into words. She seemed to sense his hesitation. "My lord, do not ask her of Gilbert— she hated him and she hated her life at Nantes. Had she the means to have seen Roger cared for, she would have left long before she did. It was hard for her to be known as my father's leman all those years." When he made no reply, she defended Glynis further. "Aye, and she left as soon as the Conqueror provided for Roger, my lord."

"I do not doubt it, Demoiselle, and I would not reproach her for that which she could not help. If there is any blame, 'tis on me and my family." A smile played at the corners of his mouth much like Roger's. "And if I am ever in need of a champion, Eleanor, I pray you will speak for me as loyally as you have for my wife and son."

The fourth bells rang. Eleanor gave a nervous start and clutched her chaplet tightly. " 'Tis nearly time, and I am not ready!"

"Nay, child go as you are. I promise he'll be pleased by the sight of you. Rannulf reports him as short-tempered as a bear in a pit from the wait." He straightened the circlet on her brow in a fatherly gesture and offered, "I'll walk you there."

"I would be honored, my lord."

A tiring woman thrust a small breviary into her hands. "Demoiselle, you must go." With a quick twist of the skirt of her gown to straighten it, the woman pushed her toward the door. "May God smile on you, my lady."

Clouds had parted to admit the sun's brightness after a morning of intermittent rain. The world seemed to have bathed and freshened itself during a respite from summer's heat. Richard took Eleanor's hand and laid it in the crook of his elbow as they came out into the open stone-paved walk. "Even the heavens smile on you, Eleanor, for this day to tell you 'tis right what you do."

"I pray it is."

He could sense her tension mounting and sought to ease it. "Tell me, child, how it is that the world calls you Eleanor and my son names you Lea?" he asked casually as he stopped to open a gate.

"When I was born, he could not pronounce Eleanor, my lord, and Glynis is said to have sounded it out slowly for him as El-le-a-nor. He still could not say it, but he marked the middle sounds and to him I have been Lea ever since. I like it."

"Aye, he told me you two shared much as children."

"He and Glynis were all I had, my lord," she answered simply, "and when he left to join William's train and she went away, I thought I should die of the loneliness." She gave a deep sigh of remembrance. "And then I went to Fontainebleau."

He patted the hand that rested on his. "Those times are over, Eleanor. Now you will have a husband to stand for you and to keep you. You are fortunate that you get one who knows and loves you. Too many of our class marry as strangers and get acquainted in the marriage bed."

She fell silent. She had many questions that she could not ask about what would happen. When she'd overheard some of the maids discussing her after her bath, saying such things as, "The little Demoiselle is too small for such a one as that" and "I'll warrant she bleeds much," she'd sought out Roger frantically. His attempts at soothing had been of little benefit when he'd told her, "All women bleed a little then, Lea, but only the once." She'd wanted to ask more, but his body servants had arrived to prepare him, and she had no further opportunity. She felt pitifully ignorant of what was expected of her. Now she realized with a start that they'd stopped walking and Richard de Brione watched her curiously.

"Is something the matter, Demoiselle?" he asked gently.

"Nay." She reddened in embarrassment at her thoughts. " 'Tis only that I wish I had some lady to speak with before . . . before . . ."

"Aye, and I regret the lack. What troubles you?"

She looked up wide-eyed and then back to the bright green grass. He seemed kind and fatherly and concerned for her well-being. With a gulp, she managed to ask, "What happens if I am too small?"

Fighting an urge to smile at her innocence, Richard

appeared to consider the matter seriously. "I've never heard of that happening, Eleanor, and I am sure your husband will use you gently. Where did you hear such a thing?"

"From the maids."

"Well, you are not as small as all that, I can tell you. In fact, you are much bigger—aye, a foot or more taller—than William's Mathilda. You say you remember the Conqueror—well, he was not a small man, was he?"

"Nay, he was only a little shorter than Roger."

"Then there is your answer."

"Thank you, my lord."

"You are most welcome, Demoiselle. Is there anything else you would know before we go on?"

"Aye, but I could not ask such questions."

"Then I suggest you seek out Roger alone when we are done and ask what you would of him. I'll warrant he can answer for you."

They managed the rest of the walk in harmony. Richard was enchanted with his son's choice of a wife. The girl had beauty and intelligence, to be sure, but she also had a candor that would serve her well. Her ignorance of sexual matters was born of a sheltered existence and could be remedied, but her innate honesty about her lack of information brought him the realization his son wed no ordinary beauty.

A slow smile broke across her face, prompting him to stop again. "What amuses you now?"

"I was thinking that the Conqueror and his lady must have made an odd-looking pair with him so big and her so little."

"Aye—she had to stand on a stool to get into bed, and everything had to be made small for her—stools, tables, everything. Her bower must have been a strange place for him." The bells tolled again. "But we tarry too long, Eleanor. If we do not hurry, Mass will have already begun."

When they reached the church, Roger and his witnesses were already there. He had come early to pray and give thanks—it was fitting to do so, since

God allowed him the two closest desires of his heart in Eleanor of Nantes and his own legitimacy. Now it would be up to him to make what he could of God's gifts.

Even as he took her hand at the church door, he was unprepared for the love, the pride in her, the exhilaration he felt. A hush fell over the assemblage as all strained to hear the priest's greeting and the couple's vows to each other. Father Alain stood before them in the doorway and asked their purpose; then Roger responded they came to pledge themselves in marriage. After asking if any there knew of any impediment to the marriage, the priest waited for any to protest. When none spoke up, he nodded to Roger.

Taking a deep breath, Roger clasped Eleanor's hand even more tightly and spoke clearly: "I, Roger de Brione, of my free will, take thee, Eleanor of Nantes, to wive, to have, to hold, to love in joy and adversity unto the ends of our lives. I so swear."

His hand was warm and strong over hers and his blue eyes, though serious, gave warmth and reassurance. For a brief moment she looked up at him before facing the priest. Softly, almost inaudibly, she began her own promise to him, and her voice gained in intensity as she spoke: "I, Eleanor of Nantes, of my free will, take thee, Roger de Brione, for my husband, to have and to honor, to love and to keep, so long as we may live. I so swear. Father, I ask God's blessing."

There on the stone threshold, they knelt while Harlowe's chaplain laid his hands over them and called on God to grant them joy of each other and children of their bodies. Rising, they followed him in to Mass.

"Half an hour—I can try to give you half an hour before they want their sport," Roger leaned over and whispered to Eleanor while the traveling acrobats tumbled to after-supper music. He could feel her tense at his side and hastened to add, "Try to be in bed before we get there, Lea, even if you have to get up and do your hair after the door is barred. 'Twill be easier that way."

"All right."

He could tell by her terse reply that she was mortified by the prospect of having a dozen or so men see
her bedded according to custom. He slipped a reassuring arm about her shoulders and pulled her closer.
"Nay, they do not stay—my father will see to that. He
has ordered more wine to be brought out so that they
may revel into the night."

"Do they have to look on me?" she managed even
as her face flamed. She caught the glimmer of amusement in Roger's eyes and flared, "Well, I have never
wedded nor bedded before—I know not what to
expect!"

"And I have never wedded before either, Lea—nay,
do not look at me like you would box my ears—'twas
not my meaning," he protested. "But I have witnessed
the bedding before and I can tell you that they will
strip me, say all manner of vulgar things, and put me
into bed with you. someone will witness that my leg
touches yours—that is all—and then they will leave if
someone drags them off." He fingered a lock of hair,
twirling it absently.

She pulled away nervously and shook her hair free.
"Don't do that!" He looked down in surprise and she
reddened again. "I am sorry, Roger—I . . . I am un-
reasonably cross."

"And you are afraid," he finished for her. "Aye, I
understand, Lea, but you fear for naught—but we can
speak of it later when we are more private. For now,
drink your wine and watch that girl in the green." He
pointed out to her where he looked. "See—I swear
her joints are not the same as ours. Look at that!
Could you walk over your head like that?"

"Well, I would not want to—you can see her legs
when she does it."

"Aye." He turned back to stare at Eleanor, his gaze
warm and intimate. "I would want you to do it only
for me, of course." He watched her color yet again,
the pink diffusing through her cheeks becomingly. Jesu,
he thought, she is beautiful and she is mine. Mine! His
heart seemed to swell with pride at the thought. For

her, everything had to be right and good and he would see that it was. She would always have the best that he could give her of himself and of material wealth. Even his legitimacy took on a special significance because it was something more that he could bring to her. In time, he could make her a countess.

Out of the corner of his eye he could see Earl Richard summon one of the maids to the dais. It was time. He stood and pulled Eleanor up after him. The music and acrobatics stopped as all eyes turned to them. With his free hand Roger lifted his cup high and called out, "I ask you all to wish my wife a long life of happiness as you join me with your cups." He swallowed a long draft to the cheers of Richard's household and guests. A slightly drunk knight yelled back, " 'Tis the custom to wish her fruitful, my lord."

Soon the hall was enveloped in chaos as everyone seemed to vie with everyone else in toasting the bride. " 'Tis now, Lea," Roger shouted over the din. "Run!"

Both Eleanor and the maid lifted their skirts and hurried for the door. Once out of the great hall, they were joined by several other maids and all ran for the tower bower where she would spend her wedding night. Richard's chamberlain lit the way for them and then stayed long enough to inspect the room to make sure servants had left everything in order. Then he withdrew and left them alone to get her ready for bed.

While one of the tiring women pulled off her gown and undershift, others turned back the bed and smoothed the fresh sheets. Still another prepared a tray with wine cups and fruits and cheeses to be set on a table near the bed. When a maid approached with her hairbrush, Eleanor remembered Roger's advice and shook her head.

"But madam," the girl protested, "it will tangle and get in the way."

"My lord likes it down," she managed as she fought rising panic. In a matter of minutes the room would be filled with strangers come to see her bedded, and then she and Roger would be alone—alone to do whatever it was they would do. By now she had a notion of what would happen from what she'd gleaned in snatches of conversations between the maids. It sounded distasteful and it sounded painful, but she'd made her commitment in Holy Church to Roger and she would not draw back now.

Footsteps sounded on the stairs. Eleanor pulled away from those who yet attempted to straighten her hair and tore open the bed curtains before scrambling frantically between the sheets. The door burst open to admit a crowd of men who pushed a half-naked Roger ahead of them. Eleanor clutched the sheets tightly under her chin and sat up. Her dark hair tumbled down over shoulders and sheets in a cascade of lustrous waves. Rannulf of Chester swaggered over for a closer look, leering and telling her that she at least knew the proper place to await her lord. Her eyes seemed enormous in her face when Roger turned around to face her. They'd finished undressing him and several pushed him toward the bed while making obscene comments about his physique and offering advice on the best way to take a virgin. Before any could lift the sheets, Roger pushed them back.

"Move over, Lea, and let me in before they do me further harm." He tried to speak lightly to hide his own tension at finally being able to lie with her. She edged away while still tightly holding the covers against her. He heaved himself into the deep feather bed beside her and sat up. "At least give me a corner, Lea, if you do not mind. After all, 'tis not your body they laugh at." His teasing fell on unresponsive ears. Finally he reached over and gently disengaged a corner for himself and drew the sheet over both of them. Sliding his foot over to rub against the calf of her leg, he motioned his father to approach. Earl Richard nodded and announced, "They are bedded. Let us go back and finish the rest of the wine—the jongleur and the acrobats stay to perform yet again."

"Aye!" Rannulf shouted. "And I get the one in the green!" He laughed at Eleanor's shocked expression. "I would see what lies above those legs of hers!"

With more ribald comments, the men gradually filed

out. Roger quickly rose to bar the door after them. "Jesu, Lea, but I thought I should never have you to myself." He stopped to pour wine into the cups and brought them back to the bed. "Here, drink this— 'twill make you feel better."

"Roger, if I drink any more, I shall either be sick or too drunk to know what happens," she protested.

"Lea—" He hesitated while he tried to calm his own racing heart. He wanted her and he wanted her now, but his mind counseled caution. She was obviously afraid. He swallowed some of the wine to wet his dry mouth. "Would you like for me to braid your hair so that it does not tangle while . . . while you sleep?" His hands seemed to shake as he set aside his cup.

"I don't care."

The wind was coming up, bringing with it the smell of new rain. Roger walked over to open the shutters and to let the breeze cool the heat he felt in his body. He wanted to get back into the bed and throw himself over her to slake the intense desire he felt for her, but this was no serving wench nor free-favored lady of Normandy's court. This was Eleanor of Nantes, his Lea, the woman he'd wanted and fought to have for years. With her, he had to go slowly, to woo gently, to teach lovingly. With her, it had to be a union of spirit as well as flesh. He moved back to sit on the side of the bed.

"Lea—" He reached to clasp her hand. It was small and cold in his. "Lea, I know you are afraid, but I will help you. I am the same man you have known since we were children, love." He tried to keep his voice even and calm, but it sounded strange even to his own ears. "If you will but do as I ask, it will be fine, I promise." He turned to watch her face in the flickering candlelight. She seemed as still as though she were carved out of a fine white stone. Only the rise and fall of the sheet against her breast when she breathed betrayed life. "Lea . . ." He sought words of explanation and could find none. Finally he looked away with a sigh. "It has been some time since I've laid with a woman, Lea, and I do not know if I can wait until you are ready. I will try not to hurt you this time, love, and I can tell you that after this once, there is no pain." He felt her hand tighten in his as she squeezed his fingers.

"Roger, I love you," she whispered in the dimness behind him. "I always have and I always will. Nothing you could possibly do to me would change that." When he turned to her, he could feel as well as see her timid smile. "Aye, I am afraid, but I will survive because I know you love me."

"Sweet Mary, but I love you, Lea," he managed as he rolled into bed and enveloped her in his arms. "I will do my best to please you." She turned against him, small, soft, warm, and trusting. An overwhelming need to protect her flooded over him. "Would you have the candles doused or left lit?"

" 'Tis up to you, my lord husband," she murmured against the hard flesh of his shoulder.

"Well, I would see what I could of you even in this light," he answered. "Aye, I would watch your face." He shifted her position slightly and bent to brush her forehead lightly with his lips. "Art beautiful, Lea." His fingers kneaded the bare skin of her shoulders as his mouth sought hers. Even as her lips parted, desire flamed through him.

He twisted and turned hungrily against her while exploring her mouth, her earlobes, her neck, and her throat with his mouth. She twined her arms around his neck and tried to press against him. She could feel the hard muscles that corded his back, shoulders, and upper arms, and his strength fed her own desire. When his mouth moved lower to savor the taste of her breasts, her hands worked ceaselessly to caress his back and then to ruffle the thick waves of his hair.

Gradually he let his hand brush lower and lower as it moved from cupping her breast to stroking the soft smoothness of her flat belly and then to the wetness below. She recoiled briefly when he touched her there, and then closed her eyes in pleasure as he began to stroke the entrance to her body.

It seemed that every sense was centered somewhere

deep within her belly as something tautened inside and strained to reach some unknown ecstasy. His mouth and his hands felt as though they were everywhere now. Finally he moved back to her lips for one last, long, deep kiss before parting her legs with his knee and easing his body over hers. Instinctively she settled beneath him and clutched at his waist.

"Do not draw away," he whispered hoarsely even as he sought her body with his own. For answer, she twined her legs over his and moved against him.

For one brief moment, when hard flesh met soft, she could feel her body resist his, then give way before him. A sharp tearing sensation made her stiffen and then there was a flood of warmth as two bodies joined. He held himself still inside her for a moment while he whispered anxiously, "Are you all right, Lea? The bad has ended."

For answer, she held him closer and nodded. Her eyes were still closed as he watched her when he began to move. "I love you, Lea," were his last coherent words as she strove to match his rhythm. It was as though they worked to meld themselves into each other, becoming one in a mindless, overwhelming desire to give and receive the extraordinary pleasure of each other's bodies. Roger fought to maintain enough control to satisfy Eleanor, but abstinence and the culmination of years of wanting made it nearly impossible to master what had become a raging need of his own. With a cry of release, he drove himself home deep within her and then collapsed breathless against her.

He could feel the beating of her heart and hear her ragged breathing beneath him. It came home again to him just how small and delicate she was in spite of her passion. He rolled over and away from her, pulling her hair. Propping himself up on an elbow, he disentangled the silky mass and then smoothed it away from her face. Her eyes were still closed, but he could watch her swallowing as she gained command of her own emotions. He bent to brush her lips softly. "Heaven . . . Lea, you have given me heaven."

She opened her eyes under his gaze and blushed

furiously at his expression. Then her face broke into a warm smile that lit his heart. He pulled her closer and hugged her to him.

"Was it bad? Did I hurt you?" he asked above her ear. His arm closed protectively around her waist. "Are you all right?"

"I am fine, my lord husband." She managed to turn over in his arms and face him. "Roger, why did you not tell me it would be like that? Why did you let me worry so?"

"I could not tell you how it would be, Lea—it is different for a woman than for a man. Besides, I feared to disgust you."

She snuggled against him and rested her head beneath his chin. "Nay, you did not disgust me. Do you remember what you said to me in Fuld Nevers' stronghold? That there was nothing wrong with me? Well, I did not believe you until tonight." She burrowed closer as his arms tightened around her. "Oh, Roger, I do love you."

"You are sure you are all right? You are so small that I feared to crush you."

"Well, you did not." She stretched out a white arm for him to see in the dim candlelight. "Behold—I still have two whole arms and two whole legs—I am alive and well."

"Ummmmm." He nuzzled the top of her head. "Your hair smells of honeysuckle." His hand brushed it away from her temple.

"Ummmmhmmmm." She stretched against him and stifled a yawn.

"Are you sleepy, Lea?"

"A little. Why? Did you want to lie with me again?"

"I am lying with you."

"You know what I mean."

"Nay—there is always tomorrow and years after then. Turn over and let me just hold you." When she did as he told her, he tucked an arm around her waist and pulled her back against him. "Go on to sleep."

"Are you sure?" Her eyes were heavy as she suppressed another yawn. The excitement of the day and the physical satisfaction of their lovemaking made her drowsy. A gust of wind caught at the bed curtains as rain began to pelt against stone walls and hit like pebbles in the lake below. He was warm, he was safe, she was secure. She settled comfortably in his arms and drifted into sleep even as the storm came up.

Sleep did not come to him for a long time. He lay close to her and savored the feel of her body against his. He felt too elated to give up his consciousness—his mind, his heart, every fiber of his being seemed to sing out, "She is mine!" After years of striving for the impossible dream, that dream had become reality and Eleanor of Nantes lay against him in the flesh. His hand moved again to push back the heavy hair that fell over her face and he could feel the soft warmth of her breath against his palm. A surge of emotion overwhelmed him—she was his to love, his to protect, his to keep. No longer did he have to imagine her coming to him in his dreams. She had given herself to him and that giving exceeded anything he could have imagined. Aye, it was more than the act itself—it was the intense union of body and spirit that gave him fulfillment.

The wind howled and the rain came down harder. He ought to get up and close the shutters against the sound and blow out the wildly flickering candles, he knew, but he was loath to leave her even for that minute. There was no clothing or furniture to damage and the candles would gut themselves soon enough. Besides, he took pleasure in looking at his sleeping wife in the faint light. It was not until a rain-drenched gale blew across the room and put out the candles that he could force himself to get up and shutter the window.

She roused sleepily when he got back into bed and sat up in the darkness. "Roger . . . I thought you'd left me."

"Nay, love—never." He caught her and pulled her back down against him. The recent memory of her passion flooded over him as he remembered the feel of her open body beneath his. He moved his hands to cup her breasts while he nuzzled the sensitive places on her neck. "Let me love you again, Lea," he whispered into the darkness.

For answer, she turned in his arms and gave herself up to his embrace. The wind swirled and screamed furiously and the rain came down in sheets to splash into the lake, but neither cared.

"Lea . . . Lea! Are you all right?" Eleanor woke to Roger's shaking reluctantly. He peered anxiously in the warm morning light as she stretched sore muscles and tried to come awake.

She opened her eyes gradually to adjust to the brightness of the room. All vestiges of the storm had passed and it appeared they had slept nearly to midday. "Aye, I am fine." Her eyes met his and their shared passion came to mind. She blushed furiously as she thought of her wanton, shameless behavior in the night.

"You are sure—you aren't in any pain or anything, are you?"

"Nay." She shook her head and sat up. He appeared seriously concerned. "Why?" she managed to ask as she sat up with a yawn.

Reassured, he managed a rueful grin. "Well, they are going to account me the greatest beast on earth, Lea, when they look at these sheets. Jesu, but they'll think I killed you."

She tumbled out of bed and looked for herself. A large dark bloodstain marked where she had lain and several smaller smudges smeared the area. Mortified, she managed to ask, "Roger, do I have to stay while they look? I mean . . . you know . . . there's certain to be more comment, and I've no stomach for it."

"Nay. Any can see you came to me a virgin, Lea." He kissed her lightly on the bridge of her nose before bending to savor the taste of her lips. Heat and desire seemed to flame between them in spite of the night's lovemaking. He drew back shakily and reached for his clothing. "Nay, I'll make you sore if we keep this up." He pulled on his chausses and tied them at his waist. Picking up his garters, he asked, "Do you want the maids or can I help you?"

She shook her head. "I can manage everything but my hair." She moved to look again at the bed. "Oh, Roger, they will see and they will know." Her face flamed again.

"Aye. Lea, 'tis what married people are expected to do—they do it every night."

"Every night?"

"Well, whenever the husband wills it, anyway." He finished wrapping his chausses and came to stand beside her.

"Aye, the husband's rights." She nodded.

"And the wife's, Lea." He picked up her brush and pushed her onto a bench before he started unknotting the tangles in her hair. "If you ever want me and I have not approached you to lie with you, just tell me and I will do my best to satisfy you. I would have you content in all ways, Lea."

She turned to lean against his leg and hugged it. "I am content."

"Well, I will have to write to Henry, of course, and tell him of our marriage. Do you send to Gilbert or do you want me to?"

"I don't care. It all seems so far away—my father, Belesme, Fontainebleau, everything."

"Aye, but we will have to go back one day. I have lands there—nay, *we* have lands there, love."

"When?" She jumped in alarm beneath his fingers.

"No time soon," he soothed. "But I will have to explain to Curthose if I want to keep the Condes. I think I'll let Henry plead my case first."

"Will he be angry that you did not tell him the whole when you asked his help?"

"Mayhap, but Henry is always Henry and we are friends. He is more likely to be disappointed that you came to me. His mind knew he could not have you, but his heart always had hope." He finished unsnarling the hair and began dividing it to plait into one heavy braid. As soon as it became known that they were awake, servants could be relied on to bring Richard de Brione and witnesses to attest to Eleanor's virginity in her marriage bed. "I could do this better,

Lea, but if you would escape more vulgar comments, we will have to hurry. Do you think you could ride after last night?"

"Of course I can ride. Sweet Mary, but you worry too much, Roger."

"Well, if the water is not too high from the rain, I have someone Earl Richard has asked me to visit. My grandmother, my mother's mother, yet lives in the village in the care of the Saxons because she cannot bring herself to accept Norman charity from my father. He would have me tell her that her daughter yet lives and ask again that she come here if my mother returns."

"She must be very old."

"I would suppose so. I have never met her and my mother spoke little of her family."

"I would be proud to go with you."

"I had hoped so. I would show her what a fine wife I have got me, Lea." He finished braiding and straightened the plait against her back. "Hurry and dress, love, and we will get out of here for a while. I'll stop in the kitchens and beg some bread and cheese and cold meat and we can eat by ourselves somewhere between here and there." He gave her an affectionate squeeze on her shoulder. "Aye, I would have you to myself before I have to share your company with a dozen other men at my father's table."

"I hope we can cross the water."

"Aye. Mayhap they will lower the level." He watched her surprised expression. "This was not always a lake, Lea, according to Brian. When the Conqueror came, Aeldrid lived in a fortified manor on a point in the river bend. As the river was spring-fed, the Conqueror suggested to my grandfather that he divert the channel and surround the high ground with a lake for security. Thus Harlowe was built on the island formed where Aeldrid's manor had stood. That is why the church became part of the fortress—it sat far enough away from the village proper that it could not be left with it. My father has since built another church there to replace the one here."

"Does it seem strange to call Earl Richard your father?"

"Aye, but I know it is so and he would have it so. Therefore, I make the effort to think of him as my father. Mayhap it will come easier to say with time. As it is now, I cannot call him other than Richard."

"He is a good man, Roger. I can tell. He has none of Gilbert's weaknesses and he strives to do right."

"Let us hope that I have not brought him trouble." Roger pulled on a plain tunic and belted it.

"What do you mean?"

"Nothing."

"Nay—you said the words, so you can explain your meaning."

"Nothing."

"Roger," she warned, "I would share your fears as much as you would share mine. Is it Belesme?"

"A foolish worry, Lea, but a worry nonetheless. Richard is a belted earl with more lands and greater power in England than Belesme. With him beside me, I do not see how we can possibly fail."

"Roger, did you have any idea when you came here?" Eleanor fastened a girdle over her blue samite gown and turned around.

"I knew he was my father and I hoped that he would support me because of the blood we share, but I had not the least idea that I was not his bastard son."

"A lot of men do not own their bastards."

"Aye, but I'd heard he was an honorable man." He stopped to listen to the sounds of footsteps on the stairs. "Jesu, but we have tarried too long, Lea." A knock sounded and Earl Richard called through the door. Roger moved to open it and found his father alone.

"I came before the rest." His eyes rested approvingly on Eleanor. "I thought she might wish to be somewhere else when they arrived."

"We had hopes of going to see Gytha, my lord, if we can get across."

"I'll have someone row you across—part of the bridge

is underwater and we have not yet opened the gates for fear of flooding the village."

"How can I find her direction?"

"Ask anyone there for Aeldrid's wife. Her husband was thane here and the Saxons still honor her—just tell them you are of her blood and they will take you to her." Richard's attention turned to Eleanor. "And you, daughter—how do you fare this morning?"

"I am well, my lord."

"So I see. Once word of your beauty spreads, my table will be full of those who would come to look on my daughter-in-law." He looked from her to Roger and back and could not resist a light teasing. "Well, I can see your fears were unfounded, little one."

"My lord—"

"Oh, leave him be, Roger. Can you not see he means me kindness?" Eleanor faced the earl with a smile. "Aye, my fears were unfounded, and I am well-pleased, my lord. Indeed, I am glad to be welcomed into this family. I hope now to be known as Roger de Brione's lady rather than Gilbert's daughter. 'Tis an honor."

"Well, you two had best be going if you are to miss seeing the sheets hung up for all to look on." He gave them a conspiratorial grin. "You'll find a basket ready in the scullery and I've left word at the gate you are to be taken across. We keep horses stabled on the other side."

"*Thank you*, my lord," Eleanor managed.

"Think you I do not remember how it was with Glynis even after all these years? Nay—get on with you."

Richard watched them leave before turning his attention to the bed. The bloodstains bore testimony to the girl's virginity better than any he'd ever seen. Jesu, could the boy not use her more gently than that? Mayhap he ought to say something to him. Nay, he decided, the girl seemed well-pleased so he ought to leave well enough alone. Hopefully, Roger had planted his seed and Harlowe would know the joys of children in its halls and courtyards. Aye, he'd been denied the

pleasure of seeing his son grow, but he could yet know
a child of his blood in Roger's sons or daughters.
Unhurriedly he summoned a page to bring up the
others. Then from the window he watched a boatman
hand Roger and Eleanor into a flat wooden boat. He
turned away content and waited. If his grandchildren
resembled either their mother or their father, they
would be beautiful.

"Salut!" Roger called out to a fellow crossing a
narrow dirt lane. "Can you lead me to Gytha, Aeldrid's
lady?" He fished in his pouch for a coin and showed
it. The fellow pretended not to understand. Finally, in
rusty Saxon remembered from his mother, Roger repeated the question, adding, "I am of her blood and I
would see her."

"Save your money, Norman," was the terse reply.

Eleanor leaned over her pommel and addressed the
man. "My husband was reared in Normandy, but he is
of Saxon blood. Please—may we see the good dame?"

"All of her relatives are dead—most in war with
your Normans."

"Aye, but she will know this one. Earl Richard
sends us."

He appeared to consider. "All right," he decided,
"if the earl sends you. My lord Richard is not like the
rest of them."

They followed him to a house set apart from the
small huts of the village. It was larger, more spacious,
and better tended than the others, guarded by two
house servants who maintained a vigil from a stall in
front.

"Earl Richard sent them—he claims to be a kinsman of my lady's."

"By what name?"

"Roger—but the name will mean naught to her.
Tell her I have the look of Glynis and see what she
says."

A servant disappeared in the house for a few minutes. When he returned, he nodded to Roger. "Aye,
she'll see you."

Roger dismounted and helped Eleanor down. Clutching her hand like two children facing discipline, he entered the house. His grandmother sat on a high chair at one end of the room and watched them with birdlike eyes. With a start, he realized that age had shrunk her until she was smaller than Eleanor. He'd had no set plan for revealing himself because he had not known her health and he'd not wanted to cause her harm. One look at the small lady told him that she was not one given to hysterics.

"Grandmother, I have brought my wife for your blessing. We were but wed yesterday at Harlowe."

"I have no living grandson, sir."

"I was born of your daughter Glynis in Gilbert of Nantes' stronghold in 1069."

"You are mistaken—my daughter lies dead at Harlowe, boy."

"Nay—Earl Richard had her grave examined but two days ago, Dame Gytha, and there is none there. Glynis was sold to Gilbert while my father went to fight the Wake, and Gilbert was supposed to have killed her. Instead, he took her back to Nantes with him."

"Your father?"

"Earl Richard."

The old woman looked at him sharply and beckoned him forward for a closer examination. "Aye, you have the look of him."

"And of her."

"I have no daughter."

"Your daughter lives at Abbeville."

"Aeldrid pronounced her dead when she went with the boy you call Earl Richard. A fine Saxon man he'd found for her and she would have none but the Norman's son." Her voice trailed off. "So you are her bastard then?"

"I am her son by her husband." He moved yet closer. "Grandmother, my mother lives and my father has hopes of bringing her back to Harlowe. He would have you there with her." Roger could not tell if he was even making her think on his words. "You have none other of your blood left and she has none but you and me. I cannot begin to tell you what she has suffered at the hands of the Normans, but if she proves willing to return, I would think you could find it in your heart to welcome her. Jesu! You are all that is left of your family!"

"She has suffered?"

"Aye—much. But it would be better for you to hear of it from her. I did but come to tell you she lives and to ask your blessing as your grandson."

"This is your wife then." She gestured to Eleanor and waited for Eleanor to come closer. "Ah, you are almost as small as I was—but not quite. I did not stand a full five feet. Turn around and let me look at you."

Eleanor did as she was asked and then impulsively knelt at the old woman's feet. Gytha leaned forward to study her face. Her gnarled hands touched the hair that pulled back from Eleanor's face and then reached to lift the chin.

"Art a beauty, child. Norman?"

"Aye. My mother was Mary de Clare and my father Gilbert of Nantes."

"The same Gilbert that carried off my daughter?"

"Aye."

"Then how . . . ?" The old woman's face turned to Roger.

"That too is a long tale. Suffice it to say that I have carried her off and wed with her. Her father would have given her to Robert of Belesme."

"*Belesme!*"

"You have heard of him?"

"Who has not? The Devil travels across the sea. And what sort of man would give his flesh and blood to such a one as that?"

"Gilbert."

"So the Saxon carries off the Norman this time, eh? Aeldrid would have liked that. Let me get down from here and call for wine and cakes, boy. I would hear the whole tale from you. Aye, a Saxon takes a Norman."

"Half Saxon," he reminded her over Eleanor's head. "You forget I am his son also."

"Pfaugh! You are my grandson and therefore Saxon."

Roger pressed his advantage. "Earl Richard names me his heir. I will rule where Aeldrid ruled. Aeldrid's blood will yet again hold sway over this land."

They passed much of the afternoon with Gytha, first telling her of their childhood at Nantes and then all that had befallen them since. She asked a few questions and bristled at mention of Old William, but otherwise seemed to mellow as they talked. Finally she stopped them and smiled at Eleanor. "It has made the circle now, or so it seems, with this Norman girl. From her, Harlowe will get an heir of both bloods and justice will have been done." She caught Roger's surprise at her acceptance and nodded. "Aye, Richard of Harlowe is a good man and rules well, but he is Norman and a reminder that we are a conquered people. Your son can claim some Saxon blood and the people will love him for it." Abruptly her manner changed. "I am tired now, but I would give you my blessing before you leave. May God in his wisdom grant you a long life and peace and happiness and give you strong sons to hold this land after you are gone."

"We would have you move to Harlowe."

"Nay, I belong among my husband's people. All I ask is that if I am alive when the babes are born, bring them to me so I may see those of Aeldrid's line."

"You will not be rid of me so easily," Roger promised. "I intend to come again and hear of my Saxon relatives. Besides, I would practice my Saxon tongue. Who knows? Mayhap Lea will learn it also."

14

Uneven-tempered in the best of times, Robert stalked the length of Belesme's open area between gatehouse and inner wall in a particularly black mood while he considered his next move. The newly arrived intelligence that Roger not only had succeeded in taking Eleanor to England but also had married her under Harlowe's protection tore at his insides like some deep hot pain. In all of his struggles with Gilbert, in all those years since the May festival at Nantes, Robert had never considered her anything but his to take and hold. He barely held his fury in check as he strode past the armory, the stables, the granaries, and the great kitchens that abutted the thick inside wall. Men scattered before his unseeing eyes and even his favorite wolfhound bitch slunk out of his way and took refuge beneath a loading platform.

He stopped where the wall met the new construction of his pretentious manor house—the house he was building for Eleanor of Nantes—and gave a timber support a mighty kick with heavy-soled boot. When it did not budge, he kicked again and again, to no avail, until at last he fell against it and slid down the partially finished side wall. His face contorted hideously to fight the sobs that rose in his throat, his chest ached with unaccustomed tightness, and still he could not hold back the hot tears that scalded the high cheekbones and poured down the planes to fall in wet spots on dry, powdery dirt. For seven years he had fought and schemed to have her, without success.

Above him in one of his towers, Piers de Sols sought out Mabille in alarm. The boy's infatuation with the

woman was over—he served Count Robert now and
Robert's strange behavior frightened him. Mabille listened impatiently while Piers recounted the tale of
Belesme's captain returning from Rennes and bringing
word at last of the Demoiselle. Mabille fought to
conceal her elation over the news.

Then she looked out her slitted window and saw her
son. Not since his cradle days had she ever seen him
cry, and then it was only with that enraged howl of
demand. Alarmed, she gathered her skirts and went
down to him.

With unusual gentleness, she touched his shoulder.
"Come, Robert, let us go up where none can see," she
coaxed.

He looked up in embarrassment and quickly wiped
his wet cheeks with the back of his hand. Nodding, he
allowed Piers to help him stand. The three of them
slowly made their way back to Mabille's solar. Robert's step was heavy and his broad shoulders slumped.
His mother longed to touch and to comfort, but she
did not dare. It was only Eleanor's precipitate flight
that had allowed any sort of a reconciliation between
them, and that reconciliation was tenuous at best. And
she knew that while his anger might be spent for the
moment, it had remarkable powers of rejuvenation.
She had to content herself with a nearly impersonal
pat on the nearest shoulder.

"Sit down, my son, and I will pour you wine, and
you can tell me the whole."

"What is there to tell?" he asked tiredly. "She is in
England now and she is wed."

"*Wed*?" Mabille's voice rose in incredulity. "When?
to whom?"

"Several weeks ago—to Roger FitzGilbert, though
he is FitzGilbert no longer."

"*What*! Robert, do not tease me with nonsense.
Roger FitzGilbert is her brother!" Mabille would have
said more but for the face her son turned to her. The
hurt and anger she saw reduced her to silence.

"So we all thought, fools that we are, Mother. In
truth, he is not her brother. He is not even Gilbert's

bastard!" Anger struggled for the upper hand in his conflicting emotions. "Aye, he is Harlowe's heir!"

"Robert, you cannot have heard it aright." Mabille was positive and reassuring. "Nay—his mother was Gilbert's whore."

"Stolen from Harlowe, who thought her dead. But not, apparently, before Richard de Brione planted his seed." Robert's face twistted at the irony of it. 'Now the Bastard is bastard no more, and lies with Eleanor in the marriage bed while I am left with naught but the humiliation.'

Mabille moved behind him and began to massage the tight muscles of his shoulders. Wisely, for once, she let him talk while she rubbed and listened.

"Aye, I have built her nearly a palace here. Her windows I have ordered from Milano, her furnishings from Florentine and Milanese craftsmen, and she will see them not. I would have used her gently, Mother."

Mabille's jealousy over this unwonted extravagance overcame her caution. "Nay, Robert"—she leaned over to encircle his neck with her slender arms, and her red hair fell like flaming satin over his shoulders—"you are well rid of the girl. 'Tis as well that she goes to him. What need have you of a convent girl?" Her voice dropped huskily. "Now that she is gone, we can be as we always were."

"Stop it!" He loosened her arms roughly and ducked away to rise angrily. 'What need have I of her? *Every* need, Mother! She is mine! Mine! D'ye hear? Mine! I would have wedded with her and sent you away! I would have given her all I could!" He turned back to Mabille. "But she feared me and ran from me, Mother. Aye, I frightened her with this temper I have of you." He advanced on her. "I am your son, Mabille, and look what your blood has brought me—nothing but fear and hatred! If I could, I would open this vein and drain all that I have from you out of me."

Mabille backed away while Piers watched uncomfortably. In his months of service with Robert, the boy had learned not to interfere in the strange quarrels between mother and son. One minute, they could be physically at each other's throats, and the next they could be almost amiable. It was too risky to interfere in something that neither of them understood. Besides, he felt nothing for Mabille anymore. His love and loyalty went to her son in spite of the man's cruelty. When Mabille would have clutched at him for safety, he moved out of the way and went to stand by the stairs.

"Robert, for God's sake . . ." Mabille was alarmed by her son's expression now.

"*God*? What can he do for one whose soul is already damned?" Robert gibed.

"It is not my fault if you disgusted her! You should have laid with her at Fontainebleau and then there could have been no question—nay, my son, 'twas not I who lost her!"

Robert stopped, arrested almost in mid-step. "What did you say?" he asked softly.

"About what?" Mabille sensed the danger had passed and stopped backing away from him. "That you should have just taken your precious Eleanor and let the consequences fall on your shoulders?"

"Aye. I had forgotten about Fontainebleau," he mused almost to himself. "Aye."

"I do not know what you mean, Robert. Has this girl addled your brains until you cannot make sense?"

"Nay, I have but just *come* to my senses. Mother, send to the seneschal—I am going to Rouen!" When she did not move to do his bidding on the instant, he caught at her hands. "Do you not see? I am going to the archbishop!"

"I see many things, Robert, but I cannot see this," she snapped. "Do not speak in riddles to me."

"I will get her back with the Church's aid."

"Are you daft? They make the sign of the Cross at the very mention of your name, my son."

"Eleanor of Nantes is worth the price of a few Masses, Mabille. When it becomes known that she was pledged to me first and that she lay with me at Fontainebleau, the Church will declare her mine."

"You would not take a wife who has lain with

another man—Robert, you have too much pride for that." Mabille caught at Belesme's arm. "Nay, you do not want her!"

"And you do not understand. I will have her if I have to kill everyone who stands in my way—I will do anything to get her and anything to keep her. She is mine."

"Art a fool, Robert. She will bring you grief."

"She cannot bring me any more grief than you brought my father, Mabille."

She winced at his meaning. "And you were too young to know the grief he brought me. We were not well-matched in anything."

"And so you killed him and then lay with every man in the keep, including your own son, to hide your guilt. And you made me as foul as you are, Mother. You cannot understand how it is that I would have a lady as fine as Eleanor."

"So fine that she lay with her brother!"

"He is not her brother!"

"You would take his leavings!"

"Aye! If the Church does not support me, I'll make her a widow!"

"Robert, listen to me! She is wed—she has lain with another man—she is not for you. Let us cast about for another bride for you."

"I would not have the flat-faced woman you would choose. Nay, Mother, it is Eleanor of Nantes for me if I have to kill to get her."

Piers watched the renewed escalation of the quarrel with detachment. Had he been Belesme, he would have sent Mabille away long before and been done with it.

"I am for Rouen—do you help me get ready or not?"

"Nay!"

"Then get out of my keep!"

"Nay! I bore you here, Robert, and I stay!"

"Then be a mother and act in my best interests. Stand with me rather than against me in this."

"I do not want her in my house!"

"You have no claim to Belesme, Mabille. If you would rule, go to your dower lands."

"I will not!"

His hand snaked out and caught her throat. "Nay? Have a care, Mother, that you do not wind up imprisoned in this keep you love so well. You have done naught but defy me where she is concerned." His green eyes glittered. "Aye, 'twould not surprise me to learn you came to Caudebec that night in collusion with mine enemies to draw me away from Rouen." His fingers tightened around her neck. "I ought to strangle you here and now for that."

"I came for your wedding."

"And defied my orders to stay away."

"You are my only son!"

He dropped his hand and sighed. "Aye, I am your son, Mabille, though I curse the blood you gave me. Let us not quarrel again over this."

"But I see your death in this. Robert, I did not tell you—have not told you—that I have dreamed of what will happen. You will lie dead in the dirt beneath Lord Roger's feet ere 'tis done."

A derisive snort escaped him. "Now I know you make up the story, Mother. The day will never come when I cannot take him by any means he chooses." He touched the red marks where his fingers had imprinted her neck. "The next time you would dream, remember this and dream of Lord Roger at my feet, for that is how it will be, I promise."

None was more surprised than the Archbishop of Rouen when Robert of Belesme was ushered into his presence and fell on his knees to kiss his ring. A shiver went through the prelate at the feel of Belesme's strong fingers around his and he fought the urge to pull away. Hastily William Bonne-Ame made the sign of the Cross over the bent black head and bade Robert rise.

"My lord, I could not be more surprised to see you," the archbishop murmured truthfully. "In fact, except for your abortive betrothal, I cannot recall your presence in Holy Church since the Conqueror died."

Robert bristled at the mild reproof in William's voice and then hid his contempt by staring at the floor in what he hoped appeared to be submission. "Father, I have come for your aid," he stated baldly beneath William's thunderstruck stare. "Aye, I ask you to stand with me in seeking the return of my affianced wife."

"Your *wife*?"

"Eleanor of Nantes."

"My son . . ." The archbishop nearly choked on the words. "I can do nothing if she refuses the marriage. Surely you must know the position of the Church on consent."

"She was pledged to me!" Robert's anger flared briefly in spite of his resolve to conciliate William. "I am sorry, excellency, but I am overwrought by what has happened."

William's curiosity was piqued enough that he unbent slightly. "I think, Robert, that you should tell me the whole. Let us share a cup of wine and I will listen—though I am uncertain what you would have the Church do." He motioned Belesme to a low table flanked on either side by two high-backed chairs.

Robert sat and began to recite the story he'd rehearsed in his mind a dozen times. The archbishop listened attentively as Robert wove his lies into the fabric of truth, telling of his contract for Eleanor with Gilbert and Curthose and of his subsequent visit to Fontainebleau. William let him go without interruption until he reached the point of Eleanor's flight with Roger. Then the wily churchman placed his fingertips against each other and broke in somberly.

"Let us return to the place where you admit you took the Demoiselle against her will at Fontainebleau. That *is* what you have said, is it not?"

"Aye." Robert flushed at the hostile tone in William's voice. "But she was pledged to me, excellency— she gave me her pledge first!"

"And she consented to lie with you?" William persisted.

"She did not," Robert admitted, "but we were

pledged. I but had my rights of her. The Church recognizes the plighting of troth."

"You forced the maid."

Belesme was uneasy at the way the archbishop dwelled on the least savory aspect of his story. "Aye," he answered finally. "She is very beautiful and she was to be mine—I could not help myself."

"Were there any witnesses?"

"Not exactly, but the abbess can attest to the fact that Eleanor was distraught and unclothed when I left. I was sorry, of course," he hastened to add under William's disapproving gaze, "but what was done was done. We were pledged to wed, after all, and I considered it no dishonor. Excellency, I expected to fulfill my marriage contract as soon as I finished Curthose's business. You remember well that she was to come to me here in this church."

"I still fail to see what you would have me do, my lord."

"She is in England, excellency, and it is claimed that she has wed the man we knew as Roger FitzGilbert, a man we thought her brother. It has since been asserted tht he is Harlowe's son and it is claimed that he is the heir."

"If what you say is true," William noted slowly, "then she was not free to wed another. Aye, I see your point now, my lord. *If* you tell the truth." He cast a furtive glance at Belesme's sword hand and found it still rested on a knee.

"Excellency"—Belesme raised those strange green eyes to meet the archbishop's squarely—"I will swear on anything you name that Eleanor of Nantes is mine."

"Even at the peril of your immortal soul?"

"Aye."

"Robert, how long has it been since you were confessed?"

"I don't know."

"You know, do you not, that to force yourself on an innocent maid whilst she was under the abbess' protection was a grievous sin—a blot on your soul?"

"Aye, but 'twas not my intent when I went there. In

truth, I could not help myself—I could not look on her and not have her. I only wanted to see if she were whole and unblemished, I swear."

"But you forced her."

"After she had already pledged herself to me. We were contracted to wed!"

William felt a surge of power over the hated Robert of Belesme. If the man told the truth, the Church would be bound to stand with him in demanding the return of Eleanor of Nantes, but William would exact a price for his support.

"You understand that I must send to the abbess and request her to prove or disprove your tale—this must be thoroughly investigated and the Lady Eleanor will have to be questioned." His lips pursed disapprovingly as he surveyed this enemy of the Church. "You have not been overzealous in your observation of the faith, my lord, and I would have some token that you mean to reform ere I begin. It goes against my very nature to compel a Christian lady to live with you."

"I mean her no harm, excellency. I would treat her well and care for her as the mother of my sons," Robert defended. "Aye, I would be good to her." He knew what William Bonne-Ame was thinking and it rankled him to give in, but he could think of no other way to get what he wanted. "Aye, I have built a place for her at Belesme—I will rebuild the chapel also for her and her chaplain."

"And for yourself, my lord? Do you confess for the good of your soul?"

"I bear the burden of all I have done."

"But do you ask for forgiveness and for God's healing grace?"

"Nay!"

"Confess yourself to me, Robert." The hairs on the archbishop's neck rose at the sight of Belesme's hand involuntarily going to his sword hilt, but he did not waver in his determination to win some concession from the count. "Repent and let God remove this burden of sin you carry."

"At what cost? You would raid my purse ere you would give me what is mine by rights!"

"You make it difficult to believe in your sincerity."

"You want my confession?" Robert's voice sounded harsh even to his own ears. "You have not the time, excellency, to listen to all I have done. I have killed, I have maimed, I have ravished, and I have blasphemed—aye—but, wherever I go, men fear me and bend to my will because your fires of hell frighten me not." Belesme's green eyes were cold and unwavering. "Aye, excellency—I'll give you my confession if you have the stomach to listen."

"Confession is only part of it, my lord, and well you know it. Absolution depends on repentance and penance."

They stared at each other for a long minute. Finally Robert reminded himself of his purpose in seeking out William Bonne-Ame, and he went down on his knees before him. Slowly he began the barely familiar ritual by intoning, "Forgive me, Father, for I have sinned . . ." His voice was clear as he began the enumeration of some of his more well-known transgressions. He spoke as perfunctorily as possible, neither glossing over nor gloating over what he had done. He had little interest in turning his own request for aid against himself, but he found it necessary to compromise with the churchman by playing William's game. When he finished what he judged to be enough sin to satisfy William's requirements, he stopped and waited.

Stunned by Robert's dry accounting of his own cruelty, the archbishop had difficulty finding his voice. Finally he managed to chide Belesme, "You should confess more often, my lord, and not save the sins of a lifetime for one confession." He sighed heavily. "I find it difficult to believe in your sincere repentance without some sign. Perhaps there is some proof you can offer God of your intentions?"

"I leave that to you, excellency."

"Ah, well . . . perhaps the building of a church for the people of Belesme and the endowment of a monastery to aid in the repose of your father's soul."

"There are not enough prayers in all of Normandy to raise my father from hell," Robert snorted.

"Nay, you forget—I knew William Talvas. He was a hard man, Robert, but he had his virtues."

"He beat my mother nigh to death." Robert averted his eyes again. "And what you ask would beggar me."

"Nay. You are a wealthy and powerful man, my lord. Share with God, and your gift will be returned to you tenfold or more. And," he added significantly, "I will grant a conditional absolution."

Belesme considered it blackmail, but he would have to at least appear to agree to William's demands if he wanted the archbishop's very necessary support in his quest to have Eleanor's marriage to Roger declared invalid. "So be it," he answered soberly.

15

The garden was still and peaceful with the somnolent sounds of a late-autumn morning. The air was crisp and cool and the leaves of a half-naked tree fell like a golden rain over the stone benches, narrow rock walk, and hedgerows below. Dew still glistened on the rows of herbs and the late-blooming flowers as Eleanor brushed aside a place to sit in this, her haven from the bustle and noise of the great fortress. It was here that she came to meditate in peace each morning before beginning the tasks she set for herself as interim mistress of Harlowe.

Earl Richard had written that he'd found Glynis and they'd renewed their vows of years before. He expected to bring her home to Harlowe by Christmas feast, but first he intended to go to Normandy's court and plead Roger's case with Curthose. Eleanor sighed and fingered the many keys that hung from an iron ring at her girdle, the symbols of her temporary authority in Harlowe. She could scarcely wait to give them up to their rightful owner. It had been difficult, nearly impossible at first, for a girl out of a convent to manage the housekeeping duties of a castle that amounted to nothing short of a small walled city. But now, when she and Roger were able to return to his own lands, she felt more than competent to run the household of the Condes.

Earl Richard had made no mention of her father, but then she supposed he could not be expected to have had any contact with Gilbert of Nantes, given the situation with Glynis. Certainly Gilbert had not deigned to reply to her letter telling of her marriage to Roger, but she could well imagine his reaction. Ah well, she consoled herself, he had been an unnatural parent and he had never loved her anyway.

Her thoughts turned to Roger as she offered a brief prayer of thanksgiving for his love. After all those years of loneliness and misery, she had not believed it possible to be so happy. Each day seemed to bring her some new discovery of his goodness, his kindness, and his love. And he valued her for more than being a woman. Less than a week before, he'd sent her with Harlowe's officer to render the lord's justice in the local court while he rode to Stamford to meet with William Rufus.

Only two nagging fears still weighed on her mind. The first was the feeling that she had not heard the last from Robert of Belesme—there'd been no word at all as to his reaction to her marriage, but she could not believe he would accept such an insult gracefully. In her heart, she half-expected to wake up one morning and find him camped with an army outside Harlowe. And the other nagging fear she harbored secretly was that she was barren. In two and a half months of marriage, her courses had come three times. Roger's attitude puzzled her in this—he just shrugged and said he was glad enough she hadn't conceived.

The gate creaked behind her and the noise brought her back to the reality of the day's business. It was Ralph d'Escrivet come to receive her orders for the running of the household, and if he thought it ironic to consult a young girl about things he'd done since before she was born, he was more than diplomatic about it. He was fatherly, he was patient, occasionally he offered suggestions—but he always followed her orders to the smallest detail.

"My lady." He knelt on one knee by her bench.

She reached to grasp the heavily veined hand. "I wish you would not do that, Sir Ralph." She smiled. "Come sit beside me and tell me what it is we do today." She brushed the leaves off the bench next to her.

"Well," he began as he eased his old bones up and

took the place she indicated, "there's the supplies for winter. I have brought the list of what we have of each item in the stores, Lady Eleanor."

She took the pages of figures and studied them briefly before turning to him. "But you are better able than I to determine the needs, sir, for you have wintered here many times."

"And you are the lady of the house," he reminded her with a gentle smile. "Here, I have brought a list of what we used last year for comparison."

To Eleanor, her sessions with the steward seemed to be lessons in management. Bending herself to the task of checking this year's supplies against last year's usage, she joined Sir Ralph in making up a list of things to be ordered or procured from some of Harlowe's other properties. By the time they'd settled on everything from candles from London to barrels of lampreys from the south and wine from Aquitaine, the sun waxed high in the sky. The old man took meticulous notes on her wishes and nodded his approval as he went over them.

"You've a fine mind in that pretty head," he told her admiringly. "The nuns taught you well."

"Nay, 'twas Roger and you, my friend. The nuns did naught but beat me for my impiety." She watched him roll up his papers. "What about the cloth merchant? If he does not come soon, there will not be enough time to make the Christmas robes. I would not have it said that everyone did not get at least one change of clothing."

"He comes today, my lady, and I have brought girls in from the village to assist in the sewing once the materials are chosen and the patterns are cut."

"Aye. And I would have some martin and vair for the lining of cloaks for my lord, Earl Richard, Lady Glynis, yourself, Brian, the bailiff, and the sons who foster here." She counted them off on her fingers.

"And for you."

"And for me." She nodded. "Aye, but first I need to find from Roger how much he can afford for that."

"Lady, Earl Richard would expect to buy your winter clothes—'tis little enough he could do for the service you give him here. Besides, you are of his family now and he takes pride in you. Order what you would have and be generous with yourself—'tis what he would tell you if he were here."

"Nay." She shook her head emphatically. "I will not be one of those wives who are said to squander their husbands' substance, and I will not hang on the sleeves of his relatives. Let me find out what Roger will pay before I order."

Privately, Ralph thought that the young lord would spare no expense for his lady, so plainly was he besotted with her, so the steward had little fear that she would lack for anything. He rose to take his leave, his notes rolled in his hand.

"Nay, I'll walk with you, sir," Eleanor decided, "for I have sent the women out washing the linens while the weather still holds warm enough." She tucked her hand in the crook of the old man's elbow. "I ought to see that they do it all."

"They will." He opened the garden gate for her and drew her along the wall where they could see workers cutting the fresh rushes for the floors. "Do you want them woven or scattered in your chamber? I've ordered them scattered in the hall because they are easier to sweep up if need be and Earl Richard cannot abide the stench of rotting food beneath his feet. We clear them away several times before the spring sweetening."

"Aye, so we did at Nantes."

"The lime-washing should be complete before supper and the rushes will go down in the morning."

"Well, I think I prefer to have them woven into several mats for the solar so they can be picked up and aired on pleasant days," she decided.

They walked along until they reached the open yard that swarmed with activity. The sounds of the blacksmith's hammer, rolling carts, herded animals, and newly arriving riders vied with the shouts of orders between masters and workmen to create a cacophony that made normal speech impossible. Eleanor had to lean against Sir Ralph to listen to his explanations of various projects. Suddenly she stiffened as she made out shouted insults across the way, and then she picked her way purposefully through the crowded yard toward the altercation. A puzzled Ralph followed and tried to shout a path clear for her.

"You!" she called out to one of the youths gathered in a corner. "What is the meaning of this?"

The boy, taken aback by her sudden appearance, stammered something unintelligible. She turned to another and demanded, "Well? I thought I heard something I did not like."

"We were teasing the stable bastard, my lady—that was all," someone off to the side explained.

"All?" Her voice rose in incredulity. "Nay, I will not stand for it! Do you hear me? I will not stand for it!"

"Lady—" Ralph was taken aback by her anger at so small a thing and sought to calm her.

"Nay!" She shook off the hand he placed on her shoulder and bent to examine the young boy whose grubby hands were rubbing away tears. " 'Tis no light thing to torment someone for what he cannot help. Here . . ." She offered a corner of her gown to rub at the smudges on round cheeks. The other boys milled around her in disbelief that she would soil her gown on the dirty child. Rounding again on them, she demanded, "Whose child is this?"

"Eadgytha's."

"His father?"

"She is a Saxon slut—who can tell who his father is?" the boldest boy ventured sullenly.

"Silence! Your countess is Saxon, fool!" Eleanor railed. "My lord's mother is Saxon!" She turned to the steward. "Do you know this boy?"

"Aye—his mother is one of the village girls we bring in here to do the laundry. She's a pretty thing and too often some of the noble sons here try to make sport of her."

By now the child had determined that Eleanor meant to champion him and he clutched her skirt with his dirty fingers. She brushed back his hair for a better look at his face.

"He's a pretty child."

"My lady," the boldest boy spoke again, "he's a bastard."

"Don't ever use that word in my presence again! Listen to me! Once my lord was being tormented for being a bastard, and do you know what happened? I'll tell you—William the Conqueror chanced on it, and do you know what he did?" Without waiting for anyone to guess, she went on, "He had the boys thrashed and he took my lord into his service. If he had not done that, my lord could have been a stableboy too, and would never have discovered that he was the legitimate heir here."

"Humph! Well, he's not legitimate." the unrepentant boy pointed at the child clutching her gown.

"Nonetheless, I will not have him called names." Eleanor had mastered her anger now as she smoothed the tangled crown of dirty blond hair. "Each of you will be birched ten times."

"But I didn't call him anything!" one of the boys in the group protested.

"And you did not stop it, either, did you? Nay, if you were part of the tormenting, you can take your punishment," she pronounced flatly. "Sir Ralph, will you see that my orders are carried out?"

"Aye." He called out the name of each boy and ordered them to the practice yard. "I'll have the squiremaster do it."

Roger had seen much of the incident from where he had been at the armorer's. At first he'd been inclined to intervene, but Eleanor had reached them before he could get there and his heart swelled with pride at her swift disposal of the problem. His memory harkened back to that other incident so long ago and he had to smile. His Lea had not forgotten.

"Well done!" he called out before he reached her. "Jesu, Lea, but you have not lost any of your fire." He turned to the steward. "Whose child?"

"His mother is a Saxon villager, my lord, and his

father is unknown. Before the boy was born, she claimed to have been ravished by one of the squires sent here for training. My lord Richard offered her justice if she would name her attacker, but she would not." The old man let out an expressive sigh. "We thought we knew who it was, but without her charge there was nothing we could do. Earl Richard gave her money and sent her back to the village, but once the boy was born, she came back. Now we suspect she lies with most of the young men."

"How awful! Roger—"

"What?"

"He is not an ill-looking child—can I not take him for my page? I mean, he would have to be washed and dressed and trained, of course."

"Aye, he would that."

"But William thought you bastard-born when he took you into his train."

"Aye. Lea, if it pleases you, do what you would. He seems over-young to me."

She knelt again at the child's side. "Your name?" When he just blinked and did not answer, she tried, "How are you called?" Again, no answer.

"Lady Eleanor, you cannot have a speechless page," Sir Ralph protested. "Let me find him a place with the monks."

"Nay! Roger, ask him in Saxon what his name is."

Roger repeated her question and was rewarded with a mumble of sorts. He leaned down and tried again. This time they heard a barely audible "Garth." Roger straightened up and grinned at Eleanor. "If you would keep him, you'll have to learn enough Saxon to talk to him until he can be taught French."

"You speak the tongue, and there are others about who do also—I am sure we can manage. Tell him what I have decided and see if he would like to live with me."

Roger bent to translate her message and was rewarded with a stream of Saxon spoken so fast he was hard put to understand. He said something else to the child and received another answer.

"Well?"

"He says he would like to stay with the pretty lady. Apparently he is small for his age, because he says he is nearly six."

" 'Tis young, my lady."

"Aye, but age is something that can be remedied with time, Sir. Ralph. By the time he learns the language and the manners, he will surely be old enough. Until then, he can roll a pallet by my door." She looked down at the grubby hands that still firmly held her skirt. "But for now, would you see him cleaned up? Aye—and get his head deloused and trimmed."

"Your charity does you honor, my lady," was about all Ralph could manage as he disengaged the boy called Garth from Eleanor's gown and led him off.

Roger watched with an amused expression on his face. He draped an arm about her shoulders and pulled her against his side. "You cannot know how proud I am that you are mine, Lea."

It was midafternoon before the cloth merchant had spread his wares and she had chosen what she would have from the large assortment he brought. She collected swatches of each selection and made her way to her solar. On the morrow, she would go over what was to be made into what with her women so they could cut the patterns. She was satisfied with herself over the purchases she had made, purchases which included rich materials for new bed hangings in Earl Richard's chamber. They would be her gift to Glynis.

As she rounded the top of the winding tower stairs, she was struck at first by the silence. At this time of day, she could ordinarily expect to hear the chatter of half a dozen maids gathered by the west-side window slits to ply their needles. Instead, she found Roger alone. His tunic lay discarded in a heap beside the table that held the washbasin.

"I sent your women away, Lea, so that I could wash the dust off me in peace." He favored her with a crooken grin. "I heard the cloth merchant you were expecting had come at last and I thought you'd be up." He dropped his washing cloth into the basin water. "Come show me what you've bought, so long as you've not beggared me."

"Ralph said you told him that I could buy the whole if I wanted, but I did not," she laughed. "Aye—I've cost you some gold this day, husband, but 'twas well spent." Ignoring his invitation to show her swatches, she laid them aside and moved closer. "Were you done, or would you have me finish for you? I could order a washtub, you know."

"Nay, if you could but rinse off my back, I'd be grateful—'tis more dust than sweat, anyway. I was showing the squires how quintains were made at Nantes and the straw was full of it." He pulled a stool close to the basin and sat leaning forward while she wrung out the rag he'd been using. As she began wiping his back, he ventured casually, "I have heard from Henry."

"When?"

"While you were in the hall with your merchant."

She stood still and silent for a moment before daring to ask, "And what said he to our marriage? Was he angry that you did not tell him?"

"He said that if he'd known you would take just anyone, he'd have pressed his own suit—that he might not be heir to an earldom but he had some prospects."

"He did not!" She tugged a lock of hair.

"Ouch! Vixen! Nay, he did not, Lea, but he was all that was gracious. He wished us well."

"But what did he say?"

"If you would know, ask him—he comes tomorrow."

"Tomorrow! Sweet Mary! We cannot be ready for him so soon."

"You obviously have never traveled with Henry, my love. He moves at whim and often rides with as few as two or three men at his side. Aye—and he will stay at all manner of hostelries without a care for luxury. I'll warrant it has been a while since he's enjoyed anything half so nice as I know you'll provide for him here. Nay—do not fret yourself over it."

"But he's a prince!"

"He allows himself few friends, Lea, but we are

among them. You serve him better by letting him just be Henry."

"But he was not surprised by our marriage? He is not angry? What if he comes in anger?" She returned to her basic fear that something could mar her happiness with Roger.

"He was surprised, but he approves your choice of a husband, Lea. He actually wrote that if it could not be Henry, then it ought to have been me." He caught at her waist and pulled her against him where he sat. Pillowing his head against the softness of her breast, he tightened his arm around her and murmured softly, "I did not send your women away to talk of Henry, love. Is it over?"

She knew immediately what he meant and nodded. "Aye, I am sorry it came yet again." Her pulse quickened as she caressed the thick, waving blond hair. "I pray daily that I may conceive."

"I told you 'twas early days yet, Lea. I would have you to myself as long as possible. Besides, God will send us a child when he is ready, and not before." He burrowed his head against her. "Ahhhh, now there's an idea I like—rub my head."

She let her fingers furrow the thick hair, parting and massaging, savoring the feel of it. Even after more than two months, it was a marvel to her that this big strong man was her husband. At night, when she would awaken beneath the weight of his arm around her, she could clasp it and thank God for the gift of his love.

His hand moved from her waist to smooth her gown over the curve of her hip. As if sharing the same thoughts, he half-whispered against her, "Sometimes I think I must be dreaming, Lea, and I am afraid I'll waken and you'll be gone—I cannot believe you have come to me."

She clasped his head tightly. "Aye, 'tis the same with me."

"I want you so much that I fear I disgust you with my needs."

Even as he spoke, both his hands slid over her hips

in a caress that kindled desire. Her mouth went dry
and her whole being responded to his touch. "And I
fear that you will think me wanton," she answered
softly, "for I never tire of this."

He pushed the bench back and stood at the same
time. "Let me bar the door and then I'll help you
undress." He released her to pad barefoot to the door,
where he slid the heavy wooden beam through the
iron rings. " 'Twould take the whole garrison to bother
us now, love," he announced as he turned back to her.
She stood naked above the pile of her hastily discarded gown and undershift, her slim white body gleam-
ing in the semi-shadows of the stone-walled room.

"Jesu, but you are beautiful—all of you, Lea."

Prince Henry followed his messenger not by a day,
but rather by a matter of hours. It was nearly dusk
when he ordered his companion to sound his arrival at
Harlowe. He'd ridden hard on his journey from his
brother's palace outside London to warn that Belesme
had landed in England in the company of William
Bonne-Ame's representative and the papal legate to
England. At least Rufus had not been in London to
welcome them. Henry was uncertain of their business,
but he was uneasy to see the Church in any sort of
alliance with Robert of Belesme. It could not augur
well for Roger and Eleanor.

As he awaited the raising of the iron gates, his
thoughts turned to her. He would see her again, this
girl of his youthful dreams, and she would be his
friend's wife. A sigh of regret escaped him as he asked
himself how fate could have allowed Eleanor of Nantes
to slip out of his reach. Nay, he had to own the
truth—his own ambition had cost him the woman he
still believed he could have loved. Had he been willing
to gamble his chances for England's throne, he could
have had her. But he'd decided several years back
when Rufus first mentioned he intended to name Henry
his heir that he would have to have a Saxon bride to
unite the country behind him in the face of what
would surely be Curthose's rage.

But for now, he would see Roger and Eleanor and wish them well. A smile curved his generous mouth as he remembered his shock, then his anger, and finally his acceptance of the news that they had wed. It was hard to fault someone for taking one's advice, and that is exactly what they'd done. He'd told Roger to find her a strong husband and he had found her the strongest man available—except for Robert of Belesme. Jesu, what he would have given to be there when Robert received the news that his intended bride had wed the man they all thought her half-brother.

In front of him, the first gate slowly creaked upward and he urged his horse onto the floating bridge. His eyes traveled upward to the marvel that was Harlowe. Well, if Belesme meant war, Henry could not imagine a better fortress for it. Aye—and he would see to it that Rufus did not stand for the amassing of too many troops on English soil.

They were standing there within the inner gate, smiling and eager to welcome him. His breath caught in his throat and his heart gave a rush when he saw her. He'd not thought it possible, but each time he saw her, she was more beautiful than his memory of her. He tossed the reins of his horse to a waiting stableboy and dismounted. Careful, Henry, he told himself, do not give yourself away—she is his now, and you might need him later.

When Roger would have knelt at his feet, Henry stopped him and enveloped him in a tight embrace. Giving the kiss of peace on both cheeks, he stepped back for a better look at his friend.

"Jesu, but the wedded state is good for you, Roger. You look well."

"Aye—come give Lea a kiss, my lord. She would have it that you are angry with us for deceiving you, but the fault was mine. She did not know."

Eleanor came forward smiling, her arms outstretched to clasp his hands. Henry caught them and pulled her closer to plant chaste kisses on her cheeks before releasing her and stepping back. There was a glow of

happiness about her that he'd not been privileged to
see before, and it gave him another pang of regret.

"My lord Henry . . ." She dipped a graceful curtsy
before him. "In the absence of Earl Richard, we bid
you welcome to Harlowe."

"In truth, I could not stay away, Lady Eleanor. I
had to come and see for myself that Roger was indeed
heir to all this and that you had wed."

"Aye—'tis unbelievable, isn't it? I pinch myself black
and blue to prove 'tis not all a dream."

Reluctantly he tore himself back to Roger. "Well,
my friend, I have much to tell, but first I need a bath
and a pitcher of wine to wash the dust from my throat.
I've ridden direct from London."

Roger nodded and clapped for a page. "Take my
lord Henry to my father's quarters," he ordered. To
Sir Ralph he added, "And send up the tub."

Arm in arm, Roger and Eleanor watched Henry
follow the boy. Then Eleanor pulled away. "I'll send
one of the boys up with his wine while I change my
clothes."

"Change your clothes?"

"Aye—you would not have me get this gown wet,
would you?"

"Lea, I would not have you bathe him."

"Nonsense, Roger. To do otherwise would be an
insult."

"You do not know him around women."

"Well, I am your wife. Surely he would not dare lay
a hand on his vassal's wife, would he? Oh, Roger, do
not look like that! This is Harlowe and I know what I
am about now."

Eleanor found Prince Henry already nearly undressed,
sparing her the necessity of removing his clothing.
Only his chausses and cross-garters remained and, when
she knelt to attend to them, he stopped her.

"Nay, I can undo them faster than you can." He felt
strange to be standing naked in front of her. Stop this,
he chided himself—you have had a hundred women—
how is it that this one is so different? She turned to lay

down the linens she carried and he hastily slid his body into the steaming water. Still, he was unprepared for her touch.

She moved behind him and started with his back. She lathered and rinsed him quickly before leaning over him to get his chest. Her dark braid fell forward to brush his shoulder and he could smell the soft scent of roses. A sense of loss overwhelmed him. Almost involuntarily he reached to clasp her wrist against his wet chest. She dropped the soapy cloth into the water in surprise.

"You are happy?"

"Aye."

"I am glad for you."

"My lord . . . please . . ." She tried to pull away gently.

He did not seem to notice as he mused aloud, "I think I have loved you since that day we met at Nantes, Eleanor."

"My lord, do not—"

"Nay, let me have my say—'tis only this once I can say it." He let her loose enough to slide his hand down to clasp hers. "Aye, I could have loved you differently, Eleanor of Nantes," he continued so softly that she could barely hear, "and there would have been no need for others."

He seemed younger, more vulnerable, almost boyish as he cocked his head upward to look at her. She resisted the urge to brush back his hair and soothe him as one would a disappointed child. If any chanced to come in, the worst would be thought.

"Henry," she said gently, "do not say anything that will stain your honor or mine."

"Nay." He shook his head and fixed her with warm brown eyes. "What I feel for you, Eleanor, cannot be dishonorable, for 'tis the purest thing I have ever felt. I would see you happy above all else, and if I cannot have you, then I am glad 'tis Roger who does. He loves you and will treat you well. Just remember— should anything happen to him, I will ever stand ready to hold for you and yours. There—I have said it." He released her hand and leaned back against the rim of the washtub with a sigh. "I would not say anything else to distress you."

"My lord, there was a time when I could have loved you, too."

"Those years in Fontainebleau?"

"Aye—you and Roger were all I had then. Your letters and your visits kept me alive."

"Nay—you were his in spirit even then. I think my hopes for you died with your mother, but I did not know it."

She leaned over and retrieved the cloth from the water and began to soap it anew. "I will always remember what you have said, my lord, and I am grateful for your friendship." She reached for a pitcher of water to wet his hair and poured a little over his head. "Let me finish this so that you can get your supper."

If the prince had intended to broach the subject of Robert of Belesme quietly with Roger over his cup, he was denied the opportunity. The covers had scarcely been lifted from the tables and the mummers had just begun their acts when a dusty rider was escorted in with a letter for "Roger of Harlowe." Roger stepped out into a corridor to better read the message and then returned white-faced and grim to the hall. When Eleanor tried to question him, he brushed her aside and turned to Henry.

"I would have a word with you in private, my lord."

"Roger, I would know—what is it?" Eleanor demanded.

"Nay, not yet—I will tell you the whole later," he promised grimly.

Henry nodded and rose to follow Roger. "You pardon, Lady Eleanor," he murmured as he passed her, "but 'tis nothing, I am sure."

Not to be left behind, she gathered her skirts and went after them, catching them on the narrow, winding stairs that led to her solar. By now, she was well aware that whatever the messenger brought, it was not nothing.

"Roger, I demand to know—what oversets you so?"

"Belesme."

"Jesu!" She exhaled sharply and crossed herself. "He comes to fight us?"

"I would that he had—I could beat him here at that."

"Then?"

Henry intervened smoothly. "Eleanor, can you not see he is disturbed? Pour us all some wine and let us look at what is to be done." He gave her a gentle push on up the stairs. "Nay—we are right behind you."

She finished the climb and lit the brazier with a torch from the stairwell with shaking hands. Belesme. What could he possibly do to them now unless he provoked a quarrel with Roger? She fastened the torch in an empty iron ring and went to a cupboard to get cups. Behind her, she could hear Roger speaking low to Henry. She poured the rest of the contents of the wineskin into three cups and turned around to watch the prince read the message. He was shaking his head in disbelief.

"Well?" she demanded. "It concerns me, does it not? I would not be protected from mere words, Roger." When he did not reply, she moved closer and could see some sort of official seal affixed to the parchment. "Please—what is it?"

Henry read it again and swore softly. "Belesme has turned to Holy Church seeking your return, Eleanor. He charges you cannot have wed Roger because you are already wed to him."

"*What!*" It was nearly a screech. "And they listen to him? Let me see!"

"Aye." Roger nodded grimly. "They listen to him. We are summoned to London to appear before the Archbishop of Canterbury and the Bishop of Durham and the papal legate to answer Belesme's charge."

"But they are wrong! How can I belong to Count Robert? How could he dare to say such a thing?"

"Eleanor, think—is there anything that could have happened, anything that could have been construed as a binding promise between you and Belesme?" Henry tried to push the thunderstruck girl to a bench, but she stood as though rooted to the floor.

Roger slid an arm around her as she began to shake uncontrollably. "Lea, in fright, did you agree to wed with him?" He drew her closer and began to stroke her hair in spite of Henry's presence. He forced himself to speak with a calmness he did not feel. "We must examine where he came up with his charges so that we can refute them."

"But I promised him nothing! Nay, I refused him and he beat me!"

"Where? At Fontainebleau?" Henry demanded. "Tell me the whole that I may better understand what we ought to do."

"Let her collect her thoughts, my lord. Lea, come sit you down and take a drink of this." Roger led her to the bench and held the cup for her to drink as one would hold for a child. "Here . . ."

She gulped obediently, pushed away the rest, and took a deep breath to calm her thudding heart. "Nay, I never said anything that he could use for this. Roger, he came to me at Fontainebleau, gloating that he had forced my father to give me to him. He was cold and direct and demanded to see what his sword had bought him. He made me disrobe." She shuddered as she remembered his coldness at first.

"God's teeth! The whore's son!" Henry's hand crept involuntarily to where his sword usually hung from his belt.

"Let her finish. Lea . . ." Roger's voice was soft and gentle as he dropped to a knee beside his wife. "Lea, what happened then? What did he say? What did you say?"

"He . . . he kissed me . . . and he touched me over my body—I thought he meant to ravish me. I . . . I asked him not to dishonor me—and he laughed. Then he turned me loose and said he was in full armor and had not the time. He handed me my clothes and tried to pledge with me." She stared unseeing into the space before her and remembered it clearly. "He said the words and bade me repeat after him, but I would not.

I remembered what you both had said about taking my vows as a nun and I reasoned it would be the same thing. He hit me several times, but I still refused to say what he would have me say, I swear. He frightened me, but I decided I would not be beaten to death like a tame animal. I began to fight back—I scratched at his face—and he began to laugh. His manner changed then and he told me we would pledge in Rouen the first of July. He picked up his helmet and left."

"He did not ravish you? He let you strike him?" Henry seemed amazed that she could have come out of such an encounter with Robert with nothing more than a bruise or two.

"She came to me virgin," Roger stated flatly, "and there's good men and true that can swear to having seen the evidence."

"There's nothing more—nothing else happened?" Henry persisted. "Did you see him alone again?"

"Aye—in Fuld Nevers' stronghold. He kissed me and tried to lie with me, but he did not ask for my pledge." She had to smile at that memory. "Roger cooled his lust with the blade of his sword." She looked up at both men and stated emphatically, "I never said anything at any time that Robert of Belesme could have construed to have been a pledge to wed with him, I so swear. And I will swear to Pope Victor himself that I tell the truth."

"Robert lies." Roger's eyes met Henry's above her. "He lies."

"Aye, but how do we prove it? He must have said something—have told something—that made the Archbishop of Rouen believe hm. William Bonne-Ame is no man's fool—my father put him where he is today." Henry paced to stare at the flaming brazier. "It could be that it is just his word against Eleanor's, but I doubt he would come forward with such flimsy evidence."

"Lea does not lie!"

"Nay . . . nay—'twas not my meaning. What I would say is that he must think he has something else to bear his charges—he has bribed or coerced someone to corroborate what he says." He caught Eleanor's indignant expression and added gently, "Whatever can be said of the Count of Belesme, my lady, it cannot be said that he is a fool. Can you not imagine the reception he received from Holy Church when he turned to them? Aye, I'll warrant William's heart paused at the sight of him."

"But I have told the truth!"

"I believe you." Henry stared into the fire as though looking for some answer to be read there. Finally he straightened. "The thing is now to decide how best to counter him."

Possessing Eleanor's hand and holding it tightly, Roger decided, "We go to London—we have nothing to hide—we were wed in Holy Church."

"It could be a trap to draw you out," Henry mused thoughtfully. "Here he cannot touch you, but there you are out in the open with almost none to support you."

Eleanor's eyes widened at the implication and she clutched Roger's hand. "What then do you advise?" she asked Henry.

"I don't know. I would think some before I decided, if it were I summoned to a strange city to answer a madman's charges."

"Henry, we cannot run again. Besides, if we fail to answer the summons, 'twill appear she is guilty," Roger reasoned, "and she will be excommunicated. We have to go."

"Why?" the prince countered. "Why cannot you steal the march on Robert and go directly to Rome and apply for a hearing with His Holiness? Aye—I would send an envoy of my own with you—or I could persuade Curthose to do so in your behalf."

" 'Twas Curthose's approval of a marriage with Belesme that brought all this about," Roger reminded him.

"My brother weaves like a plant in the wind—he bends the way the wind blows. Let me but talk to him and I can persuade him—especially if Belesme is over here."

"Nay—in Rome, I am even farther away from any help. My lands lie in Normandy and my father's are here. I say we go to London and prove Robert a liar in the court of his choosing." Roger rose and pulled Eleanor up to hold her against him. "Henry, I know you speak from love of us, but I would have this settled quickly. Don't you see—these charges make it appear that Lea is an adulteress. Aye—and she could carry my child anytime now. I will not have my children called bastard by anyone."

"Go to the Holy Father."

Roger threw his hands up in disgust. "Jesu! Think what you advise, my lord—the courts at Rome drag on for years over small appointments. What happens to Lea during that time? I can tell you—some will call her my leman rather than my wife, and I could not bear that."

"Eleanor . . ." Henry turned his attention to her. " 'Tis you this most concerns. What do you want to do?"

She leaned into Roger and rubbed her cheek against the soft velvet of his tunic. "I am not afraid to face Belesme with my husband at my side, and I would rather see him in a room surrounded by people than across a battlefield from Roger." She could listen to his heart beat beneath the warm fabric. "Aye, I have told the truth here and I can tell it in London."

"So be it then. I will ride to my brother Rufus and try to persuade him to return to London before the hearing convenes. Mayhap his presence will restrain Count Robert a little."

"But will it help Lea?" Roger countered. "He is not known for his cordial relations with the Church."

"They are made up for now."

"But why should he do anything for me?" Eleanor ventured. "From what I have heard—"

"You have heard he is only interested in men," Henry cut her off abruptly, "and 'tis true. But I can tell you this—once he is persuaded to take a stand, he is not like my brother Curthose. Aye, when Rufus stands, he stands. Besides, he will at least want to see the woman my father once thought to make him take for England's queen."

"Nay!"

"Aye—but I argued you should come to me instead. Much good it did me when your mother died," he finished with a trace of bitterness in his voice.

"When do we have to go to London, Roger?" Eleanor asked quietly to change the subject.

"November 5—we'll have to leave after All Hallows."

"Two weeks then."

"Aye."

"Oh, Roger, I had so many plans—we would celebrate Christmas feast here with your mother and father. I have ordered the robes for everyone, and the women are making new hangings for your parents' chamber . . ." Her voice trailed off in disappointment. "Sweet Mary, but I was happy here."

"Shhhh, Lea . . ." Roger held her close and spoke softly. "Lea, we have a lifetime of Christmases ahead of us. Besides, this thing surely cannot drag out that long. 'Tis probable that we'll be here anyway."

"But I won't have done it. I wanted to show everyone that I could manage it, that I could plan and make it happen . . ."

"Is this the girl who long ago at Nantes told me she had not the least ability in housekeeping?" Henry laughed. "God's teeth, Eleanor, but you put such importance to such small things."

She pulled away from Roger to face Henry indignantly. "And is it wrong to want to have the accomplishments of other women? You forget I have spent much of my life locked away behind high walls. Nay, this is the first time I have been free and I would have my husband proud of me!"

"Lea . . . Lea . . ." Roger pulled her back and attempted to soothe her ruffled feelings. "You cannot know how proud I am of you."

"Even you cannot understand that I would be valued for more than the way I look to people," she wailed against him.

"Listen, this is Roger—I know all your faults, Lea,

and I love you still." He brushed back a stray strand of dark hair from her face. "I love the way you look, the way you talk—your loyalty, your strength, your courage, and your faith in me—aye, I love everything about you."

"And I did not mean that you were not an accomplished housewife, Eleanor," Henry spoke behind her. "I but teased that you worried over small things."

She managed a sheepish smile. "The fault was mine, my lord. Here you both were trying to help me in . . . in this thing with Belesme—and all I could do was strike at you because I will not have the Christmas I had planned."

" 'Tis all right," Roger reassured. "We'll have this settled and be back here long before then. You'll be here to welcome my mother and father."

16

The eyes of the curious seemed to follow her everywhere she went. Only the fact that her accuser was the hated Count of Belesme kept her from being mobbed by those who would call her a public harlot. As it was, many felt that she could be excused on the grounds that Count Robert was hardly the husband for any woman, and certainly not for a convent-bred girl. William Rufus himself had returned to London to lend his kingly presence to the Church tribunal called to decide which man was entitled to Eleanor of Nantes. It had taken all of Henry's persuasive powers to convince Rufus he had any interest in the matter at all, but once that was accomplished, the king now stood squarely behind Harlowe's heir.

Stating flatly that she had nothing to hide and that the truth would exonerate her, Eleanor refused to attend the opening of the tribunal in the colorless gray garb suggested by the prince. She chose instead to appear clad as a lady of rank and fortune, wearing a purple samite gown and golden girdle beneath a fine cloak of russet velvet lined with sable. As she walked into the chamber at Westminster, she was flanked by Roger, Rannulf of Chester, and several of Harlowe's vassals. She held her chin high and met the gaze of those who would look on her squarely. A murmur of appreciation swept through the predominantly male crowd who sat assembled to watch these curious proceedings.

An expectant hush fell over the room as she took her seat beside the man she'd dared to marry in defiance of her father and her duke. A side door opened to admit the Archbishop of Canterbury, the Bishop of Durham, and the papal legate to England. Behind them trailed nearly a dozen scribes in black robes brought to record the testimony and to examine the evidence as it was presented. Eleanor settled in her seat and took a deep breath to maintain her calm. Another door opened and King William Rufus strode in, followed by Robert of Belesme and Prince Henry. The sight of Belesme with Rufus nearly unnerved her until her eyes met Henry's and he nodded and smiled slightly.

Belesme was magnificently dressed in cloth of gold and green velvet. He made his way to a chair at the opposite side of the room and sat down to stare at her. His face was cold and impassive.

She stared back coolly and resisted the urge to cling to Roger. They were, after all, in Westminster and surrounded by a roomful of people. Besides, she would not let Robert of Belesme know she still feared him, now perhaps more than ever. Before, she had not realized the depth of her love for Roger or of his for her—now what she had was too precious to lose. If the Church ruled against her . . . She dared not let herself even think on it. She knew she was right and she was Roger's wife. She could not conceive of wedding with Belesme now—or ever.

It was as if Robert knew he was in her thoughts. The green eyes met and locked with hers across the small open space, and she could see the triumph in them. An involuntary shiver coursed down her back when at last he smiled. Her fingers crept to entwine with Roger's and she was rewarded with a squeeze of reassurance.

As presiding judge, the Archbishop of Canterbury rose and all followed suit. He raised his arms and called on God in prayer to grant the wisdom necessary to decide this problem that faced them, to give them an open heart and mind, and to render them just. And then he called on God's blessing for all assembled there. Eleanor could sense that Belesme's eyes never left her during the prayer.

As they were taking their seats again, she was surprised to see Fontainebleau's abbess and two of the nuns come in silently and slip into seats near the side door. Idly she wondered what business they could have here in London.

The churchmen whispered between themselves briefly and then the Bishop of Durham nodded to one of the scribes who rose and addressed the crowd. His voice was stern with self-importance.

"We are met here to examine the case of the Lady Eleanor, daughter to Count Gilbert of Nantes," he intoned, "for the purpose of determining if she is the lawful wife of Roger de Brione, late called Roger FitzGilbert, or if she is the betrothed wife of Robert Talvas, Count of Belesme." He took a breath and turned to Belesme, saying, "As charging party, my lord, your testimony will be heard first. You will rise and come forward."

Robert stood and nodded before moving to a chair in front of the dais where the churchmen sat. He waited for the signal to sit.

"State your name, my lord."

Belesme's eyebrow rose a fraction, but he stared again at Eleanor while speaking clearly and precisely. "Robert Talvas, Count of Belesme, Lord of Mantes, Vyonne, and Eisle."

The clerk produced a small golden casket. "My lord of Belesme, herein lies a relic of St. Catherine. Do you swear upon this that you tell this tribunal the truth as you know it?"

Robert's green eyes flickered over the room, stopping briefly to watch Eleanor, and then he placed his hand on the metal box. "Aye, I so swear."

"So help you God at the peril of your immortal soul?" the clerk persisted.

"So help me God."

The clerk removed the box and placed it on a table near the papal legate before taking his seat. Belesme moved his chair closer to the dais and sat also.

"My lord"—the archbishop leaned forward to address Robert—"these are serious charges you would make against this woman. To find her not this man's wife is to find her guilty of adultery. Is that what you would have of this hearing?"

"Nay, I would have her still. I do not believe that she understood she was mine when she pledged to him."

A ripple of whispers spread through those in the room before the archbishop raised his hand for silence. "Then, Count Robert, we must ask you to tell us why you believe this woman should be given to you."

Eleanor listened in shocked silence as Robert settled back and told his story skillfully, weaving truth with lies until the whole seemed fact. He was clever enough to tell of his rough treatment of her, of his forcing her to disrobe, of his demanding her pledge, and then he stunned everyone by asserting she'd lain with him at Fontainebleau and had given him her pledge to marry at Rouen.

"It's a lie! He lies!" Roger jumped to his feet and took several steps forward before Harlowe's vassals managed to restrain him. Even then, he called out to Belesme, "You have condemned your soul to hell with your perjury, Robert! You know she came to me virgin!"

Instead of responding to Roger, Belesme turned to the archbishop and repeated levelly, "I had her and she was promised to me."

"By her own words she was pledged to you?" The churchman leaned forward.

"Aye—I swear it."

"Lies—all of it," Roger countered.

"Silence!" The papal legate raised his hand for order and then inclined his head to confer in whispers with the archbishop and the bishop. Nodding, he turned back to address Belesme. "My lord, would you repeat for us the words she used to exchange vows with you?"

"Aye—she said, 'I, Eleanor, daughter to Gilbert of Nantes, take thee, Robert of Belesme, for my betrothed husband. I so swear.' "

"Those were her exact words?"

"Aye."

It was Eleanor's turn to come to her feet. "Nay! I'll not listen to his lies in silence, excellencies! Those were his words—not mine—and I refused to repeat them for him! He beat me and I would not say them!" She clasped Roger's hand and held it up. "This is my husband—my only husband—as God is my witness!"

"Lady Eleanor . . ." The Archbishop of Canterbury's voice was not unkind as he addressed her. "We will hear you out when we have finished listening to Count Robert. Please be seated and refrain from screaming here—there is no need for such outbursts."

"No *need*? Excellency, my lord of Belesme has come here and all but said she is a harlot, and you would have her sit calmly and listen." Roger's voice rose angrily. "Nay, she will not!"

"Lord Roger," the Bishop of Durham addressed him, "she will answer his charges in due time. Until then, you will both be pleased to sit whilst Count Robert tells his grievance. We will question him then and ask him to provide corroboration of his testimony. When that is done, the Lady Eleanor will have her opportunity to defend herself and call whomsoever she will for witness." He cast a withering look at Eleanor as she made to speak again. "Aye, and if need be, we will have both of you wait outside before we will listen to any more such disruptions."

"Excellency." William Rufus rose and faced the three churchmen, his ruddy face bland and almost amiable. "While this is clearly a matter for Holy Church to decide, two of the parties involved are our vassals and, as such, their affairs are a concern to us. The lady . . ." He paused to look at the white-faced Eleanor. "The lady can reasonably be expected to be unhappy with these proceedings, as the very convening of this tribunal casts doubt on her honor. It should be clearly stated from the beginning that none here thinks her a willing adulteress." His gaze moved to Robert of Belesme. "Is that not so, Count Robert?"

"Aye, your grace. I believe she did not understand the binding nature of her pledge to me. I would still take her to wive with Holy Church's blessing." Robert smiled at what he perceived to be the king's support for his position.

"Exactly." Rufus turned to face Roger. "And you, my lord—you would not prejudice this tribunal with emotion when you have the opportunity to tell the truth later. You serve your lady ill by speaking out before your time." Pleased to have played the peacemaker, Rufus sat back down and announced, "You will proceed."

Reluctantly Eleanor and Roger took their seats and listened in silence as Robert told in detail of his lying with her. Roger clasped her hand in her lap and heard Belesme describe her resistance and his ravishment of her. Even the usually impassive clerks seemed shocked by the sordidness of the tale.

"You forced her?" the papal legate interrupted. "You would have Holy Church bless a union begun in ravishment?"

"She gave me her pledge! She was mine to do with as I would!"

They conferred on the dais and moved on. "And what evidence can you offer that she expected to wed with you?" Durham asked finally.

"Her father removed her from Fontainebleau and proceeded to bring her and her bridethings to Rouen for the marriage. I was called on to secure her release when Fuld Nevers took her hostage because she was my betrothed."

"Then why do you think she fled Rouen in Lord Roger's company if she expected to wed with you?"

"She was afraid of me, excellency, because I was overeager at Fontainebleau." Belesme leaned forward in his chair to make his point. "She left Rouen in the company of a man she believed to be her brother because he offered her safety here. I think she realized that she could not stay with him when it was discovered that he was not of her blood, and that was why she wed with him. Yet that does not change the fact that she belongs to me."

"Jesu, but he can lie like the truth," Eleanor whispered. "Roger, I am afraid they will believe him."

"Nay—you've not had your say yet. He has offered no proof."

As if he heard them, Robert pointed to where Mother Mathilde sat. Everyone followed his direction as he announced, "She can tell you that I had Eleanor of Nantes at Fontainebleau."

"Nay, he lies!" Eleanor was on her feet again. "Excellencies, he has twisted his own actions to show something that never happened. I never—"

"Silence! Lord Roger, pray remove the lady from the room until it is her time to answer questions."

"I will not!" She turned to where Rufus and Henry and some courtiers sat. "Your Grace—"

Rufus seemed taken aback by this direct appeal to him. "Nay, gentle lady—go with your husband until you are called."

"My lord Henry—"

"Go on—I will tell you all that is said here," Henry answered.

Rannulf of Chester was behind her and he whispered low for her and Roger, "Aye, Lady Eleanor, your friends will not let your honor be sullied."

"Rannulf," Roger warned, "the quarrel is not yours—do not do anything foolish." He put his arm protectively around Eleanor's shoulders. "Come on, Lea. His lies just upset you anyway. We will show them the truth when it is our turn."

Eleanor paced the small room provided for them in the Tower of London by the king. Behind her, Roger aimlessly cast dice and scooped them up to throw again. It seemed like they waited interminably for the summons to Westminster, and the wait wore on her nerves.

"I wish you would not do that!"

"All right." He stooped to retrieve the dice and placed them on a low table. He eyed her soberly. "Lea, you must calm yourself—it serves no purpose for you to pace like this."

"Roger, I cannot! Jesu! Can none see through his lies?"

"We have not had our day yet," he reminded her gently.

"Can you not see?" she cried out passionately. "By the time our turn comes, I shall be going in there after he is already believed! I know I did not give my promise to him, and I know I did not lie with him, but do you think they will listen? Nay— they will not! 'Twill be my words against his—and whom do you think they will believe?" Her voice flattened out in bitterness. "I am a mere woman, Roger."

He came up behind her and caught her stiff body against his, wrapping his arms about her to still her restlessness. "Hush—'tis not over yet, Lea. I can see now that we should not have come—that we should have listened to Henry—but I cannot believe any can look on you and think you capable of giving a vow and breaking it."

"But you love me!"

"Aye, more than life, Lea."

She turned in his arms and allowed him to cradle her head against his shoulder. "If only we knew what is happening."

"Henry stands our friend, Lea—he'll come and tell us what goes on."

"Roger"—she clutched the velvet of his tunic and raised her head to look up at his face—"I am afraid."

"Aye, but we can only trust God—and Henry."

"I thought the king was to be on our side, but I can see he is not."

"He is. Lea, what can he do now?"

"He sits with Belesme!"

"Nay, Robert sits with him in hopes of winning his support." Roger stroked her shining braids and sought words of encouragement. "Once you are heard, love, I cannot imagine them ruling against us. We'll be back at Harlowe ere Christmas and all will be as you've planned. And this spring, we'll go to our own lands in the Condes."

"You believe so?" she asked hopefully.

"I know so."

"You can trust my brother Rufus." Henry cleared his throat and spoke from the doorway where he had heard Eleanor's fears. "But there's little he can do—little you would have him do ere a decision is made by the bishops. His intervention may be unnecessary, you know, and if he were to speak up in your behalf just now, it could do more harm than good. You must remember that his own relationship with Holy Church has not always been cordial."

Eleanor stepped back self-consciously and Roger released her. "Have they dismissed for the day?" he wanted to know.

"Aye, and I came to tell you what was said."

"More lies," Eleanor stated flatly.

"Not all of it. After you left, the abbess spoke of Belesme's violence to you at Fontainebleau and told of the bruises he inflicted on you. Unfortunately, she assumes that he forced you."

"And he did not."

"She also told of your stubbornness, Eleanor, and of your steadfast refusal to take your vows to Holy Church. I think that will help show you capable of resisting coercion from Belesme."

"But they will condemn me for being impious."

"That was not the impression she gave," Henry continued. "She spoke of your goodness and of your ability with the sick. She condemned Robert's behavior at Fontainebleau."

Eleanor stared in disbelief. "But she never liked me."

"Well, she likes Belesme less. Her testimony was as favorable as it could be under the circumstances. She told of the bond between you and Roger and of his many visits there."

"And did they listen?" she demanded.

"Not to that," he admitted, "but you have to remember that they consider marriages between the nobility to be matters of policy and they expect a woman to love where she is given."

"Nay, they cannot expect her to love Belesme! God's

teeth!" Roger exploded. "Would they give *their* sisters
to him?" He turned to the narrow arrow slit that lit
the cramped tower room. "We should not have come
to this travesty."

"I tried to tell you," the prince reminded him grimly.
"But enough of that—Gilbert has arrived here."

Eleanor resumed her restless pacing. "Of what good
is that to me?" she asked no one in particular. "My
father does not care if I am sent to Belesme! Indeed,
he wills it!"

"Well, do not despair too soon," Henry advised,
"for you can have your say tomorrow. Rufus overheard the archbishop tell the papal legate that they
would hear your father and examine the marriage
contract in the morning, and then they would question
you in the afternoon."

She came to a halt at the prince's side. "My lord,"
she asked quietly, "what can I expect from all of
this?"

"God willing, Eleanor, you can go home to your
husband in peace." Henry avoided meeting her eyes.

"But you do not really think so."

"I do not know," he answered truthfully. "I hope it
will be so."

"Sweet Mary, but I'll not go to Belesme—they cannot make me!" she cried out. "I'll take the veil first!"

Roger placed his booted foot in the arrow slit and
rested his elbow on his knee. "Nay, Lea—we fled
once and we can flee again," he announced matter-of-
factly. "I did not win you to lose you."

"You could not do that to your father—not when he
welcomed you as his heir," she told him sadly.

"Nay, I loved you long before I knew my father. I
told you once—I will take you to Byzantium and offer
my sword to the emperor before I'll let you go to
Belesme."

"It will not come to that," Henry promised. "I have
already sent to the Holy Father asking that any promise you made to Belesme be set aside because of
coercion and that your marriage to Roger be declared
valid."

"You do that much for us?" Eleanor's eyes brightened hopefully and then she remembered their adversary. "Nay, if Count Robert suspects, he will have your messenger killed."

"My man left this afternoon in Rufus' colors," Henry continued unperturbed. "Since Robert believes him either sympathetic to him or else indifferent, he will not interfere. It is not uncommon, after all, given my brother's delicate relationship with the Church, for him to complain to Rome. Once my man gets there, he will wear my badge when he asks for audience with Victor III. I have no quarrels with the Holy Father."

Impulsively Eleanor stood on tiptoe to kiss the prince's cheek. "My lord"—she smiled through tears of gratitude—"there is no way we can ever repay you for your kindness."

"One day I may need your husband's standard raised in my behalf, Eleanor, and I will not hesitate to ask. Now I have nothing to fight for, but that might not always be the case."

"I am your man," Roger promised. "Aye, I am pledged to Eleanor and then to you."

"But what of tomorrow?" Eleanor's attention focused now on the more immediate concern. "What if they do not believe me?"

Roger stepped in front of her and caught her elbows. "Look at me, love," he commanded. "You will tell the truth, and we will call witnesses to attest to your virginity at the time of our marriage. Rannulf saw the sheets and will say so. If we can but catch Robert in this one lie, we can cast doubt on all he says."

She nodded. "Aye, if we can but do that."

It was early and the frost still clung to the browning blades of grass. The air was still chilly as Eleanor walked the Tower Hill in solitude before Roger rose. Her leather slippers were spotted with the melting frost, but she did not seem to notice. Instead, she found a spot sheltered against the wind and, spreading her woolen cloak beneath the skeleton of a big oak, she sat down, drew up her knees, and wrapped the heavy wool around her. She had come to escape the confines of the small chamber, to clear her head, and to think.

She looked up in annoyance at the sound of boots crunching on the grass, and found the king staring at her. She reached out to balance herself and rise, but he shook his head.

"Nay, do not." He seemed almost as irritated as she felt.

"Your Grace," she managed as they stared at each other.

When she did not waver, his face broke into a slow smile, and then he burst out laughing. "God's teeth! 'Tis no wonder my father liked you, little Eleanor—art as brave as a man!"

Taking his words for a compliment, she smiled back. "And I liked your father, Your Grace."

"You are out early and alone," he observed.

"I could not sleep, and I would sort out what I would say this day."

"Aye." He frowned soberly and surprised her further by sinking to the ground beside her. "Henry tells me you were nearly my queen."

"So he told me, Your Grace, but I did not know it at the time."

"Well, you are prettier than Harold's Edith of the Swan Neck," he decided, "but I want no queen. I have as little use for women as my mother had for me."

"Queen Mathilda?"

"Aye." He settled against the tree and nodded. "My mother bore eight of us that lived and had eyes only for Robert."

"Curthose?"

"Curthose." He gave a derisive snort. "Short-legged and stupid as he is—and faithless, too—yet she thought him perfect. She called me too red, but at least I grew to my full size."

"Aye, I know how it is," she sympathized. "My

parents hated me because I was not a son. Gilbert scarce speaks to me."

"He is here."

"Henry told me, but I have not seen him. No doubt he comes to support Belesme's claim."

"Aye." He crossed his heavy boots and nodded. "He and Curthose were both fools if they thought you a match for Robert. Even my father recognized that someday something would have to be done to curb him."

"Yet Holy Church seems to stand with him and his lies," she muttered bitterly.

"The Church is full of old fools—though this pope is more reasonable than the last. God knows I quarreled with *him* often enough."

"It is unjust—surely you can see it is unjust!"

"Curthose is a fool," Rufus repeated, "if he would allow Belesme to unite with Nantes. One day, the man will grow fat enough to challenge him and he will have helped it come about. My father taught 'tis easier to rule when all vassals pull against each other equally."

"He needed Count Robert's troops in the Vexin," she observed simply. "I doubt he likes Belesme any better than anyone else, but he would not quarrel with him and try to fight the French both."

"My brother sided with the French against our father and led French troops there. Now that he is Normandy, he finds they still foment unrest. What Curthose needs to do is lead his troops himself."

"I care not for politics!" Eleanor cried out passionately. "All I want is to live with my chosen husband in peace!"

"And I will support Roger de Brione in this," Rufus told her, "but not because of justice. I will stand with him because he is Harlowe's son and I would keep Harlowe loyal."

"But you support justice!"

"I am like Henry—I support what serves me best. We have already sent to His Holiness for you to thwart Belesme."

She hugged her knees tighter for warmth and looked at her unexpected benefactor. "Will it help?"

"Belesme is no match for Henry's guile. Aye, His Holiness will remember Henry is the better friend— and Henry may well wear England's crown one day. The Church will weigh that." The king stopped to study Eleanor's profile. "I admit I find Henry's interest in this intriguing—'tis not like him to do so much for nothing. I am surprised that he did not take you for himself."

"He is Roger's friend."

"We have no friends." Rufus shivered in the wind. "You ought to be inside, Lady Eleanor." He caught a low-hanging branch and pulled himself up. "And I would see to my hawks—I feed them myself when I am here."

She struggled up and brushed the damp grass from her cloak. "Wait—there's something I would know."

He turned back impatiently. "What?"

"Queen Mathilda—was she really smaller than I am?"

He nodded. "Aye, by nearly an English foot, I would say. Why?"

"I just wanted to know."

William Rufus noticed the pendant of her necklace as it slipped out the opening in her cloak. " 'Tis strange—what is it?"

She fingered the object self-consciously. "It holds a lock of St. Cuthbert's hair, your grace. Dame Gytha, my lord's grandmother, gave it to me in hopes that it would make me fruitful."

"Saxon nonsense."

She watched him go and shook her head. "Nay—I have to hope," she told herself as she started back.

"Your name, my lady?" The clerk's manner and voice were impersonal.

"Eleanor, daughter to Gilbert of Nantes and wife to Roger de Brione," she answered proudly as those around her gasped at her audacity.

"Do you swear upon this relic of St. Catherine that you tell the truth as you know it?"

She reached out to touch the golden box he held and nodded. "Aye, I so swear."

"So help you God at the peril of your immortal soul?"

"So help me God at the peril of my immortal soul."

"You may be seated, Lady Eleanor."

With her head held high and proud, she took the chair he indicated and faced the panel of churchmen on the dais. She straightened her full velvet skirt and smoothed the fabric over her lap before folding her hands carefully. She raised her eyes expectantly toward the dais and waited for her ordeal to begin.

"Lady Eleanor," the Bishop of Durham addressed her, "we have heard much testimony to support Count Robert's claim to you. Your father and your father's liege lord contracted for a marriage between you and Robert Talvas, did they not?"

Her mouth was dry as she answered, "Aye, but I was not consulted. I knew nothing of the contract until he came to Fontainebleau and told me we were to wed."

"And you consented then?"

"Nay. At first I could not believe it when he told me, because he and my father were enemies."

"But he convinced you?"

"Aye." She stared at her father across the chamber and nodded. "I came to realize that Gilbert did it to save himself. Count Robert told me that he had fought my father with the intention of forcing a marriage with me."

A buzz of interest spread through the audience. The bishop frowned irritably and raised his hand for silence. "Would you have us believe, Lady Eleanor," he proceeded, "that you defied your father's wishes and refused the marriage?"

" 'Tis the truth! He came to me cold and arrogant and forced me to disrobe, excellency, saying he would see what his sword had bought him. I thought . . ." She faced the bishop squarely before continuing, "I thought he meant to ravish me and I was afraid, but I would not bow to his will. He told me he was in full armor and that he had not the time, and he demanded my pledge. He told me what he would have me say, and I refused. He beat me until I fought back, and for some reason, that stopped him. He told me that we would pledge in Rouen on the first of July and then he left."

"That was all?"

"That was all."

"You swear that you did not lie with him—that he forced you not?"

"I swear."

"And that you did not promise to wed with him?"

"I swear."

"Lady Eleanor, do you understand the gravity of perjury?"

"Aye."

"And yet you would have us believe that you refused the Count of Belesme when he came to you at Fontainebleau, that you were still virgin when he left?"

" 'Tis the truth, I swear."

"The abbess, Mother Mathilde, stated that she found you unclothed, bruised, and crying after Robert Talvas left you, yet you would have us believe that you resisted him."

"Because I did!"

"Did you not tell her you were accursed? Did you not take to your bed after he left?"

"Aye—but not because he forced me and not because I was pledged to him! I cried because I could see no way to escape being betrothed to him at Rouen except by taking my vows to Holy Church!"

"And then the man Mother Mathilde believed to be your brother came to Fontainebleau and you planned to marry against your father's wishes."

"Nay! We were as brother and sister, and he would not let me be forced to wed against my will. He offered to help me escape to England."

"You were his leman."

"I was not his leman. I thought he was my brother

until we were safe in England and he came in search of his father. Only then did he reveal that we were not of the same blood, and he asked me to wed with him."

"So you married Roger de Brione to escape Robert Talvas?"

"Nay—I wed with him because I love him and he loves me. Earl Richard gave his blessing to the union."

"But you were pledged to Count Robert."

"I was not pledged to Count Robert! I feared and detested the man and I was determined to resist wedding with him! I would have taken the veil rather than have been given to him!"

"Lady Eleanor, you had some seven years in which to give yourself to Christ," the papal legate interrupted, "and you did not choose to do so. Yet you would have us believe that you were ready to give your vows when Count Robert saw you at Fontaine-bleau?"

"Aye! I did not want to wed with Robert of Belesme!"

"Why did you not honor your mother's dying wish and dedicate your life to Holy Church?"

"Because I was not suited!"

"Why?"

"Because I dreamed of getting out and of having a lord and children of mine own. But not Belesme!"

"Your father chose him for you."

"Excellencies, you surely cannot have lived in either England or Normandy and not know what manner of man he is—everything he is is against all the Church teaches. I could not wed with him!"

"Perhaps you did not realize that you were pledged to Count Robert—or perhaps you did not consider your pledge binding because it was given under duress," the Bishop of Durham suggested.

"Nay—I gave him no pledge."

"He says he took your maidenhead."

"He does not tell the truth," Eleanor answered evenly. "I went to my husband a virgin, and there is proof." She reddened and added, "I bled on my marriage bed."

Belesme was on his feet in an instant. "I do not accept that as proof," he asserted. " 'Twould not be the first time sheep's blood was used for such a purpose."

"You know you have borne false witness, my lord." Eleanor stood and faced him. "As God is my witness, I tell the truth!"

"We have no further questions at this time, Lady Eleanor," the Archbishop of Canterbury announced as the room broke into excited chatter.

She nodded and moved to Roger's side. He clasped her hand and together they faced the dais. "Excellency," Roger spoke out, "there are good men and true in this room who can attest to my wife's virginity at the time of our marriage."

"Nay," Belesme countered, "they can attest to having seen bloody sheets, but they cannot testify as to whose blood stained them."

For once, the prelate ignored Belesme. "Lord Roger, if you will give the names of your witnesses, the clerks will take their testimony for our review."

"I name Rannulf of Chester, Walter of Hereford, and my father, Richard de Brione, Earl of Harlowe."

"Harlowe isn't here—I see him not," Robert sneered.

"I believe the earl is in Normandy at Duke Robert's court," the papal legate answered, "and I see no reason that his statement cannot be taken there or when he returns."

"Nay! I'll not wait forever!" Belesme exploded. "I demand justice! And I would have it now! You cannot drag this on for months and let her live with him when she belongs to me!"

"Silence! My lord of Belesme, we will take all of the testimony into consideration and we will review all statements before we make any decision," Canterbury pointed out reasonably. " 'Tis no light thing you ask of us and we must proceed carefully and thoughtfully to sort everything out." He stood to indicate dismissal. "With the exception of . . ." He looked to one of the clerks, who read the names, and then he repeated,

"With the exception of Rannulf of Chester and Walter of Hereford, we ask that everyone leave us."

Belesme was not to be denied. Fixing the archbishop with his cold green eyes, he fairly bit off the words, "And when might we expect your excellencies to make some disposition in this matter?"

"My lord count," Canterbury answered, "I can promise that something will be determined within the week."

"Lea, I have failed you," Roger told her even as he followed her up the stairs to their cramped Tower room. "I should not have brought you here."

" 'Tis not over yet," she reminded him.

"Aye, but they will drag this on in spite of what Anselm, our good archbishop, says, and we will live under the taint of Belesme's charges for months, maybe even years. Henry was right." He dropped dispiritedly to a low bench and reached for a wineskin on the nearby table.

"Roger, they cannot but rule for us," she reasoned as she came up behind him and began massaging his shoulders. "If you believe in God's justice, you have to believe that." Her words echoed hollowly in her throat—too often in these last weeks she had voiced Roger's pessimism herself and it had been he who had braced her courage. "Aye, we will win."

"I pray you are right." He poured himself a cup and drank deeply.

"Did you think I did poorly today—is that what worries you?"

"Nay." He reached to pat the hand on his shoulder reassuringly. "You told the truth, Lea. What more could you do? 'Tis just that I do not believe they will rule when they say they will. Do you think any of them wants to risk Belesme's wrath? He will make it so they delay and we will have to live like this. 'Tis not so bad for me, but I cannot stand what it does to you." He slumped beneath her hand. "Do you think I cannot see you cringe when even a few call you harlot and cast stones and spit when you go out?"

"So long as we are together, I do not care."

"You are my wife, Lea—I will not have it said you are my leman." He ran his fingers through his hair and stared distractedly into the shadows. He seemed tired and vulnerable. "I would that my father were here."

"What could he do that we have not already done?"

"Stand openly with me. Henry does what he can, but he does it secretly. Just once I would have someone with power come forward and say Roger de Brione is right."

She had never before heard him express dependency on anyone and it alarmed her. For all of his twenty-three years, he had made his own fortune and taken charge of things for her. "Send for him, then," she advised.

"I fear 'tis too late," he answered soberly. Abruptly he rose and walked to the arrow slit. Outside, angry clouds had rolled in, darkening the sky and threatening a winter storm. "Ah, Lea, do not be minding me. 'Tis most probably the weather that makes me feel like this."

A gust of cold wind blew in heavy with the smell of rain. She shivered and moved to block it with his body, coming up behind him and laying her head between his shoulder blades. "Roger, you are all there is for me," she whispered against his back. Her arms slid around his waist and she pressed against him for warmth and security. He stood still and stared out into the gathering storm.

She could feel the weight of Gytha's amulet against her breast as she pressed even closer. "Roger, please . . ."

"I am sorry, Lea. I should not worry you with my foolish fears." He shivered against the wind and reached to bang the shutter into place even as the first spray of rain hit. Behind them, the brace of candles flickered and then went out, leaving the room lit only by the coals in the brazier. Outside, the wind began to howl more violently and the rain came down as though the sky poured. He turned. "You are cold, Lea—let me put more wood on the fire."

"Roger . . ." Her hand slid up the velvet of his sleeve, where drops of water stained the fine fabric.

"You once said it was my right also." She smiled softly.

"What?"

For answer, she slipped her arms around his neck and pulled him to her, her lips parted invitingly for his kiss. His response was immediate and wholehearted. There was no gentle exploration, no slow savoring of the nearness of each other this time. The chilliness of the room was forgotten, obscured by the heat between their bodies as she clung to him, molding herself to him. A low, animallike moan rose from deep within her and she tore herself away from him, whispering breathlessly, "Now. Roger, love me now."

For answer, his hands unfastened the girdle at her waist and freed her gown to hang straight from her shoulders. His mouth possessed hers hungrily while he worked the fabric of gown and undershift up over her hip to feel the bare flesh beneath. She shivered against him, but this time it was from the heat of desire rather than the cold of the room.

Her hands worked at his belt. "Love me as I love you, Roger," she whispered as the leather loosed. "Please."

"Sweetheart, I'll love you any way you want," he answered while slipping both gown and shift over her head. "Jesu, Lea . . ." His voice dropped to a hoarse whisper as he stared at her. "I've had you many times now and yet each time is new—I cannot have enough of you." His fingers trembled with desire, tangling in the cords that held his chausses. He muttered a mild oath when the knot tightened.

"Let me get it," she offered. Her head rested against his chest while she worked the cords. His hands caressed her bare shoulders and back, dropping to slide over satin-skinned hips. The knot came loose and allowed the stockings to bag down about his cross-garters. She slipped to her knees and began unfastening the leather bands while he stretched to pull his tunic off his shoulders. Naked now, he pulled her up and kissed her deeply, molding their bodies together until he could feel rather than hear the low moan of passion that rose within her breast. She twisted against him urgently now, her body straining for that ultimate closeness. "Please, Roger . . ." She was breathless when at last he released her mouth. "Now."

"Aye." He lifted her easily and carried her to bed, laying her down gently. When he would stretch out beside her, she slid beneath him and twined her arms about his neck. Her hips moved invitingly and he could deny his body no longer. Her eyes were closed, her body restless with yearning. He raised himself to watch her as he entered her, savoring both the feel of her as she received him and the sight of her pleasure. A moan escaped her and her brow furrowed in concentration even before he began to move within her.

She clutched at him, her hands grasping, kneading, raking the flesh of his back, while her hips thrashed, rolled, and strained greedily against his. The heat, the intensity of her response to him feeding his own passion, he thrust deep and rhythmically for that elusive fusion of body and spirit. Her hands drove him further and further until he could stand it no longer.

She had never experienced such acute pleasure before. Her moans turned to cries of release that mingled with his as together they found ecstasy. Both struggled to catch their breath, collapsing against each other. Roger rolled over and pulled her to rest in the crook of his arm. She pillowed her head on his chest and tried to master her racing heart.

"Art a mystery to me still," he managed between gulps of air, "the way you lie with me, sometimes lying beneath me gently and sweetly, waiting for me to give you pleasure, and other times nearly burning me with your fire." He stroked the smooth skin of her shoulder and arm and murmured, "Today, Lea, you were fire itself."

"Mmmmmm." She settled contentedly against him and fingered the relic that still twined at her neck. "Mayhap I'll conceive of you this day."

"I hope not." He could sense her disappointment and he rolled on his side to face her. "Nay." His fingers touched her lips as though to still the protest that rose there.

"Roger, 'tis right that I give you an heir of your body—to do less is to fail you." She struggled to sit up.

" 'Tis unimportant to me now, I swear. I would rather have Harlowe go to the Crown and the Condes to Normandy than to lose you, Lea." He could see she did not understand. With a sigh, he voiced his deepest fear. "Women die in childbed," he said simply, "and I would not live without you."

"Men die in battle and leave wives to mourn them," she told him quietly.

"But you are so small."

"Aye, and so was Queen Mathilda—yet 'twas not from that she died." She half-turned in the bed to stare into the near-darkness. "Roger, I love you. I pray daily to God that I can bear your child. I would look on your son and see you and me in his face and know 'tis right that we have taken each other."

"It is right."

"Is it? Then why does God deny me this? Does my mother's curse make me barren?"

"Three months is hardly a lifetime, Lea. Besides, children are a gift of God, yes—but that does not mean he withholds them for punishment. Think on it—there would be no bastards if that were so." He reached up and tweaked the nearest braid. "Lie back down and warm your husband's bones, love."

"Aye," she sighed as she settled back into the depths of the feather bed and let him draw her close. "But I do not see why I must pray for your child and you must pray against it, Roger. How can God know which to favor?"

Pulling her cloak tightly about her for warmth against the chill dampness, Eleanor walked Tower Hill alone before supper. The household guards, having grown used to her solitary walks, paid her little heed as they stood sentry over the complex that served as seat to England's government.

Out of the corner of her eye she caught sight of a man whose walk seemed familiar, and she paused to study him as he crossed the open area past the White Tower. Surely it cannot be, she told herself even as she gathered her skirts and began to run after him.

"Aubery!"

The man spun around to face her, his face breaking into a broad smile at the sight of her. He waited until she reached him before he dropped respectfully on one knee.

"My lady."

"I knew it was you—but how came you here?"

"Jean, Hugh, and I came with Earl Richard and Lady Glynis." He caught her surprised expression and nodded. "Aye, we were at Curthose's court when word of Count Robert's claim to you reached us. Earl Richard would not rest until he'd sent his own emissary to Rome in your behalf, and then he insisted on coming here to support you." He roses gracefully even as he spoke and favored her with a scarce-concealed appraisal. "You look well, Lady Eleanor."

"Well enough if this thing were over. Tell me—does my lord know you are come?"

"Nay, we are but arrived a few minutes ago. The earl would seek out the king first and test his mood."

"Prince Henry says Rufus stands with us." She rested a hand on his arm. "But Glynis—she is here?"

"Aye, and eager to see you, my lady."

"Sweet Mary, but it will be wonderful to be with her again." Eleanor could barely contain her excitement at the squire's news. "And Roger will be most pleased to see you."

"And I him." Aubery grinned as he fingered Henry's badge. "Aye, there's little excitement in serving a prince with no lands. He left us sitting on our thumbs at Rouen whilst he came over here."

"You are his man now?"

"Nay—'twas but to protect us from Curthose's and Belesme's wrath—we took no oaths to him. As soon as may be, I would tear this off and wear Lord Roger's colors—whatever they may be."

"You have heard the whole, have you not? My lord is no bastard, but Harlowe's true heir."

"Aye." The squire shifted his feet uncomfortably and avoidied her eyes as he dared to ask, "How goes the inquiry?"

"Who can tell? Count Robert lies with his hand on St. Catherine's relic, swearing against eternal damnation, and it sounds like the truth. I face them and tell them what really happened and I cannot tell if they believe me or not." She squinted into the lowering sun and shook her head. "I know not what to think, Aubery," she told him bitterly.

"They will decide for you. Aye—who could give a lady to Count Robert?"

"Aubery!" The younger man barely had time to turn around before being enveloped in Roger's embrace. "Jesu, but you grow prettier by the day, I'll warrant."

"Nay—leave me be." Aubery flushed crimson and gave Eleanor a sheepish grin as he extricated himself from Roger's arms. "I would wed as soon as may be."

"You? And break half the hearts in Christendom?" Eleanor teased.

"Your sister Adelicia has been much at Curthose's court, my lady, and the duke favors the match if my father can come to terms with Gilbert."

"You and Lissy?" Eleanor's face broke into a smile as she clasped the squire's hand. "Aye—I favor it too."

"Well, naught's settled for certain," he cautioned, "but I have hopes."

"My father is here—he speaks for Belesme against us."

"So I have heard, but I don't think that will weigh on my dealings with him." Aubery added wryly, "Gilbert will only see that I am willing to take her with little dowry."

"Eleanor, have you no kiss of welcome for me?" Glynis' musical voice sounded behind them and Eleanor turned into her outstretched arms. Beneath the bemused stares of Earl Richard and the king, the two women were reunited after more than seven years. Eleanor stepped back self-consciously and realized that now she ought to kneel before the new countess. Glynis caught her and shook her head above the dark braids. "Nay, sweet child—I gave you suck as a babe—do not be kneeling to me." Turning to William Rufus, Glynis beamed mistily. "Has my son not given me a lovely daughter, Sire?"

"Aye, she is that," he acknowledged. "Henry would have it none can compare in Christendom." Little given to the interests of women, he turned his attention to her husband. "I see you have found your son."

"Aye, and I cannot thank you enough, Sire, for the kindness you have shown him in my absence. You do me and my lady much honor by your lodging him here rather than in the city."

"Henry would have me spare the Lady Eleanor the pain of traveling amid the crowds. Londoners are a nasty lot, ready to believe the worst of anyone." Clearly, Rufus was bored with the subject as his attention turned to something dearer to his heart. "I have heard you brought new hawks from my brother Curthose's mews."

"Aye." The earl nodded. "A wedding gift from your brother when Glynis and I renewed our vows."

"If it does not rain on the morrow, I would see them fly. My brother may be a weak fool, but he keeps good birds. Who knows—I might be tempted to buy one of you."

" 'Tis still light enough to see into the cages, Sire," Richard observed. "Would Your Grace care for a look at them?"

Clearly he had found favor with the king. Rufus glanced at the lowering sky and nodded. "Aye, I think there's time—they'll not dare serve supper without us. Tell me, does FitzWarren still keep my brother's mews?"

"Men!" Glynis tried to sound disgusted, but her voice betrayed her amusement. "Well, lovey, shall we find a warmer place for a coze?"

"You are as I remember you," Eleanor murmured

softly. "Ah, how I have missed you these long years since Nantes."

"And you are even lovelier than I remember you, child. Your beauty comes from the heart as well as the skin, I think. As for me, there's more gray in these braids than I care to notice, but Richard does not seem to mind."

"You are happy then?"

"Aye—at last."

"Oh, Glynis, I am so glad for you. I pray we may all yet live together in peace."

"Well, 'tis bound to be so, for Richard and I have spent many hours on our knees praying for you, little one. Indeed, you are as dear as a blood daughter to both of us." Glynis linked her arm through Eleanor's and began walking back to the royal apartments where they had been granted lodging. "God in his goodness could not let you go to a man like Robert of Belesme."

"Nay, he could not."

"Well, let us not think on it, my dear. We have enough to tell each other of seven years apart—so much has changed for both of us, I think."

"Aye. I thought of you often," Eleanor admitted freely, "and wondered how it was at Abbeville."

"As well as might be for a sinner, I suppose. My days were spent in penance for my living with Gilbert."

"How awful!"

"Nay, 'twas better than living with him. 'Tis hard to endure a man whose touch you despise, Eleanor. But I often thought of you also at Fontainebleau."

"They were forever at me to take my vows, but I had promised Prince Henry and Roger that I would not. And Roger wrote often, so I had but to read his letters when I could not stand it. By the end, I think Mother Mathilde had to own I would be a poor nun. Jesu, but you should have seen her when Belesme came."

"Had he come to Abbeville, the nuns would have been prostrate with fear. They told such tales of him, anyway. Richard caused quite enough of a stir when he came and announced that I had never been other than his wife."

November 21, 1092, was a day that would live forever in the memory of those attending Westminster to hear the findings of the ecclesiastical court. Hastily summoned to one of the abbey's side chambers, Roger and Eleanor were met by an irate Prince Henry and a disgusted king. One look at either of them confirmed Eleanor's worst fears—they were not going to be pleased with the decision. She clasped her hands tightly to still them and waited with thudding heart.

"We have not much time." Henry spoke quickly while shutting the door behind them. "Durham has confided to Rufus that they have been unable to reach a decision."

Hope flared briefly in Eleanor's breast and then died. Henry's expression was ominous and the king did not meet her eyes. "But—"

"At least they did not rule for Robert." Roger let out his breath slowly and waited.

"It seems that they do not feel able to rule on something where the testimony was so different and both parties were under oath—"

"But he lied!" Eleanor pointed out.

"Aye, and we know he lied, but they feel unable to deal with the situation here," Henry continued.

"And so they send it to Rome," Roger sighed. "Aye, I should have expected this."

"There's more, isn't there?" Eleanor demanded with sinking heart.

He nodded. "They have considered Belesme's complaint that you continue to live with Roger when the issue of your marriage is unsettled. They . . ." He met the fear in her eyes and sighed heavily. "They will send you to Fontainebleau to await Rome's decision on to whom you belong."

"Nay!" Her hands crept to her face in horror and disbelief. "But I have done nothing to deserve this!" She clutched at Roger's arm for support. "This is unjust! This is my husband!"

Roger drew her protectively into his arms and held her close. "Nay, love, you'll not go," he soothed. "My Lord Henry, we'll not face them to hear this. I'll take her back to Harlowe and let anyone dare to come for her!"

Rufus shook his head. "The Church will call on me to enforce its will."

"Then I'll take her out of England! Aye—we'll go to Byzantium."

"Roger, consider!" Henry reasoned.

"Consider nothing! They would take her away again! Nay, I'll not let them. She is my wife and I am sworn to protect her!"

"Listen to me—both of you!" Henry implored. "We have little time, but all is not at an end. My man is already in Rome by now and argues your cause with Victor III! Do not ruin your chances by rash action or by defiance. Rufus can tell you that it does not work."

"Jesu!"

"What I would ask is that you appear to agree to the Church's ruling and that Eleanor go back to Fontainebleau until we can persuade His Holiness as to the validity of your marriage. She is probably safer there than anywhere else, and I am certain enough of the outcome that I'd wager all I had on it." Henry's brown eyes were intent on hers. "You understand me—the pope *will* rule in your favor."

"Nay, I—"

"Eleanor, if you would ever live in peace with your husband and bear legitimate children, this is something you will have to do."

"Sire—" She reached out toward Rufus.

"You cannot ask her to go back there!" Roger shook his head as though he could not believe they were serious. "I don't understand this! They had to know Robert lied."

"Cowards all"—Rufus nodded contemptuously— "except for Anselm, and I've reason to believe he sympathizes with you. If anything can be said for our good Archbishop of Canterbury, 'tis that he is uncorruptible. I expect him to write to the Holy Father also, for I can tell he does not trust Belesme."

"But we could wait years for His Holiness to decide," Eleanor protested. "And I have already spent seven years of my life in that place."

Already they could hear the clerks calling order in the other room. Henry muttered an oath and shook his head. "Do what you will, and I will stand with you, but I advise accepting this ruling so that you can win the next."

" 'Tis not your wife they would send away," Roger reminded him grimly.

"Nay, but I value her also and I would not see her called harlot the rest of her life when I knew it was not so. I would want her sons and daughters to be born in wedlock."

"As yours have been?"

"Nay, but I have not loved their mothers, so 'tis different."

Rufus opened the door a crack and peered out. "They wait for you. Listen to what my brother advises and know we will stand by you in Rome."

"God's teeth! You make it sound as though we have no choice!"

"Roger . . ." Henry's voice was tired. "You can fight it, but defiance sits ill with the Church. And this time, there will be no question of her taking the veil. She can take a maid with her and live in comfort whilst she waits. Besides, I think we can get Victor to reach a decision before summer."

"Does my father know of this?"

"Nay."

"I would speak to him before I agree to anything." Roger's palm smoothed her hair. "I would consult him in this, for I do not believe he would want Lea to go back there."

Henry shook his head. "Earl Richard is no man's fool, Roger. He will tell you exactly what I have said."

"What difference does it make anyway, Roger?" Eleanor asked, her voice toneless and flat in defeat.

"We both can see that Prince Henry has the right of the matter. We cannot fight Holy Church."

"Lea, we can flee—do not look like that, love!"

"Nay." She shook her head sadly. "Nay, you cannot shame your mother and your father, Roger. Were it just Belesme, we could fight it and they would stand with us, but this is the Church also."

A knock sounded on the door and Henry grasped Eleanor's hand quickly, squeezing reassurance. " 'Twill be all right in the end, I swear," he promised.

A heavy sigh escaped her. Squaring her shoulders, she nodded. "So be it then."

"Good. You and Roger go on—Rufus and I will come in later by another door. The less Belesme suspects us in this, the better for you."

Sober-faced, Eleanor and Roger made their way into the hearing chamber and took seats by his parents. Glynis leaned across her husband and whispered, "What is it? You both look sick unto death."

"You'll hear soon enough," Roger hissed back grimly.

"Sire, Lord Roger, Lady Eleanor, and peers of the realm . . ." Anselm of Bec, Archbishop of Canterbury, stood to address them. "We have been unable after much deliberation to arrive at the truth of this matter." He halted and faced the king. "Therefore, we are agreed that a higher authority than ours is required for disposition of this case. The Lady Eleanor will be returned to Fontainebleau from whence she came to await the decision of His Holiness, Victor III."

Richard de Brione sprang to his feet in an instant to protest the injustice. "Your excellency," he addressed the archbishop, "you do my family a wrong if you do this. Lady Eleanor came a virgin to my son's marriage bed, and I will attest to that. He is her lawful husband. Whatever lies and false witness Robert of Belesme has borne here should not be used to separate this gentle lady from my son." His voice rich with eloquence, he stretched his hand to touch Eleanor's shoulder lightly. "Aye," he continued, "they have borne much suffering and danger for the love of each other. They have been separated long years and have survived to wed. Do not do this to them."

Managing a tremulous smile at her father-in-law, Eleanor rose also and faced the dais. "As God is my witness, I swear that this man at my side is my true husband, that I have never by word or deed contracted myself to Count Robert, and I know in my heart that the Holy Father will affirm that truth." A lump formed in her throat, making speech difficult, but she swallowed and faced them squarely. "I will await his blessing on my marriage to Roger de Brione at Fontainebleau."

Even Durham was not impervious to her courage. He leaned forward from his chair, his voice cracking with emotion. "Lady Eleanor, it is not our wish to pain you in body or spirit, but in conscience we could not reach the truth. You will be escorted by your father to Fontainebleau, where you will have the privileges accorded a lady of your rank."

"My lord bishop," Roger protested, "Count Gilbert has already demonstrated that he cannot protect his daughter adequately. If she must go, I ask that she go with Harlowe's escort."

Before Belesme could voice his opposition, William Rufus stood. "And if it please your excellencies, since the foremost consideration is the lady's safety, I stand ready to guarantee her safe passage to Normandy under England's escort. I am sure my brother Curthose can be persuaded to do the same."

It was final then. Eleanor sank back into her chair and absently fingered the amulet at her neck. Nothing more that anyone in the room said made any difference to her. She was going to Fontainebleau—back to the exile from which she'd escaped. She heard nothing and she felt nothing. It was not until Roger touched her shoulder gently to indicate the inquiry was over that she could focus on reality. And as she stood, her eyes met Belesme's across the room and read the triumph there.

*   *   *

"Lea, 'tis not too late! We can leave here now and be on the coast ere morning."

"Nay."

They were alone in the Tower chamber. Prince Henry had managed that at least and they had one last night together. All day she had listened to the advice and the frustration of those around her, and now it came down to a few hours left with Roger. To part from him seemed more than she could bear, but the consequences of defiance were too great to consider. Nay, she could only make the best of this one night and trust God's ultimate justice.

"Lea, look at me! I cannot let you go!"

"Please, Roger, do not tear at me like this! We both know 'tis hopeless to resist!" Her face crumpled hideously and she hurled herself into his arms. "Oh, Roger," she wailed against his shoulder, "let us not quarrel in these last few hours we have together. Do not make this more than I can bear."

"I have failed you, Lea. I have sworn to hold for you, and I have been unable to keep my oath to you." His voice was low and anguished. "Jesu, but I would not have had it come to this."

"Don't say that!" she cried fiercely. "Roger, you have given me everything you had. Aye—you've given me happiness—more than I expected in a lifetime in these last three months. Whatever happens, they cannot take that from me." She rubbed her cheek against the hardness of his chest and whispered fiercely, "When I am lonely, Roger, I can lie on my cot and remember what it was like to love and to be loved by you. Had we not dared, I would not have even that."

"The pope will rule for us—he has to!"

"Aye, and then I will live in peace with you for the rest of our lives."

"Lea, I cannot let you go! Too long I waited for you!"

"And I for you. Roger, you are my life."

"But what if Victor rules for Robert? What then? Nay, Lea, I will kill Robert or I will die trying."

"Hush, love—'twill not come to that," she promised. "I would take the veil gladly before I'd give myself to him."

"I don't know." He released her and moved restlessly away. "All my life," he mused hollowly, "I have fought and trusted in God, knowing that I could win what I would have because it was right. And I have seen Belesme's evil triumph in spite of everything."

"He has not won—not yet. Your father has listened to Prince Henry and to the king and he believes in them. I believe in them." She slipped her arms around his waist and pressed her body against his back. "Roger," she whispered, "give me yet another memory to carry with me."

1093

17

"My dearest lord," she began, "my prayers are with you always." She paused to consider what to write. Shifting slightly on the bed, she pulled her covers more closely about her knees for warmth and realigned the writing board on her lap. Outside, the cold February wind blew fiercely and sleet rattled against Fontainebleau's tiled roof. She shivered from the dampness and the cold and stared briefly into the small, inadequate brazier where flames flickered valiantly against the draft from the unshuttered window above her. Ah, to be in his arms just now, sheltered and warmed by the heat of his body, while I tell him, she thought, and sighed. Flexing her fingers against the cold, she dipped her pen in the inkpot and continued writing.

> May God in his grace keep you safe, my lord, and grant that we may soon be together again. You are never far from my thoughts.
>
> The receipt of your last letter gladdened my heart, as did the trunk you sent. The woolen-and-vair cloak is much admired by all for its warmth as well as its beauty. Prince Henry's Christmas box is finally exhausted, but we drank of his wine and ate sweetmeats until Mother Mathilde chastised us for gluttony. I noted that she partook of it also.
>
> I fear my letters are of little comfort to you, my husband, for there is naught to write of here. One day is very like another save for whether it rains, snows, or is clear. Every day is cold and we do not go out more than necessary, for the wind chills the

courtyard between our lodgings and the kitchens and chapel.

I am treated well by all, but I am not content, for I would have you with me above all things.

She hesitated, rereading what she had written. It was a poor effort at best, and nothing like the long, passionate letters he sent her. But she would not distress him with what he could not help. A slow smile spread over her face as she dipped the quill into the ink again and pictured him reading her next news.

Yet, though I am parted from you now, I am comforted by the knowledge that I am to bear your heir. I did not tell you sooner because it was early days and I feared it could not be. Now I am sure and I pray God grants us a son of our bodies to bless our union. I judge the babe will be born in August, most probably mid-month. May the Blessed Virgin intercede that I am delivered at Harlowe with Glynis to aid me.

God keep you and your parents until we are met again. I remain your faithful and loving wife.

Satisfied, she reluctantly stirred from her bed to place a chunk of wax in the melting cup and hold it over the fire. It liquefied and sputtered. She folded Roger's letter and poured a small amount of wax over the edge, taking care that it did not run and ruin the parchment. The small puddle opaqued and hardened to where she could scratch her initials into it. A glance at the window told her none would ride out this day, but she would be ready when the weather cleared.

Once her writing was done, she could make do without the extra light from the window. Pulling a stool over, she climbed up to shutter the opening and then closed a heavy tapestry over it. This time her lot was better at the abbey, she reflected, for she had a chamber fitted with fine hangings, a feather bed, and furniture sent by the earl, and she was allowed the company and service of a page, a maid, and a manser-

vant. The latter she kept busy on the roads between
Fontainebleau and Harlowe.

"Alan!" She called to her page and waited for the
boy to come running from a nearby alcove. He appeared, his face ruddy from the cold, and bobbed her
his hasty obeisance.

"My lady?"

"I would have Thomas prepare to ride as soon as is
possible," he told him. "Send him to me."

"Aye." The boy could not resist a grin at the thought
of the messenger's chagrin when he heard he was to
ride out yet again. Even the nuns laughed at the
frequency of his trips.

"You can tell him he is not to leave until the sleet
stops and 'tis safe," she added.

The page scampered off to do her bidding with the
enthusiasm of one too long forced to endure being
cooped up. It seemed to her that he ran when he could
walk, just to have something to do. Eleanor pulled a
low table and two stools closer to the fire, and then
rummaged in her chest for the chessboard. Poor Thomas
was not much of a player, but he would have to do
until she saw Roger again.

The weather cleared briefly—long enough for Eleanor's messenger to ride out—and then a new storm
rolled in, bringing with it bitter cold and high winds. It
was a time for staying indoors and close beside fires.
At the abbey, the nuns went about their business
heavily bundled in warm robes and cloaks, their bodies swathed in somber-colored wool until they looked
like a group of fat women no matter what their actual
size. For Eleanor, it was a restive time, for she was
neither expected to participate in the strict religious
observances of the sisters nor to do any of the day-to-
day work. Instead, she kept to her chamber in the
company of her eight-year-old page and her sweet-
tempered but somewhat slow-witted maid. Days—weeks
even—were spent within the close confines with little
to do but fret and pray for deliverance.

Outside, the wind howled anew. Eleanor moved
restlessly about her small chamber, drinking mulled

wine that Trude heated with the brazier's poker and
regretting Thomas' absence. God willing, he would
have a safe trip. She glanced longingly at her chessboard and sighed. Poor Trude could not seem to learn
even the basic moves necessary to make the game
progress. Behind her, the maid placidly folded her
clothing and put her things away in the tall cupboard
that served as storage for nearly everything. Sometimes the girl's quiet acceptance of her lot irritated the
restive Eleanor, and this day was worse than usual.
"Jesu," Eleanor snapped finally, "can you not cease
the racket you make with the cupboard—and can you
not sit still?" Her voice sounded shrewish even to her
own ears and she instantly regretted her lapse of temper. "I'm sorry, Trude—I did not mean to screech at
you—'tis not your fault we are prisoners here."

"Nay, my lady—I do not mind it." The girl closed
the cupboard doors quietly and moved to stir the fire
before laying another small log on the brazier. "I like
it here," she said simply.

Eleanor stared in disbelief at the blond-headed maid.
In her seven years of residence at the abbey, she had
never considered anything but escaping, and here the
gentle Trude liked the place. "You *what*?" she managed finally.

"I like it." The girl inclined her head as though
contemplating a new idea. "Aye, I'd like to stay." She
caught her mistress' incredulous stare and nodded.
" 'Tis so peaceful here. If I were daughter to a noble
house, I'd want to be dowered here. But," she added
regretfully, "they'd not take me with nothing, do you
think?"

"Trude, are you saying you want to become a nun?"
Eleanor nearly choked on the words. "You do not
know what you say. Aye, look at me—seven long
years I spent here whilst they badgered me to take my
vows—seven long years it was that I yearned to be
free to live."

"But for you it was different," Trude answered slowly,
"for you knew and loved Lord Roger. With me, 'tis
different." She turned her pale blue eyes to Eleanor,

her grace far more eloquent than her simple words. "I am baseborn, you see, and I have no one to care for me, my lady. If I am pretty, I will be passed from one lord's bed to another for their pleasure and then left to bear the bastards I conceive alone. The best I can hope is that none find me comely so that I am given in wedlock to some dirty serf to labor in his fields until I die."

"Nay," Eleanor protested, " 'tis not so. You are a lady's maid, Trude."

"Am I?" the girl asked pointedly. "I have not your wits, Lady Eleanor, and I know it. Were we at Harlowe, could you not do better than me? Aye—had I not asked to come with you, would you have taken me?"

"Nay." Eleanor had to own the truth of the maid's words. Too often, she found the girl's limited abilities frustrating and wished for a replacement. Aye, even a moment before, she'd wished for one who could provide her with the diversion of a game of chess. "Trude, are you certain of what you say?" she asked quietly. "Do you truly wish for this life? You have not seen the labor nor experienced the long isolation of what you would choose. When the weather warms, you will work in the gardens and till the fields with naught but poor clothes and meager food for pay."

"For the love of God, I could bear it," the girl answered.

"Jesu!" Eleanor breathed. "You are sure? You would not long for the beauty of England and a fling around the maypole?"

"Nay. Had I the choice, my lady, I would be bride to Christ."

Eleanor looked at the simple village girl as though seeing her for the first time. She was kindhearted and not totally simpleminded, and she had a certain sweetness of disposition that was pleasing to those around her. But most of the nuns at Fontainebleau were of the nobility, girls who had been given by their families to express faith, gratitude, or hope to God. Yet Mother Mathilde seemed to tolerate the quiet Trude, allowing her to take her meals at the communal table.

"You would truly do this? You are not simply wishing to escape what you think will be your fate if you do not?" In justice, Eleanor realized there were those who felt called to the vocation, and she acknowledged the service they performed. "Tell me the truth, Trude."

"I would."

" 'Tis not impossible, you know. I could write to Lord Roger and ask that he endow you with enough that Mother Mathilde would accept you."

"Would you?" The girl's eagerness was almost pathetic. "I should pray for you both every day of my life," she promised.

"Aye. In truth, I would," Eleanor allowed, "if I thought you were serious in your wish for the vocation. 'Tis fair enough, I suppose, to trade you for me. Reverend Mother spent long hours and many words on me and could not win me. With you, she already has a willing novice." Before she'd gotten the words out, the simple girl was on her knees at Eleanor's feet, kissing the hem of her robe. Embarrassed, Eleanor gave her an impatient tug. "Do not be thanking me, Trude, until you've spent your seven years here," she told her firmly.

Noises came from the courtyard, drawing their attention. By the sound of it, riders were coming in. Each girl stared at the other, surprised that any would venture out in such weather. Eleanor was the first to recover. Hurrying to pull a stool to the high window, she drew aside the tapestry and opened the shutters to peer outside. Three men dismounted, led their horses to a sheltered place, and hastened to bang on the abbess' door. She could see Mathilde crack her door against the wind and then the men disappeared inside.

"Sweet Mary, but I'll warrant they were nearly frozen to their saddles," she muttered as she reshuttered the window. "What can they possibly be doing out in weather like this?"

"Mayhap they are travelers who have lost their way," Trude suggested.

"Aye, but who would travel in this cold?"

*   *   *

Responding to an urgent summons to Mathilde's apartment, Eleanor pulled her cloak close about her body and crossed the yard. The wind whipped the wool about her legs and cut through her clothing like a knife. Her fingers and face were numb by the time she reached for the door, and she did not wait to knock before wrenching it open. Inside, Mathilde and a stranger sat with their chairs pulled to the fire. Both turned around at the blast of cold air that preceded Eleanor into the room. The gentleman rose, bowing slightly to acknowledge her presence. Her eyebrow rose a fraction at the sight of his rich clothing—this then was no ordinary traveler seeking refuge from a winter's storm. She unclasped her cloak with stiff fingers and laid it aside before sweeping him a return curtsy.

"Art the Lady Eleanor?"

"I am."

Strong fingers reached to grasp hers and raise her. "You are as my prince told me," he murmured, "but even more so."

She stared up into the stranger's face. "I am afraid, sir, that you have the advantage of me, for I know you not."

"Stephen of Exeter." He smiled. "I serve Prince Henry and am but arrived from Rome, where I represented you before His Holiness."

Her mouth went dry and her heart thudded uncomfortably. The room seemed to spin for a few seconds and then right itself. "Sweet Mary!" she breathed. When he did not say anything more, she turned away and half-whispered, "Surely you did not ride all this way in the cold to look on me in my misery, sir. Pray tell me—is it decided?"

"A look would be worth the ride, Lady Eleanor," he answered, "but I come because my lord would have you the first to know of His Holiness' decision." He reached to touch her sleeve gently, his face still smiling. "Four days ago, I was summoned into Victor III's presence and told there was no question in his mind as to the validity of your marriage to Lord Roger—that if you gave any pledge at all to Robert of Belesme, it was forced from you and therefore not binding."

"Jesu!" She could not manage anything more.

"Aye—'tis over and you have won."

"We have won," she repeated foolishly as she clutched at him for support. "Mother of God! We have won!" She raised her eyes to meet his. Tears sprang up and welled uncontrollably. "We thank you, sir," she managed, "and we thank Prince Henry."

"Aye—he loves you well, lady, and has made your cause his own." Stephen watched her try to digest his news. Henry had said she was the most beautiful woman in the world, and for once he had not spoken from a moment of passion. Lady Eleanor, her face diffused with the joy he had brought her, was one no man could easily forget. 'Twas little wonder Belesme had gone to such lengths to possess her. Aloud he spoke gently, "Come warm yourself by the fire and I will tell you all."

"Nay, sir—'tis you who must be cold from such a ride. I am well with the tidings you have brought."

"I will thaw in time, but I own it *was* cold. I did not expect the storm when I left Rome, and Prince Henry would have it the utmost importance that you hear even before 'tis made known. As soon as the weather clears, I am for England to tell him also."

" 'Tis true then?" Mathilde spoke from behind them. "She belongs to Lord Roger?"

"Aye. Once it came to the Holy Father's attention, there was little question. I fear Durham was intimidated by Count Robert's presence and did not want the consequences of ruling against him—thus he swayed the legate to argue for a referral to Rome."

"Prince Henry was right," Eleanor murmured, "for he advised us to go to the Holy Father in the beginning."

"Now, child, you can return to your lord and bear this child in wedlock," the abbess told her.

"You know?"

"Aye, I have seen the sickness." She reached out to Eleanor with a bony, veined hand. "I shall pray you make a better wife than nun." When she caught Eleanor's surprised expression, she added, "Aye, I have come to see you were not destined for this. Thank God you were not destined for Belesme, either."

Unable to cope with Stephen's good news and the abbess' unexpected kindness, Eleanor threw herself into the startled Mathilde and gave full vent to her emotions. Tears flowed freely now. Mathilde hesitated and then closed her thin arms about the girl and allowed herself to stroke the shining braids.

"There . . . there . . ." she soothed. " 'Tis over, Eleanor, and you are free to love where you will—you will go home to your lord."

Stephen concurred. "Aye—'tis nearly settled. When the weather warms, you will be sent to Rouen in William Bonne-Ame's care to await Lord Roger's arrival. I doubt it should be above five or six weeks before you are reunited with your husband." Stephen nodded to Mathilde over Eleanor's head. "I have discharged my lord's duty for now, but I must needs ask your hospitality for myself and my companions until 'tis warm enough to ride. I would not spend another day like this in my saddle."

"You are welcome to stay as long as 'tis necessary, Sir Stephen," Mathilde answered graciously. "And I do not doubt that Eleanor will welcome the company. Too long I've watched her struggle to find amusement here."

18

Eleanor rolled linen bandages listlessly, her attention scarcely focused on the conversation of those around her. Trude worked patiently beside her and talked of her gratitude for being allowed to stay with the nuns. Winter sunlight filtered through high windows, giving the mistaken impression that there was warmth outside. And still she waited—waited for something to happen that would signal her release back into the world.

She missed Roger terribly—so much so that she thought she could bear it no longer—and yet no word had come from either Rouen or England that she was actually to leave the abbey. Two weeks ago the weather had cleared and Stephen of Exeter had ridden out to take his news to England and left her behind to wait.

She stopped to touch her nearly flat abdomen and wondered idly how much longer before she would feel the child there quicken. Already to her it had life and being—so much so that in moments of solitude on her bed she would speak to this son she carried. If only Roger could share in her love and hope for the child—if only he could be with her . . .

"Riders!" someone called from the bell tower to those below. "Riders!"

Before anyone thought to stop her, Eleanor was up and running for the courtyard eagerly. Surely this would be her escort to Rouen or at least would bring word of the archbishop's plans. But no sooner had she cleared the doorway than she heard cries of, "Belesme! 'Tis Belesme!" Climbing quickly to the wall, she stared unbelieving at the column of mounted men making their way toward the almost unprotected abbey. Above them floated the hated green standard of Robert of Belesme.

"Get the priest! Tell Reverend Mother!"

Nuns were running in panic everywhere and shouting at each other. Eleanor stood transfixed and helpless for a moment and then knew she would have to flee. She came off the wall and ran for the stable that sheltered the work animals and the few ridable beasts belonging to the abbey. It was cold and she wore no cloak, but she had no time to go back for one. She bridled and saddled the nearest horse and threw herself up on its back.

"Lady Eleanor! You cannot—you'll freeze!" Trude cried out as she rode into the courtyard.

"Better to freeze than die in Belesme's hands!" Eleanor yelled back. Digging her heels into the horse's ribs, she urged the beast out the west gate. From what she'd been able to make out, Belesme came armed, and that meant he and his men rode heavy with mail. Hopefully, that would prevent fast pursuit.

While not so bitter cold as it had been, the air was still chilly. She shivered and hovered closer to the animal's back as she picked her way down the narrow path to the woods behind the abbey. At least there, she would have the cover of trees to break the wind and to obscure her from pursuers. Once in the thicket of dead and naked trees, she stopped to consider just where she could go that he would not find her. The nearest shelter would be the huts of the villeins who worked Fontainebleau's lands for a share of the crop, but that would be the first place she could expect Belesme to look for her. Yet she dared not go deeply into the woods for fear of becoming lost and then freezing when nightfall came. And in spite of having lived some seven years of her life in the abbey, Eleanor had never explored any of the surrounding countryside to know what lay out beyond what could be seen from the abbey walls.

She kept to the edge of the forest, staying no more than twenty feet from cleared fields, and followed the path of the clearing. She was finally rewarded by the sight of another of the Conqueror's abandoned churches. Allowed to overgrow as part of his game reserve, it could barely be seen from open ground. She urged the horse toward it and hoped the place still had walls enough to provide some shelter.

Rounding the corner, she was grateful to find that all walls still stood and that much of the roof was still intact on one side. She dismounted and led the animal into the corner that faced against the wind. Just the shelter of the wall seemed to warm the air somewhat. A quick glance around told her that she would have to make do with what she wore—altar cloths and hangings had long since been carried off. No benches remained, either, but then, she had no means of making a fire and could not risk the smoke. She sat down to contemplate her chances for survival.

If she could but wait until dark without freezing, she could ride along the road until she reached one of those crude huts she'd passed when she was brought back to Fontainebleau. Mayhap she could beg a night near a fire at least. She hugged her knees to her and thought of her child. If for no other reason than the heir she carried, she had to survive. She chafed cold hands against the rough wool of her day gown and huddled closer to the wall. Her horse backed closer to shelter itself.

It was a long wait for darkness, a wait unbroken by the sight or sound of anything except the few movements of her or the horse. The temperature began to drop even before the sun lowered in the sky, and Eleanor had to admit to herself that she could not last until it set. Cold and numb, she rose and stood on limbs that were almost too stiff and painful to use. She hobbled slowly over to the horse and managed to pull herself back into the saddle.

The wind had died down mercifully, but the dip in temperature still threatened survival. She forced her mount out onto the open road and gambled it would be deserted. She had scarcely come into the open before the sound of horsemen told her she had made a grievous mistake. Half a dozen men led by the green-cloaked Belesme came into view almost immediately. A frantic kick to her horse's ribs coupled with a strong yank on the bridle caused it to rear. Before she could react to control it, she lost her seat and was thrown to the ground. She rolled away from flailing hooves and lay in a heap in the cold dirt. Tears of anger and frustration scalded her cheeks while she waited.

He reined in and dismounted. She thought briefly to feign injury and closed her eyes. She could hear the clink of his spurs and his mail and the crunch of his heavy boots on the rough road as he came to stand over her. Looking up through veiled lashes, she thought he seemed ten feet tall. He reached down and hauled her up roughly. She sagged like a limp rag. The flat of his hand struck her across the face, the mail of his glove cutting into the numb flesh of her cheek. She reeled away, only to be caught and shaken savagely until she thought her bones would come apart. Her eyes flew open and she raised her arms to protect herself. With one last furious shake, he let her fall to the ground again.

"Fool!" he shouted above her. "You might have frozen!" He nodded at a boy who'd ridden up beside them. "Piers, get blankets and tell the others we camp here. I would have a fire and food before the tent is set."

"My lord," the boy protested, "can we not go back to Fontainebleau, since we have found her?"

"Nay—can you not see she is nearly done?" Besides, we are already on the road to Belesme."

"Belesme," she repeated foolishly.

"Aye." He turned his attention back to her. "What did you think to do—kill yourself to thwart me?" he asked as he pulled her up.

"What does it matter?"

"I ought to let you freeze," he muttered, "but too much of me would have you still." He unfastened his fur-lined cloak and wrapped it around her. "Here—you will be fortunate if you do not suffer in the lungs for this."

She would have liked to recoil and to repudiate the gesture, but the cloak was warm with the heat of his body. She shivered and pulled it close. Nay—let him freeze, she decided.

"Where were you going?" he demanded.

"I sought safety."

"Out here and alone?" he gibed.

"My lord, I claim the protection of Holy Church—I ask to be returned to Fontainebleau at once."

His laugh was harsh and derisive. "I see no church here, Eleanor."

"You know I am under Holy Church's protection already!" her temper flared momentarily. "You defy the Holy Father in this!"

"An old man in Rome," he scoffed. "I have had enough of the Church! They would beggar me with the promise of you and yet they have not delivered."

"You perjured your soul in London! They will damn you for this!"

"D'ye think I care? What would they give me that I cannot get for myself—heaven? Nay, I am Talvas—Mabille's spawn also—there is no heaven for me."

"My lord . . ." Piers brought up a couple of blankets and hesitated. He did not like to inject himself into any of his lord's quarrels, but he knew Belesme wanted the blankets.

"Oh . . . aye. Is the fire started?" Robert's manner changed abruptly.

"It smokes a little so 'twill soon catch, my lord. Would you bring her closer?"

"Aye—she is nigh frozen." Robert threw another covering over her and pushed her toward the others.

He brought a steaming cup of spiced wine to her. "Drink it," he ordered curtly. She took it and sipped, burning her mouth. " 'Tis hot, but will warm you inside," he added at her discomfiture.

Her teeth still chattered even with her body warmly wrapped in the fur of his cloak. He set down his own cup and moved closer. "I pray you do not sicken before I get you to Belesme."

"I did not think you prayed at all, my lord."

"A manner of speech. Nay—I doubt He would listen to me."

The flames of the fire flickered and cast an eerie glow on the handsome black-visaged face. The pupils of his green eyes seemed to reflect the red and gold of the flames. Eleanor furtively crossed herself and turned away.

It was obvious that he was used to moving about in the conduct of his petty wars, for he came well-prepared. A group tent was speedily erected against a steep slope for protection against the wind, brush was collected to lay beneath pallets, and fur robes were spread over them. Several fires were set and blazed in a wide semicircle outside to warm the air and to provide cooking heat. Salted meat was unpacked and soaked in a kettle of water and potatoes and onions were added to it for a stew. These were no household knights come out for pleasure, but were seasoned soldiers used to force marches and cold ground. They gathered away from Eleanor and Robert while supper cooked and entertained themselves with ribald ditties sung without accompaniment.

If Belesme found her lack of conversation discouraging, he gave no sign. She rolled up in his cloak and feigned sleep while he sat and stared into the dancing flames. The worst of all her nightmares had come to pass now and she had fallen into Robert of Belesme's hands, but she would survive. She had to for the sake of Roger's heir.

She must've managed to doze, because the next thing she knew, Belesme was thrusting a small bowl of potage and meat at her and telling her to eat. She tried to push it away, but he was insistent. "I will not have it said I starved you. Besides, you need your strength—'tis a long way to Belesme."

She struggled upright and tried to take a bite. "My lord"—she shook her head desperately—"I would not go to Belesme."

"And I will not take you back."

"My husband—"

"Let the Bastard come after you," Belesme cut in contemptuously. "I'll not let you go again so long as there's breath in this body."

"He is no bastard!"

"Nay?" A black eyebrow shot up quizzically. "Bastard or not, his mother was Gilbert's whore."

"His father is Earl Richard."

"Aye, I have heard the tale, but I believe it not."

"I cannot go to Belesme!" She turned to him. "Do you not understand? I am wed to another, my lord—I am wife to Roger!"

"Nay—a widow soon enough," he growled back. "Eat your food and be still."

"I am not hungry for this."

"Eleanor"—his voice dropped in warning—"do not provoke me to violence this night. Would you have me beat hunger into you?"

"Nay," she sighed tiredly, "but I hunger not."

He took out a small knife and began expertly to cut the chunks of meat in her bowl. Spearing a piece, he held it out for her. " 'Tis not what you are used to, but it serves," he told her. "Eat it."

With a sigh of resignation she did as he asked, taking bowl and knife and trying to eat. He set aside his own untouched and watched her. Her dark braids fell down her back like two thick ropes of hair bound with golden thread. Her profile was fine-boned and straight with delicate features and her eyes were as dark as any he'd ever seen.

"Do not stare at me!" she flared. "Jesu, but I cannot stand this game you play!"

"I like to look at you." He reached out and touched one of the braids. "I remember when you wore it loose like a maid, Eleanor, and I would see it thus again."

She shook her hair free. "My lord, what can you gain by taking me with you? Surely you must know that my husband and his father will stand against you—aye, and Rufus and Curthose, and Holy Church. You cannot win in this."

"Let them come for me then—they cannot take Belesme."

"I am not for you."

"I have wanted you since Nantes." He stared absently across the fire to where his men ate. "Aye, if the Church holds you to be his, I will make you a widow."

The food she'd eaten rose and gagged her. She fought the urge to vomit, but it was as though everything in her stomach rebelled at once. She struggled to her feet and ran to a nearby tree, where she leaned and retched until nothing but bile came up. Belesme shouted for Piers to attend her, and the boy ran up with a wet cloth for her face.

"Nay—'tis over," she managed when he began to wipe her forehead. "I am all right now."

Belesme kicked savagely at the fire, his heavy boot scattering ashes and live coals into the night air. It galled him to think the thought of him made her sick. "Put her in her pallet and see she is warm," he ordered curtly.

The boy nodded and helped her to the tent, where she stumbled in the darkness among the pallets. He pushed her to one near the side and got out another fur to cover her. She rolled in between the thick skins gratefully and closed her eyes.

When she awoke, the small tent was filled with the sounds of night breathing as those around her slumbered. The chill that had gnawed at her bones was gone, and her body was warm. They were packed into the sleeping area so that she lay between two she judged to be Belesme and Piers. Robert's arm lay across her, holding yet another blanket over the both of them, and his breath was oddly soft above her head.

"Mother of God," she whispered aloud into the darkness, "deliver me."

19

The gray mists of dawn still hung over into morning, shrouding everything with a chill, damp haze. Eleanor shifted her weight uncomfortably against the saddle pommel and tried to ease the stiffness she felt. Belesme's steel-clad arm held her so tightly that she could feel the links of his mail through the heavy green cloak. She stole a glance upward but could see little of his face that was not obscured by the nasal of his helmet.

She leaned back to fight another wave of nausea, but her breakfast was resisting all her efforts to keep it down. Her stomach churned and her food seemed to be rising to her throat. She barely had time to grit out between clenched teeth, "My lord, I am unwell."

He let out a string of oaths and reined in viciously. "Piers!" he shouted. "Halt and tend my lady!" With the hand that held her he pushed her head down over the horse's shoulder as she retched.

A stout fellow dismounted and rushed forward to pull her down as Belesme lifted her hurriedly over the pommel and then dismounted himself. Piers caught her and helped her stand, but her legs were weak from riding and she stumbled. Belesme circled her waist with his arm and pushed her head forward. "Try not to soil my cloak if you can," he ordered brusquely above her. "Piers!"

"Aye, my lord!" Piers dropped to his knees beside her and pulled her braids out of the way while she vomited. "Jesu, lady, but you are sick," he muttered in a soft underbreath. "Here—let me get you cleaned up."

When she finally stopped retching, Belesme pulled

her back from the mess she'd made and forced her to sit on the damp grass. Piers began washing her face with water from one of the skins.

"Nay—I am better," she protested weakly when Belesme would have made her lie down. " 'Tis over."

"You are certain? I would not have this happen again whilst we ride." His eyes narrowed while he studied her damp face. "You do not travel well."

"Nay."

"Well," he encouraged her as he pulled her up then, " 'Tis not much further to Belesme—you could see it now were it not for the mists." He supported her with his arm and walked her slowly back to the horse.

His men were bemused by his kindness to her. Hardened soldiers all, used to their lord's violent temper, they watched and gave her a wide berth, uncertain of how to treat her. They waited silently until he put her up in front of his saddle and ordered everyone to remount.

Belesme swung up behind her and unstrapped his helmet, pulling it off with an effort and tying it behind his saddle. Deep creases lined his face like hideous scars where the nasal had rested and his hair bore the imprint of the padded shelf. He ran his fingers through his thick black hair before taking the reins from her.

"I do not believe you are riding bareheaded, my lord," she gibed. "Indeed, I had supposed you slept helmeted."

"I am nearly home," he told her as he flicked the reins against his horse's shoulder and nudged it forward. "Aye—I wear it more than most, I suppose, but if I learned naught else from the Conqueror, 'twas to look for mine enemies everywhere."

"And with good reason, I'll warrant."

"I have more than my share," he admitted almost cheerfully before he raised a mailed hand to indicate the road ahead. "Look up there—you can see Belesme if you try."

She strained to follow his direction and made out

the hazy outline of a great gray mound in the distance. "Is that it?"

"Aye—'tis not a pretty place, but it serves me well. There's not an army anywhere that could take it in less than a year." The pride in his voice was unmistakable.

They picked their way up a rocky path that zigzagged steeply until the grim, stone-walled stronghold emerged from the fog and haze like a giant rock above them. Unlike Harlowe, there was no beauty to the fortress with its ugly and asymmetrical towers positioned at odd angles in its curtain walls.

They crossed finally beneath the barbican through the curtain and between inner gates so narrow that no more than two columns could pass at a time. People scurried to make way for them, and ostlers ran forward to take reins.

Almost immediately, Eleanor's attention was caught by a woman ascending the stairs of the nearest tower, a slender redheaded woman who started to run toward them. She stopped still when she saw Eleanor, and her face twisted from joy to hatred.

Robert swung down and lifted Eleanor after him, resting his hand proprietarily on her shoulder as the woman came closer. Eleanor recoiled at the woman's expression. Robert's fingers tightened on Eleanor's shoulders while he leaned forward to murmur succinctly, "Mabille."

"Your mother? Nay, she cannot be old enough!"

"You fool!" Mabille's green eyes flashed and her fingers curled like talons as she faced her son. "You bring death to this house when you would bring her here! You stupid fool!"

"Eleanor"—Robert ignored his mother's diatribe and moved closer—"behold my mother, jealous woman that she is."

Out of courtesy to Mabille's rank, Eleanor would have dropped low in obeisance, but his fingers on her shoulder stayed her. Instead, he reached with his free hand to brush back his green cloak from her face. The whole yard lapsed into silence at the gesture.

"Look on her and look well, Mabille," he taunted

his mother. "Aye—you said there was none to compare with you. Look on her and weep."

The color left Mabille's face. "Robert—"

"Nay. Belesme has a new mistress now, Mabille," he continued cruelly, "and you'll not gainsay her if you would stay."

" 'Tis another man's wife you make your whore and set above me! Nay—you shall not! You inherited this place through me!"

"I make her my countess!"

"She is Lord Roger's wife!"

"And she will be his widow! Have done, Mother, and accept it!"

"Nay!"

Eleanor shrank from the suppressed violence between them, but everyone else seemed to take it in course. Robert had loosed his hold on her and stepped forward to where he and Mabille stood yelling in each other's face.

"Sweet Mary!"

"Aye—'tis always so between them," Piers whispered behind her. "Do not mind it."

"Until the house is finished, she will need your solar." Robert had suddenly lowered his voice to end the confrontation.

"You would put your whore in my bed? Nay, you will not!"

His temper flared anew and he slapped her openhanded, a blow that sent her reeling. She wiped her stinging mouth with the back of her hand and looked for blood. He stood over her, his fist clenched, his jaw tight. "Whore?" His voice dripped with sarcasm. "Call that to your mirror, Mother. She is convent-bred and I have not lain with her."

Mabille's green eyes flashed venom. "Nay!" she spat. "You'll not keep her! When she knows how it is with you, how you—" Her words were cut off with another slap. She sank her teeth into his hand and drew blood, enraging him. This time, he struck with clenched fist, and she rolled away in a heap. He raised his boot to kick, but Eleanor could stand it no longer.

"Nay!" she cried as she caught his arm. "She is your mother, my lord—she gave you life!" She held on tightly and tried to pull him back. "Stop it!"

The heat seemed to fade as he stood there. "Aye." He nodded slowly.

Someone leaned down to help Mabille up, but she struggled to her feet on her own and faced Eleanor. "Welcome to Belesme, Lady Eleanor—I wish you misery here," she told her bitterly.

"And so you have met Mabille." Belesme took Eleanor's arm and pushed her past his mother. "Stay away from her—her evil would taint you."

"You'll not keep her!" Mabille spat after them.

Bathed and dressed in the bride clothes that had been sent to Belesme the previous summer, Eleanor felt better. Her refusal to take Mabille's chamber had been met with a shrug, and another, smaller room had been found for her. Not that it was lacking in comfort, she mused, for the place was sumptuously furnished, the bed hung with embroidered silk curtains, the walls covered with thick tapestries depicting a stag hunt, and the floors swept clean except for thick woven mats of wool laid by bed and brazier.

Piers carried in another box of her bridethings and opened a cupboard. Idly Eleanor wondered if what Roger had told her were true—that there were no other women in Belesme's fortress save Mabille. She shuddered as she recalled the strange scene between mother and son. Jesu, but they were a hostile pair to be of the same blood. She wandered to look out the tall, narrow window into the yard below, and discovered much of that portion of the yard was taken up with new construction. "Piers"—she motioned the boy over to point—"what is it?"

"A manor house, I think, patterned after some he saw of the English thanes. But my lord is not such a fool as to put it outside of the fortress. This way he has his safety and his comfort both."

"You serve him . . ." She hesitated, uncertain as to

how to phrase the question, and then plunged on, "I mean, how can you serve such a one as he?"

The boy appeared to consider for a moment and then shrugged. "He teaches me to be a man—and he saved me from Mabille."

What had Henry said of Mabille once—that she lay indiscriminately with young boys? Surely not Piers— the boy did not look depraved or evil. "You were her lover?" she asked incredulously.

"Aye—and so was everyone else here at one time or the other—some still are."

"Jesu!"

"But as for Count Robert, he is many men," Piers continued, "and some are vile and others are not. Nay—he is but what she made him."

"Mabille?"

"Aye—he should have killed her long ago," he answered dispassionately. "But he will not. I think that in spite of all, he loves her." He caught himself and feared he had said too much. He bent to pick up a painted box and placed it in a cupboard behind him. " 'Tis done," he announced as he backed toward the door.

"Wait—am I to have a maid?"

"There is none, but we have sent to the village for a girl." He met her eyes and grinned. "The difficult thing is getting one to come here—most are terrified of us."

Realizing that his confidences were at an end, she let him go. Pacing the room, she pondered her situation and looked for comfort in what she had heard. Belesme had told Mabille that he did not intend to make her his whore, so there was hope there. If only the Church could bring enough pressure on him through Curthose, mayhap he would have to release her. Nay, she knew better—he wanted Roger to come for her so that he could kill him and be done. Then he would take her. Well, she would survive Belesme—she had to. She would survive for the sake of the child she carried.

Absently she opened the cupboard and stepped back

as though burned. Piled next to her things was Count
Robert's clothing. She strode over to the nearest trunk
and jerked it open to find folded linens. But inspection of the one next to it revealed a neat pile of
embroidered tunics that could only be his. Jesu, but
she had been a fool to think he might treat her honorably. There was no means of escape, and no help
could come soon enough to save her from him. Yet
she could not dishonor Roger by lying with another.
"Sweet Mary," she whispered to herself, "what am I
to do? I have to save my son."

It did not come to her at once, but rather evolved
slowly in her brain—she would tell Belesme of the
child. He was far too proud to accept another man's
child, she was certain. It would be a risk telling him—he
might kill her in anger—but she did not think so. Nay,
maybe he would not even care and would take her for
his pleasure anyway.

Her tumbled thoughts were interrupted by the sound
of his boots on the stairs. She had nowhere to run and
nowhere to hide. Resolutely she prepared for face
him.

"You are looking better."

She spun around at the sound of his voice and her
mouth suddenly seemed too dry for words. "Aye."
She licked her lips nervously. "My lord, may I speak
freely?"

"You have a tongue."

She eyed him cautiously. He appeared calm and
reasonable and perhaps it would be best to tell him
now and get it over with. "My lord," she began, "I
would not be dishonored." To her horror, her words
brought that strange smile to his face, and he moved
closer. "Nay—hear me out!"

"I did not bring you here to hear you tell me nay."
His hand reached to stroke the nearest braid that hung
over her shoulder. "I would see your hair unbound
again." There was a soft, hypnotic quality in his voice
that made her shiver.

"Listen to me! Jesu, are you mad?" she cried out as

his fingers began unworking her braids. "You told your mother that I would not be your leman!"

"I would wed with you."

"I am not free!"

"But you will be." He combed out the hair as it unwound and then moved to the other side. She tried to shake her head free, only to have him twine his fingers in her hair and pull her head back. The green eyes were warmed with fire as he bent his head to hers. She twisted in spite of the pain and turned her face away.

"Nay."

"Say not nay to me, Eleanor," he half-whispered, "for I would have you."

"Do not do this to me!" She pushed at his chest even as he caught her to him. "For my sake—for the sake of the child I bear—do not do this!" Abruptly he dropped his hands and she stumbled away.

"Liar! You would cheat me with your lies! You carry no child!"

"Aye." She grabbed at the bedpost for support and faced him. "I have my husband's seed within me, my lord, and I will bear his child." Her face whitened as he advanced on her with raised hand, but she stood her ground. "The sickness I have had—'tis from the babe."

To her horror, his hand stayed suspended in midair as though he meant to strike her, and then he reached roughly for the shoulder of her gown. With a swift rending jerk he tore it down to expose breasts that already were showing signs of change. He stared at their fullness a moment and then forcibly stripped both the gown and undershift to her knees. She stood stock-still while his eyes traveled to her already thickening waist and then to the gentle curve of her abdomen in dawning belief.

"I'll kill him." His voice was flat and toneless as he looked away. "Would that I could tear the babe from your body and still keep you." He ran his fingers through his black hair and shook his head. "I ought to kill you for this."

To Eleanor, the toneless quality in his voice was more frightening than his rage. "Nay . . ." She tried to keep her own voice calm while moving toward him. "You would kill me for what I cannot help, my lord. I have loved Roger all of my life."

"Then you love a dead man." Without turning around, he walked slowly to the steps, leaving her to stare after him.

Eleanor pondered his reaction and worried. For the time being, her revelation had cooled his ardor, but could it save her? She was an obsession with him, and he'd proven that he'd go to any lengths to possess her. And, supposing he let her live and she bore the babe in this grim fortress. Would he let the living proof of her relationship with Roger live? She had no faith that he would. Resolutely she dressed herself and decided to seek out Mabille.

It was not an easy decision. From all she had heard of the beautiful Mabille, the woman was a witch capable of anything. Sweet Mary, but the lady was at least forty and did not look half that. But mayhap she could reason with her, because one thing was certain—Count Robert might want her, but his mother did not.

She found Mabille almost by accident, glimpsing her red hair as she disappeared into the new building in the yard. Eleanor picked her way past workmen hammering inside the doorway and slipped inside unchallenged. The place itself was enough to make one stare. A great open hall with high, beamed ceiling and tall stained-glass windows occupied the entire front of the building. At either side of the huge room were hallways going behind. There was no sign of Mabille there so Eleanor forced herself to cross the room to the nearest passageway, where she found several spacious chambers. And, behind them, a covered walk led to the castle kitchens.

"What are you doing here?"

Eleanor spun around guiltily and faced Mabille, who seemed to have appeared from nowhere. The woman was cold and haughty, her voice like ice. A quick glance revealed they were alone in the passageway between chambers.

"I came in search of you," Eleanor answered simply. "You would not have me here, Lady Mabille, and I would not stay."

"And you think I will help you?" Mabille asked disdainfully. "Nay—he would kill me."

"You are his mother—surely for the love he bears you, he could forgive," Eleanor tried. "Help me escape this place."

Mabille's green eyes glinted like glass. "Look around you, Eleanor of Nantes, and see what he has built for you." Her mouth twisted in hatred and jealousy. "For you," she repeated. "What we had was not good enough for the Demoiselle of Nantes—nay, he would give you everything. He would turn me out to have you." A wave of her white hand indicated the building that surrounded them. "For you, there had to be a palace." She spoke bitterly. "I would not help you if I could."

"I did not make him do any of these things—nay, I would not have him."

"Does it matter? He would have you. I am not enough for him."

"You are his mother still."

"I bore him—aye, in travail, the fruit of his father's lust. He nearly tore me apart with his birthing and I would not have another." Mabille looked away as though remembering some distant thing.

"But you are his mother," Eleanor persisted. "As I will be mother to the child I carry." She had the satisfaction of seeing the other woman start. "Aye—I bear my husband's son." She reached out to touch the white arm. "Please—aid me."

"Nay!" Mabille shook away and drew back. "I would see you in hell first!"

"But *why*? You do not want me here," Eleanor tried to reason, "and you could be rid of me."

The green eyes flashed. "Make no mistake about it, Lady Eleanor—I *will* be rid of you. Robert will tire of this passion soon enough and you will be gone, but you will not leave." With that cryptic pronouncement, the redheaded woman turned on her heel and walked away.

Eleanor pushed ahead of her and blocked her path. "You have not listened—I have no wish to take your place as mistress here!"

"You will not."

"Eleanor!"

Both women turned guiltily to face Belesme. Mabille recovered first and sneered. "The little fool thinks I would help her escape."

He paid her no attention, facing Eleanor instead. "I told you to stay away from her. Why must you always defy me?"

"I would leave!" she cried. "Jesu—are you both mad? You cannot keep me here! I have a husband and a family who will fight for me now. The Pope has ruled me his, and the Church will ride against you if you hold me. Even Curthouse will have to stand with him."

"And I tell you that even if the Old Conqueror lived and came for you, I would keep you. I'll hear no more of this!"

"Robert, she bears his child." Mabille gloated over her news. "You would not have her after that, surely!"

"I already know."

"Kill her then."

Green eyes met green eyes, but it was Mabille who wavered when he answered, "Nay, I cannot."

"She will bring your death."

"Nay—her next child will be mine. When Roger is dead, I will send this one to his father for heir, but I will keep Eleanor." He reached for Eleanor and pulled her roughly by the arm. "You have no business with my mother. Come away before you mark your babe."

Eleanor made the sign of the Cross over her breast and nodded. "Aye—I should not have come."

"Mabille, you will take your meals in your chamber and stay out of Eleanor's sight until I can provide escort to your dower lands."

"You dare not send me away—nay, you dare not!"

"I cannot have you both here and rest. You will be packed within the week and ready to leave."

Mabille grasped his sleeve and fell to her knees. "Robert, this is my home. You cannot do this! For what we have been to each other, let me stay!" Her voice rose shrilly as she pleaded, "Do not send me away for your dark-eyed whore."

"Witch!" He struck her with his free hand across the face. "You'll not call her thus!"

"Your whore!" she shouted.

He struck her again. This time Eleanor wrenched free and ran for the doorway to escape the confrontation between son and mother. "Mother of God!" she cried out at the sight of Piers de Sols. "Stop them!"

He came running to her aid. Eleanor leaned against the side of the building and caught her breath before explaining. "Count Robert and Mabille fight in there."

"God's blood!" the boy muttered under his breath. "I would that he sent her away."

"He sends her." Nausea gnawed at her belly and the courtyard before her floated. She closed her eyes and held to the wall. "Please . . . stop them before she is killed."

"Nay. They are like two fighting dogs, Lady Eleanor, and when they are separated, they turn on he who intervenes." His brows knit in concern as he watched her. "Besides," he decided, "I think you have the greater need of me just now."

"Nay, I am all right," was all she was able to get out before violent retching sent her to her knees and she was sick. Piers stood helplessly waiting for her to stop and then tried to wipe her face with his sleeve. "Get my lord!" he yelled to a startled sentry. "He's inside there!" He pulled Eleanor over to sit on one of the stairs and felt her clammy forehead. "Jesu, lady, but you are sick."

"Nay, 'tis from the babe—'twill pass."

"Holy Mary!" He sank to the step beside her. "Does my lord know?"

"Aye." She closed her eyes and tried to stop the spinning courtyard. "Some women have it only in the mornings, but it seems to strike me at any time. I have heard it is a sign that I carry a son."

His quarrel with Mabille forgotten, Robert ran toward them. One look at Eleanor's ashen and damp face stopped him cold. He pushed Piers aside impatiently and sat beside her to brace her.

"She is better now, I think," Piers offered.

"Better? You call this better?" Belesme cut loose with a string of blasphemous oaths that cowered those around him. "Eleanor, listen to me—you cannot go on like this. I am going to carry you up to your bed and then send for a physician from Rouen."

"Nay," she protested wearily. "He will tell you 'tis the child and that it will pass in another month or less."

"I have seen men broken in torture that did not vomit thus. Here—let me get you up."

He lifted her effortlessly and carried her toward the tower. "Piers! Get watered wine and stale bread! I've brought more than one stomach around with those."

He climbed the stairs, kicked open the door with heavy boot, and thrust her onto the bed, ordering brusquely, "Do not be getting up until you are better. And do not defy me in this, Eleanor. I swear I did not bring you here to die." He pushed the heavy bed curtains aside and leaned over her to slide a pillow under her head. "Piers will come and we will get something into your stomach and you will lie still until it settles."

"I never thought you to be skilled with the sick," she muttered.

"Nay, but I have revived those who would faint on me often enough that I know the means of dealing with it."

It was strange to hear him admit matter-of-factly that he brought around those he tortured so they could endure more. She shuddered at the implication and rolled onto her side away from him. He patted her awkwardly and drew back.

"Eleanor . . ." He hesitated as though trying to find the right words. "I have wanted you since that first

day I saw you at Nantes." He paused, his green eyes
serious. "Aye, I am everything you have ever heard of
me—and worse—but I would not willingly harm you. I
see you as mother to my sons." When she opened her
mouth to protest, he stilled her impatiently. "Nay—
let me finish. I am not given to pretty, courtly speeches,
but I swear I have never seen your like." He rose from
the bed and stared unseeing across the room for a
moment. "I have my pride, Eleanor, but I would have
you in spite of all. I meant what I said below to my
mother. Your babe will be sent to Harlowe to claim its
inheritance, but you will stay here. Learn to accept
your lot and 'twill be easier for you."

"I could die easier."

Brutal, violent, and capricious, Robert of Belesme
nonetheless cherished beautiful things, and nowhere
was that more evident than in his castle. Indeed, he
lived in the splendor of a prince behind those grim
stone walls. There was nothing even in Eleanor's experience at Nantes or Harlowe to compare with what
she saw when she picked her way behind Piers into
Belesme's great hall. From the scrolled iron sconces
instead of pitch torches to the tables laid with linen, it
was apparent that Robert's home rivaled the palace at
Rouen.

She soon discovered, however, that the company
was less exalted than their surroundings. The poorest
of the lesser nobility, those reduced to mercenary status, mingled with each other and with the richly attired members of Belesme's own household guard. As
she passed by them, her face flamed crimson from the
ribald remarks made about her. At one point, Piers
rounded on a drunken fellow bent on accosting her.

" 'Tis the Lady Eleanor, Count Gilbert's daughter,
you fool! Stand aside!"

Ignoring Piers, the man leered at Eleanor and reached
to touch the rich brocade of her wide sleeve. His voice
was thick as he mumbled, "Gilbert's daughter or
Belesme's fancy whore—'tis no difference."

From out of nowhere, a knife cut through the air

and sank hilt-deep in the mercenary's chest. His silly
grin faded to the vacant stare of the dead and he
pitched forward at Eleanor's side. She let out an involuntary scream that drew the attention of everyone in
the hall, while Robert stepped from behind her to
retrieve his dagger. When he straightened up, he swept
the large room with angry eyes and demanded loudly,
"Is there another who would slander Gilbert's daughter?" It was strangely silent as the men there watched
their lord wipe his blade on a nearby tablecloth. Finally Belesme motioned to a serving man. "Clean up
this mess."

Piers pulled the horrified Eleanor away, murmuring
low for her ears alone, "There's none that will trouble
you again at Belesme, my lady. Come—let me get you
to your seat."

"Sweet Mary! Think you I could eat after that?" she
asked as he led her to the high table.

"It's over," he answered simply.

His temper cooled, Robert joined her, casually dip-
ping his bloody fingers into the small washbowl they
shared. She watched him dry his hands on a napkin
before beginning to carve the meat before him.

"You killed that man!"

"Aye."

"Because he said what the world will think if you
keep me here?"

He shifted a slab of meat onto their trencher before
answering, "He touched you. By rights, he should
have died more slowly, but I was angered."

"You cannot kill everyone who will call me whore,
my lord."

"Nay—I make it known that I mean to wed with
you."

It was futile to dispute him on the subject and she
had no wish to anger him further. Slowly, bite by bite,
she forced herself to eat in spite of the curious stares
around her. Much to her relief, Belesme seemed to be
in a good mood. She glanced at the empty seat on the
other side of him and thought of Mabille.

"Do you really mean to send your mother away?"

"I have sent ahead to prepare a place for her." He frowned at the thought of something. "But she will have to be well-guarded."

"Surely no one would harm your mother."

He gave a derisive snort and fixed her with those strange green eyes. "Nay—'tis not for her I fear. She will strike back if she can."

Eleanor shivered at the cold way he spoke of his own mother. Apparently her thoughts were transparent, for he nodded and told her, "In my twelfth year, I saw my father die by her hand. He was much as I am"—his voice turned harsh with the awful memory—"but she was his wife and he trusted in her. She gave him poisoned pudding and then watched hours while he died, his belly on fire. Then, while they were burying him, she took his squire to bed."

"Mother of God!" Eleanor breathed in shock at the story. Impulsively she laid a hand on the rich material of his sleeve. "It must have been terrible to you."

"Nay—I wished him dead also. There was no affection between us." He dropped his eyes to his arm. "Art softhearted, Eleanor of Nantes."

Self-consciously, she drew back. "I felt sorry, my lord. A man should love his son."

"As your parents loved you?" he gibed back. "Nay, I would not have your pity."

"Aye, my parents were not kind either. I thought I should die at Fontainebleau."

"You were not sick enough of the place to pledge to me," he reminded her grimly.

"I was not."

He traced her jawline with his knuckle and leaned closer. "Art beautiful, Eleanor of Nantes," he murmured huskily. "Aye—your hair, your eyes, your fine bones—all of you."

"My lord . . ." She closed her eyes rather than recoil at his touch. "I do not feel well. Please—I would retire."

He dropped his hand reluctantly and nodded. "Aye. You have been through much these three days past. Seek your bed if you will."

* * *

With no maid to attend her, Eleanor struggled out of her gown and began unbraiding her hair, working out the tangles with her fingers before she attempted the brush. Clad only in her thin shift, she moved closer to the fire and leaned her head forward to let the hair cascade before her in ripples. Beginning at the back, she brushed with long strokes.

"I see you are recovered."

She dropped the brush as though it were a brand and sat stone-still. The flesh at the back of her neck crawled and she shivered in spite of the fire. He moved closer and lifted the dark mass, letting it slip through his fingers and fall against her back.

" 'Tis like silk." His hand dropped to her shoulder and his fingers lightly traced the seam of her shift. "Take it off," he whispered hoarsely.

"Nay!" She ducked away and rose in alarm.

"You will." His eyes flicked over her hungrily. "I would see all of you again."

She backed away from him, her arms crossed protectively across her chest. "Nay! If you take me, it will be because I have not the strength to stop you, but 'twill not happen before I have fought you with all I have."

"So be it then."

He circled her like a wolf around its prey. The firelight danced in his eyes and frightened her. "Fight if you will," he whispered as she broke for the door. He lunged and caught her at the waist. She kicked and flailed furiously while he dragged her toward the curtained bed. When he reached it, he shifted her into one arm and began undressing himself with the other. She sank her teeth into his forearm and tasted salt. He cursed but did not relax his grip. While he unfastened his chausses and removed them, she drove her elbow repeatedly into his ribs. With his foot he slipped off his shoes and worked his clothes down. Then he pushed her against the bedpost and blocked her escape with his body while he drew off his tunic. She kicked at his groin and missed.

"Nay," he laughed harshly, " 'tis enough of that." He flung his tunic into the corner and faced her, his body aroused and ready.

In desperation she threw herself at him, clawing at his face and kicking for his manhood. Her fingernails drew deep scratches across his high cheekbones before he managed to catch both her hands in one of his. With her free hand he slapped her and then caught her against him when she reeled from the blow. He forced her head back and bent to kiss her, his mouth hard and demanding on hers. His hands moved to explore her hips eagerly while he worked the thin shift upward. She twisted against him until their bare thighs met. She bit his lip and held on. He slapped her so hard that she finally cried out and released the lip. Blood dripped from the tooth wound, but he did not seem to care. He caught her again by the waist and pushed her over his arm to pull up the shift over her shoulders. With a quick change of arms, he had it jerked over her head and discarded at her feet.

Too proud to let any witness her shame and humiliation, she fought the urge to scream out when he threw her on the bed and covered her with his naked body. He made no attempt to woo her, forcing her legs apart in spite of her frantic bucking and kicking. He stilled her with his weight and forced entry into her body. She stiffened and then fell slack beneath him in defeat, clenching her teeth and enduring his hard, rhythmic thrusting while he drove relentlessly in pursuit of his own pleasure. Tears of pain and humiliation streaked her face.

Finally he gave an animal cry and collapsed breathlessly against her. His breath came in hot gasps against her ear until he finally mastered himself. Slowly it evened out and he rolled away to lie facing her. "She-wolf." He grinned as he fingered his swollen lip. "I hope it does not fester." He pushed himself up on an elbow to stare at her in the semidarkness. "You are crying."

"You have shamed me." She closed her eyes and turned her head away.

"Nay, I have loved you," he murmured. He spread her hair out over the silk pillow and continued studying her. "You are so beautiful." When she made no response, he rose with a sigh and poured himself a cup of wine. Draining it, he poured another and returned to the bed. "Here—'twill ease you," he offered. She ignored him in stony silence until he set the cup down and slid back into bed.

"Come here," he ordered while he pulled her stiff body against him. He lay quietly for a time and then began gently tracing her profile, her bare shoulder, and then the curve of her breasts. "I did not want to hurt you, Eleanor, but you would not come willing." His fingertips played with her nipples until they hardened and stood taut.

"Don't do that!" She brushed his hand away angrily. "Jesu, but you would ravish me and then try to make me like it!"

"Aye," he whispered against her ear. His hand dipped lower to stroke the inside of her thigh. "Do not fight me this time, and I will not hurt you."

20

A late-winter storm rolled in and prevented Mabille's leaving Belesme. By the time its fury was spent, Robert had other problems that demanded his attention more than his mother's departure. In his obsession with Eleanor, he had not counted on the furor that arose from his invasion of the abbey. Even the weak and vacillating Curthose felt compelled to protest strongly, issuing a written ultimatum to Robert, demanding Eleanor's release to the Archbishop of Rouen and threatening the force to bring it about.

As for Eleanor, she sustained herself during those days with her determination to live and bear Roger's child. She went through the motions of living calmly, eating in Belesme's great hall, sleeping in his bed, and dreaming of freedom. She suffered a deep feeling of humiliation every time Robert took her, but she no longer fought him. And she worried over her husband's reaction, knowing full well that he would hold her blameless, but nonetheless fearing that it would change things between them. She prayed fervently that it wouldn't.

"What is this nonsense?"

Eleanor jumped guiltily from where she knelt in prayer. "My chapel," she answered quietly. "I found these in my bridethings and I chose to set them up."

Robert eyed the hanging crucifix and the cloth-covered altar table with disdain. She had set golden candleholders with fine wax candles on either side. He frowned at the sight of a makeshift chapel in his bedchamber, but he held his tongue. "Turn around."

She didn't move. "You are displeased," she answered tonelessly.

"Nay," he sighed, "keep it if you will, but do not expect me to pray with you." He longed to get some more positive response out of her, some sign that he could make her care for him. As it was, he could make her wear the fine clothes and share his bed and his table, but he could not make her enjoy any of it. Even at night when she yielded to him, she yielded her body and nothing more.

Reluctantly she rose and turned around to face him. Her eyes widened at the sight of his full mail beneath his gold-embroidered surcoat. The three white plumes of Belesme were appliquéd over the fabric, and a white plume was fastened to the top of the helmet he carried.

"Aye"—he nodded—"you will be rid of me for a few days, Eleanor. I am come to bid you farewell to spare you your public display of grief at my leaving." The sarcasm in his voice was unmistakable.

"Godspeed."

His eyes flicked over her for some sign of concern before he moved closer. "I go to answer Curthose for you, but nothing will come of it. I do not expect to be gone above a week or two at the most."

"It doesn't matter."

"Eleanor—"

"I cry you Godspeed, my lord—what else would you have?"

"Nay, not so quick." He caught her hands and pulled her against him. "Warm my memory with a kiss, Eleanor."

She dutifully closed her eyes and tilted her head back to allow him to kiss her, but she did not respond to the pressure of his lips on hers. Her passivity infuriated him, and he crushed her against his mail while he possessed her mouth. It was not until she finally cried out in pain that he released her and stepped back. His bare hand reached to touch her forehead and he frowned.

"You are warm, but not from desire for me—how do you feel?"

"My head aches—'tis all."

"You are sure? I would not leave you unwell."

"Nay, I am all right."

He pulled her back into his arms and held her more gently. "The boy Giles will look after your needs while I am gone, and you will sup here to spare you the company of the men. I have given orders that you are to have anything that you want."

Not many hours after he'd ridden out, it became apparent that Eleanor was very ill. Alarmed, the boy Giles sent for Eustace, Belesme's seneschal, and asked that someone ride out for Count Robert. Eustace wavered, afraid of Belesme's anger at being called back and afraid of his anger if she were indeed sick. But when her fever climbed to the point that she lost touch with reality, the seneschal decided to dispatch Wald of Thibeaux out into the night to seek their lord.

It was not unknown for a fever to strike someone down so quickly that he was gone in the space of a day or two. With that in mind, both Eustace and Giles hovered over Eleanor until it became apparent that she was not getting any better. Finally Eustace sought out Mabille in the confinement of her solar and asked for help. She met his appeal with an incredulous refusal, laughing in his face and telling him that she hoped "the whore of Nantes" died. But sometime in the night she changed her mind and sent word that she would do what she could for Eleanor.

A meeting of every person left in authority in the stronghold yielded as many remedies as there were people. Only the most bizarre were discarded as the seneschal determined to try anything to save the girl. Six sheep were slaughtered and skinned and the warm, bloody skins were wrapped around Eleanor's naked body to draw out the poisons from the fever. Leeches were applied on her arms and legs until they grew fat with her blood, and still the fever raged. Finally Mabille ordered cold water from the melting snow put in a tub and had Eleanor plunged into it. Only the latter treatment had seemed to revive the girl somewhat, but she still suffered from confusion. She sat with teeth chattering in the cold water and called out for Roger.

The boy Giles leaned over the tub in front of her face. "Lady, do you know me?" he asked loudly.

Her eyes flew open. "Aye," she croaked.

"Who am I?"

"Roger."

"Nay, lady, you are at Belesme."

"Belesme. Aye—I remember. Sweet Mary—Belesme." Her lips were cracked and parched from the fever. "I thirst."

"Put her back to bed," Mabille ordered. "I'll bring her a fever potion."

She was pulled from the tub unceremoniously and swaddled in a thick blanket. Her teeth chattered and her lips were blue. Two men supported her between them and started toward the bed.

"What is the meaning of all this?"

They nearly dropped Eleanor at the sound of his voice. Giles was the first to find his voice and he cried out with relief, "My lord, you are come! Praise God you are come! Jesu, but she has been sick!"

"So I see."

He was mud-spattered and unshaven and his green eyes revealed the fatigue he felt, but he took in the scene before him thankfully. The man Wald had given him to believe that she was on her deathbed, and he had ridden straight back. He moved to take her. A quick sweep of tired eyes revealed the extraordinary measures used to save her.

"You look like death," he muttered as his mail-clad arms closed around her.

"I feel like death."

"We did not hear your lordship arrive," Eustace apologized, "for we were busy with the lady, but there'll be a bath as soon as the water can be heated."

"Nay, I am too tired. I came alone, leaving the others to break camp." He looked down to see the mud on his surcoat for the first time. "My boots are below and are nigh ruined."

Mabille rounded the top of the stairs and paled at the sight of her son. "You are returned," she uttered foolishly. "But how?"

"I rode alone." He spied the cup and frowned. "What's that?"

" 'Tis for her fever."

"Drink it," he ordered curtly.

"Nay—'tis not for me!"

"I'll warrant it's not. Drink it, Mabille."

"Stop it!" Eleanor weaved in his arms and had to lean into him.

"She would give you poison, Eleanor." Robert's eyes never left his mother. "Go on—drink it."

"Nay!"

He pushed Eleanor into Giles' arms and advanced on Mabille. She backed away, cup in hand. "Well, do you drink it?" he asked softly. "Or do I pour it down you?"

"Robert, listen to me! Let them tell you that I have nursed her!"

He reached to wrench the cup away, spilling nearly half its contents on the floor. Slowly, deliberately, he raised it to his lips, his eyes still on his mother.

"Nay!" She lunged for it, knocking the vessel from his hand to spill the rest of it. And then, suddenly conscious of what she had done, she turned to the others, crying, "Tell him! Tell him I have saved her!"

"Mabille!" he barked as he struck her. "Get down on the floor and lick up what you have spilt—lick like the dog that you are!" He drew the dagger from his belt and stood over her. "Lick, damn you! Lick!"

"Nay, Robert, you are a fool," she babbled. "You are too blind to see what she does to you. Robert, listen to me!"

"Robert, please . . ." Eleanor had pulled away from Giles and stood weaving crazily in the middle of the room. "Do not . . ." She appeared to lose her balance and Robert lunged to catch her.

"Art too sick to stand," he muttered. "Eustace!

Strip the bed and lay fresh sheets!" Nodding in Mabille's direction, he ordered, "And lock her in her solar until I can deal with her."

"Robert, I thirst," Eleanor told him tiredly, "and I am so weak."

"Get her some wine!" he barked at Giles as he sat and cradled her on his lap. "Aye, but you will mend now that I am here," he soothed her.

21

"I cannot believe in the old dog's impudence!" Robert raged as he consigned William Bonne-Ame's letter to the fire. "He would mediate your release, he says!"

Eleanor looked up from where she sat stitching an altar cloth for the chapel he'd finally allowed her to open. "I would like to see him, my lord."

"Resign yourself," he told her angrily. "You do not leave me!"

"I know, but I would confess to someone, and there's no priest in Belesme."

"What have you got to confess?" He sneered. "You are blameless and can lay what is between us on my soul."

"I did not think you had one," she reminded him mildly. "Have you changed your mind?" She stabbed at the ivory satin and pulled a strand of golden thread through it. The irony did not escape her as she realized that her captivity had taught her more about praying than seven years in a convent and more about sewing than Herleva would have guessed possible. She held up the cloth to admire the golden cross she had worked in the center.

"Do you want to see him?" he asked finally.

"Aye."

"I'll not change my mind, Eleanor. Nothing the old man can say will move me."

"I know."

"Does a priest mean so much to you? God's teeth, but you could not wait to leave Fontainebleau!"

She folded the altar cloth carefully on her lap and

looked away. "But that was before I had been to Belesme, my lord."

"Eleanor . . ." He moved awkwardly to stand behind her chair. "I have not forced you in some time now." He could watch the muscles in her shoulders tense at the thought that he might touch her. He swallowed hard above her dark head and tried not to think of how much he wanted her. "All right—you can have your damned archbishop. I'll send word that he can see you, but that I do not negotiate. But I warn you—I'll not have him in these walls above one day."

"I doubt he would wish to stay."

He felt a hopeless sense of loss as he looked down on her. Finally he sighed heavily and asked, "Can we not begin anew?" He reached to touch the soft silk of her crown, but she ducked her head beneath his hand.

"Nay, my lord. You can take me to your bed whenever you wish it, but you cannot make me like it. If that satisfies you, you have that."

"You know that does not satisfy me!" He kicked the chair leg so violently that she cringed as though he meant to strike her. "Look at yourself, Eleanor! Look at your clothes! Look around you at what I give you! God's teeth, but you are stubborn, woman!" He jerked her roughly up from the chair and shook her, forcing her to look at the newly finished chamber. "If you defy me much longer, I fear for you. I cannot always check my temper before 'tis too late." Suddenly his grip relaxed and he reached to touch her chin gently. "I did not mean to frighten you. You are the most beautiful woman I've ever seen—I would not look at another."

"But you do frighten me, my lord. Even if it were not for my husband, I could not live my life with you. Sweet Mary—what if I bore no sons? What if I angered you beyond what you could check? Would you skin me alive like you did Fuld?"

"You'd bear a son for me. If your mother had no son, 'twas because your father got none." He released her and stepped back. "What you need is time. Once

the Bastard is no more, you'll turn to me. I swear I
can make you content, Eleanor."

It was useless to provoke the argument further and
she knew it. He stubbornly refused to face reality and
nothing she could say would change that. She managed not to flinch when his hands slid down her arms
and took her hands. He bent to brush her lips with his.
"I'll show you."

Apparently William Bonne-Ame lay nearby waiting
for Robert's reply, for it did not take him long to
reach Belesme's gates. That he came at all was a
triumph of personal courage over a deep-seated fear
of Robert of Belesme. Somehow, he viewed it as a
personal atonement for what he had done to Eleanor
of Nantes.

With a very real sense of foreboding he entered the
great castle and passed beneath the eyes of an un-
friendly crowd. It was not until he had crossed beneath the barbican and found himself actually within
the walls of Belesme that he remembered some of the
details of Count Robert's awful confession. The hairs
on the back of his neck prickled and beads of perspira-
tion formed on his high forehead. His free hand crept
to touch the crucifix on his breast.

The lone attendant allowed in with him leaned over
to whisper, " 'Tis scarce a tumultous welcome, excellency."

"Nay, but we are safe enough, I think."

They crossed the inner gate and into a small courtyard faced on one end by Belesme's new manor house.
Robert himself, bareheaded and splendid in a long,
flowing robe of green silk belted with gold, stepped
forward to take the archbishop's reins. A faint smile
flitted across the coldly handsome face as he brushed
the prelate's ring with his lips.

"You are timely arrived, excellency," Belesme told
him with a straight face, "for Eleanor has but lately
furnished our chapel. You could be the first to say
Mass there in many years."

"Ah . . ." William opened his mouth and then

thought better of whatever he'd intended to say. He twisted in his saddle and looked over the crowd around him. "The Lady Eleanor?" he inquired finally.

"Inside." Robert nodded toward the new building. "Piers, take his excellency's mount," he told the boy behind him. He stepped back and waited for William to swing down.

"I would see the lady. I have promised the duke and her father to ascertain her condition."

"She has been unwell," but she mends. If you will but come with me, you can see that she is not ill-treated here."

Bonne-Ame followed Belesme to the low, single-story building and Robert opened the massive double doors for him. William was totally unprepared for the splendor he found as he surveyed the white plastered walls, the clean-swept floors covered with woven reed mats, and the ornate sconces fastened to the walls. There in the main hall, the great vaulted ceiling was as exquisite as those in churches. " 'Tis beautiful, Robert," he breathed.

"I built it for my marriage," Belesme murmured sardonically behind him. "But we tarry—I believe you wished to see Eleanor."

"Aye." Bonne-Ame gave the hall one last look. "You are a wealthy man, Robert."

He turned and followed Belesme through one of the side doors and found himself in a corridor that led to the count's living quarters. At the entrance, he stopped, uncertain as to what he would find within. From the moment he'd heard that Robert had taken her, he'd been afraid of what might have happened to the girl. In his mind, he'd imagined that Eleanor of Nantes must be the most unfortunate lady on earth.

Belesme stood aside and waited for the archbishop to pass. "Behold the Lady Eleanor," he announced proudly.

She was seated before a tall casement, her fine profile outlined by the spring sun. At the sound of Robert's voice, she turned around and William Bonne-Ame stared, suddenly bereft of speech at the girl

before him. She was small, but she was the most
perfectly formed female he had ever been privileged
to see. It was no wonder that both men wanted her
enough to fight for her.

She rose with a questioning look and came to kneel
gracefully at his feet in spite of her obvious pregnancy.
He looked down when she kissed his ring reverently
and he fought an urge to smooth the shining satin of
her dark hair. As he raised her, he could see that she
was richly dressed in ruby samite trimmed with gold
embroidery at the neck and around the wide sleeves.
Her undertunic was of the deepest blue silk. She was
pale, but he could see no marks of violence on her.
Her eyes were large and luminous against her white-
ness, and it was easy to see that she had indeed been
very ill. He finally found his voice.

"You are all right?"

She glanced at Belesme before answering, "I have
been unwell, excellency, with a fever." She gently
disengaged her fingers from the archbishop's grip and
managed a smile. "I am glad you are come, for there
is no priest here and I would confess."

"Mayhap you can persuade William to say Mass for
you before he leaves in the morning." Robert's message was pointed—he'd allowed Bonne-Ame to see
her but the had no wish to prolong the visit. He
dropped his tall frame into a carved high-back chair.

"My lord, if she would confess, it must be private.
Her sins, if any, are between her and God."

"Nay, she is blameless."

"Please, Robert," Eleanor appealed to Belesme, "it
will not take long."

"Aye." He heaved himself back up and took a few
steps toward the door. "Just do not be thinking he has
the means of taking you away. Confess if you will, but
do not expect his aid if you would have him leave here
alive."

As soon as the door banged behind him, Eleanor
hastened to bar it. Turning back to Boone-Ame, she
again dropped to her knees at his feet to begin the
ancient rite of repentance. "Forgive me, Father, for I

have sinned against God and am heartily sorry." She paused as though uncertain where to begin and then with a deep breath continued in a low voice, "I set my face against God's service, excellency, for I felt no call to the sisterhood, I loved against the wishes of my family and my family's liege lord and took a husband not of their choosing, and now I have lain with a man not my husband." Her voice fell even lower and he had to strain to hear her. "I pray Roger can be brought to forgive me."

He could feel the depth of her anguish and sought words of comfort for her. "Nay, child," he told her gently, "you have sinned in none of this. It is not wrong in God's eyes to follow the conscience he gave you. I know Lord Roger, and he is a good Christian lord, Eleanor. The pope confirms you in your choice of a husband and your marriage is valid." He laid a comforting hand on her head. "As for lying with Robert, there is no doubt but that you were forced, and therefore the sin is his, not yours. Life is precious, my daughter, and God expects us to guard it while we have it. For the sake of yourself and your unborn babe, I cannot see how you could have survived had you spurned Count Robert. You did not go willingly to him, did you? You did not seek pleasure in lying with him?"

"I hate it!" she whispered vehemently. "But I do not try to stop him anymore."

"God knows that, child, and so does Lord Roger. Nay, Holy Church would tell him he must take you back, but I know it will not come to that. He would have you for what you are, anyway."

"I hate the beauty God gave me, excellency! I would that I were ugly and that Robert of Belesme had found me so!"

"Nay—there's your sin, daughter," William told her gently, "for we must learn to accept whatever burdens He gives us and make the best of them. For that, I ask you to get on your knees and pray forgiveness. As to the other things you fear, there is nothing to forgive."

He made the sign of the Cross over her head. "I absolve thee, child. Go and sin no more."

"But I have dishonored my husband!" she cried out.

"Nay—Count Robert has. 'Tis between them, little Eleanor." He extended his hand for her to kiss again. "Come—get up and tell me how you are really treated here that I may tell your father. And Prince Henry would know also how you fare." He assisted her up and put a fatherly arm about her shoulders. "Do not despair, little one. Already the armies gather."

22

On April 30, 1093, Roger landed at St. Valéry in Normandy with a force of four hundred men levied from Harlowe's vassals and carried across the Channel in Walter de Clare's ships. He was met there by Prince Henry, who brought another hundred from Roger's levy in the Condes, and Curthose, whose resolve Henry had managed to stiffen enough to face Belesme. From the port, the army moved to Breteuil, to be joined by men gathered by Gilbert of Nantes and William Bonne-Ame. Given the uncertainties of spring weather and the sometimes indifferent response to the call to arms, Roger had made exceptionally good time.

At Breteuil, while he waited for Gilbert, Roger found that Victor III's patience with Belesme was at an end—Robert would be excommunicated and his vassals absolved from their feudal oaths to support him. Had they faced a pitched battle, the news would have been momentous, but Roger knew in his heart that Belesme could be held a year with as few as ten men.

By May 3 his patience was wearing thin and he decided to press on to Belesme without Gilbert, a decision supported by his vassals and his allies, who had spent much time arguing as to where the cowardly count of Nantes should be placed in battle. No one wanted Gilbert in front of him in case he should break and run, and no one wanted his protection on the flank for the same reason.

As the army prepared to move on to Belesme without further delay, the archbishop, clad in full mail with flowing Cross-emblazoned surcoat, rode the length of the train, blessing the troops and exhorting them to give Eleanor of Nantes justice. When Bonne-Ame reached the front, Roger dismounted, removed his helmet, and knelt in the dirt before him.

"God grant you his aid, my son," William intoned over Roger's bare head, "and make you the instrument of his justice." He signed the Cross. "In the name of the Father, the Son, and the Holy Spirit, amen." Raising Roger to embrace him, he nodded encouragement. "With God and these good and true men, we cannot fail, my lord."

"Look at him," Curthose leaned to whisper to Henry. " 'Twas he who began this whole affair with his damnable inquiry into her marriage."

"Nay," Henry reminded him abruptly, " 'Twas you and Gilbert—you who would have given her to a man like Belesme in the first place."

Curthose reddened but made no rejoinder. Instead, he rose in his stirrups and looked back down the columns curiously. "And where do you suppose Gilbert stands when all's said, brother?"

"Though he loves his daughter not, he'll come—he'd not risk his immortal soul or your goodwill. Aye—he'll answer the call because you and the Holy Father will it."

"Well, if he does, I have spoken with Lord Roger and 'tis agreed he shall guard the packs so none of us will have to depend on his fighting."

"Knowing Gilbert, he'll thank you for the service."

They watched as Roger remounted and Bonne-Ame swung into his own saddle. Roger lifted his hand to signal everyone down the column to fall into line and then he moved his horse between Henry and Curthose.

"We leave without Gilbert or Nantes' standard—he can catch up at the gates of Belesme for all I care. Let us move on."

"You do not suspect he means to betray you and join Count Robert?" Curthose asked.

"Nay." Roger grinned. "Nothing on earth could get Gilbert willingly within the walls of Robert's stronghold. He will be with us or he will stay safe at Nantes."

A cheer could be heard rising from the back of the columns. Aubery wheeled and spurred his horse to ride back for a look. Returning shortly, he reined in beside Prince Henry, his surprise evident.

"Gilbert comes—and he brings a host of archers!"

"Mother of God!" Roger turned to stare down the road behind them. "Foot soldiers and archers—aye, I should have known the men of Nantes would demand to fight for their demoiselle."

"I told you he'd not dare fail to answer the call," Henry reminded Curthose.

"Jesu!" Walter rolled his eyes heavenward. "God provides where one least expects it! Now, if you will but put him in front of Earl Richard where he can be cut down if he would run."

All eyes in front turned to the Earl of Harlowe and it suddenly came home to those present that this would be the first confrontation between Glynis' husband and the man who'd made her his leman for so many years.

"Nay—I'll not quarrel with him. 'Tis over and he reared me a fine son in spite of all." Richard raised a mailed hand to gesture to Roger. "And you'll not put him in front of me in case he should fall. I'll not have it said I murdered him to secure my son's claim to Eleanor's inheritance. Leave him with the pack as we decided."

Unaware of the almost universal contempt of his fellow lords, Gilbert rode the length of the columns to reach them. "I would have been here sooner, my lords," he explained, "but those damned fellows cannot walk as fast as we would ride, and to a man they wanted to come." His gaze swept over those around him. "Your Grace. Excellency. My Lord Henry. Roger." He stopped when he saw the earl and went white.

"Gilbert." Richard sat straight and tall in his saddle, his blue eyes cold but not openly hostile. "It has been a long time, my lord."

"Aye. We were both boys then, Richard," Gilbert managed uncomfortably.

"And now you are both men come to aid the Lady Eleanor," William Bonne-Ame injected smoothly, "and to save your grandchild that he may rule."

"She is with child?" Gilbert seemed surprised and then a slow smile spread across his face. "Praise God! I pray she has a son of my blood for Nantes!"

"And I pray she is safely delivered," Roger cut in coldly. "I count it God's blessing either way so long as she survives and is well."

"Amen," Bonne-Ame agreed. "Well, my lords, do we parley all day or do we ride to Belesme?"

"To Belesme."

They came, in Roger's words, looking like a small horde of brightly colored ants wending their way through the hills to Belesme. Saddle-weary, their bodies chafed raw in places from the stiff leather and mail they wore, they drew up in front of the high fortress and stared soberly at what they faced. Though Roger and many of the others had been there before in the time of the Old Conqueror, Earl Richard had not.

"God's teeth!" he muttered involuntarily. "But it sits up there! You told me how it was, but I thought you overgenerous in your description. Nay—you did not do it justice!"

"Aye," Roger agreed grimly. "I know not where to start to reduce it."

"Mining."

"Nay—'tis solid rock beneath. The fill does not go down under it."

"There will be a weakness somewhere, I think. I cannot believe it is naturally situated like that."

"It is. Besides, I doubt Robert will let us inspect his walls carefully enough to discover a flaw without covering us with pitch." Roger appeared to consider the length of the wall above him. "Unless, of course," he mused aloud, "we position Gilbert's archers across. If we built a tower for them, they could provide a hail of arrows as cover."

"Curthose would fire the village so they cannot plant."

"Nay"—Roger shook his head—"not unless we have to."

They could see movement on the wall above them as Belesme's archers took to the bow slits. Standing at the very top directing them from a place on the curtain wall itself was a man Roger could identify only by the ankle-length robe of Belesme green. He touched his father's arm and pointed.

"We'd best move if we are not to be cut down." He hastily jammed on his helmet and adjusted the nasal. "The man up there in the green—'tis Robert, and we are seen."

Even as Richard looked upward, an arrow fired from one of the lower slits whirred past him. He broke for cover as another fell a few feet short.

"Roger, draw back!" Henry shouted as he rode toward them. "Jesu, but you are fools to come so close!"

"Aye," Roger called back, "but I wanted him to see the defenses."

They pulled back out of the line of fire and watched the arrows fall harmlessly on the rocks below. Roger shaded his eyes against the sun and looked at the man in green. He was certain it was Robert, and the identification was confirmed when the man made a baiting gesture and called out loudly, "Come and get me, Bastard!"

"Come out and fight!" Roger shouted back.

"Hell will freeze first!"

"Arrogant bastard!" Henry muttered under his breath. "A pity my father did not drown him when he was a whelp and save the world the trouble."

But Roger wasn't attending. He stared bleakly at the huge rock-walled stronghold, taking in every detail he could see and counting every arrow slit. "I see no weakness," he managed finally, "and Eleanor lies within those walls."

23

The weather warmed as spring turned into summer, and tempers began to flare from the enforced idleness in the camp. The archers' towers had long since been built and rolled into place, and it seemed that Roger's men traded arrows with Robert's bowmen for exercise more than anything else. Nighttime mining attempts had made no dent in the walls above them and everything was at a sultry standstill. Quarrels developed among the besiegers almost daily and four bodies swung in the hot summer wind as testimony that the lord of the Condes tolerated no rapine.

The only encouragement they had was the public excommunication of Robert of Belesme and much of that was the result of conjecture. No troops came to reinforce Belesme, and apparently some inside, fearful for their immortal souls, had tried to leave. For several weeks after the ban was proclaimed, the screams of the tortured could be heard within and new heads appeared almost daily on the pikes. Then apparently the disaffection had died down quite literally when the number of gruesome skulls ceased to grow. The crows that had picked them clean moved to the corpses in Roger's camp.

Occasionally the castle gates would open under cover of darkness and a few would venture out to harry the besiegers, driving off livestock and killing sleeping soldiers. They came with such ferocity that many took to sleeping armed in the summer heat.

On June 14, such an attack occurred, but this time the camp was ready. The riders were pulled from their horses and most were hacked to death gleefully by the

soldiers from the Condes set to guard the food supplies. This time, Belesme's harriers did not return
unmolested.

The clash came as Roger prepared for his pallet and
the sound of it sent him running loose-gartered in the
direction of the melee. He nearly collided with Aubery,
who came to tell him of the attack.

"My lord, this time they are taken and all are dead!"

It was over by the time Roger pushed his way through
the crowd that had gathered. As he neared the animal
pens, he could see broken green-shirted bodies lying
about grotesquely in the dirt. A few were already
headless where the men of the Condes had axed them
cleanly, and the rest gave testimony to the viciousness
of the defense by the great gaping wounds in their
bodies.

"Nay—here's one that thought to get away!" A
half-dressed knight pushed a tall, slender boy toward
Roger. "Caught him trying to take his shirt off behind
my tent."

Roger stared in the torchlight at the white-faced boy
who wore a fine coat of burnished mail beneath his
tunic. "Does Robert send boys to lead his raids?" he
asked incredulously. "How old are you, anyway?"

"Nearly seventeen," was the sullen reply, "and he
did not send me—I begged to come, for there's naught
to do up there but sit and wait."

"And so you thought to taste war." Roger nodded
soberly. "Well, you have tasted and seen it, and 'tis
not a pretty sight, is it? Or are you used to it, I
wonder? Are you one who helps him torture?"

"Nay—I am his squire."

"How many rode with you tonight?"

"Sixteen." The boy looked at the hostile faces around
him and was certain that he would die. He swallowed
hard to fight the terror he felt in his heart.

"Release him to me," Roger ordered the knight
who still held Robert's squire, "and I will see you have
the ransom."

"Nay, my lord," the knight protested, "I say we kill
him."

"And I say nay," Roger snapped. "He is but a sixteen-year-old boy on his first raid."

"I crave your protection, my lord!" The youth pulled away from his captor and knelt in front of Roger.

"You should not wear armor, boy, for you are ill-prepared for war." Roger jerked the boy up to face him. "But you have the protection you seek. How are you called, anyway?"

"Piers de Sols."

"Well, Piers, look around you and learn." Roger moved a headless corpse with his foot contemptuously. "Behold the most common fruit of battle. 'Tis not the glory or riches that many get—'tis this."

"A coward's speech, I think," Piers scoffed. "You'd not hear my lord of Belesme speak thus."

"Fool! 'Tis Lord Roger!" Aubery hissed behind Piers.

Piers' eyes widened and he stared at the man he'd heard called the Bastard and the FitzGilbert as long as he could remember. "Your pardon, my lord," he managed, red-faced, "for I've heard none call you craven."

"Nay, none of us would die," Roger told him more gently, "and all of us will. I would just remind you that it happens too soon to too many in battle. Be wary when you fight, Piers." Turning to Aubery, he ordered the boy taken to his tent.

After most of the crowd had dispersed back to their pallets, Roger walked among the dead. He bent over one corpse, a young man whose belly had been ripped open with an ax. "Jesu," he muttered to himself, "but 'tis hell to die like this." The fellow's mouth was still twisted in the agony of his dying. Roger knelt and signed the Cross over the young man's waxy face and murmured his prayer for the dying. "May Almighty God receive your soul into his keeping and grant you peace in the name of the Father, the Son, and the Holy Spirit. Amen." He felt helpless in the face of death.

He moved to each body and repeated the ritual until he was finished and then he wandered aimlessly in the warm, starlit night along the outer edges of the en-

campment. It all seemed so pointless, these raids and
counterraids that cost lives and solved nothing. His
cause—nay, Eleanor's cause—was at a standstill. She
lay so close by and yet so far away that she might as
well be in Byzantium. He had to bring Robert out of
his castle—he had to—not just because he longed for
Eleanor, but because he could not bear to even think
of what she must be suffering at Belesme's hands.
Restlessly he picked up a rock and skipped it along the
ground.

"Halt!"

"Nay," he called back, " 'tis Condes."

"God aid you, my lord!" the sentry answered.

Oddly the man's words echoed in Roger's brain and
it suddenly came like a revelation. He had the means
to bring Robert out if he had the strength of will to
use it. He was Eleanor's sworn champion, and, afore
God, he would give her justice or die trying. He made
his way back to his tent with a new sense of purpose.

He found Piers and Aubery struggling over his chessboard much as he and Henry had done when in the
Conqueror's service. Moving behind the green-shirted
boy, he leaned over to move Piers' king.

"My thanks, my lord. I am not very good at the
game, though I have played it with Count Robert
before. Now that she is here, however, he prefers to
play it with the Lady Eleanor." Suddenly realizing
that he spoke to the lady's husband, he reddened and
mumbled, "Your pardon, my lord."

"Nay—I would hear of her," Roger answered softly.
"Do you see her often?"

"I serve her, my lord. There are no maids in Belesme
and it falls to me to attend her. I have learnt to do her
hair now that she is heavy with child, but mostly I sing
to her, play the lute for her, and bear her company
when she wills it."

"But she is well?"

"Aye. She had the fever and we thought to lose her,
but she has recovered. The babe wears heavily on her,
I think, but she does not complain. Before the siege,
my lord had all manner of delicacies brought in to

tempt her appetite." Piers could tell that Roger could
not bear to ask the obvious and he admitted, "But she
is not happy. Nothing he does can make her happy."

"Would you take a message back to him?" Roger
noted the boy's hesitation and hastened to explain,
" 'Tis no trick, I swear. I offer you your freedom to go
back if you will carry word that I wish to parley with
him."

"Aye, but he will not trust you."

"He knows me. I think he will if you tell him what I
want. I would speak with him on the open field below
the wall where we have burned the grass halfway
between here and Belesme's walls. That way we shall
both be out of bowman's range."

"And if he will parley?"

"I'll ride out with you in the morning and wait
across from where the curtain wall meets the outer
gates. Tell him that if he agrees to meet me when the
sun is highest, he is to hang a goodly sized piece of
green material over the wall where I can see it. I will
wait an hour after you ride inside for my answer."

"How is he to come, my lord?"

"Alone and unarmed, as I will be. I intend to ask
Curthose for witness, but he will not approach Robert
directly."

"All right."

As soon as the sun rose, Roger rode to the edge of
the camp with Piers and then watched as the boy
returned inside the great fortress. He dismounted and
led his horse near a large rock that offered a clear
view of the front of Belesme's outer wall. The air was
still cool, but the sun that beat down on his neck was
hot. Settling against the rock, Roger waited alone.
He'd taken no one into his confidence because he
could not risk letting anyone talk him out of the course
he'd set for himself. It was the only answer and, if he
succeeded, it would bring Lea back safely to him.

He spent the time he waited thinking of her, remembering things they'd shared in a lifetime of loving
each other, and he ached with longing for her. With-

out her, his wealth and his newfound power meant
nothing. It was for her he'd striven and it was for her
that he would win again. He shifted his weight against
the hardness of the rock and looked up again at the
high walls. Suddenly he caught movement on the top
and realized that Robert did not mean to make him
wait his hour for an answer. A cloud of material
billowed out over the ramparts and then fell to hang
against the stone side. Roger watched the green cloth
fall into place and he felt suddenly lighthearted in
spite of the task that faced him. He rose, dusted off
his clothes, and mounted his horse for the ride back to
camp to see Curthose.

It was not an easy task to persuade the duke to
accompany him unarmed to meet with Belesme, but he
managed with the explanation that Curthose could
watch from a safe distance. Then he returned to his
tent to face further opposition from his father and
Prince Henry, who watched him prepare for his meeting.

"Surely you mean to wear mail," Henry protested
as Roger drew on a light gray undertunic and then
belted a blue-and-gray surcoat over it. "I mean—think!
Even out of archers' range, Robert could carry a
dagger."

"Aye," his father agreed, "and I cannot see what is
to be gained in speech with the man. He is no more
like to give her up today than he was yesterday or will
be tomorrow. It is to his advantage to wait."

"He won't have to wait—I mean to put it to combat."

"*What*!" Henry gasped. "Nay! Sweet Jesu—nay!"

Richard sucked in his breath and let it out slowly to
still the spinning sensation he felt. "Roger—*think*! Were
it any other than Belesme, I'd say aye, but now I say
nay!"

"Do you not think I have thought it out? I know
what I am up against, probably better than either of
you. He's heavier, has longer arms, and never loses,
and the world is afraid of him." Roger's blue eyes
were sober as he met his father's. "But I know he is
mortal and bleeds like I do. God willing, I can take
him."

"You *think* you can take him, Roger," Henry pointed out, "but what if you cannot? What happens to Eleanor then?"

"There are worse things than dying, Henry. She is in hell in his hands and I see no hope for getting her out unless I can kill him. I have to."

"Do you think he will meet you?" Richard asked finally. "He already has what he wants and may not want to risk losing."

"As long as I live, he has no real claim to her, and I've come to realize that Robert wants Lea as much as I do. He'll fight."

"You give him what he wants!" Henry muttered angrily.

"I intend to give him the fight of his life. I do not do this lightly, and I've no more wish to die than you do."

They followed him out and watched as he stepped into the stirrup and swung up on the back of his big bay. A wry smile crossed his face as he looked down on the two men he loved most. "You think me moon-mad, but I swear I am not." Turning to Aubery, he asked for his glove.

"Mother of God!" Henry still did not want to believe that he meant to do it. "You are moon-mad if you would fight him in single combat."

Roger nudged his horse with his knee and made his way through the camp to where Curthose waited anxiously. The duke's nervousness was evidenced by the fact that he had chosen to wear his mail even to sit his horse a safe distance from Robert of Belesme. There seemed to be nothing to say between the two men and they rode slowly together toward the open field. Finally the duke asked, "You are sure he will be unarmed?"

"I am sure of nothing, but I expect no treachery." Roger spurred his horse into a gallop, leaving the duke to pursue. When he reached what he judged to be the midpoint in the fire-blackened earth, Roger reined in and waited.

Belesme watched them from the open gate of his

barbican until he saw Roger pull away from Curthose. Looking behind him regretfully at the empty bow slits, he shrugged. If he had thought he could maneuver Roger into range, he would have considered trying it. Slowly he walked his horse forward to meet the enemy who stood between him and Eleanor of Nantes. Roger moved forward to meet him just past mid-field.

"Bastard!" Belesme taunted as he drew near. "Well, I am come to hear you."

Without speaking, Roger lifted the mailed glove that lay across his pommel and flung it to the ground in front of Robert. Belesme's eyes narrowed and then his face broke into a triumphant smile. With athletic grace, he swung out of his saddle and bent to pick up the gauntlet. He walked the few steps to where Roger waited.

As he approached, Roger called out clearly for both Robert's and Curthose's hearing, "Robert of Belesme, as Eleanor of Nantes' sworn champion, I demand justice for her on the field of honor. I challenge you to submit your claim to her to trial by combat before witnesses. May God aid the right!"

"May God aid the right—if He cares, Bastard," Belesme responded. "Aye, so be it." And then he could not resist gibing, "I thought you had more brains, but I am not like to look a gift askance."

Roger's challenge had taken Curthose by surprise and he was not pleased. Nonetheless, he rode forward far enough to set the terms. He looked first at Roger. "When do you wish to meet?"

"Tomorrow."

"Is that acceptable, my lord?" Curthose asked Robert.

"Aye—the sooner the better."

"Then as your suzerain, I set the tenth hour tomorrow for combat. You will each come armed with mace and broadsword unless you prefer the ax."

"Nay—'tis too unwieldy," Belesme muttered.

"And you will continue until one is the undisputed victor, which shall be when one is killed or yields. If the vanquished chooses to yield, the victor will not strike him down. Agreed?"

"So be it," Roger declared solemnly.

"So be it," Belesme agreed.

"My herald will set the rules according to custom and you will abide by his calls to commence or halt."

"Aye."

"Robert, you will bring the Lady Eleanor and place her in the custody of the Archbishop of Rouen," Curthose continued, "until the matter is settled. God grant that justice is done!"

Belesme hesitated and frowned. "She is unwell and but some two months before her time. I would not have her watch."

The duke nodded in understanding. "Aye—we will set up a tent where she may remain until 'tis settled. She will be delivered to the victor."

Belesme remounted and saluted. "Until tomorrow, then."

Curthose waited until he judged Robert out of hearing before rounding angrily on Roger. "Art a fool, my lord," he snapped, "and make fools of us all! We raise our levies for you and find we have emptied our pockets for naught!"

"I have submitted my cause to God."

"And you will lose your wife and your life. You, of all people, know his skill."

Roger's earlier euphoria had evaporated when Belesme had picked up the glove, and the tension he felt was nearly unbearable. He knew the odds and he knew he had to take them, but he had no wish to spend the rest of the day hearing of his folly. "Leave me be—I know what I have to do. If he had your wife, you might do the same."

"Never."

Robert of Normandy cut off from Roger as soon as he reached camp and Roger could hear him already telling any who could hear, "Lord Roger means to meet Belesme tomorrow!"

24

"On the morrow, I will deliver you into William Bonne-Ame's custody," Robert told her first. "It is agreed."

He watched the transformation from disbelief to hope in her face, and her obvious eagerness to leave him hurt. "Aye." He nodded. "You will go out with me to the field below, where you will wait with Bonne-Ame."

"Wait?" He was not making sense to her—there was something strange about his manner. He seemed far too even-tempered—pleasant almost—and he was watching her carefully. She warned herself to be wary.

"You will wait with him while the Bastard and I determine who has the better claim by force of arms."

"Nay! Robert, you cannot—you would not!"

" 'Robert, you cannot—you would not,' " he mimicked cruelly. "Aye, I would, Eleanor, and I will. Tomorrow night, you can tear your clothes and pull your hair and weep in widow's weeds, because it will finally be over between me and him, and I will come for you the victor."

"And I will hate you," she told him evenly. "If you kill him, I will hate you."

"You will forget! I swear you will! When the babe is gone to Harlowe and Roger lies with his flesh rotting from his bones, your memory of him will fade. And you will turn to me because there is no other."

"You lie about this to torment me! You cannot stand it that I cannot love you!" She twisted uncomfortably in the high-backed chair and leaned against the arm. "Leave me be!"

"Nay." He shook his head. "By my sweat and by my blood and by my sword arm I won you, Eleanor." His voice had dropped to a low intensity that was scarcely above a whisper. "I pushed Gilbert until he had naught but his miserable life, d'ye hear? And for what, I ask you? *You!* He gave you to me then, Eleanor."

"I was not his to give, my lord. He was no father to me."

"He gave you to me! Aye—and Curthose too! Both said I could have you if I would but draw back and cry peace with Gilbert."

"Robert, that is over. Listen to me. I wed another—I wed Roger. If he dies tomorrow, I will still be his." She reasoned with him as one would reason with a child who refused to understand. "You cannot change that."

"Do not speak as though I am a fool!" He dropped on his haunches beside her chair. "I will prove to the world you are mine tomorrow, I swear. And when you are recovered from your grief, we will wed." He reached to possess one of her hands. "My sons will come from your body, Eleanor. We will get fierce, strong sons to rule Nantes and Belesme after us." He brushed the outline of her full breasts with his other hand. "When 'tis my son that sucks there, you will feel differently about me."

"God aid me! Can I not make you understand that I cannot love you? Not now—not ever! Jesu, but you do not listen to me!" she cried out in frustration.

"Nay—you do not listen to me. I have just told you that I will meet Roger in combat tomorrow and you will belong to the victor. Accept it! 'Twas he who challenged me, Eleanor. He has agreed that it will be so."

"I am not a hide of land the two of you can fight for, my lord. I am Eleanor of Nantes, a flesh-and-blood woman. Land does not care who owns it. I care who has me! I want my husband!"

They were getting nowhere and they both understood that. Reluctantly he released her hand and pulled himself up with her chair arm. "Resign yourself any-way, for 'tis me you'll get. You can watch it for your-self if you do not think it will mark your babe when I kill him."

"Death is in the hands of God, my lord. I will pray."

"I have been known to help Him send some to hell then." He touched her chin with his hand, forcing it upward until she had to look at him. "Think you I have not heard men pray for their miserable lives? Think you I have not heard them pray to die quickly? I have yet to see God stay my hand." His tone was oddly gentle and his mood had changed with baffling suddenness. "But I would never hurt you, Eleanor," he told her softly. "I have threatened, but I could not. Once I wanted you for my pride, because the Old Conqueror said you were fit to be a warrior's bride, and because you were the most beautiful creature I had ever seen. But when Wald came for me and told me you lay dying, I thought I could not survive. I love you, Eleanor, and I would give all I have to make you love me."

"If you would love me, my lord," she answered quietly, "then let me go. I cannot be what you would have me."

He stared hard at her face as though if he willed it hard enough, it would happen. She met his gaze quietly and waited. Finally he dropped his hand and stepped back.

"I have spoken nothing like this to any other!" he told her harshly. "Damn you! You are more a witch than my mother! You have caught me and yet you will not have me. I swear that I cannot save myself." He turned and walked to the door, flinging over his shoul-der, "You confound me, woman!"

Eleanor did not join Robert at the high table for supper. Her absence irritated him, but he had no wish to quarrel further with her before he met Roger. In-stead, he ate sparingly and drank little to keep his head clear for the morrow. All through supper he had to listen to those who would tell him how easy it would be for him to take Roger. Only old Eustace seemed strangely silent.

"You do not think it will be so easy, do you?" Roger asked his seneschal finally.

"I would not underestimate the man's skill, my lord. Who has not heard of FitzGilbert? I have heard his deeds sung these four years and more."

"At least you are truthful. Aye, I do not see it a simple task either." The euphoria he'd felt earlier over his meeting with Roger had left him and now he just wished it were over. Abruptly he heaved himself to his feet. "It grows late and I would sleep. Let the others eat and drink their fill."

He made his way to his new quarters and undressed himself in the near-darkness so that he would not disturb her. Easing his body into his curtained bed, he found it empty. He rolled out in alarm and went naked into the hallway to take a candle from an iron ring. Bringing it back into the chamber, he used it to light the candles that stood by the bed and those by the brazier. The room was neat and orderly, but she was not there. Cursing, he threw on his clothes and went looking for her. She did not like Belesme's rowdy and barely civilized men and therefore did not move about the castle alone, and certainly she never went about at night.

The garderobe was empty, the passageway to the kitchens was empty, and the courtyard was deserted. She did not have the means to escape—she had to be close by. On impulse, he walked to the chapel she'd refurbished and he found her on her knees with two wax candles glowing on the rail above her. Without his boots, he made little noise as he came up behind her. He could see now that her eyes were closed and that her lips were moving, but he could not hear any words. The intensity of her expression told him that she prayed fervently and desperately. She was so very beautiful that he almost needed to touch her to prove that she was made of flesh and blood. He watched her hungrily, taking in every detail of her fine profile, her thick dark lashes, her slender neck, the curve of her shoulder, and that dark, glossy hair. Even her swollen belly was not displeasing to him. He closed his eyes to still the raging desire he felt for her. If he could have had but one wish in his life, he would have wished her to love him; if he could have had two, he would have wished she carried his son.

Though they were separated in the chapel by only a few feet, the gulf between them was as wide as between heaven and hell. He stepped closer and reached to touch her bent head. "Eleanor . . ." It was a bare whisper that escaped him.

He could feel her inhale sharply and recoil beneath his hand, but she recovered quickly. "You startled me, my lord."

"Aye, but you should be in bed asleep, Eleanor. You need your strength."

"I could not sleep."

"Two candles—you have lit two candles," he murmured softly. "One is for him, isn't it?"

"Aye—I have prayed for his life, Robert."

"The other?"

"For you." She turned beneath his hand and looked up at him. "I ask God's mercy on your soul, my lord."

"If God answered such prayers, Eleanor, there would be no heads on my gate. Come—you need to be in bed." He lifted her up gently as the heat faded from his body and he was overwhelmed by a sense of loss. "Come on."

"Aye."

"You are barefoot," he noticed suddenly, "and in naught but robe and shift."

"I could not sleep once I was in bed."

"Do you want me to carry you back?"

"Nay—I would walk."

"Eleanor . . ." He took her hand and began leading her back to his chamber. "I do not have to kill him." He took a deep breath and watched her stop still. "Aye. If you will stay with me, I will only force him to yield."

"You would make me your willing whore."

"I do not want to! But if that is the only way I can have you willing, I will accept that."

"Nay"—she shook her head slowly—"I could not rob my husband of his honor. I will have to leave it in the hands of God."

"Then I will kill him."

25

The morning dawned clear and bright, and the spectators gathered early in an almost festive mood. Lines were drawn to mark the field and ropes were staked to hold the crowds back. A small tent was pitched at one end to shelter Eleanor of Nantes from the curious and to protect her from seeing the carnage that everyone expected. Many eyed the blue tent with disappointment as they hoped to glimpse the woman they had been called to fight for. Belesme's sense of the dramatic, however, gave them the look they wanted.

The gates of Belesme opened a few minutes early and he rode out with a full retinue of men in rich green silk surcoats. At his side, Eleanor of Nantes sat a white palfrey caparisoned in green and gold. She was very pale and she was far gone with child, but she struck men dumb as she rode past. In spite of her pregnancy and in spite of the fact that two men claimed her for wife, Robert had made her wear her glorious hair unbound like a maid and it streamed like rich dark silk over the green gown she wore.

Walter de Clare ran to take her reins and lifted her down. "Jesu, sweet cousin, but we have worried."

"So have I—I thought never to see any of you again." She glanced up to where Belesme sat impassively above her and then back to Walter. "But I am all right now."

"Aye." Walter hugged her briefly. "You are all right now. You are safe here and 'twill soon be over."

Her eyes scanned the field anxiously. "Where is Roger? I would see him before . . ." Her voice trailed off, unwilling to put into words the impending duel.

"In his tent, I would suppose, but I will get him for you."

"Nay!" Belesme's voice was harsh above them. "I surrender her to Bonne-Ame and none other!"

Neither was paying attention. At the far end of the roped-off list, Roger rode in full battle dress. The sun glinted off the highly polished mail and the soft breeze carried the blue-and-gray silk of his surcoat like a trailing cloud. Across his chest he wore his new device—a black falcon in full swoop.

"*Roger!*" It was a shrill cry of recognition as she sought his attention. "*Roger!*"

He reined in and looked around for the source of the cry and then he saw her. He urged his horse forward until he was between her and Robert before he dismounted. In an instant she was in his arms, pressing her awkward body so close that he could smell the rosewater she'd used to scent her hair. His arms closed around her and they stood locked together, totally oblivious of all but each other.

A shout went up from the crowd as Belesme, unwilling to watch the drama beneath him and unable to stop it, wheeled his horse angrily and rode to seek Curthose's herald.

Roger finally stepped back shakily and held her at arm's length. "Careful—I would not hurt you. Jesu, but I feared never to see you again, Lea."

She tried to smile through a mist of tears. "I must look awful now," she managed as she touched her abdomen hesitantly.

"Nay, you are as I have remembered you—and more."

"Roger," she whispered desperately, "I love you with all my heart, but—"

"Shhhh." He touched her lips with a fingertip. "I know." For a fleeting moment he wanted to just throw her up on his battle horse, to ride off with her, and to let Belesme come after them if he dared. But he'd challenged him and he'd have to end it with Belesme first.

"I would not have you do this for me."

"I do it for me too."

"Aye." She sucked in her breath and exhaled slowly. "Do you remember that day at Fuld Nevers'—when you were angry with me?" she asked.

"I do not remember being angry with you, Lea."

"When you asked if I were like all the rest where Robert is concerned?"

"Aye—I remember. I should not have said that."

"Well, 'twas true then—but not now. I believe you will win this day." In spite of her best efforts, her eyes filled with tears, and her smile twisted. "But take care anyway—for my sake."

"My lord . . ." Roger felt a touch on his shoulder and turned to face Curthose's herald. " 'Tis nearly time. I would discuss the rules with you and Count Robert."

"Aye." His mouth was dry and his stomach knotted, but he drew away from her. "Take care of yourself and the babe, Lea—I love you both." He fingered the small enameled brooch pinned on his surcoat. "I wear your token again for luck—'tis the one you gave me at Nantes."

She could feel herself losing her composure completely and had to turn away to hide her face. Strong arms enfolded her from behind and she turned into Henry's chest. It was as though he braced her for strength and she held on to him gratefully.

The prince nodded over her head. "I will take her to Bonne-Ame, Roger, and I will join you before the start."

"Nay—stay with her until 'tis over." Roger could see Eleanor's whole body shake as she fought a losing battle for control. "God love and comfort you, Lea." Reluctantly he tore himself away and swung himself up on the big bay charger.

Henry's arm slid beneath Eleanor's arm and supported her. "Come on, love," he said softly. "Let us go inside and wait. Soon enough it will be over and you can look to your husband."

*   *   *

Roger listened to the herald explain the standard rules of combat, from the start, to breaks if both should become disarmed, to the manner of yielding. The irony of it all was not lost on him as he realized that the barbarism of a battle to death was cloaked in civility and blessed by religion. He nodded soberly when asked if he understood the terms and then waited for the Archbishop of Rouen to pray aloud for God's justice.

Both he and Robert knelt solemnly, their heads bared, their bodies side by side, while Bonne-Ame exhorted God to guide the right man to triumph. There was no question in the minds of any of the spectators when the archbishop laid his hands over Roger's head and blessed him as to which side Bonne-Ame considered to have the right of the matter.

Roger remounted his charger and waited while Aubery checked over the saddle girth, the horse's trappings, the blinders, and the bridle bit. Finally satisfied, the squire handed up the well-padded helmet. Roger jammed it on his head and adjusted the nasal over his nose, taking care to ensure that he still had the best vision available. Aubery checked the evil-looking mace and tested the spikes and the chain for looseness before passing it up also. Roger made a few swings to get the feel of it and laid it across the saddle pommel. Across the field, he could see Belesme and Piers doing much the same things. Roger had to fight the nausea he felt at the pain and awful physical punishment he knew were coming, and he closed his eyes.

"Are you all right, Roger?" his father asked anxiously. "If you are sick, we can draw back for today."

"Nay—I could not do this again."

Richard possessed himself of Roger's still-ungloved hand and kissed it. "Then fight for Eleanor, son! Fight for your own son!"

"Aye."

He took Avenger from Aubery and put the broadsword in the saddle sheath. It felt light for its purpose but well-balanced in his hand. His new shield, with its diagonal division between blue and gray and its swoop-

ing black falcon emblazoned over the center, was next.
He slipped his left arm through the strong leather
bands on the back and adjusted it as comfortably as he
could. Finally he reached for the thick leather gloves
with the tiny metal plates across the back and pulled
them on. He was ready and his whole body felt taut as
a pulled bowstring. Belesme's squire signaled to
Curthose's herald that his master was ready. Roger
lifted the handle of his mace, swung it in a circle
again, and nodded.

He eased his horse out to one end of the list to a
mixture of ill-assorted cheers. He could hear cries of
"Bastard! Bastard!", "God aid you, FitzGilbert!", and
"Roger! Roger!" It made no difference what they
called him, for by the sound of it, he was not only
Eleanor's champion against Belesme—he was the
crowd's champion.

At the other end, he could see Belesme lean down
for a quick last word with his squire. Roger had nothing more to say to anyone. Indeed, he felt that if he
opened his mouth, he would disgrace himself by
vomiting.

Both men watched the herald intently now as he
lifted a red silk scarf high in the air and released it.
They were supposed to charge when it touched ground.
The breeze caught it and it wafted briefly before it
drifted downward. Roger took a deep breath of fresh
air and poised his spurs.

He dug in the instant he saw it touch, and his
charger leapt forward, gaining speed until it thundered
the length of the list. The ground seemed to shake
beneath them by the time the two men met in the first
pass. Roger could see the twirling spiked ball come at
him and he raised his shield to ward off the hit. There
was not time for him to strike a blow before he felt the
weight of Belesme's strike. It thudded against his shield
and glanced off. He swung his own mace and fell wide
of the mark. He felt like he could hear Robert laughing.

Oddly, the blow he'd taken with his shield seemed
to clear his head. The nausea evaporated and so did
the terrible tension. Now it was as though he were

detached from his body like a spirit hanging behind his ear and telling him how to strike, how to counter, and when to dodge. He took another blow before he landed one and this one nearly tore the shield from his arm. Jesu, but Belesme did not mean to take his time this day! Roger wheeled his horse for another pass, hoping to come by on Robert's left even though that was the protected side. He had to show Belesme he could strike just as hard if he were to hold his own at all.

Robert whirled just as he came upon him and they nearly collided. Roger swung with all of his weight and hit the corner of Belesme's shield with such force that the count reeled and the corner bent inward. Robert's eyes glittered with fury above his nasal. And then they began flailing in earnest, charging, reining in, wheeling awkwardly, and trading blows.

Roger took a lot of hard hits on his shield, far more than he gave, and his left arm began to ache. He longed to go for Robert's less-protected right side, but he dared not chance leaving himself open to his opponent's longer reach. The mace was not his best weapon and Belesme knew it. Robert, on the other hand, used the tools of his trade with equal skill. Roger took a crushing blow that sent his shield into his rib cage with a heavy thud that nearly unseated him. He swung high and wide more to regain his balance than anything and he heard rather than saw the iron ball hit Belesme's helmet on the side. For an instant Robert reeled precariously in his saddle, and the crowd seemed to give a collective "ahh," but then he righted himself and pulled his horse back for another charge in an effort to give himself time to clear his senses.

This time, when he charged, he did not even swing at Roger. Instead, he passed on the shield side and leaned over to strike the big bay's knees. The horse pitched forward, neighing in terror and pain to the cries of "Foul! Foul!" But he could not rein in time to take advantage of the immediate confusion and had to continue his pass.

Roger fell to the side and managed to extricate himself before the horse's weight landed on his leg.

He yanked Avenger free and waited for Belesme's next pass. It was an unequal contest now, with him on the ground and Belesme able to swing downward with the heavy mace. Roger half-crouched, his left arm above him to take the blow and protect his head, his right arm braced with the broadsword's blade upward. His detached feeling intensified as he waited, and it seemed that time slowed. He watched Belesme rein in and then spur his black destrier viciously. Roger waited and the crowd was strangely quiet. The ground beneath him seemed to shake with the thunder of the destrier's hooves and then the black horse loomed above him. Belesme's arm was raised to swing. Roger dodged at the last second and drove his blade deep into the horse's belly. It reared as Roger drew back the bloody blade, its nostrils flared and it screamed hideously, and then it fell heavily. Belesme tried to roll free, and although he did not fall beneath the horse, he could not get his foot out of the stirrup. Before Roger could raise his sword again, the herald blew a halt.

Belesme had been shaken by the fall. He managed to gain his balance finally and bent to draw his own broadsword. He faced Roger with green eyes that glittered hatred and waited for the herald to start them anew. Roger took several deep gulps of air as though to store it for later. The trumpet sounded again, and Belesme moved forward, his shield in front of him and his right arm holding his broadsword upright.

They circled each other, measuring distances and judging defenses, until Robert thought he saw an opening. He arched his swing to come in on the right side in hopes of disabling Roger's sword arm. Roger pivoted against the blow and took it on his already battered shield. It cut into the metal covering before Belesme drew back.

"Another instant and I'd have cut you in half, Bastard," he muttered through clenched teeth.

"Aye." Roger made a few thrusts to test Robert's defenses and only succeeded in tiring his arm further.

The green-and-white shield held solidly against the blows.

Both men took stock of the situation now and fell to short jabbing thrusts and easy swings designed to conserve strength. Occasionally Robert would swing hard and put his weight behind it as though to remind Roger of his strength. They were tiring now and neither had any hopes of finishing the other quickly anymore. The weight of armor, shield, and heavy broadsword was taking its toll. If they were not careful, the combat would end not on the basis of skill but on the ability to hack wildly.

Belesme was breathing heavily, his strength ebbing from weight and the heat of the sun. He sought to bait Roger into making a mistake. "Bastard! Fool! She moans at my touch and you would fight for her!"

"Liar," Roger answered mildly. "She flees from you."

Robert lunged to try again for Roger's ribs on the right side. Roger swung hard and hit the blade side-on and almost disarmed him. Furious, Robert threw all of his weight into another blow, trying to come in under Roger's shield. Roger came around high and hit Robert's helmet first with all his strength. Belesme staggered and reeled away unsteadily as though he'd lost his direction. Roger leaned on his sword hilt and tried to catch his breath. His chest ached, his arms ached, and he thought his lungs would burst from the air he would put in them. When Belesme got his wind and his direction, he turned around. A deep dent creased the side of his helmet and even the nasal was out of line. Blood ran down beneath both the nasal and the side of the helmet. Robert still seemed disoriented even though he had his sword and shield raised again. Roger was sure he had him now and he closed in.

Another blow delivered to the green shield was barely fended off. Roger raised Henry's Avenger to try cleaving from the shoulder downward, his heart racing with the excitement of winning. Robert made one last wild swing when he saw Roger raise his blade and he took him heavily on the shield. Roger reeled

and lost his balance. Robert staggered over him, swaying
and still obviously confused. Slowly he raised his sword.

"Nay! Stop it! Nay!"

Robert's head pounded with pain. He could feel his
own blood running down his face. He could barely see
where he was. But he could hear her screaming. He
stood there holding the sword above Roger's neck.

"Roger! It was a wrenching scream of horror and
terror.

Henry tried to catch her before she could get any
closer. He would not let her see Belesme kill Roger if
he had to carry her back forcibly, but she eluded him
as she ran onto the field.

Belesme turned to look for an instant. With a sudden roll, Roger pushed against his legs and brought
him down. He fell heavily and the blood poured
from the bottom of his helmet. Roger pulled himself to a half-standing position and then stood up
shakily. He lifted Avenger to place it at Robert's
throat. Robert's eyes betrayed his pain as he stared
upward.

"Do you yield, my lord?" Roger croaked through
parched lips.

"Nay."

Every muscle in Roger's body ached and he was
tired unto death itself. He raised the sword and held it
above Belesme's neck, positioning it for one last quick
and final stroke.

"Have mercy, sweet lord! Have mercy!"

Before Roger could drive the blade downward to
end his eight-year struggle with Belesme, Mabille was
on her knees in the dirt, crying and clutching at the
hem of his surcoat. He hesitated, his eyes fixed on
Robert of Belesme. Sucking in his breath, he asked
one last time, "Do you yield, Robert?"

"He yields!" Mabille cried. "He yields!"

"Nay," Belesme gasped.

"Jesu." Roger looked up at Eleanor standing white-
faced beside him, her whole body shaking. "Lea?"

Before Eleanor could respond, Mabille had crawled
to cover Robert's body with her own. And Curthose,

both men's liege lord, intervened by pushing his way onto the field, yelling, "Art beaten, Robert—yield!"

Belesme closed his eyes and swallowed some of his own blood. Slowly his lips formed a silent "Aye." Roger raised the blade higher and drove it down with such force that it stood vibrating in the ground a bare inch from Robert's neck vein. Mabille screamed and rolled away.

"Then I leave God's justice to God," Roger said finally. He could see Belesme's eyes fly open and he could hear the gasps of astonishment around him. Using the embedded sword for balance, he leaned over his vanquished enemy. "Do you need a priest, Robert?"

"Nay, I shall live," Belesme whispered hoarsely. Breathing was an effort and talk almost impossible. The blackened grass and earth were stained with his blood. He closed his eyes again and then opened them, trying to focus on Eleanor. "Take her," he rasped. " 'Tis over between you and me, Roger." Taking in more air, he gathered his strength before continuing, "I give her back as I found her—she never lay with me."

Eleanor stared down at him in astonishment, unable to believe that he'd lied to ease Roger's taking her back. She could not speak for the lump that formed in her throat while tears of emotional release flowed unchecked down her cheeks. She looked up at Roger, who stood waiting, and she flung herself into his arms. He crushed her against the bloody surcoat until she could feel every link of his mail and her babe kicked indignantly at the lack of room. He pulled off the heavy globe and smoothed her hair in that familiar gesture.

"Lea, I am come to take you home."

"Aye," she whispered through her tears. "I was afraid, but I never doubted you." Her cheek pressed against his shoulder gratefully. "Merciful God—'tis over."

"Shhhhh," he soothed. "For us 'twill never be over, Lea. We've a lifetime together."

Epilogue

Eleanor lay back, too exhausted to assist those who worked to clean up after the birthing. Her body, still aching from her effort, now felt strangely light from the poppy juice the physician from Milano had given her. Roger, who'd defied Glynis and the others by staying with her, still clasped her hand and smoothed her damp hair. At the narrow arrow slit, Glynis and the physician examined the babe.

Satisfied, Roger's mother brought the still-screaming infant closer for them to see. Overcome with emotion, Roger squeezed her hand and whispered, " 'Tis a daughter, Lea—we have a daughter!" Eleanor opened her eyes and could barely see for the tears that filled them. "A daughter?" she managed to whisper back. "Nay." Incredibly, she could tell he was smiling and crying at the same time. "You are not disappointed?" she murmured foolishly. "You do not care?"

"Nay, love." He took the babe and held her closer for Eleanor to see. "Look, Lea—she is a beauty like her mother. If we could be blessed with ten like this, I would love them all," he declared sincerely. He caught her still-stricken expression and knew she thought she'd failed him. "Nay—I swear that if I am surrounded by images of you, Lea, I am content."

"But I wanted to bear your heir!" she muttered miserably.

"And you have."

"But—"

"Just look at her, Lea—look at her!" he urged.

With a sigh, she turned her attention to the babe. It had stopped crying and was staring solemnly at her.

She tentatively reached to touch the tiny nose and lips. It appeared small, but seemed healthy enough. They took stock of one another while Roger waited and watched. Finally the babe screwed its tiny face up and yawned. A slow smile spread over Eleanor's face as she discovered the wonder that God had wrought from their bodies. "Aye—she *is* beautiful," she decided softly. "She is."

He gently eased the infant into the crook of her arm and leaned over to kiss Eleanor. "Aye, and she is ours to keep, love."

"If you truly do not mind, I do not." She twisted her neck for a better look at the babe that lay soft and warm against her arm.

"Henry would stand her godfather, Lea."

"I know—he told me that day we waited on the field at Belesme." Her face clouded at the memory of that awful day. "He said he would hold for my babe no matter what happened."

" 'Tis over and done with, sweetheart, and you never have to think of it again. Look to us and to the child instead." As if to look forward himself, he reached to touch the dark thatch of hair on the babe's head. "What think you of Catherine for a name?" he asked casually.

"Catherine? But I had thought to call her Glynis," she protested.

"Nay." Roger's mother stood by the bed and studied her new granddaughter. "Nay, give her a happier name for a happier life."

" 'Tis your choice, Lea. I thought of Catherine for the saint that witnessed my oath to you at Nantes."

The babe yawned again and stretched tiny clenched fists. Eleanor's arm tightened protectively and she smiled. "Aye, Catherine—my little Cat."

About the Author

Anita Mills lives in Kansas City, Missouri, with her husband, four children, sister, and seven cats in a restored turn of the century house. A former English and history teacher, she has turned a lifelong passion for both into a writing career.